The Raven

The Famiglia Secret Society
Book Two

Amber Joi Scott

Table of Contents

Copyrights	IX
Dedication	XI
Chapter One	1
Chapter Two	13
Chapter Three	27
Chapter Four	39
Chapter Five	49
Chapter Six	61
Chapter Seven	73
Chapter Eight	85
Chapter Nine	99
Chapter Ten	111
Chapter Eleven	123

Chapter Twelve	135
Chapter Thirteen	145
Chapter Fourteen	157
Chapter Fifteen	167
Chapter Sixteen	177
Chapter Seventeen	187
Chapter Eighteen	197
Chapter Nineteen	207
Chapter Twenty	217
Chapter Twenty-One	229
Chapter Twenty-Two	243
Chapter Twenty-Three	253
Chapter Twenty-Four	265
Chapter Twenty-Five	275
Chapter Twenty-Six	287
Chapter Twenty-Seven	297
Chapter Twenty-Eight	309
Chapter Twenty-Nine	319
Chapter Thirty	331
Chapter Thirty-One	343
Chapter Thirty-Two	353
Chapter Thirty-Three	363
Chapter Thirty-Four	375
Chapter Thirty-Five	387

Chapter Thirty-Six	399
About the author	405
Also by	407
Follow Me	411

Copyright © 2024 by Amber Joi Scott

All rights reserved.

No part of this publication may be reproduced, distributed, or transmitted in any form or by any means, including photocopying, recording, or other electronic or mechanical methods, without the prior written permission of the publisher, except as permitted by U.S. copyright law.

The story, all names, characters, and incidents portrayed in this production are fictitious. No identification with actual persons (living or deceased), places, buildings, and products is intended or should be inferred.

Book Cover by CD Rodeffer Designs

To my loyal readers and friends who love reading sexy mafia romance stories as much as I love writing them.

Chapter One

Davide

Darkness veiled the moonlit night as I tread stealthily through the dimly lit alleyways of the city. Taking deliberate steps, each one calculated and precise, I move through the shadows with the grace of a predator. The streets and shadows are my kingdom.

As I walk through the dark streets, my mind is consumed with thoughts of my responsibilities and duties as the head of the Bonanno Crime Family. It's not just about running a successful criminal empire. It's about carrying on the legacy my father handed me upon his death.

The Bonanno Crime Family is one of the five families that dominate organized crime in New York City. We are known for our ruthless tactics and powerful influence. Only a select few know that a secret society called The Famiglia unifies us.

The Famiglia is composed of members from each of the five families. It serves as a way to communicate and make deals without outside interference. It's a delicate balance, but it has kept our operations running smoothly for decades. However, the five families aren't the only members.

While I make my nightly rounds, ensuring our illegal businesses are operating smoothly, I can't help but feel the weight of my position. The role of the Bonanno Crime Family leader carries distinct challenges and responsibilities.

I must constantly be aware of threats from rival families or law enforcement agencies. Any misstep could result in losing everything we've worked so hard to build. But despite the pressure and dangers of being part of a powerful crime family, we also have a sense of camaraderie. We may be seen as enemies in public, but behind closed doors, we are like brothers.

We have each other's backs and work together to protect our interests and keep our grip on this city and world tight. And as I continue on my journey through these streets, I know I am not alone. The Famiglia stands behind me, supporting me every step of the way.

My legacy may burden me, but it also strengthens and drives me forward. I will do whatever it takes to uphold the honor of the Bonanno name and keep our family's legacy alive.

As I turned a corner, a figure emerged from the darkness, their face obscured by the hood of their jacket. My hand instinctively reaches for the handle of my concealed knife, ready to defend myself if necessary. But as the figure drew closer, their identity became clear. It was none other than my trusted informant, Marco.

Marco steps toward me, his eyes darting nervously from side to side. His presence alone signals that trouble is brewing in the city's underbelly, and I need to know what it is. In a low, commanding voice, I ask. "What news do you bring me, Marco?"

Marco fidgeted with the hem of his jacket before finally speaking. "Boss, word on the streets is that the Russians are making a move. They've been encroaching on our territory, causing unrest among our men."

My grip tightened around the handle of my knife. Russians, a constant thorn, now exceed audacity. It seemed they were no longer content with their own piece of the pie. Now, they were reaching for mine and, unknowingly, The Famiglia.

I take a deep breath, trying to contain my anger. Losing my composure would only lead to chaos and bloodshed. I had to remain calm and calculated to protect my family and preserve the delicate balance of power in the city.

Rage simmers beneath the surface as I take several deep breaths to pull it back. "Tell me everything you know, Marco."

Marco hesitated for a moment before launching into his report. He spoke of secret meetings between a mysterious Russian and other criminal leader to expand their operations into our territory. The Famiglia were particular about whom they chose to become part of the organization.

I give him a nod. "Thank you, Marco. You've done well."

He disappeared back into the shadows, and as he did, my mind worked quickly to devise a plan. I had to inform the other leaders. However, I also had something else I needed to take care of with Luca. He was my brother by loyalty, not by blood, the leader of the Gambino crime family, and my best friend. Unsure of his reaction, I had no choice but to speak my mind.

Six months ago, I rashly staked my claim on his sister Lucy. When she endangered herself, my heart felt like it would stop. Without a second thought, she broke into the hangar where the Cuban mafia was holding Giovanni's wife. She then got into a gunfight. Thankfully, she was unharmed at the end and rescued Angelina. My emotions were a mix of anger and fear. I secretly loved her when it was inappropriate.

I was twenty-six, and Luca's father had just turned over the family business to him. Giovanni, Andrea, Danti, and I were invited over to celebrate. The drinking began early, and before long, I was feeling no pain. I excused myself and went outside to get some fresh air and clear my drunken fog.

As I stepped out onto the deck, my eyes were immediately drawn to a figure emerging from the pool. She walked with fluid grace, her long hair cascading down her sun-kissed back. Clad in a itsy bitsy black bikini, she was the picture of effortless sensuality. My heart raced as I took in every inch of her form, from the curve of her hips to the swell of her breasts. The goddess before me had a tempting ass, yearning to be touched, whipped, and bitten in passion. Society may dictate that men like me prefer plastic-perfect females, but they would never understand my true desires. Give me a woman with soft curves and natural beauty any day. And this woman standing before me embodied everything I craved.

Who was this woman? Had Luca hired someone for us to play with?

I shifted my weight and reached down, feeling the heat of my straining cock pressing against the zipper of my tight jeans. I adjusted it with a quick pull and sighed in relief as the fabric loosened around me.

My hand still gripped my aching cock as the goddess turned towards me. Her body was a masterpiece, with perfectly round and ample breasts that matched her curvaceous, full ass. The sight of her was enough to make my heart race and my desire grow even stronger.

She walked toward me, her tits bouncing with each step and her nipples straining against the flimsy bikini top. I tear my eyes from her chest after imagining me doing all kinds of filthy things to them. Others won't stand a chance with her. She is mine.

My eyes glanced upwards, eager to assess her appearance, and upon doing so, I was shocked. It was Luca's little sister, Lucy.

As soon as my eyes landed on her face, a jolt of recognition shot through me. With time, she became a breathtaking woman. My mind raced with thoughts as I took in her perfect hourglass figure, silky hair cascading down her back, and a radiant smile. The sudden realization of her age hit me like a ton of bricks. She was only sixteen, but how she carried herself made it easy to forget. My internal monologue cursed at the situation and reminded me she was still just a child.

My mind raced with conflicting emotions as I looked at her, water droplets glistening on her sun-kissed skin. She had a mischievous smile, not fully comprehending the power she held over me. It was dangerous territory, the allure of forbidden love pulling at my heartstrings.

"Hey there, Davide." her voice was laced with playful innocence.

The pungent scent of alcohol filled the air, mixing with the overpowering desire pulsing through my veins. I struggled to form coherent sentences, as my mind was clouded by both intoxication and lust. Thoughts were hazy as if seeing through dense fog. My inhibitions were lowered, and my desires heightened. They created a chaotic swirl of emotions within me that made it nearly impossible to vocalize my thoughts. At that moment, words seemed obsolete as primal instincts took over my body.

As I stood there, mysteriously entranced by her beauty and the echoes of my own heart, I couldn't help but imagine a life with her. However, reality inevitably resurfaced.

"Lucy, you have grown up."

Her full pouty lips turn up in a sultry smile, and she rubs her hand down her sexy as fuck body. "It seems to happen overnight. One day, I was a beanpole with legs, and next, I had tits and a round ass."

"Lucy! Such language for a young girl.".

She sticks out her bottom lip and bats her long eyelashes. "What?"

"Little girls who use such language get their bottoms turned red."

With slow, purposeful steps, she closes the distance between us. Her face is upturned, her emerald green eyes fixed on mine with a fiery intensity. As she reaches out her hand, I can feel the warmth of her skin against my chest. She licks her bottom lip, leaving behind a glistening trail of moisture. "Will it be you who gives me a well-deserved spanking?"

Before I could answer, Luca stepped out on the deck and yelled. "LUCY GAMBINO, put some clothes on."

Lucy narrows her eyes and places her hands on her hips. "I've got a bathing suit on."

Luca walks over. "Where did you get that?"

"Italy. Mother helped me pick it out."

Luca grumbles something under his breath. "Well, you are in America. Go put something over it."

"But, Lu, it is not that bad. Davide likes it. Don't you, Davide?" Her eyes raced over me, lingering on my very noticeable erection.

My eyes met hers, and I hesitated momentarily, my mind racing as I fought to maintain control. I couldn't deny the truth. Lucy became a stunning woman, and my attraction to her grew stronger. I knew pursuing a relationship with her was forbidden by both blood and our world's rules.

With a heavy sigh, I turned my gaze towards Luca, who was still standing there, his expression a mixture of anger and concern. "Lucy, put on something else. Davide's correct; your choice of attire is... unfortunate."

I noticed her disappointed look as she reluctantly walked back inside. I couldn't help but feel a pang of regret for my part in the situation. As much as I wanted to explore my feelings for her, I knew I couldn't.

Six years later, she was even more beautiful but also headstrong and opinionated. After making arrangements with her brother for her hand in marriage, I had six months to think about it. The more I thought about marrying her, the more I knew I couldn't. I couldn't tie her to a man who would always break her heart.

My bloodline is tainted with deceit and infidelity. Generations of men in my family have dishonored their vows, their wives, and their honor. My father took my mother's virginity on their wedding night as part of the tradition. The Commission's men, part of The Famiglia, gather near the marriage bed to witness the husband consummate the marriage. After he finished, he promptly went to The Famiglia brothel reserved for members called Disorderly House and bedded not one but three women. The legacy of betrayal runs deep in our veins, and I am just another link in this chain of infidelity.

He often boasted to me about it before smoking took its toll. Lung cancer is a horrible way to die, but how he treated my mother was justice for her. My father wasn't the only one in my family who cheated. There were stories of all their conquests.

I need to tell Luca before Lucy comes home from Italy.

> Davide: Hey man, are you at home?

> Luca: Yeah.

> Davide: Sure, I'll be there soon.

> Luca: Okay.

I quickly text Mici, my trusted private security guard and driver, requesting that he bring the sleek black vehicle around. I slip on my tailored suit jacket and stride confidently out the door. As I approach, Mici swiftly exits the car and opens the back door of the imposing Bentley

Bentayga, the preferred mode of transportation for most members of The Famiglia. Its glossy exterior exudes both luxury and strength, with its bulletproof design providing an added layer of protection.

The Bonanno family crest was embossed in the back of the seats. The royal Raven had a crown on his head and blood on his claws.

As I climbed into the luxurious car, Mici closed the door behind me, and we began our journey to Luca's house. The streets buzzed with life, yet I felt detached from the city's excitement. My mind is consumed with thoughts of Lucy. I wondered about her well-being and enjoyment in Italy.

When we arrive, Mici opens the door for me, and I step out, my heart pounding in my chest. Taking a deep breath, I approach the door and knock gently. Luca opens the door, his expression unreadable. "Come in." He stands to the side and welcomes me in.

Inside, he closes the door, and we stand, facing each other. "Hey, man. I have something important to tell you."

Luca nods, his eyes boring into mine. "Okay. Let's go to my study."

As we walk down the hall, the walls are covered with photographs Lucy took. She was a talented photographer in high demand.

Luca leads me into his study, and I sit on one of the chairs in front of his desk. He walks over to the bar and pours dark amber bourbon into tumblers.

He returns and hands me a glass before sitting behind his desk.

"What's on your mind?"

I take a big drink, hoping it will settle my nerves. "I have been thinking a lot about the arrangement."

"Good. I haven't informed Lucy about the details of the arrangement yet. I assumed you'd like to be here. She is.."

I held up my hand because my heart couldn't take hearing about her. "Luca, I've carefully considered the arrangement. I've decided to break the arrangement."

His brow furrows, and I see him balling his hands into fists. "Why?"

I couldn't bear to confess my long-standing love for his younger sister, not since she was sixteen. The weight of my deceit settled heavily in my chest, the only barrier keeping our friendship from crumbling. "I let my rage cloud my judgment when she recklessly hot-wired that car and charged into a hangar filled with dangerous Cubans. I may see Lucy as a decent girl, but I'll never be able to form any kind of bond with her." My words tasted like ash on my tongue, a bitter reminder of the secrets I harbored.

A gasp catches my attention, and I see Lucy in the doorway.

Chapter Two

Lucy

"*Ladies and gentlemen, we will be landing at JFK in fifteen minutes. Please secure your seatbelts and put away all electronic devices.*"

The tug of homesickness pulls at me, urging me to return to where I was born and raised. The bustling New York has always been my home, with its towering buildings and crowded streets. It's where I first discovered my love for capturing moments through a camera lens. Every corner holds a memory, every street a story.

Countless model agencies practically threw money at me, desperate for me to become their top photographer. But the idea of photographing emaciated, self-absorbed girls who believed they were above everyone else made my skin crawl. My genuine passion lay in capturing the gritty and enigmatic snapshots of the ever-evolving New York cityscape. The towering skyscrapers seemed to reach up endlessly towards the sky. Meanwhile, the bustling streets below held a certain allure that no amount of wealth or fame could match. In those moments behind the lens, I felt I was immortalizing a constantly shifting and changing city, capturing its raw and unfiltered beauty for all to see.

For the last six months, Italy had been my sanctuary. I spent my days in the most breathtaking location imaginable, nestled between rolling hills and shimmering water at Lake Como. The endless expanse of water stretched out before me, a sparkling blue jewel embraced by nature's embrace. On the hills surrounding me were villas and gardens, their vibrant colors blending seamlessly into the landscape. And there, perched on the edge of it all, was my father's grand mansion. Its ornate facade and regal furnishings perfectly complemented the luxurious atmosphere of the Italian countryside. At dawn, I would wake to the gentle lapping of waves against the shore and the heady scent of roses and lemons wafting through my windows from the nearby gardens. It was like living on a postcard, where every turn revealed another stunning vista. But even amidst this paradise, I couldn't feel like I was truly home.

My father requested I take some time away from New York. The tension between my brother Luca and the other members of The Famiglia was palpable. They were livid with me for taking matters into my own hands. I eliminated all those despicable Cuban assholes before Luca and the other founding sons arrived at the hangar. Angelina's husband, Giovanni, expressed gratitude for saving his beloved wife. Dante and Andrea joked about me teaching them car hot wiring tricks. Even though Luca scolded me for putting myself in harm's way, his eyes showed a glimmer of pride. Then there was Davide. He looked at me with a mix of anger and concern, as if he wanted to turn me over his knee and spank me. His look confused me, as he had treated me like a plague for the past six years. I couldn't understand why he held such animosity towards me when all I had felt for him during those six years was love.

I hadn't planned on staying in Italy for six months. However, a few weeks after I arrived, Luca called and informed me he had arranged a marriage for me.

From a young age, the weight of expectation bore down on my shoulders like an impossible burden. In The Famiglia, arranged marriages were the norm for young women. Love and romance were seen as unimportant and replaced by practical considerations of joining two families for mutual benefit and stability. As I matured into adulthood, I couldn't shake off the looming reality that one day, the leader of our family would orchestrate a marriage. It made me wonder if love should be considered when choosing a life partner, even though it helped with alliances and wealth.

It had been six years since my father, the powerful leader of the infamous Gambino family, gracefully stepped down from his position. After he left, my older brother Luca effortlessly took over as the leader, inheriting both the legal and illegal businesses and the duty to protect and guide me as a member of The Famiglia. His broad shoulders bore the weight of this duty with ease and confidence, much like our father before him. Every decision made within our organization held grave consequences, with lives hanging in the balance and fortunes rising and falling with each calculated move in this high-stakes game of power. We lived in a harsh reality for which we were born and bred.

My heart races as I return home to marry a stranger with no name. The weight of this arranged union crushes me, and I shut off my phone, refusing to acknowledge any messages from Luca. I cannot bear to hear his voice or read his words, knowing that my heart already belongs to another. But duty and tradition bind me, dragging me towards a future I never wanted.

In the modern world, arranged marriages are seen as outdated and archaic. However, they were still a prevalent and profoundly ingrained tradition within The Famiglia. The Famiglia, a clandestine organization founded by five powerful Italian mafia families, operated in complete secrecy from the outside world. To most, these five families were bitter enemies, but in reality, their bond ran deeper than blood. The influence of The Famiglia extended far beyond the realm of mafia members; it seeped into every level of society, giving them power and control behind closed doors. Only those initiated into the inner workings of The Famiglia knew its true reach and influence to outsiders. It was just smoke and mirrors.

A surge of adrenaline courses through my veins, causing my heart to race and my palms to grow slick with sweat. The plush leather seat in first class is a welcome luxury, but it does little to ease the intense jolt that reverberates through my body as the Lufthansa Airbus touches down on the runway. Panic rises in my chest like a wave, threatening to drown me in fear and desperation. My mind races, searching for any semblance of calm as I struggle to catch my breath. Despite growing up in a family with multiple private planes, I have always felt more at ease in the massive commercial aircraft. As we speed down the runway, claustrophobia grips me intensely. I can feel the tightness in my chest, and my knuckles turn white from gripping the armrests with all my strength, trying to ground myself in reality.

The deafening roar of the engine dissipates as the massive plane screeches to a stop. We were safely on the ground and taxing toward the terminal. I reach into my pocket and retrieve my phone, scrolling through my contacts until I find my bodyguard's number. Sam protected me briefly before my departure to Italy. My previous bodyguard met his untimely death while trying to protect me and Angelina from kidnappers. I left Sam behind while I traveled to Italy. My father may not be the official leader in our family, but his power and influence were undeniable. No one dared cross the formidable Francis Gambino or any of his family.

The plane is a hive of activity as passengers gather their belongings and prepare to disembark. I feel a surge of anxiety as I stand up from my seat, preparing to face the life that awaits me back in New York. The familiar sights and sounds of the bustling airport offer me no comfort. It only reminds me of the impending marriage that hangs over my head like a dark cloud. As I walk through the throngs of people, my eyes search for Sam. Spotting him near the exit, his imposing figure offers me security amidst the chaos.

As I approach him, Sam nods in acknowledgment before stepping beside me and takes my suitcase. We weave through the bustling crowd together as we make our way toward the sleek black car that awaits us. The polished exterior gleams under the city lights, symbolizing the wealth and power that my family holds. As we settle into the plush leather seats, the familiar scent of rich leather and expensive cologne fills the air. The towering skyscrapers loom over us like giant sentinels, casting long shadows that seem to stretch out and envelop me in their darkness. My heart races with each passing block, knowing that my inevitable fate awaits me at my family's estate on the outskirts of the city. The weight of my arranged marriage presses down on me like a heavy stone, suffocating me with its suffocating expectations and obligations.

As we arrive at the massive gate to our grand estate, I take a deep breath to steady my nerves. The car stops, and Sam opens the door for me. I step out and walk towards the front door.

The heavy oak doors swing open, revealing the opulent interior. My brother Luca stands in the center of the room. His gaze fixed on me with a mixture of happiness and concern. He approaches, reaches out, and pulls me into a hug. "Welcome home, Lulu. I've missed you, little sis."

His embrace reminds me of the delicate balance between his brotherly love and his obligation to The Famiglia. As he pulled away, I saw the creases etched around his eyes—evidence of his heavy responsibility as the head of our family. I know his worries for me are genuine. The weight of my impending nuptials settles heavily on my shoulders like a dense, suffocating fog, extinguishing all possibilities of a blissful marriage. I nod in response to his greeting, mustering a facade of acceptance I do not truly feel.

The mansion's grandeur surrounds us. Its opulent decor is a stark reminder of the untouchable power and boundless wealth that defines our lives. The world I was born into demands a price for privilege and protection, leaving me uncertain. Every intricate detail of this lavish estate is a testament to its inhabitants' immense influence and extravagant tastes. This is my home, yet it feels like a gilded cage, trapping me within its luxurious walls.

"Thank you, Luca. I've missed you too. Is my intended here?"

He shakes his head and gives me a weak smile. "Did you sleep on the flight?"

I shake my head. I can never sleep on long flights, regardless of their duration. Whenever I close my eyes, I feel the plane closing around me.

"I didn't think you would. Why not head up to your room? I'll have Victoria bring up some food."

I glance around. "I thought he would be here when I arrived."

"No need to rush that business. The Commission hasn't been informed about the engagement."

My heart raced with excitement. "Oh. Has something changed?"

"No. With your extended stay in Italy, we thought it would be best to wait until your return. An event will happen at the compound on Friday evening. We will make the announcement then. You may go tomorrow to select a dress for the event."

"Wouldn't he wish to make that selection? I was confused as to why he didn't take charge of my life. This is The Famiglia's way. The husband or household leader makes all decisions.

"He is fine with you selecting your gown."

I needed to find out their identity. I couldn't rest until I knew who I'd be tied to forever. "Lu, what is his name?" I thought using the nickname I gave him when I first spoke would show him how much I needed the answer.

He wraps his large, muscular arm around my shoulders and pulls me close. I allow the warmth of his grasp to calm my nerves. He might be the badass mafia Don of the Gambino family, but to me, he will always be my loving brother. "Lulu, don't worry about who it is. I promise you it will be okay."

Tears prick my eyes. "But Lu."

"He's a good man. You'll see it was the right choice. Now go up and rest."

My body slumps, my muscles weak, and my stomach twists into a tight knot as I contemplate the enigmatic stranger who holds my fate in his hands. With a heavy heart, I slowly ascend the grand staircase, each step amplifying the daunting silence of the sprawling mansion. At last, I discover solace in my room, a refuge from the tumultuous events surrounding me. The soft light filtering through the window casts a serene glow over my surroundings. It urges me to gather my thoughts and fortify my resolve for the trials that await me.

As I sit on the edge of the bed, a sense of unease washes over me. The luxurious furnishings and decor only reminds me of the constraints that bind me within these walls. I walk over to the window, gazing at the sprawling estate that stretches before me. The moon hangs low in the sky, casting an ethereal glow over the landscape below.

My thoughts swirl and spin with a barrage of questions and doubts, each one pressing upon my mind more urgently than the last. Who is the man I am destined to marry? Will he show gentleness and compassion or be consumed by power and ambition like others? The uncertainty gnaws away at me, a ceaseless torment clawing at my very being. It feels as though it could devour my soul if I let it.

With a gentle tap on the door, Victoria appears with a tray of food. Her kind eyes meet mine, offering the silent comfort I desperately need in this moment of turmoil. She sets the tray on the table beside me and gives me a warm smile.

"Miss Lucy, Mr. Luca asked me to bring you some food. I made your favorite."

"Thank you, Victoria. No need for the trouble."

"Of course I did. I've missed cooking for you. Now eat up."

I offer her a weak smile in return, grateful for her thoughtfulness. She exits, and I sit at the table, picking at the food in front of me. The taste of the meal is lost on me as I grapple with the whirlwind of emotions swirling inside me. Each bite feels like lead in my mouth, a bitter reminder of the life that stretches before me like an endless abyss. I push the plate away, my mind consumed by thoughts of the man I will marry. Mindlessly, I strip my grummy clothes off and walk into the shower. Hot water beats the stress out of my body and washes it away.

I lay in bed, tossing and turning as the moon slowly made its way across the sky. Sleep evades me even though I haven't slept in over twenty-four hours. My thoughts are consumed by the unknown man I am to marry, an enigma whose identity remains a mystery.

As my mind drifts into the hazy edges of slumber, fragmented images of him flash through my mind like snapshots. He is a tall figure cloaked in shadows, with piercing eyes that seem to hold secrets within them. His voice is deep and commanding, yet strangely alluring in my mind.

My heart quickens at the thought of him, a mixture of fear and fascination pulsing through my veins. Who is he? What does he want from me? The questions swirl around me like a whirlwind, taunting me with their unanswered curiosity.

But as exhaustion finally overtakes me and pulls me into its embrace, my mind gives in to the darkness, and I fall into a restless sleep.

I am wandering through a vast forest, unable to find my way out. The trees loom above me like towering sentinels, their branches reaching out like gnarled fingers ready to ensnare me. The air is thick with an eerie silence, broken only by my footsteps echoing through the woods.

As I continue on aimlessly, something catches my eye in the distance. A figure standing among the trees, watching me intently with eyes that glow in the darkness.

My heart races as I draw closer, trying desperately to make out any features I can recognize. But as I step into a moonlit clearing where the figure stands waiting for me, everything fades into blackness again.

I wake up with a start, gasping for air as if I had been holding my breath all along. My heart is pounding against my chest as I try to shake off the remnants of the dream, feeling as though I am being pulled under.

My eyes adjust to the darkness of my room. The heavy drapes, made of deep blue velvet, hang over the tall windows, blocking any glimpse of sunlight. I checked the time and gasped - it was already ten o'clock. The hours seem to have slipped unnoticed as I slept for fourteen hours. With a deep sigh, I finally drag myself out of bed and make my way to the bathroom. Before my day starts, I need another shower to wash away the sweat from my dream. Warm water flows over me in the shower, awakening my mind for the day. I must go out to acquire my gown for Friday's event, but first, I must prepare.

After my shower, I entered my closet to find Victoria had already unpacked my suitcases. Since I would be in the public eye, I slipped on my black Dior sheath dress and matching pumps. I dried and straightened my hair before putting on a tight coat of makeup to cover up the dark circles under my eyes. As I was putting on my lipstick, I heard my phone ringing. I looked at the screen and smiled.

"Angelina."

"I heard you are back from Italy."

"Yes. I got in last night."

"I bet you are happy to be back."

"Yeah. How are you?" During my time in Italy, I hadn't connected her or anyone else.

"Really good. How are you?"

"I'm good. Do you plan on going to the Friday event?"

"Yes. I've already got my dress. Giovanni even let me pick it out."

"I'm going out today to get mine."

"Why don't we go to Bella Luna for lunch?"

I pause, my mind racing as I consider the situation. My dear friend would be invaluable with her sharp wit and wise counsel. Her marriage to Giovanni was not one of love, but arranged by her father. Despite unexpected circumstances, they quickly found a strong bond and fell deeply in love. Their love was palpable and undeniable to all who witnessed it.

"I would love that. I'll meet you there."

"Wonderful. I'll see you at 12:30."

With a deep breath, I hang up the phone and reach for my bag. It was time to brace myself and face the situation head-on, to put on my metaphorical big girl panties and stop letting it consume me. The weight of uncertainty still lingered in the air, but I refused to let it overwhelm me any longer. Determined, I stepped out into the unknown, prepared to control my fate.

Chapter Three

Lucy

I am sitting at the table, waiting for Angelina to show up. I quickly found a gown. If I were to be showcased, like a prized animal at a fair, I would strive for an impressive appearance. I was going to look amazing. I wore a stunning black gown for my farewell to the man I loved.

The gown's bodice was a dazzling display of opulence, shining like a million stars in a dark sky. The Swarovski crystal pattern shone in the light, creating a beautiful display of colors. It had a deep plunging neckline, teasingly revealing glimpses of my full breasts, while the low back added an air of sensuality to the ensemble. Crafted from layers of jet-black feathers, the skirt was a living work of art. When I turned, the feathers rustled softly like whispers from another realm, adding to the ethereal quality of the dress. As I gazed at myself in the mirror, I felt transformed into a majestic raven - mysterious and alluring, yet still exuding a sense of untamed power and beauty.

I could feel my heart racing as I imagined the impending doom of Luca's reaction to the credit card bill. The dress I had chosen was stunning, but its price tag alone could give even the most composed person a heart attack. Not to mention the pricey shoes and lingerie that completed the outfit. When I tallied everything, the bill surpassed fifteen thousand dollars. I could only hope that the beauty of the dress would soften his anger at my reckless spending.

Within The Famiglia, punishment was a taboo topic among the girls and women. It lurked in the shadows, unspoken but ever-present. The household leader wielded the power to dispense punishments as he saw fit, and it was not a decision taken lightly. Female members of The Famiglia were expected to follow the leader's rules. Punishments varied from household to household. Some punishments were more painful than others.

Typically, I refrain from using the credit card provided by Luca. Instead, I rely on the one I pay for with my hard-earned money. Unlike most women in this exclusive society, Luca supports and encourages my passion for photography. Initially, I only sold a few prints a month for a meager amount. But now, my photographs command prices in the hundreds of thousands and are proudly displayed in galleries across New York City and beyond. During my recent trip to Italy, I contacted a local gallery and presented them with my portfolio. The owner was intrigued by my unique perspective and edgy style, and they asked me to exhibit my works in their esteemed establishment.

The weight of my hard-earned money sitting in the bank was comforting. However, it wasn't all of my fortune. Being Francis Gambino's daughter from The Famiglia, my wealth is stashed in secure locations worldwide. My father always prepared for any potential threats, ensuring safe houses and stashes of cash scattered across the globe. It was a constant reminder of The Famiglia's power and influence, even against outside forces. Despite the dangers surrounding us, there was a sense of security in knowing that my family always had a backup plan.

I look up and see my friend walking toward me. I jump up and pull her into a tight hug. "Angelina."

"Lucy," she cries, holding me tight. We pull apart, and she motions for me to take a seat. "You look great," she says.

"Thank you. I love your hair." Before her kidnapping, she had never cut her hair. The monster who took her sliced it off, leaving it for Giovanni to find.

She runs her fingers through it and smiles. "Yeah, I love it. So tell me all about Italy."

"Good." I hated lying to Angelina, but couldn't tell how miserable it had been.

Angelina reaches out and places her hand on top of mine. "Did you get in trouble for what you did to save me?"

"Not really. Luca was upset, of course, but Father strutted around like a rooster, telling everyone in the town what I did," I say. I loved visiting my parents, and typically, I enjoyed my time there. Luca's disclosure of the marriage arrangement ruined any possible enjoyment. Tears formed in my eyes, and I willed them to stay put as I remember how hurt I was.

"What is wrong?"

My eyes dart around the room before returning my gaze to her. "Luca has decided it is time for me to marry. So, he has selected a husband for me."

Her hand shoots up to her mouth and her eyes grow wide. "Oh. Who is it?"

My bottom lip quivers as I try to hold my emotions together. "I don't know."

"Lucy, I am sure Luca has made a perfect match for you," she says, holding my hand tight. I want to believe her, but I can see the doubt in her eyes.

"Angelina, I could never love whomever he picks."

"Lucy, love found its way into my heart despite my initial thoughts."

"You don't understand. I can't ever love him because," I say as my voice breaks on a sob.

"Because what?" she asks.

The tears I have tried so hard to keep from falling spilled from my eyes. "Because my heart and all my love belong to another," I confess softly.

"Oh, Lucy," Angelina says.

She wastes no time pulling me into a tight embrace, knowing that's exactly what I need now. As the first sob racks through my body, I press my face against her shoulder, feeling the warmth of her familiar embrace wrap around me like a security blanket. She is my rock in this vulnerable moment, and I cling to her tightly.

"Lucy, tell me everything," Angelina whispers, her voice filled with concern.

I struggle to compose myself, inhaling deeply, my voice a mere whisper. "There is someone who I have loved since I was sixteen. But I'm sure he is not the one Luca has chosen for me."

Angelina pulls away, her gaze searching mine. "How can you be sure?"

"Because he hates me." I wipe away the tears running down my face. Angelina reaches into her bag and hands me a pack of tissues. I take one and blot my face. After a few minutes, the tears slow, and I take a deep, cleansing breath. I give Angelina a faint smile.

"Lucy, who is it?"

I shake my head. No one would know his name ever. "Angelina, I can't tell you. I must bury these feelings and prepare myself for my upcoming."

She gives me a sympathetic look. "Alright, but I am here for you anytime."

My heart weighed like a bolder with doubt and fear, consumed by the thought of betraying my true feelings. Being bound to someone I didn't love felt like a suffocating cage closing in on me, leaving me trapped and unable to break free.

Despite my efforts to banish him from my thoughts, his presence lingers like a haunting specter. Davide Corvo Bonanno. The mere thought of his name sends shivers down my spine and ignites an inferno in my body. He possessed an irresistible danger, like a starless night, his eyes penetrating my soul, leaving me breathless.

After we went to the restroom and I fixed my makeup, we ordered lunch. The rest of the time, we kept the conversation light. When we left, I had made up my mind. I would show my future husband how strong Lucy Gambino was.

When I arrived at the estate, I instructed the staff to take my purchases to my room. Victoria is standing by the staircase.

"Is my brother in his office?"

"Yes, Miss Lucy."

I give her a warm, determined smile and stride towards the office. My curiosity about my future burns within me, driving me forward. Luca's rich timber reaches my ears as I approach, accompanied by another unfamiliar voice. Intrigued by the person's identity and their conversation with Luca, I approach the slightly open door. The other voice speaks, and I notice it is familiar.

"I let my rage cloud my judgment when she recklessly hot-wired that car and charged into a hangar filled with dangerous Cubans. I may see Lucy as a decent girl, but I'll never be able to form any kind of bond with her," Davide says.

A sharp inhale escapes my lips, startling even myself. The man Luca arranged a marriage with was the one I loved intensely. My thoughts spin in disbelief as I repeat his comment, trying to grasp its meaning. He doesn't want me. He is breaking the arrangement to join our families and secure our future together. A lump forms in my throat and tears prick at the corners of my eyes. How could he do this? My heart aches with betrayal and longing as I struggle to understand everything.

A searing pain shoots through my chest, radiating outwards and suffocating me. My heart feels like it's being crushed by a thousand pounds of pressure as Davide's rejection settles in. Instantly, my rage boils over, breaking free from its cage like a wild lioness set loose. His cruel words echo in my mind, each one a dagger plunging into my already shattered heart. How could he have easily turned me away without giving me a chance? My composure crumbles as I push the door open fully, entering the room with a facade of control that barely masks the turmoil raging inside me. Every breath is filled with the raw ache of betrayal, threatening to consume me whole.

Luca and Davide whip their heads around to stare at me, their expressions mixed with surprise and apprehension. I can feel the tension radiating off Davide's body, his features taut with nervous energy. A flicker of regret dances across his eyes, but it only further enrages me. My hands ball into fists at my sides as I confront him, my heart pounding like a drumbeat.

Rage burst through me. "So, this is your impression of me, asshole? You let your rage cloud your judgment? You never wanted to form any kind of bond with me?"

Davide meets my gaze. His jaw clenched in a tight line of silent resignation. The atmosphere in the room shifts, heavy with the weight of unspoken words that suffocate me. My chest feels constricted as if held captive by the tension between us. A surge of defiance rises within me, fueled by hurt and anger at Davide's dismissive attitude towards me. Luca shifts in his seat, sensing the volatile energy pulsing between us like an electric current. Our eyes lock in a silent battle, each daring the other to break first.

"Lucy, please," Luca begins, but I hold up a hand to silence him. My attention was solely on Davide, the man I silently loved for years, only to have my feelings tossed aside.

"Can you really decide that I'm not even worthy of a chance to bond with you?" I continue, my voice growing stronger and more forceful. "You may be the head of the Bonanno Crime Family, but you are nothing but a coward when facing your own emotions."

Davide's eyes narrow, a flicker of something unreadable passing through them. I can see the mask of indifference slipping, revealing the raw vulnerability beneath. We lock gazes, daring one another to a battle of wills. The tension between us crackles like electricity.

Luca breaks the standoff with his powerful authority command. "Lucy, calm down."

But his words fall flat, unable to penetrate the intense focus of my gaze on Davide. Holding his steady gaze, I sense a maelstrom of emotions brewing within him, mirroring the chaotic storm raging in my heart.

After what feels like an eternity of charged silence, Davide speaks, his voice low and tinged with regret. "Lucy, you deserve better than what I can offer you. My life is filled with darkness and danger, and I cannot subject you to that kind of existence."

His words strike a chord deep within me, igniting a spark of defiance amidst the pain. "BULLSHIT! Who are you to decide what I deserve?" With rage, I poke my finger at his chest. "I'm already part of this dark, dangerous world. I never thought you were a fucking coward."

"Lucy, you need to watch your mouth before I turn you over my knee and turn your ass red," Davide growls.

Without a second thought, I reach up and slap his face. "My father has the right. Luca has the right. However, you, Davide Bonanno, have lost the right to spank me. You will never control me."

"Luca, are you going to allow her to talk to me this way?" Davide growls.

"Davide, she is right. You gave up on the right," Luca answers.

Davide's eyes bore into mine with a fierce intensity, a mix of frustration and something else I struggled to identify. His tall frame looms over me, his presence commanding and intimidating. But I refuse to show any sign of weakness or fear, standing my ground against him. The anger that has been simmering within me finally reaches its boiling point, bubbling up and fueling my determination to stand up for myself.

"Just because you're afraid to face your own feelings doesn't give you the right to treat me like some fragile flower, Davide," I challenge, my voice unwavering. "I am not a possession to be protected or a damsel in distress waiting for her knight in shining armor. I am Lucy Gambino, and your fears and insecurities will not dictate to me."

The tension in the room thickens, suffocating us all in its embrace. I know Davide will not back down. There is no way I can see him anymore. I step aside from Davide and shift my gaze towards Luca.

"I'm going to call Father and ask him to find me a match in Italy."

Pain etches on his face. "Lulu, are you sure?"

I fight back the tears. Despite being six years older, Luca and I have always been close. "I just ask if you will allow me to tell Father."

"Of course," Luca says in an emotion-filled voice. "No rush, Lula."

"No, I'm leaving in a few weeks." I give Davide a final glance. "I really hope you find someone who you can give them your heart. Goodbye, Davide."

With a sharp inhale, I pivot on my heel and swiftly exit the room. My chin is raised in defiance, determined to hide the glistening tears that threaten to spill onto my cheeks. I refuse to let him see how much his words have wounded me. Each step I take feels like a weight lifted off my chest, freeing me from the suffocating atmosphere of the confrontation. I can feel his gaze burning into my back as I leave, but I do not slow down or turn around. I am stronger than this, and I will not let him break me with his cruel words.

.

Chapter Four

Davide

A sharp, searing pain stabbed through my chest as I watched Lucy Gambino walk away. It felt as though a jagged knife had carved out my heart and left it lying on the ground. Its once-strong beats now fade into nothingness. With each step she took, it was as if she was stomping on my heart, crushing it beneath her feet. Nothing would ever be the same again, and I could feel the weight of that realization dragging me down into a pit of despair.

The weight of my actions hit me like a ton of bricks. My intention had been to spare Lucy from the pain of the arranged marriage, but now I saw I had only caused more harm. Watching her leave her home behind was not what I had intended, filling me with deep regret. The guilt swirled around me like a thick fog, suffocating and all-consuming. How could I have been so blind to the consequences of my impulsive decision?

"Well, I hope you are happy." I glance toward Luca and see his jaw clenched and sadness in his eyes. "You have driven my sister away."

"Luca, I didn't want that to happen."

"Well, wanting and doing are two different things. I think you need to leave Davide."

"Luca, you are like a brother to me."

"Whether your family or not, if you can't see the harm you've caused, I don't know who you are anymore." He walks away and leaves me alone in his office.

As I reflect on my choices, a heavy sense of guilt and remorse consumes me. I truly cared for Lucy but couldn't bear to hurt her even more by marrying her. My heart and mind were at war, torn between my love for her and the knowledge that it would only bring her pain in the end.

I squeeze my eyes shut as a barrage of memories of Lucy assaults my mind. The sound of her laughter, like a symphony playing on repeat in every corner of my heart; the feel of her touch ignites a wildfire within me. But now, all that lingers is a yawning void, a cavernous emptiness threatening to swallow me whole like a vacuum, sucking out all joy and light from my being.

I inhale deeply, trying to calm the storm of emotions swirling within me. My inner demon, The Raven, stirs restlessly within, tempting me with promises of wild and forbidden pleasures at the infamous Disorderly House.

Founded by The Famiglia, this establishment was a safe haven for its members to indulge in any desire without fear of consequences. Inside, the women's only job was to cater to our most depraved and decadent fantasies.

With a heavy heart, I slowly make my way out of Luca's office. The disappointment in his eyes weighs on me like boulders, crushing my spirit with every step I take. Walking down the long corridor, I am drawn to the photographs. Each one is a stunning capture of raw, unfiltered beauty, a testament to Lucy's talent behind the camera. I can't help but run my finger over the glass as if trying to touch the images and feel their emotions. A deep sigh escapes my lips as I continue, lost in thought and emotion.

In a voice so faint, I whisper. "Goodbye, Lucy."

I walk out and climb into the back of my car.

"Where to Mr. Bonnano?"

The Raven inside me caws with anticipation, eager to drown out the pain with fleeting pleasures. "To the Disorderly House."

"Certainly, sir."

For years, Mici has been my unwavering guardian and trusted driver. I have seen him fight by my side countless times, his bravery and loyalty never wavering as he risked his life to protect mine. The scars on his body tell the tales of battles won and enemies defeated, a testament to his fierce dedication and unwavering sacrifice. There is no one I trust more than Mici, my faithful protector.

As I approach the Disorderly House, I try to rid myself of the image of Lucy's face. I can still hear the softness of her voice and see the sadness in her eyes as she walked away from me. The car ride feels suffocating, the weight of my guilt pressing down on me like a vise. The Raven inside me stirs, his whispers growing louder and more insistent with every passing second.

The streets blur past me in a dizzying array of flashing neon lights. The deep-shadowed alleys, each building standing as a stoic witness to the turmoil raging within my soul. My fingers curl into tight fists, trying desperately to resist the magnetic pull of temptation that constantly taunts me. But the alluring facade of The Disorderly House looms ahead. Its siren song lures me closer with seductive promises of a temporary escape from my inner demons.

As we pull up to the entrance, I hear the muffled sounds of revelry and debauchery emanating from within. The air is heavy with the scent of smoke and perfume, mingling with the faint undertone of desperation that permeates this place.

I step out of the car, my footsteps echoing on the pavement as I approach the entrance. The bouncers recognize me immediately and part ways, allowing me to slip inside without a word. The music pounds in my ears, the bass reverberating through my chest as I navigate the throngs of people.

The air was thick with the scent of seduction as women, adorned in barely their clothing, brushed against me. The heat of their perfumed skin lingered in my senses, tempting me to give in to their advances. The Raven perched on my shoulder, whispering enticing promises of pleasure, offering fleeting moments of ecstasy to comfort my sorrow. It was a dangerous game, one that threatened to consume me entirely if I gave into its charms.

I find myself in a hidden alcove, the dim lights casting eerie shadows across the faces of those around me. A bottle of rich, amber-hued bourbon materializes before me, its alluring contents beckoning me toward oblivion. I pour myself a generous serving, watching as the liquor glides effortlessly into my glass and swirls hypnotically. With a deep breath, I bring the drink to my lips and feel the fiery liquid singe its way down my throat, spreading warmth and comfort through every inch of my body. The taste is smooth yet potent, balancing pleasure and danger.

As the clock ticks on, I find myself consumed by a thick fog of smoke and the pungent scent of alcohol. The harsh burn of each sip sends shivers down my spine, but I grasp for another, hoping to numb the tumultuous emotions swirling inside me. Lucy consumes my thoughts, her intoxicating presence still lingering in my mind. And then there's Luca, his piercing gaze filled with judgment and disappointment. His disapproving stare only adds to the chaos, forcing me to question my actions and desires. I reach for another drink, hoping the alcohol will allow me to escape the overwhelming grief temporarily.

A seductive figure glides towards me, her body moving with a sinuous grace that draws all eyes to her. Her hips sway in a hypnotizing rhythm, accentuating the curves of her hourglass figure. As she reaches me, she leans in close, her voice a smooth purr that sends tingles of pleasure down my spine. The delicate fabric of her barely there-shelf bra barely contains her full and inviting breasts. Her ruffled skirt and matching thong leave little to the imagination. The scent of musk and jasmine surrounds us, adding to the sensual atmosphere. Her presence heightened every sense, from the sight of her alluring form to the intoxicating aroma in the air.

I meet her gaze, momentarily captivated by the depths of darkness swirling within her eyes.

"What brings you to the Disorderly House tonight, Mr. Bonanno?" Her voice was like velvet.

The Raven within me stirs with restless anticipation, pushing me towards the alluring woman standing before me. Her seductive promises of escape pull at my very core. Yet, I cannot shake off the memory of Lucy, her haunting eyes imploring me not to repeat the same mistakes that plagued my family for generations. The struggle between my desires and conscience rages on. A battle fought with every fiber of my being.

"I'm looking for something to take my mind off things."

She smiles, her eyes flickering with understanding. "Then come with me."

I down the rest of my glass and her hand slides into mine, the warmth of her touch seeping into my veins. The Raven caws excitedly, eager to taste the forbidden pleasures her lips promise.

As we enter the dimly lit room, I am immediately struck by the chilling depictions covering its walls. The paintings depict The Famiglia's sinister rituals, their twisted forms, and eerie symbols sending shivers down my spine. Candles dot the walls, casting flickering shadows that seem to come alive and threaten to devour us whole. The air is thick with the scent of incense, its heavy aroma promising hidden desires and dark secrets waiting to be uncovered. My heart races as I take in the unsettling atmosphere of this place.

She leads me towards a large, four-poster bed, its canopy draped in black velvet. The mattress is piled high with pillows, beckoning us to surrender to our carnal desires. Her hand glides up my arm, her fingers tracing the tattoo of the black raven on my shirt-covered back, sending shivers down my spine.

Her eyes lock onto mine. "I want you to take me, Davide. I crave the sting of your touch, the power of a man that commands respect and fear."

My heart races as she draws closer, her lips brushing against my ear. "Let loose the beast within you, Davide.

Unleash the darkness within your soul, and claim me as your own."

The weight of my guilt and the ache of losing Lucy fade away, overshadowed by the alluring promise of escape that this dark entity offers. Its talons dig into my thoughts, pulling me towards a tempting oblivion. My heart races with excitement as I struggle to resist its pull, knowing that giving in could mean losing myself forever.

As she pulls back, her lips glistening with desire, I take a deep breath and decide. The Disorderly House was always where I could find solace in fleeting moments of pleasure, a temporary escape from the life I led. And perhaps it would serve as a temporary salvation from my guilt and heartache tonight.

My hand reaches out, grasping her roughly, and pulls her close. Our bodies press together. My lips crash against hers with a desperate, almost primal hunger. Her warmth engulfs me, melting away any thoughts or worries that may have been lingering in the back of my mind. In this moment, it is just us, lost in each other's embrace.

"Take me, Davide. Use me for your pleasure."

I let out a deep, guttural groan of desire as my hand eagerly reached for the button of her skirt. The fabric resists, teasing me and igniting my yearning even more intensely. Every inch of her body is like fuel to the fire of my desire, driving me forward with an almost primal hunger.

As I strip her naked, the satisfaction of my dominance fills me with a heady sense of power. I am the captain of this ship, the master of my destiny, and I shall have her beneath me. My mind is a whirlwind of thoughts, desires, and expectations.

With a swift and forceful movement, I toss her onto the soft expanse of the bed. Her gaze locked on mine with a mixture of anticipation and surrender. Her bare skin is like a tantalizing fruit, ripe and ready for the taking. Every curve and contour of her body beckons to me, begging to be explored. The heat between us is palpable, aching with desire as I give in to my primal urges.

"What is your name?"

She licks her lips. "Lucida."

I recoil in shock, my body tensing up as if I've been stabbed in the gut. With the force of a freight train, the truth hits me, leaving me gasping for breath and struggling to regain my composure. The woman who walked away from me with tears streaming down her face, her heart shattered by my foolishness. The woman who should have been my wife, if only I hadn't been so damaged.

Her name was a blade that pierced my heart, a constant reminder of the pain and regret I carried. I pushed Lucy away and let her slip through my fingers because of my cowardice and doubts. And now, standing before this stranger named Lucida, I was about to desecrate her memory with a single act of betrayal. The guilt and shame threatened to consume me as I struggled to keep up the facade of indifference.

The Raven inside me cawed triumphantly, its nails digging into the deepest parts of my mind, reveling in my vulnerability. It relished in its victory, believing it had dragged me into a never-ending abyss of darkness and sin. But I refused to let it consume me. With every ounce of strength left in me, I fight against the relentless creature, determined to reclaim control of my thoughts and actions.

I force myself to focus on the scent of her jasmine. This was not Lucy, and this was not what I wanted.

I jerk away from her, my mind clear. This was something I couldn't do. I couldn't betray Lucy. I couldn't let The Raven win.

"I can't do this."

Lucida gives me a look of confusion and disappointment. "What do you mean?"

"I mean, I can't do this."

Her piercing blue eyes bore into mine, searching for any hint of what had transpired. I could feel the weight of her gaze, like a pressure building in my chest. But my expression remained blank, revealing nothing. In an act of frustration and perhaps guilt, I retrieved my black leather wallet from the inside pocket of my tailored suit jacket and carelessly tossed several crisp hundred-dollar bills onto the blood-red satin sheets of the king-sized bed. As a high-ranking member of The Famiglia, I did not need to pay her. The women who worked for us were well-compensated, with access to top-notch health care and luxurious high-rise apartments fully funded by our powerful and wealthy organization. It was one of the many perks of being part of this secretive and formidable family.

I adjust my jacket and exit the room. A wave of guilt and shame hits me like a ton of bricks. Sleeping with another woman to numb the pain of hurting Lucy would only make things worse.

Chapter Five

Lucy

As I stared at my reflection in the ornate mirror, my emotions were a swirling storm within me. The dress hung on my body, mocking me with its beauty. It was the same dress I had purchased with thoughts of Davide and my love for him. Now, it represented something entirely different. It reminded me of yesterday and the heartache clinging to me like a heavy cloak. I am torn between setting fire and never seeing it again. Or confidently stride into the ballroom, defying all who would dare pity me. The dress radiated both pain and hope, and I couldn't decide which emotion would win out in the end.

Even with the seething anger that burns within me toward Davide, the fiery love that still blazes in my heart could not be extinguished. It is a bittersweet sensation, like licking honey off a razor blade. The sweetness of love mixed with the sharp pain of hurt and betrayal. Every fiber of my being yearned to let go of him, but his hold on me was unbreakable, a tight knot tied around my heart that refused to loosen. The thought of striking him, of inflicting even a fraction of the anguish he had caused me, only added to the turmoil churning inside me.

My thoughts play on an endless loop of scenarios. Had I demanded Luca's arrangement partner, what would have occurred? What would have happened if I hadn't let six months pass before finally returning home? What if I mustered the courage to confess my true feelings to him? Endless "what ifs" suffocated me with anxiety, unable to shake off the weight of uncertainty and regret.

"Lucy," Luca calls out from outside my door. "Are you ready to go?"

I take one more look and straighten my shoulders. Davide Corvo Bonanno will not control me. Picking up my purse, I walk over to the door and open it.

Luca looks at me, and his mouth gaps open. "Lulu, are you sure you want to wear this?"

I offer him a small, confident smile that reaches my eyes. "Yes," I say with determination. "I carefully selected this dress and intend to wear it tonight." My gaze sweeps over the elegant fabric and intricate beading, feeling a sense of pride. "I want my last event at The Famiglia compound to be memorable. I want to look my absolute best."

"So you are still leaving?" he asks. As I look into his eyes, I see the pain this is causing him. It doesn't match my pain, but it was closed.

"Luca, I refuse to be in a place where I'm gossiped about."

"Lucy, no one other than the founding sons knew about the arrangement. You know they wouldn't say anything to anyone else."

"Are they aware of the broken engagement?"

"Yes. I didn't want them to say something that would cause you pain again. I hope it was okay," he says, concern on his face.

"It is, but it doesn't change my mind about moving. I can't live here and know I could run into Davide anytime. He is your friend, and I don't want to stand between you."

"But you are my sister, and I love you," Luca says, wrapping his big arm around my shoulder.

Luca's powerful arms wrapped around me, and I could feel the warmth of his embrace seeping into my bones. His familiar scent of pine and vanilla calmed my nerves but also brought a twinge of guilt to my heart. He has been my rock, always by my side through every obstacle and challenge. As I prepare to move away, the weight of leaving him behind troubles me. It will be incredibly difficult for me to say goodbye to him.

"I love you too, Luca," I say softly, resting my head against his chest momentarily before pulling away.

Hand in hand, we emerge from the house's grand entrance and enter the waiting car. The leather seats envelop us in their warmth as we settle in for the drive to The Famiglia compound. The silence between us is familiar, comforting even, as we both retreat into our own contemplations. People dressed in their finest filter through ornate wooden doors to the ballroom. Luca helps me out of the car, and we walk into the ballroom. The twinkling lights of the ballroom cast a magical glow, enticing us to become a part of the glamorous affair within. It's like a scene from a fairytale, with its opulent surroundings and the buzz of excitement permeating through the air.

My heart races with a mix of anticipation and apprehension. The room is full of familiar faces, all wearing polite smiles to hide their true motives and private conversations held in secret. I've grown accustomed to this scrutiny as a member of the founding families in The Famiglia. Our every move is watched and judged, and our reputations are constantly on the line. The children of the founding five families in The Famiglia are homeschooled by top-notch tutors. While the rest go to the organization's private school. It's not that I think I'm above anyone else, but my status as a daughter of a founding son places me in a different echelon. I hold my head high and stand tall, determined to show these people that Lucy Gambino is not someone to be underestimated or trifled with.

The music swells, its enchanting melody wrapping around the room like a warm embrace. As I listened, sadness filled my heart because this was supposed to be the night when my engagement to Davide would be announced. Navigating through the crowd, we exchange pleasantries with guests and offer polite nods to acquaintances. Brightly colored dresses and sharp suits adorn the room, adding to the festive atmosphere. The scent of freshly cut flowers and delicate perfumes lingers in the air, mingling with the sweet strains of music. Despite my heavy heart, I'm still captivated by the event's beauty and grandeur.

"Oh my God, Lucy, this dress is killer," Angelina gushes, pulling me into a hug.

"Thank you. Yours is stunning as well," I say. Her gown was shimmering gold with an all-over sequin in an erupting fireworks design. It had a cape with the same sequin design.

"Thanks," she says with a small smile, her gaze fixed on her husband, Giovanni.

I gaze into her eyes. Their love is almost tangible. A lump forms in my throat as I am overcome with emotion. Giovanni's expression mirrors hers, his eyes sparkling with adoration and tenderness. Seeing their unwavering love for each other fills me with awe. It's like watching a mesmerizing dance between two souls that are truly meant to be together, wholly intertwined, and in perfect sync.

"I'm...excuse me," I say. Turning before anyone can answer, I rush toward the bathroom.

I stumble into the bathroom, barely able to support my weight against the cold marble sink. My heart thunders in my chest, threatening to burst through my ribcage. Tears prick at the corners of my eyes, but I fiercely blink them back. I refuse to let these vultures see me vulnerable. Not here, not now.

I inhale deeply, attempting to steady my racing heart as I reach for a tissue. My eyes are slightly swollen and red. The closed door can't contain the lively sounds of the ballroom, filling the silence with merriment. It starkly contrasts with the turmoil brewing inside me, threatening to overflow at any moment.

A sudden movement catches my eye as I gather my thoughts and fix my appearance in the mirror. Whirling around, I am met with Davide lounging against the door. His dark eyes, filled with an intense gaze, penetrated my very being and sent shivers down my spine. The air between us crackles with an unspoken tension, leaving me breathless.

"Davide," I say, my voice coming out as a whisper.

"Lucy," he snarls his voice a guttural growl. "Why did Luca allow you to leave the house like this?" His hand clenches into a tight fist as he aggressively steps toward me. His eyes were ablaze with seething rage. "Do you even realize how vulnerable you are in that dress? Every man desires you passionately, imagining fucking you."

"Excuse me."

"This dress clings to every glorious inch of your body, baring too much skin."

I seethe with rage, my voice sharp and filled with venom. "This is my body, and I will wear whatever the hell I want."

He steps closer, and I am enveloped in the intense heat radiating from his body. His proximity is suffocating, overwhelming me with a tumultuous mix of longing and anger. The familiar scent of his cologne engulfs me, mingling with the heady aroma of my expensive perfume to create a dizzying concoction that threatens to unravel my composure. My heart races as our eyes lock, the tension between us palpable in the air.

"Davide, you have no right to comment on my choices. I am not yours to control."

A flicker of emotion, too fleeting to decipher, passes through his dark eyes before they harden into cold stone again. His jaw clenches, and I can see his muscles ticking as he struggles to maintain control. In that brief moment, I catch a glimpse of the internal conflict raging within him.

A sudden jolt runs through me as he viciously grabs my neck, forcing my head towards his. His lips ravage mine in a fierce, demanding kiss that sets my body ablaze with an unknown heat. It's my first kiss, but there's nothing innocent about it. The intensity grows with each passing second until it becomes almost unbearable. I never imagined it could feel like this. It's a volatile mixture of ecstasy and peril, melding into a dangerously enticing concoction.

His rough, calloused hand trails up my body with a sense of urgency. As it reaches the front of my dress, he tugs at the fabric, exposing my skin and sending shivers down my spine. His touch is firm and possessive as he cups my breast and presses his fingers against it, eliciting a gasp from my lips. Then, with a sudden twist, he captures my nipple between his fingers and applies just enough pressure to send sparks of pleasure through my body, causing my core to clinch. My senses are overwhelmed by the intensity of his touch, and I can feel myself surrendering to his every move.

A sharp gasp escapes my lips as I feel the sting of pain shoot through my body. The intensity of the sensation is overwhelming, causing my body to tremble and my mind to swirl with desire. Every nerve ending is on fire as his lips press against mine, sending sparks flying through me. It's a delicious agony, one that I can't help but crave more of.

His voice was rough and heated as he groaned into my ear, his fingers still pinching and pulling at my nipple. I could feel the warmth of his breath on my neck. "Do you like that? Seeing you in this dress, you made so fucking hard. Black feathers, just like a raven's wings. Corvo has been begging for release since he first laid eyes on you in this dress." His words sent a wave of heat through my body. "Why did you choose this dress? To drive me wild with want?" The intensity in his voice matched the fiery passion in his eyes as he devoured me with his gaze.

"Before I knew you were the one, I had picked out this dress." He pulls my earlobe between his lips and suckles on it. "Davide, please." The feelings coursing through me were nothing I had ever felt before. I had no control over my body. Despite my lack of romantic relationships, I have still experienced pleasure. But the sensations Davide is causing are unlike anything I've ever felt. The intense pressure of his kisses and fingers on my nipples brings me immense pleasure, almost to the point of being unbearable.

He tugs on my nipple and groans. "Who has made you feel this way?"

"No one."

With a firm grip on my ear, he whispers my name in a low and serious tone. Slowly, he releases me and steps back, his gaze never leaving mine. The intensity of his eyes sends shivers down my spine, and I can feel the weight of his words hanging between us like a heavy curtain.

I try to recover from the seeming betrayal of my own body. "Davide."

He nods once, his face expressionless. "This shouldn't have happened."

I choke back tears, my mind racing to make sense of the tumultuous events unfolding. He turns on his heel and strides out of the bathroom, leaving me frozen in place, my heart slamming against my ribcage and my core throbbing with need.

My mind, like a hurricane, swirls and crashes as I struggle for air. My body trembles with an overwhelming surge of unfamiliar sensations, my heart racing with a primal desire

I can't control. Confusion battles with desperate need as I try to make sense of this chaotic storm of emotions raging within me.

I straighten my shoulders, preparing myself for what's coming. My heart races with frustration as I try to make sense of Davide's sudden appearance and departure. The lingering feeling of almost reaching climax lingers in the depths of my core, leaving me both aching and angry at his absence. Damn him for leaving me hanging so close, tantalizingly close, but ultimately out of reach.

I slowly turn to face the full-length mirror. My reflection reveals a disheveled sight. My once flawlessly applied lipstick is now smeared and smudged across my lips. Strands of hair have escaped from their elegant updo and now frame my flushed face in an unkempt halo. Furthermore, the delicate silk fabric of my dress was pulled, exposing my left breast. The evidence of my exertion is visible on my skin, glistening with beads of sweat and adding to the chaotic state of my appearance. I am a vision of wild abandon, completely undone by passion and desire.

With shaky fingers, I hastily fix my appearance. Smoothing down the wild tangles of my hair and tucking back a few stray strands. My dress feels tight and uncomfortable against my skin, but I refuse to let it ruin the rest of my evening. Gathering courage, I again enter the opulent ballroom, intent on making the most of what remains of this evening.

Rejoining the festivities, I can't help but feel Davide's presence lingering in the back of my mind. His kisses, gaze, and touch overwhelmed me with intensity. I can't help but feel a strange mix of excitement and apprehension as the night carries on.

I see Angelina and Giovanni twirling around the room in a graceful dance. Their laughter echoes through the air, filling the room with infectious joy and energy. They move together like watching two puzzle pieces fit perfectly into each other. I can't help but feel a twinge of longing as I watch their genuine happiness and love for one another.

Through the tall windows, I see the moon rise higher in the sky, casting a soft glow over the festivities. I consciously try to be present and engage with those around me. The lively music fills the air, urging me to sway and twirl to its vibrant rhythm. As I move through the crowd, several single members approach me with inviting smiles and outstretched hands, asking me to join them on the dance floor. Without hesitation, I accept, determined not to let Davide's disapproval dampen my spirits for the night.

The comforting embrace of melodies and laughter carried me through the night. Yet, even with the festive atmosphere, I couldn't escape the lingering feeling of Davide's lips on mine and the intensity of his gaze. It was like he could delve into my inner self, unveiling all my thoughts and feelings. His touch still burned on my skin, like a brand I couldn't shake off.

As the lively party slowly ended, I stood by the bar. I'm savoring a delicate glass of wine and observing the members as they bid their farewells. Suddenly, a hovering presence catches my attention. I turn to see Davide standing there. His deep, intense gaze is fixed on me, leaving me uneasy and vulnerable in his presence.

"What are you doing here?"

"I couldn't leave without seeing you one last time. When are you leaving for Italy?"

The anger in my voice is palpable as I retort. "Your constant rejection has left no room for doubt. You don't want me. You shouldn't be concerned about my departure. Trust me, it will be sooner than you think, and then you won't have to bear the sight of me any longer." I sit my glass down and walk away.

Chapter Six

Davide

Realizing my foolishness hit me like a ton of bricks, I couldn't help but curse myself. Why did I bother coming tonight? Was I some kind of masochist seeking punishment? My mind felt foggy and sluggish, barely functioning on my few hours of sleep. A dull ache throbbed behind my eyes, a constant reminder of my poor choices.

A suffocating sense of dread envelopes me as I toss and turn in my bed, haunted by relentless nightmares. Each one begins with Lucy, naked and willing, in my bed, her body beckoning me toward ecstasy. My desire turns to confusion and horror. Lucy's tears stain her once beautiful face, and a chilling voice whispers from the darkness, urging me to claim her. I reach out for Lucy, desperate for some sense of reality, but my hand passes through her like she is nothing but a ghost in my tortured mind.

When I arrived at the grand formal event at The Famiglia compound, I scanned the crowd to find a hidden spot where I could observe Lucy. I couldn't believe I had resorted to acting like a stalker. I unexpectedly bumped into Andrea and Danti when I approached a secluded corner. These two were not just fellow leaders of their respective families but also founding sons of The Famiglia. We shared a bond beyond friendship. We were brothers in arms, bound together not by blood but by our unwavering loyalty to each other and our families.

"Hey, man," Andrea says. "How are you holding up?"

Andrea, Danti, Giovanni, and Luca were the only ones aware of the arranged marriage. Luca must have notified them of the broken arrangement after I left yesterday.

"I'm okay," I answer, even though the lie leaves a bitter taste in my mouth.

He raises an eyebrow, knowing I am far from okay. They all know about my family's heritage. The infidelity of the Bonanno family was legendary.

"Davide, I think you need to reconsider this. You have had feelings for Lucy for a long time," Andrea says.

My head whips around, my heart racing in panic. How could he possibly know this? I had never confided in anyone about my feelings for Lucy, yet here he was, calmly stating them as if they were common knowledge. My mind raced, figuring out how this information had been revealed. Was it written all over my face, or did he have some secret means of reading my thoughts? Fuck, Giovanni was the one who could read minds. He denies it, but I have seen him in action on more than one occasion. The uncertainty and fear swirled inside me like a turbulent storm, leaving me feeling exposed and vulnerable.

"She is just Luca's sister." A bitter taste forms on my tongue as I say the words. For so long I hadn't seen her as Luca's sister, but the woman who I loved with all my being.

Andrea's reply catches me off guard. "Davide, it's clear that you've always had feelings for her. You never kept your emotions hidden from me. I saw how you looked at her and how your breath hitches whenever her name was mentioned."

His words strip me bare, exposing me to the harsh truth. I feel a primal urge to flee, to hide from the brutal reflections of my desires. I cannot escape the cruel reality that has consumed me for years. Inferno raged in my veins as the demon clawed and screamed. Release the Raven, but only when true love burns within me, not mere carnal lust.

Danti looks at me sympathetically, sensing the turmoil within me. "We all care about you, Davide. I know you wouldn't want to hurt Lucy. But consider marrying her. Unlike the others in your family, this match wasn't just an arrangement. There is love involved, and it could make an enormous difference. Since you love her, you won't want to hurt her, and this will prevent you from straying."

"I didn't say I loved her."

They both shake their heads. "You don't have to. It is a fact."

"Well, it is too late. She is moving to Italy." The thought of never seeing her again, of never feeling the warmth of her touch or hearing her laughter, or worse yet, watching her marry someone else, causes an invisible knife to plunge into my dying heart. Each breath feels like a struggle, like I am trying to fill a balloon punctured with tiny holes. The weight of my sorrow sits heavily on my chest, threatening to crush me. But all I can do is stand there, numb and helpless, as she slips away from me forever.

"What?" Danti asks.

"Yeah. After she overheard me telling Luca I was breaking the arrangement, she told Luca she would let her father arrange a marriage with someone in Italy. She is leaving."

"Fuck, man. Luca didn't tell me," Andrea says.

"There is nothing I can do. She hates me."

"HOLY FUCK!" Danti says, looking across the room.

I follow his eyes and gasp. My heart races as Corvo's presence surges within me, a violent storm brewing and ready to unleash its wrath. He thrashes and roars, consumed by a primal desire to possess the goddess standing beside Luca. His electric energy courses through my veins, urging me to unleash his power upon her. He craves every part of her, determined to make her his and his alone. Nevermore will she belong to anyone else but him.

Lucy stands beside her brother. Her slender form was adorned in a gown meant to be my undoing. The dangerously low cut of the top revealed the swell of her breasts, a sight that hadn't graced my eyes in six long years since she stepped out of that pool. As my gaze lowered, I felt my breath catch in my throat. The bottom of her gown was made entirely of black feathers.

I'm unsure how she did it, but seeing her in that dress was a brutal reminder of the passion that still burned within me. Corvo roared, urging me to release him, to claim her as his own.

"You can't have her." My silent thought to my inner demon.

Corvo's voice reverberated like thunder in my mind, a primal growl that consumed every thought and sense. I couldn't deny the undeniable truth surging through me, fueling a ravenous craving to claim her as mine. Every fiber of my being, every dark impulse, roared with an insatiable desire for her, the beast inside me clawing and thrashing with an overwhelming hunger that could not be ignored.

I feel someone putting their hand on my arm. "Davide, don't," Andrea says. "Come, let's go get some air."

With all the power I have left in my body, I turn away. "Yeah, I need some."

We slip through the side door, and Danti's hand darts into his jacket pocket, retrieving his shining silver flask. My lips curl into a wicked grin. For as long as I can remember, Danti has carried this damn flask with him everywhere he goes. The cursed object is like a talisman to him and the only reason he's still alive today.

Five years ago, Chinese bastards ambushed him outside his apartment. They aimed for his heart. However, this cheap flask in his inside pocket took the bullet instead. Its smooth surface is now adorned with a dent as proof of its sacrifice. Miraculously, not a drop of blood spilled, and Danti killed every one of the motherfuckers. Despite everything it's been through, that thing remains intact and always held Danti's finest bourbon. It is a reminder of all the close calls and narrow escapes this trusty flask has seen alongside its owner.

My hand trembles with anticipation as I reach for the flask, its smooth metal surface cool to the touch. With a gentle twist of the lid, I take a long, satisfying drink. The rich aroma of smoky oak and sweet spices dances on my tongue as I swallow, savoring every drop. As it travels down my throat, it leaves a pleasant burn, igniting a fire within me. A contented sigh escapes my lips as I close my eyes, letting the alcohol's soothing warmth settle my nerves.

Handing it back to Danti, I take several cleansing breaths. I had to control myself. It was for the best for Lucy to marry someone who would treat her with the respect she deserved. "Thanks. I appreciate the support."

"I think you are an idiot, but I will help you get through this," Danti says. "Let's go inside and continue staking her."

Andrea laughs at the apparent joke.

We walk in, and I go directly to the bar, needing alcohol to dull the pain. The bartender immediately poured my drink without asking what I wanted. The Famiglia staff were trained to know members' preferences, especially the founding sons.

I raise the glass to my lips and take a sip, savoring the expensive taste. Nevermore will I lose control. I owe it to myself and to Lucy.

With each sip, my mind sees Lucy in that dress. My heart pounds in my chest, and Corvo roars in my mind, demanding control. But I am strong. I will not let him win. I will not become the monster he wants me to be.

I take a deep breath, turning from the bar to gaze at the party. As soon as I do, my eyes fall on Lucy talking to Giovanni and Angelina, his wife. Angelina makes a comment and then looks up at Giovanni. They share a look of tenderness and something else. Lucy turns suddenly and rushes across the room toward the bathrooms. What happened? Is she sick?

I slam my glass down. The sound echoes through the room as I spring up from my seat. Determined to find out what's wrong, I approach the bathroom with a sense of urgency. I approach and pause for a moment before slipping inside. She's standing by the sink, her breaths coming in ragged gasps. When I see her reflection in the mirror, I feel a sharp pain in my chest from the anguish on her face.

She dabs a tissue at the corner of her emerald eyes. I groan. Suddenly, she whirls around, and I am sucked into her beauty. Corvo chants in my mind. *"Take her, taste her, make her ours."*

Her voice is a soft, delicate whisper that makes my heart skip a beat. I can't help but drink in every inch of her as she stands before me. The gown she's wearing hugs her body tightly, attracting the attention of every man in the room, but no one appreciates her like I do now.

Fury over the thought, I stomp toward her and don't stop until I am inches away. Fury runs through me. "Lucy, what the hell was Luca thinking, letting you leave the house like this? Do you have any idea how dangerous it is for you to be dressed like this? Every fucking man is lusting after you. They all want to rip this dress from your body and buy their cock deep inside you. This dress hugs every curve of your body, revealing too much skin."

"So. It is my body, and I love my dress." Usually, I like my women who obey my every demand with a respectful yes, sir. Lucy is not that type of woman. I blame Luca for her strong will. Instead of making her to stay at home and prepare herself for her future husband. He encouraged her to pursue her passion for photography.

I move closer, breathing in her sweet aroma of honey-suckle. But there is another smell which Corvo moans, the tangy scent of her arousal.

"Davide, you have no right to comment on my choices. I am not yours to control. You made it perfectly clear you don't want me."

I reach behind her neck and yank her face to me. My lips claim hers with all the passion and wanting I have. She tastes so fucking good. Why did I resist this for so long? I am sure I could live the rest of my life off it. I skim my other hand up her body and pull back the front of her dress. Not breaking the kiss, I squeeze her full breast before taking her nipple between my fingers and pinching it. Hard.

She breaks the kiss to cry out. I lean into her ear and murmur. "Do you fucking like that?"

I pinch and pull the hardened nipple, basting in her cries of pleasure from the pain. Did you realize how much you excited me in that dress? You are wearing black feathers. Fucking black feathers. Corvo has been demanding release from his cage since he saw you in this dress. Why did you select this dress? Was it your intention to make me desperately crazy?"

Her words come out in short breaths. "I picked it out before I knew you were the one."

I took her earlobe between my lips and sucked.

"Davide, please."

God, I love hearing her begging.

"Who has made you feel this way?"

"No one."

"Lucy." I release her ear and step back. I gaze into her emerald eyes, full of passion and something I've never seen before. Her arousal.

"Davide." Her voice was like a warm caress. The moment stops time. In a blink of an eye, she willingly gave herself to me. She trusted I would take care of her wants and needs. Her trust was so precious that I knew if I allowed myself to have her, I would break it and her. I couldn't do this to her. I loved her too much to hurt her.

I remove all emotions from my voice. "This shouldn't have happened." I release her and walk out of the bathroom, leaving my broken heart and soul on the floor.

I am destroyed, but I need someone to check on Lucy. Looking around the room, I am relieved to see Giovanni and Angelina. I make my way over as quickly as possible.

"Giovanni."

Giovanni looks at me, and I know he can read my thoughts. "Angelina, sweetheart, why don't you go find Lucy? Davide and I need a moment."

Angelina's brows furrow before giving him a nod and taking off toward the bathroom.

Giovanni takes a step closer to me. "What the fuck did you do?"

I swallow hard, trying to regain control of my emotions. "I... I don't know what came over me. She... she was just there, and I... I couldn't help myself."

HIs face darkens. "Did you fuck her?"

"No, no, not like that! We just... kissed. That's all."

Giovanni's expression softens slightly. "You know, Davide, if you ever hurt her, you'll have to deal with Luca and me. You decided to break the arrangement, so you must stay away from her. She is no longer yours."

His words wash over me. He is right. Lucy was no longer mine. Why does that hurt so much?

"I know. Thanks for allowing Angelina to check on her."

"She is like a sister to me, and she is Angelina's savior. Go get yourself a drink and take some time to think?"

I pat him on the arm before going to the bar and getting a drink. With a drink in hand, I find a table against the wall. From this spot, I see Angelina walk back in with Lucy. They go back to Giovanni. A few minutes later, Luca joins them. I don't know what they are talking about, but I see Lucy smile several times.

As the party winds down, I watch Lucy walk to the bar and get a glass of wine. No one else was around, so I went over to apologize and find out when she was leaving.

"What are you doing here?"

"I couldn't leave without seeing you one last time. When are you leaving for Italy?"

"You have made it perfectly clear you don't want me. So you should worry about when I will be leaving. It is soon, so you won't have to see me much longer."

I watch as she links her arm to her brothers, and they leave the room. It wasn't as if I couldn't go to Italy to see her, but there was no way I could go see her with another man who was her husband.

Chapter Seven

Lucy

An overwhelming sense of panic washed over me as the reality of my situation sank in. What was I going to do now? All my plans and preparations for moving to Italy and having my father arrange a marriage with a suitable member of The Famiglia seemed futile at this moment. The certainty of my future now feels unstable.

In contrast to New York, where the founders of The Famiglia lived and ruled. The Italian organization comprised foreign leaders and wealthy Europeans. Because his family was one of the original five, my father sat on The Commission, which is the governing body of the society.

In the world of high-ranking members, any one of them would be acceptable to become my husband. After that unforgettable kiss and Davide's electrifying touch in the bathroom, I knew I could never be with anyone else. His touch had seared into my skin, branding me as his and his alone.

If I went to Italy, my father would arrange a marriage, and if I stayed here, Luca would. Davide was my only choice for marriage.

With great sadness and desperation, I saw just one way out. I need to escape from The Famiglia. This meant leaving behind my beloved family, friends, and the man I had secretly loved for years. Perhaps he would eventually find the perfect woman to marry if I disappeared from his life. After all, The Famiglia organization was filled with eligible women who met the high standards required to become the wife of their founding son and Don. As the weight of this decision settled upon my shoulders, I couldn't help but wonder what awaited me on the outside. Would I find freedom or simply trade one prison for another? Only time will tell.

I always knew that marrying Davide would be challenging because of his family's history of infidelity. But despite it all, I couldn't deny the connection we shared, the way he made me feel alive in ways I never thought possible.

But the reality of our situation was harsh and unforgiving. The weight of expectations and obligations pressed down on me, threatening to crush any hope for a future with Davide. With a heavy heart and determined spirit, I would leave everything behind.

However, it was going to be a daunting and nearly impossible task. To completely vanish from the most influential organization would require unmatched intelligence and expertise. The thought alone sent shivers down my spine, but I was determined to see it through.

It has been four years since I was detained by the Bratva. Even now, I remember every detail.

It was a warm spring day, and I was enjoying the new camera I had gotten for my 18th birthday. My brother, Luca, encouraged me to pursue my passion for photogra-

phy. I lost track of where I was and ended up in Gravesend. Unfamiliar with the place, I stumbled upon an alleyway. The light beautifully illuminated the stone walls, casting unique shadows. I was snapping shots at every angle and didn't hear them until it was too late. When I turned, I found two men in designer suits standing behind me. Taking them in, I put to memory every detail. They were at least six foot four inches, with jet black hair slicked back, broad shoulders, dark brown, practically black eyes, well-manicured beards, and tattoos. I could see them on their necks as they peeked from under their crisp white dress shirts and on the back of their hands and fingers.

"*Well, what do we have here?*" *the biggest man says in a thick European accent.* "*A malen'kiy vorobey (Little Sparrow) has landed in this dark place.*"

I stood rooted to the spot, my body trembling with fear as I faced the menacing figures. Their imposing presence seemed to tower over me, making my heart race and my muscles tense up to hold on to some semblance of composure. My ears rang with my pounding heart, its beat erratic and loud in the silence. Desperately, I searched for any potential escape route, but they had their bodies forming a solid wall that I couldn't break through. The cold sweat on my neck amplified the consuming dread. I weighed my options, knowing that running was not a viable one in this dangerous predicament.

The man, shorter in stature but with a menacing air, stepped forward with calculated steps. His dark eyes gleamed with a predatory hunger as he spoke. "*You seem to have wandered into our territory, Little Sparrow.*" *His voice sent a chill down my spine. I couldn't help but step* back, trying to create distance between us. "Why are you in this desolate corner of the world?"

Summoning every ounce of courage within me, I pushed myself to speak, my voice trembling slightly. "I... I was simply capturing some photographs. My apologies if I have trespassed." The words spilled out of my mouth like marbles, each tinged with uncertainty and unease.

The burly man made a deep, guttural sound and exchanged a knowing glance with his partner. A faint glint of suspicion flickered in his eyes as he asks. "Photographs, huh? Do you have a hidden talent, or are you just causing trouble?"

Before I could respond, the man circled around me, his dark eyes scrutinizing my camera, with a mischievous smirk playing on his lips. His gaze was sharp and calculating, like a predator sizing up its prey. His leather boots scuffing the ground echoed in the quiet street, adding an ominous undertone to the encounter. I could feel his curiosity and amusement radiating off him as he continued to inspect my equipment.

A sinister chuckle escaped his lips as he studied the camera, his eyes alight with a dangerous glint. His deep baritone only emphasized his dark assessment of the situation. "Quite an expensive toy for such a small bird."

My heart raced in my chest as I felt the tension in the air thicken, and I struggled to maintain a calm facade.

The towering figure advances, a menacing predator stalking his prey. "Little bird, where did you get this camera?" His deep growl sends shivers down my spine.

My throat tightened, and I struggled to find a plausible explanation. "It was a gift from my older brother.

My voice trembling ever so slightly. The weight of the truth hung heavy in the air, like a loaded gun pointed in my direction. In this tense situation, it felt like my only weapon.

They exchanged another glance, communicating silently in a language I couldn't understand. The tension was palpable as they seemed to deliberate their next move. The prominent man moved closer, his intense eyes locking onto mine, causing me to recoil.

His words dripped with a menacing tone as he towered over me, his eyes blazing with an unsettling intensity. My heart raced as he reached out, causing me to flinch, but his grip was as tight as a vise when he grabbed my arm. The smell of alcohol and cigarettes washed over me as his breath invaded my nostrils. "Your brother must be quite generous. Does he have knowledge of your precise location, Little Sparrow?"

The air around us felt thick, the tension between us palpable. I panicked, searching for an escape from this perilous moment.

A shiver of ice ran down my spine as his words sunk in, the gravity of the situation hitting me like a ton of bricks. I stood frozen in fear, realizing I had stumbled into dangerous territory. It was controlled by the notorious Russian mafia, infamous for their brutal ways. Panic surged through my mind as I desperately searched for an escape route from this perilous encounter. My heart pounded with each passing second as if it were trying to break free from my chest.

My heart raced as I tried to regain some semblance of control in my voice. "I... I was just exploring. I didn't mean to cause any trouble."

The smaller man laughed derisively, his eyes glinting with malice as he leaned closer, invading my personal space. His hot breath blew against my ear as he spoke. "You're in our territory now."

"And in our territory, little bird, we don't take kindly to intruders." The bigger man growled, and his grip tightened on my arm. I winced at the pressure, feeling a surge of panic. The realization of my danger crashed over me like a wave, threatening to drown my resolve.

The smaller man's grin widened as he studied me with predatory eyes, enjoying the fear that gripped me. "What should we do with her, Dom?"

My heart races as Dom's unyielding stare bores into mine, his voice dripping with cold malice. "Ivan, she is nothing but a helpless, lost bird. Let's show her the consequences of straying too far from her cage."

I feel a shiver run down my spine at the sheer cruelty in his words, knowing that whatever lesson they have planned will be vicious and unforgiving.

Ivan's sudden movement jolts me and before I can even blink, he has ripped the camera from my hands. I look and see the malicious glee dancing in them. "A little memento for your dear brother." He flips the camera around and unleashes a barrage of snapshots, capturing the terror etched on my face as a twisted keepsake.

"What is your name, little bird, so we can send the photos to your brother?"

With steely determination, I straighten my back and lock eyes with Dom. Memories flood back of my father and brother doing the same, a silent show of strength and defiance. I say with a voice dripping with pride and conviction of my family's legacy. "Lucida Esmeralda Gambino."

In an instant, Dom's facade of cockiness crumbles into a mask of pure malice. As soon as my name falls from his lips, his gaze darkens into a smoldering inferno, burning with recognition and hatred. The air around us crackles with tension, the atmosphere shifting to one of imminent danger. His grip on my arm becomes a vise, squeezing tighter and tighter as he speaks my name in a menacing growl. "Gambino." When he repeats the name, his face contours like my name is poison on his tongue. Each syllable dripping with venom and rage.

My muscles tense, and my heart races as I prepare for the inevitable onslaught. With a steely determination, I push aside the gnawing fear in the pit of my stomach. My surname holds immense power in these streets. It stirs up a treacherous underbelly of alliances and rivalries within organized crime that can shift at any moment.

Ivan's eyes widened in surprise as he glanced at Dom, a silent exchange passing between the two men. It was clear that my identity had sparked something significant to them.

With a sudden, decisive nod from Dom, Ivan reluctantly handed back my camera, his expression unreadable as he stepped back. Dom released my arm. His gaze was still fixed on me with wariness and curiosity. I could feel the tension in the air slowly easing like a predator deciding to spare its prey for reasons unknown.

"Lucida Gambino." Dom repeats my name, his voice quieter now, as if testing the sound of it on his lips. "You're far from home, Little Sparrow. You should be more careful where you spread your wings."

His words sent a chill down my spine, a warning wrapped in a cloak of ambiguity. I nodded slowly, the weight of the encounter settling heavily on my shoulders. Clearly, my family name carried both influence and danger in these dark corners of the city.

Without another word, Dom turned on his heel, gesturing for Ivan to follow as they disappeared into the shadows of the alleyway. I stood there momentarily, my heart still pounding in my chest, trying to steady my nerves and gather my thoughts. The encounter had been a close brush with danger, a reminder of the precarious tightrope I walked between the safety of anonymity and the perils of my lineage. A cold resolve settled in my heart as I watched their retreating figures. In a world where Gambino is a shield and a target, I must not be naïve or careless.

With trembling hands, I checked my camera to ensure it was undamaged, thankful that they hadn't resorted to violence. The captured images felt heavy, significant snapshots of the world and reminders of lurking dangers.

Their voices lingered, a warning of forces in this underworld. The streets grew quieter, holding their breath, anticipating what would come.

As soon as I stepped into my home, I rushed to tell Luca about what had transpired. But before I could even open my mouth, Davide and the other founding sons were already there, their eyes ablaze with a dangerous fire. Tension thickened the air, and I feared that one wrong *move would ignite a full-blown war between The Famiglia and the Bratva.* Without hesitation, Davide pulled out his phone and made a call, his voice dripping with venomous rage and an ominous intensity that sent shivers down.

A short while later, the room fell silent as Davide hung up the phone, his jaw set in a steely expression. His dark eyes bore into mine, a storm of unspoken emotions swirling within their depths. Tension filled the air, as if the room held its breath.

"Davide, what did you do?" Luca's voice broke through the heavy silence, his tone a mix of concern and caution. The other founding sons exchanged uneasy glances, sensing the gravity of the situation.

Davide's gaze remained fixed on me, his features unreadable as he finally spoke, his voice low and measured. "I made a call that was required."

His words hang in the air like a veiled threat.

His words were powerful, making me feel uneasy. Davide's actions had significant consequences in their world of alliances and vendettas. I knew better than to pry further. The complexities of his role as the face of the Bonanno Crime Family wore heavy on him. Davide's reputation preceded him, a shadow that loomed over every decision he made, every alliance he forged, and every enemy he faced. I was filled with conflicting emotions as I observed him - fear and a strange admiration for his unwavering determination.

The room's atmosphere was suffocating. Invisible tendrils of power intertwined between us, pulling at our loyalties and tempting us with betrayal. Davide's gaze broke away from mine, his eyes darting to Luca with a guarded *yet unmistakable hint of emotional turmoil. I could feel the tension rising like thunder in my chest, threatening to explode at any moment.*

Davide's voice cut through the silence like a hot knife through butter. "We need to be vigilant. I don't trust Dom."

"I am thankful she wasn't injured. Lucy, from now on, you'll always have a guard."

Ever since I had someone with me when I left the house. I had to figure a way out. If I traveled abroad, it would be easier to stay under the radar. If I stayed in the United States, it would be more difficult. No guard accompanied me during my travels to and from Italy. Maybe, just maybe, this is the solution.

Chapter Eight

Davide

Tonight is the night. As dread blankets my heart, I finish getting ready to attend Lucy's going-away party. For the last three months, I have buried myself in work, trying not to think about her and how much I will miss her.

The Russians were up to something, their stoic silence unsettling me like a ticking time bomb waiting to explode. We had captured two of their footmen on our territory, and despite hours of brutal torture, they remained resolute in their refusal to divulge any information. My frustration and rage boiled inside me as I sent a menacing message to Dominic Mogilevich, the notorious head of the Russian mafia. A mysterious package arrived at his opulent mansion in Brighton Beach, containing the grotesque contents of severed eyeballs and a single black raven feather. I could only imagine the look of horror on his face as he opened the parcel, knowing it was a warning from me. The raven feather was my signature calling card, a chilling reminder that I was not a force to be underestimated or trifled with. Despite my expectations for retaliation, there was no response from Mogilevich. The silence only fueled my unease and suspicion of their sinister plans.

Grudgingly, I slipped into my finely crafted suit, the smooth fabric clinging to every contour of my body. As I gazed at my reflection in the floor-to-ceiling mirror, I couldn't help but be reminded of the turmoil that lurked beneath my polished exterior. The Raven within me stirs. Its presence is a constant weight on my shoulders, a reminder of the sins I carry with me. Though I may present myself as Davide Corvo Bonanno, inside, I am nothing but a vessel for the insatiable darkness that threatens to consume me whole. My facade may deceive others, but I can never hide the truth from myself.

Mici drives me to the party. My heart races as we draw near the Gambino estate. I needed to calm down and reign in my feelings for her.

We pull up to the Gambino estate. The mansion's grandeur is illuminated by lights, starkly contrasted with the darkness that gnaws at my soul. I take a deep breath and exit the car, ignoring the heartache.

Stepping into the lavish party, I'm surrounded by the elite of The Famiglia organization. The air is thick with tension as I scan the room for Lucy. I found her with Luca and the other founding sons. Her laughter echoes through the crowd, her beauty more captivating than ever. I can't help but feel a pang of jealousy and regret, knowing that in a few hours, she'll be gone from my life forever.

With a deep breath, I force a small smile and head toward her. Luca is standing beside her, and as he sees me near, I see a flicker of warning in his eyes. He wouldn't think twice about beating me to a blood pulp if I upset her.

"Davide, thanks for coming."

As our hands meet in a handshake, I feel the strong, firm grip of his hand, a warning not to harm his sister. We release each other's hands, and I turn towards Lucy, who immediately catches my breath. She is a vision of seduction in her black dress, hugging every curve of her body as if it were tailor made for her. Memories flood my mind of how she moaned beneath me as I teased her puckered nipple, sending shivers down her spine. Her long blonde hair cascades down her back, gently pulled back at the nape of her neck in a low ponytail. I can't help but imagine grabbing onto it as I thrust deep inside her slick, wet core.

Consciously, I push aside any thoughts that may dampen the moment. I lean in, my lips gently touching her soft, velvety cheek. My voice shakes with emotion. "You look absolutely stunning, Lucy."

Her skin feels like silk against my lips, and the scent of her perfume fills my senses. It's a moment of pure bliss amidst the chaos of the world around us.

She looks up at me with her big, green eyes full of longing and pain. "Thank you, Davide. I'm so glad you could make it."

My mind is consumed with an insatiable hunger for her, a burning desire that has only amplified since our first encounter. The darkness within me growls relentlessly, demanding that I take her as my possession to make her mine for eternity.

But I can't do that. Lucy is not mine, not now, not ever. I plaster a fake smile. "I wouldn't miss the opportunity to see you one last time."

Our eyes lock in a fierce gaze, communicating a whirlwind of emotions that threatens to knock me off my feet. They bore into my soul with an unyielding intensity, causing my knees to tremble and threaten to give out beneath me.

"Great party, Luca," Andrea says, slapping me on the back. "Davide, you don't have a drink. Let's go take care of that problem."

My heart aches as I cling to her gaze, not wanting to break the connection. But I know I must, for my own sanity. With a deep breath, I gently grasp her hand, bringing it to my lips. I tenderly kiss her hand, trying to convey all the love and longing in my soul through this simple gesture. My eyes search hers, hoping she can see how much she means to me. My voice is full of raw emotion I murmur. "Goodbye, Lucy."

As I reluctantly remove my hand from Lucy's, her fingers trail along my palm, igniting a fire that spreads through my veins. Her sweet and alluring scent tickles my nose, lingering long after she's gone. With a sly smirk dancing on his lips, Andrea stands waiting for me at the bar, gesturing for me to join him with a glass of dark amber liquid.

I take the glass and slam back the drink in one swift motion. The fiery liquid scorches my throat as it slides down. But even as the burning sensation dissipates, I can't escape the overwhelming pain of Lucy's leaving. My body shudders with the intensity of my emotions. Andrea makes small talk, but I really don't hear him. My mind is consumed by what it would be like when Lucy is gone. After I finish my drink, I motion for another, then another, allowing the alcohol to numb my feelings. I stumble away from

Andrea, my feet carrying me toward the back, where I seek solace in fresh air and isolation.

A chilling sense of familiarity washes over me as I return to the exact spot where it all began. The once clear pool water now appears as a deep, foreboding pool mirroring the haunting full moon above. Its mocking brightness taunts me, a constant reminder of my unrequited love for her. My inner darkness churns and roars like an untamed beast, threatening to consume me whole as I stand in this cursed place once more. My heart weighs heavily, with memories and emotions trapped within this endless cycle of longing and pain.

As I stand there, transfixed by the inky depths of the pool, a primal fear grips me, and I feel my hold on reality slipping away. The darkness within me grows more potent, its tendrils engulfing me in its suffocating embrace. My heart pounds furiously as I struggle to keep control, but the burning rage inside threatens to erupt at any moment, tearing through my composure like wildfire. I take shaky breaths, trying to calm myself, but the overwhelming force of my inner demons is too much to bear.

The sounds of the party become distant echoes, and for a moment, I feel like I'm alone in this world. But I'm not. I'm never alone. My inner demon is always with me, a constant reminder of the blood on my hands. The darkness within me is not just a part of me; it is me. It's who I am and who I will always be.

"I remember that day."

I don't have to ask which day. It was a day that I will always remember.

"It was the first time you looked at me like I was a woman, not a little girl."

"Lucy."

"It was the day I knew I loved you, not as a crush, but as a life-changing love."

"Lucy, you can't love me. I am no good for you."

She looks up at me, her eyes filled with tears. "I don't care about that. I just want to be with you."

I can't help but feel a pang of guilt. How could someone as pure and innocent as Lucy love someone like me?

I sigh heavily, my heart heavy with the weight of the decision I have to make. "I'm sorry, Lucy."

She looks confused, and for a moment, I see her lips quiver in anticipation of my answer. But then her eyes fill with understanding, and I see a fire ignite within her.

"I understand, Davide. But I ask you to do just one thing for me before I leave forever."

I watched as her eyes filled with tears, a physical manifestation of the pain I had caused her. But I couldn't turn back now. "Tell me. What do you want from me?"

Her graceful movements bring her to stand in front of me. I look down at her, mesmerized by her beauty and captivated by her presence. With a gentle tug, she pulls apart the tail of the bow at her waist, causing her dress to fall open and reveal her flawless, naked form. My heart skips a beat as I am overcome with desire for her. "I want you to be my first."

Her low, sultry voice sends shivers down my spine. At this moment, I am completely lost in her, and all thoughts of hesitation or doubt dissipate into thin air.

"Lucy, you can't mean that. You know that women must be pure for their husbands within The Famiglia."

"Davide, I know this, and there are ways around it."

"Once it is gone, it is gone." I needed to change her mind. Even though my cock is so fucking hard it is painful as I think about sinking into her hot wet pussy.

"I know, but do you think women have figured out ways to get around this over the years? We are not as stupid as men think we are."

"But you are leaving tomorrow."

"Yes, and I want to have one memory of joy when I am forced to have sex with a man I don't love. Davide, please make love to me."

Her words were like a knife twisting in my heart. I knew she was right. I knew that for her, this was the only chance she would ever have to be with someone like me. Someone who could give her what she truly wanted. But I couldn't do it.

I shook my head, my voice barely audible. "I can't do that to you, Lucy."

Her face contorted with anguish, tears streaming down her cheeks as she locked eyes with me. "You've already decided for me, Davide. I have no say in the matter." Her voice shook with emotion. "All I want is one night. One night to feel wanted, to be with the only man I have ever loved. To feel like a woman, not just a commodity you can dispose of." Each of the pleading words is filled with heavy desperation and longing.

I met her gaze, finding a world of emotion within her pleading eyes. The depths of pain and longing shone through, tugging at my heartstrings. My chest tightened, feeling the weight of her unspoken words and wanting to ease her burden. I inhaled deeply, steeling myself against the all-consuming darkness that threatened to overtake me. She needed me to be strong, to provide her with the comfort and love she so desperately craved. It was a daunting task, but I was willing to take on it for her sake.

"Okay." Taking her hand, I led her over to the pool house and walked in. It was a large room with a large bed with plush pillows which overlooked the pool.

As she fell into my arms, our bodies fused together perfectly. The warmth of her skin against mine was electric, sending shivers down my spine. Her scent enveloped me, a heady combination of sweet perfume and her alluring musk. I kissed her slowly, savoring the taste of her lips and the feel of her softness against me. My hand trailed down to her waist, tracing the delicate curve of her hip with my fingertips. She moaned softly into my mouth, igniting a fire within me that mirrored the intensity in her eyes.

As my lips left hers, I continued down the curve of her neck with tender kisses, savoring the softness of her skin. Her gasps and quickening breaths only fuel my desire, and I can sense her heart pounding beneath my touch. My fingers map out every inch of her body, tracing the graceful lines of her collarbone, her shoulders' gentle slope, and her arms' delicacy. Each touch, each lingering kiss, is a gesture of my devotion to her, an expression of how deeply I value and cherish her presence.

As I lower my lips to her chest, the soft fabric of her dress brushes against my cheek. Every touch ignites a fire within me, but I know what I do is dangerous. Yet, at this moment, all that matters is the sensation of her skin against mine, a tangible reminder that this moment is real and not just a dream.

As my lips press against Lucy's skin, her breaths become shallow and rapid. Her body trembles under my touch, her pulse racing and her heart beating against my lips. Her skin is like silk beneath my fingertips, and I can feel a primal fire igniting within me as I trail my kisses lower, each one leaving a trail of desire in its wake.

But as I reach her waist, a sudden wave of guilt washes over me. It feels like a heavy shroud, suffocating and all-consuming. My mind screams at me to stop, but my desire and inner darkness take control. With trembling hands, I commit the ultimate sin, knowing that this moment will forever haunt my conscience and damn my soul.

I look up at Lucy, her eyes locked on mine, filled with desire and fear. She knows what I'm about to do, and she can't stop me. For a moment, I see the fire in her eyes die, replaced by a look of acceptance. She knows that this is the only way she can have one night of pleasure before her fate is sealed.

As I slide down her waist, my fingers brush against the thin material of her dress, and I can feel her heart pounding against my touch. I want to savor every moment with her, to make this one night the best she will ever have. But it's too late for that. I know what I'm about to do is wrong, but I can't deny the darkness that consumes me.

As I gently push the dress off her shoulders, my fingers glide over her smooth, pale skin. My heart hammers in my chest, the adrenaline coursing through me like a raging river. The darkness within me stirs, clawing to the surface as desire consumes me. Part of me wants to turn away, to flee from this temptation, but I cannot resist its pull.

I can feel the weight of my decision bearing down on me like a heavy stone. My heart is racing, and my hands are shaking as I reach and touch her skin. It's warm, silky, and soft, like the finest silk.

As I gaze upon her bare form, every inch of her body is intoxicating and alluring. I am overcome with a sense of guilt. This is not the righteous path, yet I am drawn to it like a moth to a flame. The darkness within me consumes my thoughts, overpowering any sense of morality or reason. Despite my inner turmoil, I cannot resist the temptation before me.

When we're both naked, I guide her to the bed. The fire in her eyes has been replaced with a comforting and unnerving warmth. I can't help but feel like I'm betraying everything I stand for, but I know that this is what she wants.

We lay on the bed, our bodies pressed against each other, the warmth of her skin seeping into my own. I can feel her heart beating against my chest, the rhythm matching my own. Her breath is soft and warm on my neck, and I can't help but feel a sense of calm wash over me.

As we kiss, I can feel the fire in her eyes burning brighter, consuming us both. It's as if we're two sides of the same coin, the darkness within me mirroring the light within her. I know this is not right, but I can't help but feel we're connected in a way that defies explanation.

"Lucy, are you sure?"

"Yes, Davide."

I devour her body with hungry kisses, tracing a fiery path down to her core. With a primal growl, I part her legs and plunge myself between them, inhaling the intoxicating scent of her arousal. My fingers dance along her folds, slick with her desire as she moans and writhes beneath me. It's like she's begging for me to lose control and take her over the edge. And I am more than willing to oblige.

A beautiful moan escapes her lips as she lifts her hips. "Davide."

"Shh, my love, I need you to get you ready for my cock."

I gently brush my lips against her sweet, slick pussy, savoring the heady taste that fills my mouth. My tongue slowly traces along her folds, tracing patterns and flicking over her sensitive clit. With each passing moment, her moans grow louder and more desperate, urging me on. Her hips grind against my face, seeking out more stimulation. I delve deeper, sliding my tongue inside her and feeling her walls clench around it in response. She arches her back, surrendering to the waves of pleasure coursing through her body. Every touch, every lick sends shivers of ecstasy through her, causing her whole body to tremble with delight.

As I continue to eat her out, I can feel my own desire growing, the darkness consuming me. But I know this is what she wants, and I can't deny her this. I'll do whatever it takes to make her feel good, even if it means facing my inner demons.

My fingers glide up and down her thighs, slowly teasing her and building her anticipation. I can feel the heat radiating from her body, and I know that I'm getting her closer and closer to the edge. I slide two fingers inside her, feeling her muscles contract around them, pulling them deeper inside.

"Oh, Davide." She reaches down and grips my hair and guiding my mouth back to her wet folds. "Please, more. I need more."

I gladly oblige, increasing the pace of my fingering and licking, sucking on her clit, causing her to scream out in pleasure. Her body arches, her muscles tighten around my fingers, and I know she's about to come.

I feel her pussy pulsating around my fingers as she releases her orgasm, her juices coating my hand. Her legs shake uncontrollably, and I can hear her breaths becoming ragged, her heart pounding against my face. I keep going, wanting to give her the most intense pleasure she's ever experienced. Her body writhes beneath me, her moans getting louder, her voice hoarse with passion.

Finally, she's still, her body spent, her breaths slowing down. I slide my fingers out of her, my hands glistening with her juices. I lean up and kiss her, tasting her on my lips, feeling her breath hitch as our tongues dance together.

I don't even recognize my voice as I whisper. "You're incredible, Lucy."

She smiles, her eyes filled with happiness and lust.

I grasp my cock and place it at her wet opening, rubbing it against her wet folds. Her eyes flutter shut as her mouth drops with a long drawn-out moan. I don't want to hurt her, but I am not a tiny man, and she is a virgin. "Lucy." She opens her eyes and looks at me. "Don't take your eyes off me."

Chapter Nine

Lucy

I gazed into his eyes. I couldn't help but get lost in their deep, piercing blue. For years, I had harbored feelings for this man. But now, as we stood here together, my heart raced with the realization that my dreams were finally coming true. As he left, I was overcome by a deep feeling of longing and finality. This would be our first and last chance to be together. Desperate to make the most of our time, I asked my dear friend Angelina to cover for me. Her knowing look and comforting hug promised she would do everything she could to help me seize this opportunity before it slipped away forever.

I thought for sure he was going to refuse, but he surprised me.

As I descend from the peak of the most intense orgasm I have ever experienced, I feel his engorged head pressing against my entrance. My mouth goes dry when I see his throbbing and sizable cock. It's been described countless times, but seeing it in person takes my breath away. How is this massive member going to fit inside me? The anticipation and desire coursing through my body only add to the overwhelming feeling of arousal and excitement.

"Baby, I can go slow or fast. Both will cause pain, and I am sorry."

"Fast." Whatever pain would be involved was worth it.

He leans down, his breath hot against my skin, and captures my mouth in an all-consuming kiss. The taste of mint and desire dance on my tongue as our lips move in perfect sync. As he pulls back slightly, his eyes find mine, revealing a combination of intensity and longing, delving deep into the core of my being. My heart races, and I can feel the heat rising between us, a tangible force threatening to consume us both. "I'm sorry."

His hips sway in a fluid, practiced motion, and I steel myself for the inevitable ache that will follow. The anticipation builds, a tight knot in my stomach, but with Davide by my side, I have complete trust and confidence. I know he will do everything possible to ensure my comfort and pleasure in this experience, and I am grateful for his care and consideration.

I gasp as he thrusts into me, his cock forcing its way past my quivering lips and plunging deep into my slick, eager depths. The sensation is a combination of pain and intoxication, making me moan uncontrollably as I am filled to the brim. He briefly pauses before forcefully taking my virginity, causing immense pain. It feels like he's ripped me apart, but I'm consumed by the intense pleasure that follows. Every nerve ending ignites in a fiery inferno as he takes me completely, claiming me as his own with possessive fervor.

Hot tears stream down my face, burning like acid as they leave a trail of dampness on my flushed skin. The more I wipe my trembling hand on my face, the more the prickly heat intensifies. It's like my emotions are taking over my body. The pleasure and pain collide in a chaotic mix, leaving me gasping for breath as I struggle to control the overwhelming sensations washing over me.

"Shh, my love, I am so sorry." His gravely voice repeats over and over again.

He holds me still, letting the initial shock of pain transform into a deep and satisfying pleasure. My body is consumed by a warm, tingling sensation that radiates from within. Soft, sultry moans escape my lips as he moves inside me, each thrust igniting a euphoric rush throughout my entire being. Each touch we share brings me immense pleasure, like an electric current running through me. Every nerve ending comes alive with sensations, and I am lost in the overwhelming pleasure of our passionate encounter.

Every movement is deliberate and calculated, each touch expertly crafted to elicit the most intense pleasure within me. Davide's piercing gaze bores into my very being, setting off sparks of desire that ignite a fiery passion within. Our bodies move in perfect synchronization, every thrust sending wave after wave of ecstasy through me. The slight pain of my torn virginity is eclipsed by the overwhelming pleasure of his skilled lovemaking. I eagerly entwine my legs around him, pulling him closer with a fierce need that only he can satisfy. My body responds eagerly to his touch, every nerve on fire as I cry out in ecstasy. Consumed by desire, longing for him to claim me completely. My moans grow more urgent, desperate for him to take me deeper and fill me completely with his love.

His movements become frantic. Each thrust is a powerful burst of pleasure that courses through my body like electricity. The intensity grows with each new motion, bringing me closer and closer to the edge of ecstasy. I can feel his muscles tense and strain as he struggles to hold back his climax. However, I know it's only a matter of time before he gives in to his primal desires. Our lips meet in a desperate kiss, fueled by our shared need and the intense heat between us. His lips are slick with sweat and passion, adding a layer of sensation to our overwhelming connection.

When we reach the peak of pleasure together, the room explodes into a blur of sensations. The sound of our heavy breathing, smelling our combined sweat and lust, and feeling pure ecstasy as his hot, throbbing cock pulsates inside of me. Our bodies collapse onto the bed, limbs interlocked, and hearts racing as we bask in the aftermath of our passionate encounter. Finally, a sense of complete fulfillment washes over me. A feeling that can only be described as pure bliss and completion.

I surrendered to the warmth of his embrace, melting into the comfort of his chest. The steady thump of his heartbeat against my cheek was a soothing lullaby. His gentle, warm breath tickled my neck's sensitive skin, sending shivers down my spine. My fingers glided through his hair, each strand feeling like velvet between my fingertips. The sense of intimacy intensified as we lay entwined on the bed, with his cologne wrapped around us like a familiar cocoon. Each touch, breath, and moment felt eternal in our blissful togetherness.

I tilt my head up, drinking in the intricate features of his face with an unquenchable thirst. Every line and curve is etched into my mind. The steadfast set of his jaw, the mighty arch of his eyebrows, the alluring dip of his lips. In this moment, he holds me spellbound, and I am helpless to resist the magnetic pull he exudes. I pray for time to stand still, never wanting this fleeting moment to end.

The warmth of his touch surrounds me, yet a voice warns that this moment is fleeting. I give in to the rush of emotions I feel when I'm with him, despite knowing I shouldn't. The feel of his fingers intertwined with mine sends shivers down my spine and sets my heart ablaze. I cling to each passing moment, desperate to hold on to the sweet memories that will soon become distant echoes.

"I love you, Davide."

His arms envelop me like a warm, protective cocoon as he pulls me closer. I can feel the strength and devotion in his embrace, each touch filled with love and tenderness. Every muscle in his body radiates affection and comfort, and I am grateful for every moment spent in his arms.

"I love you too, Lucy. And I wish I could give you more."

With a deep breath, I hold back my swirling emotions. It was his only offering, but it would remain imprinted in my memory. I force a grateful smile. "I understand. Thank you for this moment. I pray that one day, someone who can battle the demons alongside you will come into your life." My words hang in the air, heavy with unspoken meaning and wistful hopes for our futures.

"There will be no one."

I gathered my dress and shoes, and a wave of harsh reality crashed over me like a ton of bricks. Guilt and shame dragged me down as I stumbled out of the pool house. Every fiber of me screamed regret, but a small part longed for the intense pleasure and connection I had just experienced. He was the only man I desired. How could I deny that? Each step, a painful trudge through irretrievable loss. Not my virginity, but Davide Tomorrow would come, and with it, my vanishing act, leaving nothing but bittersweet memories and an aching void in my heart.

For the last three months, I have been planning my escape from The Famiglia. I wasn't going to Italy. After hours and days of thinking each scenario out, I decided I would lose myself in a city with 8.5 million inhabitants of New York City.

I had to navigate through a crowded airport, surrounded by travelers and security. My trusted bodyguard would leave once I passed through the metal detectors, leaving me to execute my risky plan alone. I would scan the crowds for a potential ally. Someone boarding an international flight who resembled me. With a sizeable amount of cash and my first-class ticket as leverage, I approached her with a proposition. If she agreed to help me, I would reward her and provide her with my designer clothes while I transformed into a disguise, complete with a dark red wig. Once I left the airport, I would make my way to the cozy home I had purchased under the name Lucy Mitchell. Anticipation filled me as I prepared to start anew, leaving behind my past and taking on a new persona in this unfamiliar town.

With my cameras in hand, venturing into the gritty streets of New York City meant befriending those with questionable pasts. A man, shrouded in mystery, specialized in providing people with new identities. His rugged appearance and sly grin suggested a life of deceit and danger, but his confident demeanor drew in curious souls like a moth to a flame. He was the master of reinvention, and his connections ran deep within the city's underbelly. Rubbing elbows with him meant gaining access to a world unknown to most, where secrets were currency and loyalty were paramount. The rewards were endless for the brave.

My new identity granted me the power to purchase my home, even if it wasn't in my desired location. The Famiglia controlled most of New York City, with only a few pockets controlled by rival mafia families. The Irish were in charge of Hell's Kitchen, the Chinese controlled Chinatown, and the Mexican Cartel ruled Bushwick. I hadn't returned to Southend since the traumatic incident at eighteen, but I knew that hiding in Brighton Beach would be my best bet for escaping.

Money wasn't an issue, and over the last few months, I had taken money out of my private account in cash. Then, I would take it and deposit it into my new account under my new name. If, down the road, I found I was running low, I could also find a job.

Quietly, I ascend the back steps and slip into my bedroom. I desperately needed a few minutes alone to clean the sticky residue off my thighs and to make myself presentable again. In my private bathroom, I gaze at my reflection in the mirror and gasp in shock. My once carefully applied makeup is now smudged and smeared, with long tracks where tears had cascaded down my cheeks. The mascara and eyeliner have turned into black rivers, while my lipstick is barely visible on my trembling lips. The image in front of me contrasts the composed person I try to portray to the world.

As I stand in front of the mirror, I can't help but feel a sense of loss and longing. Davide is, and forever will be, the only man I'll love. And now, I was leaving him behind, disappearing into the sprawling chaos of New York City, never to be seen again.

I splashed some cold water on my face, hoping to wash away the pain and the memory of that night. As I dried my face, I couldn't help but think about Davide's words. "There will be no one." I knew he was right, but it didn't make it any easier. I had fallen for him, and as much as it broke my heart, I had to leave him behind forever.

Tears well up as I grab a washcloth to clean up the remnants of my lost virginity. It wasn't about losing it, but the realization that Davide would be the only one I would ever experience this. My heart aches at never experiencing this intimacy with anyone else. As I rinse the cloth under the faucet, I can't help but feel like I'm washing away a part of myself, yet I know I have to let move on. I throw the cloth in the laundry hamper and fix my makeup. After completing, I exit the bedroom and head back to the party.

When I enter the room, Angelina catches my eye. I make my way over and grasp her hand.

"Thank you. Did anyone notice?"

"No. Luca was engaged in conversation with several people. Davide came in a few minutes ago. I never seen him so broken."

Swallowing back my tears, which threaten to fall. "I said my goodbyes."

Angelina wraps her arms around and squeezes. When she pulls back, I see fire in her eyes. "I wish he would get the stick out of his ass. He is in love with you."

"But love sometimes is not enough. My heart can't take seeing him, knowing he will never change his mind."

"I'm going to miss you." She looks around, and in a quiet voice, she says. "And you won't be here to see this little one born."

"You're pregnant?"

"Hush, keep quiet. No one knows, but I wanted to tell you. Lucy, you are my very first friend."

Nestled within the secure walls of her family's estate, Angelina lived a sheltered life, protected from the outside world. Her marriage to Giovanni introduced her to a new world filled with intrigue and danger. Unlike her, I had no excuse for never making friends. Growing up in The Famiglia, a notorious organized crime syndicate, girls my age were often superficial and untrustworthy. Their desire for power in the organization hindered them from building real connections or friendships.

"I'm sorry I won't be around."

"Well, after he or she is born, I'll make Giovanni take us to Italy."

As I spoke to Angelina, the weight of my deceit sat heavily on my chest like a boulder. Each word felt like a sharp blade piercing my heart, knowing that I would not be there to witness the birth of her child. The guilt weighed on my conscience, threatening to suffocate me with its crushing force. But despite the pain and turmoil, I could not bring myself to marry someone whom I did not truly love. It was a bittersweet decision, one that tugged at my heartstrings and threatened to drown me in an ocean of conflicting emotions. Ultimately, I knew it was right. It would liberate me from a future filled with falsehoods and counterfeit love.

Chapter Ten

Lucy

With a heavy heart, I take one last look around my childhood room. It had transformed so much over the years, reflecting my shifting interests and dreams. From the pastel hues of a nursery to the whimsical decorations of a fairy princess, my mother had lovingly crafted this space for me. But as I grew older, I longed for something different. A room like Luca's, with its dark walls and edgy decor. However, the thought of disappointing my mother and seeing the hurt in her eyes made me push aside my own desires and prioritize her happiness above mine. Despite my struggle, this room holds countless memories and remains special to me.

The once vibrant and colorful walls now stood bare, stripped of all personal touches. The photograph that used to hang in its frame with pride now rests in my house, surrounded by the familiar comfort of my belongings. Each box, filled with memories and possessions, was painstakingly packed, shipped to Italy, and then sent back to the States. And finally, it made its way to my current home in Brighton Beach. It was like a shell game, a diversion for my family as they slowly realized I had left.

I picked up my backpack and grasped the handle of my carry-on bag. I stepped outside my room to find Victoria standing by the door.

Tears welled in her eyes. She mumbled. "I am going to miss you, Lucy." Our beloved housekeeper had been a constant presence in our lives for as long as I could remember. While my mother was The Famiglia's glamorous face, Victoria tended to me when I fell and scraped my knees and comforted me when I experienced my first period.

I embraced her warmly, my arms circling around her and holding her close. My heart swelled with emotion as I whispered. "I'll miss you too, more than you could ever know." Gratitude poured from every fiber of my being for this woman who cared for and loved me like her own child. She had been my rock, my guide, my mother.

Victoria's arms wrapped around me, offering warmth and security as I prepared to face the unknown. As we parted, the lingering touch of her embrace felt like a protective shield against the uncertainty that awaited me. With tears welling in my eyes, I realized that leaving this house would also mean leaving behind a piece of my heart, a cherished memory that would forever be etched into my being.

While walking through the familiar halls, memories came rushing back to me. Images of birthday parties, family dinners, and whispered secrets shared with Luca's late-night dance in my mind. Now, memories felt bittersweet, overshadowed by the weight of my chosen future.

As I enterTears roll the crisp morning air, I notice Luca waiting patiently by the car. His tall, lean frame is silhouetted against the rising sun, casting a golden glow around him. His deep blue eyes reveal an unspoken sadness. Despite our six-year age gap, we have always been close. Ordinary boys wouldn't want their little sister tagging along, but not Luca. He always made me feel included and invited me to hang out with him and his friends. Our bond was unbreakable, forged through years of adventures and shared secrets.

I was exposed to knowledge that little girls were not meant to possess, and I witnessed sights that no innocent child should have encountered. Yet, despite the unconventional upbringing, I wouldn't trade it for any other childhood experience. It was a unique journey filled with lessons and experiences that shaped me into who I am today.

"Lu."

"Lulu, are you sure you don't want to take the private jet? I can go with you."

I shake my head. "You know I can't do that. I'll be okay, and I promise to text you as soon as I land."

He faces the ground and pushes the stone with the toe of his shoe.

"Luca, please look at me," I implore softly, reaching out to tilt his chin so our eyes meet. His pained gaze pierces my heart, confirming the equal difficulty of this goodbye for both of us. We've always been each other's rocks, our unwavering support amid our family's turbulent dynamics.

"Lu, I want you to know that I will be okay. I have to do this. I squeeze his hand tightly before letting go. The weight of his unspoken words lingers between us, heavy with all the things we both hold back for the sake of our family's facade.

With a heavy heart, I gaze toward the waiting car, its metallic exterior gleaming in the sunlight. The thought of leaving Luca behind makes my stomach churn, but I know it's for the best. As I sink into the plush leather seat, I can't help but watch him recede in the distance through the small window. His figure grows smaller and smaller until he's just a speck on the horizon, a bittersweet reminder of what once was.

We pull out the massive gate and turn. While looking out the window, I notice Davide standing beside the gate. He still wore the suit from the previous night and appeared sleepless. Swiftly, the vehicle sped up, and I glimpsed him lifting his hand. Tears begin rolling down my face. If possible, I would have him run towards me, hold me tightly, and never release me. Life isn't a romantic movie or fairytale. Davide didn't want forever with me. He was very clear on this, so I had to leave. My heart ached as we turned the corner, and Davide's figure disappeared from view. A silent sob caught in my throat, and I swallowed hard, willing myself to be strong. This was the only way.

The bustling streets of New York whizzed by as we drove further into the city. I took in every detail, determined to commit it all to memory. The bright lights flashed and dazzled, illuminating the buildings that towered above us. My heart raced with excitement and fear, knowing I couldn't risk returning to the city after I disappeared because I could be recognized. Even my planned disguise, which included colored contacts and dyed hair, couldn't guarantee safety from facial recognition software. We were entering a world where anonymity was nearly impossible, and I could feel the weight of that knowledge pressing on me with every passing block.

I desperately tried to distract myself as the buildings and streets passed by. But Davide's haunting gaze remained imprinted on my mind. His dark eyes, like pools of swirling emotions, seemed to penetrate into the depths of my soul. A tumultuous mix of longing and inner turmoil danced within them, leaving me both enchanted and unsettled.

After what seemed like forever, we arrived at JFK and entered the busy international terminal. Sam hastily parked and grabbed my carry-on bag from the trunk as I flung my bookbag over my shoulder and impatiently opened the car door. Sam gave me a hard stare before I could even step out, sending shivers down my spine.

"You know better than to get out of the car alone. What kind of guards do they have in Italy? If they allow this kind of recklessness, I'll have to go there myself and show them how it's done." His voice was sharp with frustration, and his eyes blazed with a protective ferocity, making me feel both grateful and slightly intimidated.

"Sam, they do make me stay in the car. Thank you for your service, and I wish you all the best."

"Just because you're getting married in Italy doesn't mean you can't come home for a visit."

Forcing a smile and a nod, we walk into the terminal. Sam walks with me to the TSA entrance and rolls my carry-on toward me. I grasp the handle, ready to pass through TSA. I couldn't help but feel a sense of finality wash over me. It was my final encounter with everyone, him included. The hustle and bustle of travelers whizzing by added to the chaotic atmosphere. "I've got to get in there." I tried to keep my voice steady. My heart felt heavy as I realized the gravity of this moment. A wave of gratitude surged through me, prompting me to add. "Sam, thank you once more."

"You have a safe trip and call when you land," he instructed.

I nodded my head and walked up to the TSA worker, who checked my ticket and passport. As always, the airport was busy. Being an old pro at TSA checks, I sailed through quickly. Once on the other side, I started toward my gate. With every step, I prayed to find someone who could assist me. It was the only thing I couldn't plan.

I rounded the corner, my heart pounding as I scanned the crowd waiting to board. I tried to blend in, casually glancing at each person without drawing any attention. But it was impossible not to notice the cameras positioned everywhere, capturing every movement and moment. My family would be searching for me soon, using every piece of footage to track down my whereabouts. The pressure of being watched only added to the intensity of the moment.

My heart raced, pounding against my chest as I scanned the multitude of faces in the crowded terminal. My palms were slick with sweat, and I could feel the weight of my decision to leave everything behind settling heavily on my shoulders. The hustle and bustle of the airport swirled around me like a chaotic vortex, but amidst it all, I was searching for just one person. The one who held the key to my freedom. My eyes darted from person to person, desperately trying to find them before it was too late. Each moment passed, urging me to go faster. There was no turning back now, and I knew my fate would be sealed once our eyes met.

And then, like a mirage in the desert, she appeared before me. A woman with long, sun-kissed blonde hair cascading down her back, just about my age and height. She stood by a quaint coffee stand, her demeanor serene, unlike me, who had tumultuous emotions brewing inside. She held a worn book in her hand, its pages well-loved and dog-eared, and her gaze darted up occasionally to scan the bustling crowd around us.

"Flight 562 to Rome will be boarding first-class passengers in twenty minutes."

Panic coursed through me as I realized I was running out of time. The woman quickly gathered her things and packed them into a backpack before standing. With purposeful strides, she made her way towards the ladies' bathroom. Her attire mirrored my own - faded jeans, scuffed tennis shoes, and a worn sweatshirt that looked like it had seen better days. At that moment, we were nearly identical reflections.

I trailed after her into the ladies' room, my footsteps echoing against the tiled floor. The room was quiet, except for running water from a few sinks. I looked around and saw a few more women in the mirror. From a stall, she emerged, catching my eye. My heart pounded as I took a deep breath, knowing this was my chance to confront her.

I smile at her. "Hi."

"Hi."

"Where are you off to?"

"To Rome. I am spending the summer backpacking through Europe. Well, until my money runs out. What about you?"

"Actually, I'm running away from a dangerous situation, and I think I could help with your money problem if you would do something for me."

The woman's piercing blue eyes widened in surprise at my sudden and unexpected confession. She took a hesitant step back, her posture guarded and assessing as if trying to gauge my intentions. I could practically see the gears turning in her mind, weighing the potential risks and rewards of whatever proposition I might have for her. The wary glint in her eyes gave way to a flicker of curiosity, and I knew she was intrigued despite her caution.

"I... I'm not sure what you mean." She was clearly unsure about getting involved in something that sounded like trouble.

With a heavy sigh, I inhaled deeply, the cool air filling my lungs and bringing clarity. The clock was ticking. The seconds slipping away like grains of sand in an hourglass. I knew I had to choose my words carefully, for they held the power to either make or break this crucial moment. My mind raced with various options and strategies, trying to find the perfect combination that would bring success.

"I must vanish without leaving any evidence. And I can help you with your money problem if you're willing to switch identities with me for a while."

Her eyes widened like saucers, and she darted her gaze around the restroom in a frenzy of nerves. Leaning at me with a sense of urgency, she whispered in my ear.

"Are you serious? What kind of trouble are you in?"

I hoped she would understand the gravity of the situation without needing all the details. "I can't say much here, but let's just say I need to disappear from some people who will stop at nothing to make to stay."

The woman bit her lip, torn between curiosity and fear. After a long pause, she finally nodded slowly, her expression determined.

"Okay, I'll do it. But you have to promise me I won't get caught up in anything illegal."

I nodded in agreement, my heart swelling with gratitude for her kind help without probing further into my personal situation.

"Thank you. We'll switch tickets. I have already checked in, so you will take my first-class ticket and cell phone. Once you land in Rome, send the text I saved to Luca and smash the phone. After that, you'll be free to enjoy your backpacking trip with a little extra financial support."

I reached into my bag and pulled out my ticket and the envelope with the cash.

"Here is the ticket and twenty thousand dollars. Do we have a deal?"

She looked inside the envelope and back up at me. I'm sure she is trying to decide if it is worth it. "Alright."

"Thank you so much. Do you mind if we trade sweatshirts and wear this hat?"

"No problem."

She starts removing her sweatshirt as I take off mine. I handed her mine, and once she had it on, I gave her my ticket and the money.

"First-class passengers for flight 562 to Rome can now board."

"Well, I guess it is time for me to go."

"Thank you again. I'm Lucy Malone, by the way." It was the name I used when I traveled.

"Tonja Stewart."

"Have a pleasant flight, and I hope you have a great summer."

She gives me a bright smile and holds up the envelope. "I am sure I will. Good luck with your situation. Stay safe."

With a firm grasp on her luggage, she strides out of the bathroom and disappears from sight. As soon as she's gone, I slip into the now-empty stall and change my clothes. The rough, worn fabric of my jeans is replaced by sleek black dress pants that hug my legs, and a soft, flowing blouse with intricate flower patterns adorns my upper body. My feet slide into black heels, completing the transformation from casual traveler to polished businesswoman. Next comes the most crucial part of my disguise. I pull back my natural hair and place a jet-black wig atop my head, adjusting it until it looks natural. I stuff my old outfit back into my suitcase, leaving no trace of my previous appearance behind.

As I pushed open the stall door, my heart raced with anticipation. Stepping out, I approached the full-length mirror with a mix of curiosity and nervousness. Who would I see looking back at me? The reflection revealed a woman that was not me, at least not in appearance. A long, dark red wig cascaded down my back, concealing my natural hair and shielding my face from recognition. With trembling hands, I reached for the oversized, dark sunglasses and slipped them on, completing my disguise. For the first time since coming up with this plan, I felt a glimmer of hope that it might work. Staring at myself in the mirror, I couldn't believe how different I looked, unrecognizable even to myself.

With my spine rigid and jaw clenched, I gripped the case handle and marched out. The bustling airport crowd parted around me as I pushed through. Finally, outside, I spotted a taxi and climbed in, giving the driver my first destination. I would change taxis several times before going to my new home. As we sped away, I leaned back and sighed. This was not how I imagined my life would turn out, living in fear all the time and under the control of The Famiglia. But as I reflect on this daring escape, a slight sense of pride swells within me for accomplishing what seemed impossible.

Chapter Eleven

Davide

The absence of her presence was like a gaping void, a deep chasm that seemed impossible to fill. It was a permanent loss that weighed heavy on my heart, dragging it down with each passing moment. With tear-filled eyes, I stood outside the ornate iron gates of the grand Gambino estate, watching and waiting for her final procession to pass by. The desperate ache to catch one last glimpse of her face consumed me, overtaking my entire being like a black hole sucking in all light and hope. It felt as though I couldn't breathe. The very air I needed to survive eluding me in this moment of grief.

As the last music notes faded into the night and the guests dispersed, I slipped away from the crowded house and sought solace in the pool house. My mind was consumed with thoughts of her, but a deep sense of guilt restrained me from going any closer to her room. The temptation to be near her, to feel her warmth against my skin, was overwhelming. But I knew it would only bring more complications to our already tangled situation. So, instead, I retreated to the quiet sanctuary of the pool house, where the only sounds were the gentle lapping of water against the sides and my racing thoughts. Oh, how badly I longed for her embrace, but I knew that for now, it was best to keep my distance.

The path I was considering treading was fraught with danger. With her pure heart and virtuous ways, Lucy deserved someone better than me, and our union would surely be doomed from the moment we exchanged vows. Yet, as the first rays of sunlight peeked over the horizon, I felt an irresistible urge to find her one last time. The sky was painted in shades of pink and orange, casting a warm glow over the landscape. Dew glistened on the grass, and the birds sang their sweet morning melodies. It was a picturesque scene, but my thoughts were consumed by the woman who had captured my heart.

I saw her emerge from the grand doors of the estate. Her figure was shrouded in the morning mist like a ghost of my desires. She hugged Luca and climbed into the vehicle. It sent a shiver down my spine, awakening the dormant beast within me. *She is ours. Stop her and keep her.*

As she passed by me as I stood by the gate, I felt an overwhelming urge to reach out and grab her, to confess all the forbidden thoughts that had been swirling in my mind. But I remained rooted to the spot, watching her disappear into the distance.

Tears threatened to spill from my eyes as I turned and walked away from the imposing Gambino estate. The weight of my own demons bore down on my shoulders, dragging me deeper into the pits of despair. Within me, The Raven cawed with frustration. Its call echoing through my mind like a never-ending scream. It craved to be released from the prison within. But most of all, it craved

Lucy. I knew the consequences of giving in to its dark desires. The chaos it would bring into her life was too great a risk for me to take. Each step I took from the estate felt heavier than the last, as if the darkness within me had grown even more vital in its disappointment and longing.

I made my way back to my estate. Thoughts of Lucy lingered in my mind like a haunting melody. The broken marriage agreement loomed over me like a dark cloud, threatening to suffocate any chance of happiness. How could I bind her to a man who would break her heart over and over again?

I returned to the safety of my home thanks to Mici. In the confines of my office, I poured a large glass of bourbon. The smooth liquid easing down my throat and numbing my senses. Collapsing into the plush armchair in my study, I felt the heavy weight of my decisions pressing down on me like an anchor, dragging me deeper into a dark, twisted labyrinth. The Famiglia was more than just an organization. It was our legacy, passed down from the founding sons to their heirs. We were willing to do whatever was necessary to protect it and keep it thriving. Whether we acted as assassins, judges, or any other role required, secrecy and prosperity were paramount in our minds.

As the leaders of The Famiglia, the founding sons were expected to set an unbreakable example for all members. The rules and regulations were sacred, never to be defied. For years, I upheld them with unwavering diligence, but last night, I succumbed to temptation and broke one. My desires overtook my rationality as I took something that did not belong to me, a transgression that weighed heavily on my conscience.

I stared into the swirling depths of my drink, the amber liquid reflecting the turmoil in my soul. The Raven circled within me, its dark wings brushing against the edges of my conscience. "Nevermore," it croaked, a reminder of the power it held over me, over my very being.

I took a deep breath, trying to find some semblance of peace amidst the chaos that threatened to consume me. The walls of my study seemed to close in on me, suffocating me with their opulence and cruelty. Everything in my life felt like a cage, trapped in a web of obligations and blood-soaked loyalties.

But then, amidst the oppressive silence of the room, a whisper reached my ears. A soft voice that cut through the darkness like a beacon of light in a stormy night. It was Lucy's voice, her laughter echoing in the chambers of my heart.

My heart ached as I reluctantly stood from the embrace of the plush armchair. My steps were heavy and slow as I approached the floor-to-ceiling window, its grand frame adorned with intricate designs. The view that stretched before me was one of opulence and wealth, with meticulously manicured gardens sprawling out beneath the gray sky above. Vibrant colors of every hue burst forth from the carefully placed flowers and foliage, creating a stark contrast to the bleakness of the world outside. My eyes roamed every inch of the yard, taking in each detail, as if trying to etch them into my memory forever. A soft sigh escaped my lips as I whispered into the stillness of the room, "Goodbye, my love." The words hung heavily in the air, filled with sorrow and longing for what could have been.

I am so fucking tired. For the last two weeks, I have been trying to find out who was hijacking our gun shipments. Every time I thought I figured out who I was, I met with a dead end. Marco was as baffled as I was.

The sleepless nights blend together, each one a tapestry woven with threads of exhaustion and frustration. The elusive perpetrators seemed to be always one step ahead, leaving behind a trail of chaos that threatened to unravel the very fabric of our operations.

My heart pounded like a ticking time bomb as I paced the study, the flickering light casting grotesque shadows that seemed to mock me. The Raven within me cawed and clawed, its dark presence looming over my every thought like a vulture waiting to feast on my soul. The feeling of impending doom consumed me, suffocating me with its unrelenting grip.

I poured myself another drink, the amber liquid offering a brief respite from the tumult of my thoughts. The familiar burn as it slid down my throat was a welcome distraction from the relentless cycle of suspicions and dead ends that plagued my mind and the constant thoughts of Lucy. When I close my eyes, I see her naked body, and I swear I can still feel how tight her pussy wrapped around my cock as I took her virginity. In the dark of the night, I hear her moans of pleasure play over and over in my mind.

Then, I wonder how she is doing. Had her father arranged her marriage? Was he a nice guy? Who was he?

Did I know him? Which family did he come from? Would he figure out she was not a virgin? How was she going to hide this from everyone? There are so many questions and no way to get the answers.

Luca and I usually have a daily routine of talking to each other. But ever since she left, our conversations have come to a grinding halt. Our once close relationship had become strained, and it was all due to my own actions. I threw myself into work to fill the void she left behind, desperately trying to cope without her presence in my life. Day after day, I buried myself in paperwork and meetings, determined to keep moving forward despite the emptiness inside me.

A knock sounded on my office door. "Yes." I look up to see Luca walking in. His face is marred with worry.

"What's wrong?"

"Lucy has disappeared."

My legs gave out beneath me, and I desperately clung to the edge of the desk to avoid collapsing to the ground. The words hit me like a physical blow, causing my heart to race and my vision to blur with panic. "What... what do you mean?" I struggle to steady myself against the overwhelming surge of emotions crashing over me.

"She never went to Rome. Or if she did, she never reached our parent's home. Hell, they didn't even know she was moving over. She lied to me. She never called our father."

My heart was a pounding drum, beating against my ribcage with such force I thought it might burst through my chest. A cold sweat coated my skin as I desperately searched for her, my mind racing with endless possibilities.

Had she been abducted? Was she safe? My pulse thundered in my ears, drowning out any rational thoughts as fear consumed me. Where was she? What had happened to her?

"You haven't even bothered to contact her in two weeks? What the hell were you thinking, waiting this long?" I was seething rage.

Luca stomped over until he was inches away. "Davide, I don't like your tone. Where do you get off questioning me? You are the one who caused all this. She would still be here if you hadn't backed out of the arrangement."

He was right it was my fault. "I was going to hurt her, anyway. It was only a matter of time."

"I don't believe that. How many women did you sleep with in the six months she was away? Better yet, how many women and you fucked since breaking it off?"

The truth was like a heavy weight on my tongue, begging to be let out. But I couldn't bring myself to say it, not to him. Because if I did, it would confirm his suspicions, and he would be right. Every time the thought of another woman crossed my mind, my body rebelled against me, and my once eager cock wilted away in shame. It was a constant battle between what I wanted and what I knew was right for our relationship. And it tore at me every day like a relentless storm that refused to pass.

Luca shakes his head. "Damn, Davide, I thought she was with our father. She was so upset when she left. I was giving her space."

The panic in my chest is uncontrollable, a fiery inferno that consumes every rational thought. My mind swirls with endless scenarios of Lucy's disappearance - each one more terrifying than the last. Guilt and worry mercilessly pummel me like a heavy stone, suffocating me under its unbearable weight. I am drowning in a sea of fear, unable to escape its relentless grip.

"Have you contacted The Commission?" My voice hoarse with unspoken fears.

Luca shook his head grimly, his usually stoic demeanor cracking under the weight of uncertainty. "No. I didn't want to go before the entire Commission until I had more information. I did call Andrea, Danti, and Giovanni. They are working on collecting information from the last time we knew where she was." He runs his hand through his hair. "Davide, we must find her before it's too late."

My mind raced as I tried to piece together any clue leading me to Lucy's whereabouts. Had she left willingly? Was this part of a sinister plot against the Gambino Family? Was it one of my enemies?

I would not rest until she was safely home. "I will find her."

"It has been two weeks. You know how a trail goes cold after just a few days."

"When was the last time you heard from her?"

"I got a text that she had landed in Rome the day she left."

"We need Justin to pull her call logs and find out where the last text came from. Jack Carter needs to be called and have him send the airport surveillance footage to Justin. Call your father and have him call his contact at the Fiumicino Airport and send their surveillance footage to Justin. When he gets the videos, I want the five of us to go over them. Once we get concrete evidence of what happened, then we will bring it before The Commission."

We spent the next few days combing through the surveillance footage, every grainy frame filled with hope and dread. But the more we searched, the more we realized Lucy had vanished without a trace. There are no passenger lists with her name on them or CCTV footage of her leaving the airport. She was gone, and we were left with a thousand questions and no answers.

As the days dragged on and blurred into weeks and months, I was in a perpetual state of panic. Whenever I dared to close my eyes, her face would appear before me, her unsettling grin imprinted on my mind. She was like a ghost haunting my thoughts, an unshakeable memory that tormented me day and night. The mere idea of her being harmed or, worse, filled me with a gnawing dread that consumed me from the inside.

I spent several weeks in Italy, combing through any possible lead we came up with. However, none of them panned out. When I returned to the States, I followed every morsel of leads, but it was as if she had just disappeared into thin air. With each passing day and no one demanding a ransom, only two things were left. She planned to leave and didn't plan on returning. Or she is...dead. I didn't want to even think about that. The very thought caused my inner Raven to cry out in pain. She has to be alive.

My mind raced with possibilities, each one darker than the last. But deep down, I knew only one thing for sure. I would stop at nothing to find her. I could feel the pulls of my inner demon growing stronger, urging me to take matters into my own hands and seek vengeance for my lost love. The thought of her being hurt or worse was too much to bear.

The shadows in the study seemed to seep into my soul, engulfing me in a suffocating darkness. Each bitter sip of alcohol burned down my throat, numbing the pain momentarily but never truly easing it. My heart throbbed with every second that passed, each beat an agonizing reminder of her absence. But giving up was not an option. I would search for her until my final breath, if needed, determined to find her, no matter the cost.

Chapter Twelve

Lucy

Disappearing from my prior life was easier than I ever could have imagined. In a state of desperation and fear, I fled to my new home in Brighton Beach. During the initial month, I rarely ventured outside my sanctuary. Instead, I concentrated on crafting a space that mirrored my tastes and wishes. As someone who came from a privileged background, I failed to realize the joy of choosing furniture according to my own taste instead of conforming to societal norms. Each piece was chosen not for how it would be perceived by others. It was for the way it made me feel and the beauty it added to my surroundings. Every day, a new box arrived with something else to make this place not just a house but my home. It was liberating and invigorating all at once. I was living my life outside of The Famiglia, and even though I missed those in my life, I embraced my future.

Luca and The Famiglia, not wanting to draw attention to themselves, had no intention of reporting me missing, as I expected. It was a blessing in disguise for me. Only The Famiglia and my family watched, not the whole world. This became possible by hiding in Brighton Beach, the stronghold of the Russians. Despite knowing their absence, I remained vigilant whenever I left home.

I admired my transformation with a sense of pride. I couldn't wear the red wig forever. Once again, I'm encountering the unfamiliar. I dyed my own hair. Hard to believe vibrant red was just hair dye. My once light blonde locks now glimmered with a newfound depth and shine. And when I added the deep brown contact lenses, my eyes took on an unfamiliar depth, making them appear larger and more alluring than ever before.

My hair and eyes weren't the only things that underwent a transformation. Even my features changed under the skilled application of makeup. My cheeks were perfectly contoured, my lips a lush shade of red, and my eyes accented with just the right amount of shadow and liner to enhance their shape.

As I stood before the mirror, carefully observing every detail of my altered appearance, I couldn't help but feel amazed. This simple solution of changing my hair color and adding makeup completely transformed me into a new version of myself.

Every aspect fell into place. Gone was the blonde-haired, blue-eyed Lucy Gambino. In her place is a fiery red-headed, brown-eyed Lucy Mitchell.

Today was the day I planned to explore. In an attempt to calm down my racing heart, I took a deep breath before stepping outside and locking the door behind me. The bright sunshine beat down on me, reflecting off the oversized, dark sunglasses perched on my nose. My plan for the day was simple. The first thing was to go shopping for much-needed food and other necessities. The second reason was to familiarize myself with the area. After extensive online research, I discovered a local market within a reasonable distance.

I climbed into my plain black four-door sedan. It had been so long since I had driven a car. I double-checked and triple-checked my mirrors and seat before pulling away. While going down the street, I couldn't help but notice the stark contrast in traffic compared to downtown Manhattan. No blaring horns or impatient drivers were cutting each other off. Instead, it was a peaceful and orderly flow of cars. I hated driving in the city. The only time I drove was when I visited my parents in Italy. Driving here was actually nice.

I navigated the unfamiliar streets with caution and excitement, my hands gripping the steering wheel a little tighter than necessary. I finally arrived at the local market after a few wrong turns and missed landmarks.

The smell of fresh produce and baked goods enveloped me as I entered, reminding me I had never shopped for myself before. The staff at the Gambino mansion took care of this task and everything else.

I wandered through the aisles, taking in the colorful displays of fruits and vegetables. My fingers grazed over the fresh produce as I tried to remember what ingredients it took to make a simple pasta dish. It was both liberating and daunting to have such autonomy over my own meals. I was excited to eat something other than frozen dinners and fast food delivery that I had been living off.

I moved through the aisles with purpose, carefully selecting items to stock my barren kitchen. A nagging feeling at the market overshadowed the excitement of choosing between brands and varieties. The fear of being recognized or discovered clawed at my insides, threatening to unravel the fragile peace I had built for myself.

In the process of making my way to the checkout counter, I felt like someone was watching me. Instinctively, I tensed, my heart hammering in my chest as I tried to maintain an air of nonchalance. The cashier, a middle-aged woman with a warm smile, greeted me cheerfully as she began scanning my items. "Finding everything okay?" she asked, her voice bright and friendly. I smiled in return, nodding as I handed over the cash for my purchases. As she bagged my groceries, I casually glanced around the store, trying to spot anyone who might be paying too much attention to me. I didn't see any staring, but the hairs on my neck tingled.

I give her a smile. "Yes, thank you."

She finished bagging my items. "You have a nice day."

With the last bag safely in the cart, I turned and bid her a cheerful farewell. As I walked across the sprawling parking lot, I couldn't help but scan my surroundings with wary eyes. My heartbeat quickened as I imagined someone watching me from behind a nearby car or lurking in the shadows of a building. Despite my presence, I went unnoticed by everyone. Every step felt like a monumental feat, and I couldn't shake off the lingering sense of paranoia that came with being in public again.

When I returned to my little house, I was exhausted and happy. I brought the groceries in and organized them in the kitchen, feeling proud of myself for finishing my task. As I stored away the items, I couldn't shake off the lingering unease from my trip to the market. The feeling of being watched persisted, always in my mind. I tried to dismiss it as paranoia brought on by my heightened state of alertness, but deep down, I knew better. The familiar chill raced down my spine as a shadow flitted past the window, too swift to be anything but a figment of my imagination or a bird flying by. It would take me a while before I could feel like no one was watching me.

Needing something to take my mind off my uneasy feeling, I attempted to make spaghetti. After chopping the fresh tomatoes, basil, and garlic, I placed everything in a pot. Remembering the many times I watched Victoria make the sauce, I added the other herbs. An hour later, I stirred the tomato basil sauce on the stove. Picking up the spoon, I dip it into the pot and bringing a taste to my lips. It was a little bland, so I added a pinch of salt. I was actually cooking, and it wasn't bad; it was good. Not as good as Victoria's, but I wouldn't starve.

As the sun dipped below the horizon, casting a warm orange glow over the landscape, I diligently went around my house. I double-checked all the locks on the windows and doors. Satisfied that everything was secure, I set the alarm and headed to my bedroom. After quickly grabbing a soft, silk nightgown from my dresser, I went to the spacious bathroom. The cool marble floors felt heavenly under my bare feet as I filled the bathtub with hot water and added a generous amount of luxurious bath bubbles. One of the few items I brought from home was this little indulgence. It was the one I used the night of my going away party. As I settled into the tub and let the warm water soothe my tired muscles, I closed my eyes and fully relaxed for the first time in weeks. I close my eyes and allow the scent of lavender and vanilla to envelop me, sending me back to the night when I gave my virginity to Davide.

The memory of Davide's touch lingered in my mind, a bittersweet reminder of the passion we once shared. As I soaked in the comforting warmth of the bath, I let myself drift back to that night. The steam rising around me seemed to carry echoes of whispered, heated desires that had sparked a forbidden connection between us. Despite all the warnings and barriers that should have kept us apart, our souls were entwined in a dance of danger and desire.

I had lost myself in him, in the intensity of his gaze and the strength of his touch. With his dark allure and commanding presence, Davide had been an irresistible force that drew me in like a moth to a flame. And in that moment of surrender, I had willingly offered him not just my body but also a piece of my heart. It was a reckless choice that could shatter the fragile balance I had tried so hard to maintain.

My fingers trace the outline of my body, aching for the touch of Davide's hand. They glide over my breasts, down my stomach, and finally reach my swollen clit. The intense desire consumes me, and I know it's time to give in to my cravings. With eyes tightly shut, I conjure his image beside me, his hands exploring every inch of my body. And in that moment, my hand becomes his, guiding me towards a mind-blowing release.

Every fiber of my being ignited with fiery desire, consumed by the memory of our wild and passionate encounter. His lips leave a trail of fire down my neck, his skilled fingers exploring every inch of my trembling body. His hot breath on my ear sends shivers down my spine as he whispers promises and dirty secrets, fueling my heart to race faster and faster. My mind surrenders to thoughts of him taking complete control, dominant and unapologetic, leaving me powerless in his grasp.

My body trembled as he forcefully plunged his thick, pulsating cock inside of me. Each thrust felt like a lightning bolt that tore through my insides, splitting me apart and melding me back together. The pain was intense, but it only fueled the fire burning between us, igniting a primal desire within me. My nails clawed desperately at his back, leaving bloody trails in their wake as I marked my territory over his flesh. Our bodies moved in a frenzied rhythm, our hearts beating as one in a symphony of lust and need. The bed groaned under our weight, bearing witness to the raw passion and intensity of our love-making. The air was heavy with the intoxicating scent of our sweat mingling with the sweet aroma of sex. In that moment, time stood still as our souls merged into one, consumed by an all-consuming inferno of desire.

My body convulses with the force of his release, his seed spilling deep within me, marking me as his. I know that in this forbidden love, he has given me more than just passion and affection, but a part of himself that will forever be intertwined with mine. Our bond burns like an unbreakable curse as we part ways, reminding me he forever claims me.

A guttural moan escapes my lips as wave after wave of intense pleasure crashes over me. My body tenses and spasms as I reach the pinnacle of ecstasy, fingers frantically pinching at my clit until I shatter into a million pieces. Slowly, I emerge from the euphoric haze, my legs trembling as I awkwardly crawl out of the lukewarm bathtub. I wrap a plush towel around my quivering body. The warmth soothes my sensitive skin, but it is nothing compared to the fire burning within me. My reflection in the mirror reveals a woman consumed by her desires. Her eyes are clouded with desperation and regret as she struggles to make sense of the tangled mess of emotions that threaten to suffocate her.

The crisp air replaced the lavender steam in the bathroom, yet a hint of memory lingered. I paused, lost in thoughts, before tearing myself from the past and leaving the bathroom.

I slipped into my nightgown, the silky fabric gliding against my skin. As I slid under the cool sheets, they enveloped me in their comforting embrace, soothing my overheated body. The room was bathed in a soft, moonlit glow as I closed my eyes and allowed sleep to overtake me. My thoughts drifted to Davide and the bittersweet realization that he could never be mine, a pang of longing coursing through my heart. In the night's stillness, I found solace in the gentle rhythm of my breath.

As I drifted off to sleep, I was consumed by mixed emotions. The joy of the memory, the regret of my choices, and the burning desire for Davide. Ultimately, I knew I needed to move forward. I couldn't keep reliving the past, even if it was the most exhilarating and heartbreaking experience of my life.

The next day, I threw myself into my routine, cleaning and organizing the house, ensuring everything was in perfect order. I went for a long walk in the park, enjoying the fresh air and feeling the sun on my face. For the first time in weeks, I felt a glimmer of hope that I could find some semblance of normalcy in this new world.

The memories of Davide will always be with me, and I will always love him. No man will ever be able to fill the void. But life must move forward, and healing will take time. I can't help but wonder if fate will bring us together again one day. Until then, I will focus on building a new life for myself, surrounded by love and happiness. And maybe the memory of Davide will bring me the strength to face whatever challenges come my way.

Chapter Thirteen

Lucy

What was wrong with me? I had been living in Brighton Beach for three months now, and while I was acclimating to the solitary lifestyle, trepidation still plagued me every time I ventured outside. Despite encountering no actual danger or having anyone approach me, an unshakable feeling of being watched lingered at the back of my mind. The bustling streets of Brighton Beach felt like a maze, with shadowy figures lurking around every corner. It was as if the city was watching and judging my every move. Every day, I fought between my desire for independence and the constant fear. I persevered, resolved to create my own life.

The morning started like any other until I stepped into the shower. The warm water cascaded down my body as I ran the washcloth over my breast, a routine task that turned alarming. A sharp, shooting pain shot through me, causing me to drop the cloth and clutch at my chest. Tentatively, I reached a shaking hand to my breast, my fingers brushing against a small yet unmistakable lump. Panic surged through me like a tidal wave, threatening to drown out all reason and logic. I tried to ignore it, but fear took hold of me and wouldn't let go. I worried that something serious might be wrong with me. Every breath felt heavy and strained as I tried to process this new and terrifying reality.

Breast cancer was the curse that ran through my family. It took my grandmother, a strong and fearless woman, leaving us all in shock and grief. She never thought to check for lumps until it was too late. Disease ravaged her body at forty, stealing a fulfilling life. Her memory now stands as a perpetual alarm, urging constant watchfulness in the battle against this lethal adversary.

My mother was unwavering in her determination to do her monthly checks. I can remember the day it happened, like it was just yesterday. The sky was a dismal grey, with thick, dark clouds looming overhead and frigid winds whipping through the air, sending shivers down my spine. My parents hurriedly left the warm comfort of our house, leaving me behind with our trusted housekeeper. An uneasy feeling settled in the pit of my stomach. The trees outside bent and swayed in the relentless wind, creating an eerie symphony that matched the dread building up inside me. Hours later, they returned, and I saw tears rolling down my mother's face. I had only seen it twice before when my father got hurt, but this time felt different - raw, painful. I couldn't recognize my mother at first. Her usually composed demeanor was shattered, revealing a vulnerable and distraught woman.

It wasn't until I turned thirteen, on the cusp of adolescence, that I learned the truth about my mysterious father. The notorious Gambino crime family was headed by him, a name that caused much fear. It was a shocking revelation that my mother had kept hidden from me for so long. But she assured me we were part of something bigger than a criminal organization. We were part of The Famiglia, a knit community bound by loyalty and tradition. With that, my formal education in our way of life began.

Tension hung heavy as we gathered in the library before dinner. Mom sat beside Dad, her hand trembling in his grasp. Their faces were grave, and my stomach clenched in fear. In a hushed whisper, they shared Mom found a lump and got tested for cancer. The words hit me like a hurricane as I remembered the stories of my grandmother's battle with breast cancer. Fear and uncertainty consumed us all as we waited for the results.

Luca and I, along with our parents, gathered once the results were in, finding ourselves in the library again. My heart sank as the weight of the news settled in. Cancer. That one word echoed in my mind, bouncing off the walls of my thoughts like a haunting specter. I sat there, frozen, staring at my parents, trying to absorb what they told us. The room felt suffocating, the air heavy with unspoken fears and uncertainties.

My father's usually stoic expression was now etched with deep worry lines, his brow furrowed and his lips trembling. His piercing blue eyes, steady and unwavering, now betrayed the fear he tried to hide. As I looked at my mother, her normally strong and composed demeanor had crumbled, replaced with a fragility and vulnerability I had never seen before. The realization struck me hard - the woman who always guided me through life's trials was now in a battle she may not win. My heart ached at the thought of losing her, and I could see the same pain reflected in my father's eyes.

As the news sank in, I felt a surge of emotions - anger at the unfairness of it all, fear of losing her, and a fierce determination to do whatever it took to support her. Cancer, a formidable foe, never deterred my family from fighting. We were fighters, warriors on our own, and we would confront this.

Days turned into weeks, filled with endless doctor's appointments, tests, and waiting. The uncertainty was a heavy mantle that draped over our household, casting a shadow on everything we did. I watched as my mother bravely faced each new challenge with unwavering strength, her resolve unwavering even in the face of uncertainty.

One evening, as I sat by her bedside, holding her hand and trying to offer whatever comfort I could, she turned to me with a look of fierce determination in her eyes. "Lucy," she says, her voice barely above a whisper. "I need you to promise me something."

I felt a lump form in my throat as I gazed at her, seeing the vulnerability beneath her brave facade. "Anything, Mom."

She squeezed my hand tightly, her gaze locking onto mine. "Promise me you will never lose hope, no matter how dark the road ahead may seem. Promise me you will always remember the strength within you and never let fear or doubt cloud your spirit," she implored, her eyes searching mine for reassurance.

Tears welled in my eyes as I nodded, my voice just a whisper. "I promise, Mom. I promise to never lose faith, to stand strong even in the face of adversity."

A faint smile flickered across her lips, a mix of pride and gratitude shining in her eyes. "That's my girl." Her fingers brushing against my cheek. "You are stronger than you know, Lucy. And I do not doubt you will carry on our legacy with courage and grace."

The words crashed against my mind like a relentless wave, leaving deep scars in the depths of my soul. I could see my mother's face contorted with pain, fighting her battle with unbreakable strength. And then, after endless days and sleepless nights, we received the news that she was cancer-free. I experienced a bittersweet sense of relief. She made me promise to never skip a monthly check and to seek help right away if something didn't feel right. The weight of that promise settled onto my shoulders like a heavy burden, a constant reminder of the fragility of life and the strength of a mother's love.

I slipped on my clothes, the urgency coursing through me. With a trembling hand, I pulled up a list of local gynecologists on my phone and began making calls to see who could see me today. Only two offices were listed in the area, and I knew that if neither could accommodate me, I would have to risk going to a doctor closer to Manhattan. My first call was disappointing, as the receptionist informed me they were booked for several weeks. My heart pounded as I dialed the next and final office, my mind racing with worries and possibilities.

"Good morning, Dr. Richardson's office. How may I help you?" the receptionist answers in a cheery voice.

"I need to see a doctor today."

"What is going on?" she asks.

Fighting back the tear, I croaked out. "I felt a lump this morning."

"Stop worrying. Most times, it is nothing," she encourages.

"Breast cancer runs in my family. My grandmother died of breast cancer, and my mother battled cancer over seven years ago."

"Let me see what I can do," she says. A minute later, she comes back on the line. "We had a cancelation. Can you get here in an hour?"

"Yes. Thank you."

I snatch my purse with a trembling hand, my heart thudding against my ribs, and I make my way towards the doctor's office. Every footfall feels like dragging through quicksand, the weight of my anxiety and fear pulling me down with each heavy step.

Sitting on the hard plastic chair in the cramped waiting room, my mind was consumed with a storm of terrifying possibilities. What if it was cancer? An icy chill crept down my spine at the thought. What if it was already too late? My heart pounded as I tried to push away the fear. Each tick of the wall clock dragged on, mocking me. Finally, after an endless wait, my name was called, and I made my way toward the ominous door marked "Doctor's Office."

"Lucy Mitchell."

"That is me."

The nurse gives me a smile. "Come this way, please."

I follow her down the hallway and into the small, sterile examination room. My regular gynecologist's office was similar to a fancy lounge, complete with cozy chairs and a comfortable exam table. This room was built for efficiency rather than comfort. Designed to discourage lingering, the chairs were hard and uninviting. Covered in a thin layer of paper, the examination table had a cheap, clinical appearance. The cabinets were made of utilitarian materials, lacking any sense of elegance or style. This room served only one purpose. To get the job done quickly and efficiently.

The kind face of the nurse asked about my health history, and I shared every detail with her. She noted each entry in my file, asking follow-up questions. With a gentle smile, she instructed me to change into the plain gown provided and climb up onto the padded examination table. The room was devoid of warmth, with a chilling atmosphere that sent shivers down one's spine. Following her instructions, I couldn't help but feel vulnerable, but I trusted that this was for my well-being.

The minutes felt like endless hours as I waited for the doctor to arrive. My heart pounded in my chest, and my hands shook with nervousness. After what seemed like forever, the door opened to reveal a middle-aged woman wearing a pristine white coat. Despite her warm smile, a hint of weariness in her eyes betrayed the weight of her responsibilities. She took slow, deliberate steps toward me, her shoes clicking against the linoleum floor.

"Hello, Lucy. I'm Dr. Richardson," she introduced herself, her tone professional yet somewhat detached.

I greeted her with a nervous nod, my heart fluttering. She took a moment to review my medical history on the file, the silence between us almost suffocating. When she turned her attention to me, her gaze was sharp and cold, studying me with clinical precision. The air was heavy and tense, like a courtroom awaiting a verdict.

"You found a lump this morning," she stated, more than a fact than a question.

I whisper. "Yes."'

She nodded and motioned for me to lie on the sterile examination table. As her hands glided over my skin with cool precision, I couldn't help but feel a surge of anxiety churn in my stomach. Every touch, every prodding movement seemed to send shivers down my spine, as if her fingertips were electric and sparking against my flesh. The bright overhead lights illuminated the room, casting stark shadows on the white walls and gleaming medical equipment. Despite the controlled atmosphere, a feeling of vulnerability consumed me, leaving me exposed to her clinical scrutiny.

Dr. Richardson's expression remained impassive as she continued the examination, her gloved fingers moving over where I had felt the lump. I held my breath, my heart pounding in my ears, waiting for her to say anything. The silence stretched on, suffocating me with its weight.

After what felt like forever, she retreated and discarded her gloves. Her face betraying no emotion. I sat up, my gaze unwavering as I searched her expression for any clue about what she had discovered.

"Lucy," she began, her voice calm but tinged with a hint of seriousness. "I understand your family history and your concerns. It's good that you're vigilant about your health."

My heart thumped against my chest like a caged bird desperate to escape. I braced for her next words, my mind swirling with all the worst-case scenarios. Was it the C-word? The one that had haunted me in my darkest thoughts? My palms grew clammy and cold as I waited for her answer, feeling like I was teetering on the edge of a precipice. Would this be when my worst fear was realized?

"But," she says, her expression softening ever so slightly, "I don't feel a lump. Your breasts are tight and swollen. When was your last period?"

Her question hit me like a train wreck. When was it? I remembered it a few weeks before I left. But I couldn't remember having one since I disappeared from my family and The Famiglia.

"I can't remember the date."

"Could you be pregnant?"

My mind raced at the mention of pregnancy, a dizzying mix of emotions swirling within me. Could it be possible? I hadn't even considered the idea until now. The thought of carrying a child, especially under these circumstances, sent a wave of both fear and wonder through me.

"I... I don't know."

Dr. Richardson studied me, her gaze searching mine for any hint of confirmation.

"Let's do a quick pregnancy test just to rule it out." Her gentle tone calmed me.

She handed me a cup, the smooth surface cool against my palm. She smiled and pointed towards a wooden door, indicating that the bathroom was there. I followed her instructions and soon stood in a small, sterile room with white-tiled walls and floors. Running water echoed in the small space as I relieved myself into the cup and then washed my hands. My heart raced with nervous anticipation as I returned to the examination room. Time stretched endlessly as Dr. Richardson finally turned to me, clutching a fresh printout.

"It's positive."

Positive. The word echoed in my mind, sending me a rush of conflicting emotions. It was positive for pregnancy. I felt a mixture of disbelief, fear, and a strange glimmer of hope all at once. How could this be happening? How could I be carrying a child amid all the chaos that surrounded me? My mind raced with questions, doubts, and uncertainties as Dr. Richardson's words hung heavy between us.

"Positive?"

Dr. Richardson nodded, her face softening with a hint of understanding. "Yes, Lucy. You're pregnant."

The weight of her words settled over me like a heavy blanket, wrapping me in a cocoon of shock and disbelief. I would be a mother - a thought that filled me with joy and terror. How can I have a child alone? However, as scary as it was to raise the child on my own, there was no way I would abort the baby. The tiny baby was part of Davide. It's the only part I could ever possess.

I sat there, stunned by the news of my pregnancy. A rush of conflicting emotions washed over me - fear, joy, uncertainty - mingled in a tumultuous storm within my mind. The possibility of creating life amid the dark world I was entangled in terrified me.

Dr. Richardson's voice brought me back to reality, her words breaking through the haze of my thoughts. "Lucy, I can see you're overwhelmed. It's natural to feel this way, given your circumstances."

I nodded, grateful for her understanding tone amidst the chaos within me. "What do I do now?" I ask, my voice tinged with vulnerability and determination.

The doctor offered me a reassuring smile before explaining the next steps. "First and foremost, we must ensure you receive proper prenatal care. I can refer you to an obstetrician who specializes in high-risk pregnancies, considering your family medical history."

Chapter Fourteen

Davide

My days are shrouded in unending darkness, a heavy cloak that weighs down my spirit. Ever since the day I last laid eyes on Lucy, the light has abandoned me. Even Corvo, my inner Raven, has grown still and silent. Rarely does he remain hidden. His presence always felt like a familiar weight on my shoulder, but now he, too, seems to have disappeared into the shadows of my mind.

The hope of Lucy's return diminishes with every excruciating day that passes. Justin has poured thousands of hours into meticulously scanning through every second of airport surveillance footage, his mind consumed by the task at hand. He exhausts every resource and technique in his arsenal, straining his eyes to catch even the tiniest hint or clue. But all his efforts yield nothing. The void left by Lucy's absence grows deeper with each fruitless attempt, driving Justin to the brink of madness.

Lucy went through the TSA and boarded her plane. When the plane arrived in Rome, there was no video of her, but the text she sent to Luca pinged outside the airport.

"Davide," my mom, Nan, called out as she walked into the room carrying a tray of food. The smell wasn't appealing. "You need to eat."

"Not hungry."

"You need to keep your strength up. When you find her, she will need you."

My heart clenched as I voiced what I had been thinking. "I don't think I'll ever see her again."

Each word felt like a ton of bricks crashing down on me, crushing my spirit and leaving me gasping for air. The mere thought of Lucy's absence created a gaping hole in my heart, a black void that threatened to swallow me whole. My soul felt suffocated by the weight of her absence, a shroud that threatened to consume every inch of my being.

Corvo's silence was suffocating, his absence a stark reminder of the darkness that threatened to consume me. The Raven who had always guided me through the shadows was now nowhere to be found, leaving me adrift in a sea of uncertainty.

My mother's delicate hand, warm and comforting, pressed gently on my shoulder and brought me back to the present. She was my anchor in this chaotic world, keeping me grounded when everything felt like it was slipping away.

"Davide," she whispered with a hint of worry, "you can't lose hope." Her words were like a lifeline, pulling me back from the brink of despair.

I turned to look at her, seeing the worry etched into her features. "I don't know if I have any hope left, Mom. Lucy is... gone."

"David, you don't that."

"Seven agonizing months have passed with no sign of her. Every day is a mental torture, wondering if she's alive or dead. Our team has scoured every lead and found nothing. Not a single clue to her whereabouts or even the possibility of a ransom. It's like she's vanished into thin air, leaving us grasping at shadows and haunted by the unknown."

I feel my mother's arms around me. "As hopeless as it might seem, you must keep positive that you will find her, and when you do, you need to allow yourself to love her. She is your other half."

"I can't do that. She deserves someone who loves her and is faithful. I am not that guy."

"Bullshit. Answer this. The six months she was in Italy with her parents, how many women were you with?" she asks.

"None," I murmured.

"Okay, and how many women have you been with since she disappeared?"

"None."

"So, let me get this straight. The man who knows he won't be faithful to her hasn't slept with anyone for over a year," she says with a smirk.

I let out a bitter chuckle at my mother's words. She always had a way of cutting through my self-pity with her blunt honesty. "You, Mom, always alter my perception."

"Davide, because I know you, I can understand your actions. You have a good heart, even if you try to hide it under layers of darkness."

I collapsed onto the couch, my body sagging under the unbearable weight of grief. My breath came in ragged gasps as I confessed to my mother, "I ache for her, Mom. It's as if something has been forcefully taken from me, leaving behind an immense emptiness."

Mom took my hand in hers, giving it a gentle squeeze. "You will find her, Davide. No matter how long it takes, you will bring her back home."

Her words sparked a glimmer of hope, a tiny flicker of light in the endless darkness surrounding me. I finally let myself believe that Lucy was still out there, waiting to be found. The thought of her being alive and in need rekindled a long-lost fire within me.

With renewed determination, I silently vowed to not rest until Lucy was safe and sound in my arms. I owed it to her and us to fight for our love and not succumb to the shadows that threatened to consume me whole. I had been a fool. I should have listened to my friends and mother. My father's and grandfather's infidelity didn't define me.

I reach out and gently intertwine my fingers with my mom's, grateful for her presence. With gratitude in my heart, I pick up the fork and dig into the food on my plate. Though I wasn't hungry before, the aroma of the dish beckons to me, and my stomach growls in response. As soon as I take a bite, my taste buds come alive with flavor, and my hunger is awakened in full force. I quickly devour every bite on the plate, savoring each morsel until nothing remains. Thanks to the delicious meal and my mother's love, my belly feels warm and satisfied.

As the delicious meal settled in my stomach, my mind sharpened, and I pulled up the videos from the day Lucy disappeared from the airport. The footage showed her arrival, stepping out of her sleek vehicle confidently. She had a brief exchange with her guard before effortlessly lifting her black hardcover carry-on by its handle and strolling through the busy airport. The next camera captured Lucy in the TSA line, her pre-screening status allowing for a quick and smooth process through security. She placed her bag on the conveyor belt and confidently walked through the metal detector, retrieving her belongings on the other side. Camera after camera documented her journey through the airport, a lone figure amid the bustling crowds.

An announcement is made concerning her flight, and I watch her walk into the ladies' room. Unfortunately, there was no camera in the bathroom. I continue to watch until she emerges and rushes toward the gate. What am I missing? I've watched this video at least five hundred times. Hell, I can almost tell you how many steps she makes.

As I stare at the screen, I reach out to switch to the next camera video and notice a woman exiting the bathroom. She is tall with long red hair and wearing a tightly fitted skirt and jacket. I stop the video and zoom in on her face. The quality isn't good, and she is wearing a pair of black, oversized sunglasses.

Her blurry features were unrecognizable, yet something about her resonated. The way she moved with purpose and the confident tilt of her head seemed oddly familiar. As I leaned closer to the screen, trying to discern any distinguishing marks or features, a sense of unease settled in the pit of my stomach.

Could this woman be Lucy? Or was she a mere bystander caught on camera? My mind raced with questions, each leading down a different path of possibilities and suspicions.

I swiftly accessed footage from nearby cameras during that time. There she was again, moving swiftly through the crowd, her red hair a vivid contrast against the sea of muted colors. It was as if she had intentionally made herself not stick out.

As I continued to analyze the footage, a nagging feeling crept up. We believed Lucy had been targeted for harm all along. What if she left willingly? Why would she want to do that? Did she decide at the airport or plan it beforehand?

Lucy's mind was a dazzling and complex machine, filled with talents that society deemed inappropriate for a proper young woman. However, unlike most women in The Famiglia, Luca had encouraged her to pursue her passions and develop her skills. And oh, what a gift she had! With one click, she could transform any unappealing view into a captivating work of art. It was as if she possessed a magic touch, able to capture the essence and beauty of every scene she encountered.

But she was also a constant presence in our group, sitting with Luca and the rest of us as we discussed family business. While seemingly quiet and unassuming, she absorbed everything like a sponge. It wasn't until she hot-wired a car and expertly took out the men from the notoriously ruthless Cuban Cartel that we realized just how much she had learned. With precise aim, she dispatched each target with only one bullet, leaving Giovanni speechless at her display of skill. Even our most skilled marksmen could take notes from her tactics.

With my gaze fixed on the screen, I analyzed the red-haired woman once again. Who was she? Where did she come from? Changing the video to the one near the bathroom, I began the video and watched as she walked out after Lucy. I don't remember seeing her walk in. Rewinding the footage before when Lucy walked into the bathroom. As the moments ticked by, I didn't see the redhead. The redhead never goes into the bathroom. I switch cameras and look for her somewhere else in the terminal. But I don't find her. This was too peculiar.

I urgently require additional perspectives on this woman. I reach for my phone and dial Luca's number with trembling fingers. He answers after the first ring, his voice laced with genuine concern.

"Davide, what's wrong?" Luca's voice sounded urgent on the other end of the line.

"I need your help, Luca. I've found something. No, someone in the airport footage from the day Lucy disappeared. A woman with red hair."

"A woman with red hair? What are you talking about?" Luca's confusion was palpable through the phone.

"She comes out after Lucy from the bathroom. However, I can't seem to find her on any feed. The only time is after she walks out of the bathroom. I have a feeling she might be connected somehow. Can you all come and view the footage with me?" I needed Luca's keen eye for detail and a strategic mind would be invaluable in unraveling this mystery.

There was a short pause before Luca responded. "I'll call the others and be there in twenty minutes. Wait for me before making any impulsive decisions, Davide."

After ending the phone call, I shifted my attention back to the screen, eagerly following the mysterious woman's fluid and alluring movements once more. Her every step and gesture held an air of intrigue and danger that captivated me.

Twenty-five minutes later, Luca, Danti, Giovanni, and Andrea walk in. I bring them up to speed on the red-haired woman. They don't look like they believe me, but a picture is worth a thousand words.

I pull up the video and cast it to the large-screen TV. They watch the screen and see Lucy leave the bathroom, and then five minutes later, the redhead emerges.

"So a red-headed woman comes out of the bathroom," Giovanni says.

"But I can't find how she got there or anywhere else in the terminal. Hell, I watched hours of TSA check-ins, and I never see her come in."

"What about afterward?" Danti asks.

Fury courses through my veins, fueling a frantic search for her that has consumed me. But now, as I desperately try to retrace my steps and find her again, I can feel the panic creeping in. "I haven't looked yet," I confess, desperation seeping into every word. "But she has to be connected to Lucy's disappearance. And if we don't find her, we may never see Lucy again." My voice trembles with fear and determination as I continue the hunt, knowing it may be our only hope.

Chapter Fifteen

Lucy

"Lucy, the baby's heartbeat and growth are great. However, I am very concerned about your blood pressure and the swelling of your legs and ankles."

My ankles were non-existent, mere cankles that blended seamlessly into my calves. The only shoes I could squeeze my swollen feet into were clunky house shoes, reminiscent of something my great-grandmother would wear. Ever since I discovered my pregnancy, I devoured every book I could find on what to expect. However, not a single one mentioned the vanishing act my ankles had pulled. Instead, they warned of high blood pressure and the potential for a condition called preeclampsia.

"Are you talking about preeclampsia?"

"Yes, Lucy." The doctor's voice was gentle yet serious. "I am going to run a blood test to check for any presence of protein in your blood. This could be a precursor for preeclampsia, a potentially dangerous condition during pregnancy. Do you have someone at home who can be with you?"

I couldn't help but feel a twinge of fear at the mention of such a scary word. I shook my head, feeling alone and vulnerable in this moment.

"How about the father or a family member? Can you call them and ask for help?"

"The father is out of the picture, and I don't have any family." It was a lie. She could never know the truth because it was too dangerous.

I was all alone, just as I had planned. As scared as I was, I couldn't go back. I am sure my family is mad about my disappearance. However, I also had to worry about what The Famiglia would do to me. Even though I was a daughter of a founding family, it didn't make me immune to their punishments for breaking the rules. I had no clue what they would do to me, but I could handle whatever they handed out. Though I didn't know what they would do to my child. I would do everything possible to prevent them from finding me or my child.

A wave of pure adoration washed over me, engulfing every fiber of my being as I fell madly in love with the baby. This tiny being, a priceless gift from Davide, is my sole link to him. But despite the overwhelming joy, a deep ache settled in my heart - a reminder that I was alone in this world, isolated by my choices.

Dr. Richardson looked at me sympathetically and patted my arm. "Lucy, you are not all alone. I am here for you and your baby. There are ways you can get some help. Let's take this test and see what we're looking at."

Dr. Richardson's words hit me like a ton of concrete bricks, crushing my chest and suffocating me with the harsh reality of my loneliness. I lay on the cold steel examination table, feeling each word stab at my heart with the force of a thousand sharp knives. As I closed my eyes, all I could think about was Davide. The man who had given upon me this bittersweet gift, a constant reminder of my deepest desires and darkest secrets.

While Dr. Richardson prepared the instruments, I sensed impending doom. The looming threat of preeclampsia paled compared to the storm brewing within me, a storm of emotions, fears, and unspoken truths.

But as the sharp, stabbing needle pierced my skin and the rich, crimson liquid filled the vial, a sudden sense of determination washed over me. The needle's sting was worth it for this precious life inside me. Davide's baby. My heart swelled with fierce love and protectiveness as I set my resolve to do everything in my power to keep this child safe from harm. Fear and uncertainty could not cloud my judgment; I would do whatever it takes to ensure this baby's well-being.

"I will rush these results. Rest here, and I will be back as soon as I can."

She walks out of the room, and I let the tears I had been holding back flow. I couldn't lose this baby. I just couldn't. The past seven months were incredibly difficult. So often, I caught myself picking up the phone to call Luca to come get me. The feeling I had about someone watching me has never stopped. Every time I walked out of my house, the hairs on my neck stood on end. I carried a snub nose 9mm revolver wherever I went. No one ever approached or tried to talk to me, but the feeling remained.

As my tears mixed with the sweat on my face, a fierce determination took hold of me. I refused to let fear paralyze me, not when my child's life was at stake. I had to summon every ounce of strength for both of us, even if it meant pushing myself to the brink of exhaustion. Nothing would stand in the way of protecting my child.

Despite the overwhelming loneliness that weighed on my heart, I found solace in the thought of Davide's child growing inside me. This baby symbolized a forbidden love, a love that could never be openly acknowledged. But it was a love nonetheless, and I would protect it with every fiber of my being.

I waited for Dr. Richardson to return with the blood test results. I closed my eyes and whispered a silent prayer to whatever forces may be listening. Please let my baby be safe. Let us make it through this storm together. I couldn't imagine losing the one thing that tied me to Davide. The door opened, breaking my concentration. Dr. Richardson entered, her expression grave.

"Lucy, I'm afraid the test results show that there is indeed protein in your blood. It's not a definitive diagnosis of preeclampsia yet, but it's a warning sign we can't ignore."

As her words hit me like a sledgehammer, my heart plummeted into the depths of my chest. A frigid terror crawled through every inch of my veins, threatening to freeze me in place. The dangers of preeclampsia swirled in my mind, devouring any sense of hope. But I couldn't let fear consume me. Not when the lives of both myself and my unborn child hung in the balance.

My mind raced with a million questions and fears. "What do we do now?" Dr. Richardson's expression softened as she sat beside me, her eyes filled with empathy and understanding.

"We need to monitor you closely, Lucy. I'll schedule more frequent check-ups and tests to monitor your condition. In the meantime, it's important that you take care of yourself physically and emotionally." Her voice was a soothing balm to my frayed nerves.

As her words sank in, I felt a flicker of hope ignite within me, like a spark catching hold of dry kindling. Maybe, just maybe, we could navigate through this storm together and emerge on the other side unscathed, stronger and braver for it. With a deep breath to center myself, I nodded with renewed determination, my eyes shining with both fear and determination.

"I'll do whatever it takes to keep my baby safe." With unwavering resolve, I vowed to do everything I could to bring our baby into this world healthy.

Dr. Richardson gave me a reassuring smile before gently touching my shoulder. "You're stronger than you think, Lucy. And you're not alone in this. We'll face this challenge head-on, together."

I stepped out of the sterile white walls of the clinic, and the weight of the doctor's words settled heavily on my shoulders. The looming threat of preeclampsia hung over me like a dark storm cloud, casting shadows of doubt and fear across my mind and heart. Yet deep within me, a fierce determination burned bright, fueling a fire of resilience and strength in the face of adversity.

I made my way home, the streets bustling with life around me. People hurried past, lost in their own worlds, unaware of the storm raging within me. And yet, despite the chaos of the outside world, I found a strange sense of peace settling over me.

Entering my little house, I let out a long sigh and sank onto the couch. The familiar surroundings offered some comfort, grounding me in reality. I rubbed my hand over my belly, feeling a flutter of movement beneath my touch. A surge of love and protectiveness washed over me as I whispered words of reassurance to the precious life growing inside me. Every kick and every flutter reminded me of the fragile yet resilient bond I shared with this little one. It was Davide's child, my beacon of light in a world darkened by secrets and danger.

The evening sun cast long shadows through the window. I found myself lost in contemplation. Thoughts of Davide haunted me like a relentless specter, his enigmatic presence weaving through the fabric of my existence. Despite the circumstances that kept us apart, I couldn't deny the love I still harbored for him.

The weight of my impending motherhood pressed upon me with both joy and trepidation. Davide would never know about his child, about the silent sacrifices I made to protect our secret. He would never see the depth of my love.

Night descended like a velvet curtain over the city. I remained in the stillness of my living room. The quietness wraps itself around me, comforting me and giving me a sense of security. I picked up the photo book on my coffee table and opened it up. The first picture captured all the guys at the pool. Each was holding a tumbler of bourbon and wearing nothing but their swim trunks. It was one of the few times they were kicking back and relaxing. Luca's blonde hair slick back from where he had been in the pool. It was one of the few pictures where his scar was fully displayed. He wore his hair long so it would hang over it. He would never admit it, but I know how much he hates it. It was a reminder of how close he lost his life.

Andrea and Danti were showing off their muscles while Giovanni made kissy lips. My eyes drift to the last person in the photo, Davide. He was looking directly at the camera. I had seen this picture countless times, yet now it took my breath away. I always thought he was angry with me. However, now I see something I missed. I see the same intensity in his powerful eyes as the night we made love. Why couldn't I see it then?

It was as if his gaze bore into the depths of my soul, unraveling the layers of my defenses with each passing moment. The photograph captured a moment frozen in time, a fleeting glimpse of a man torn between duty and desire. His eyes held myriad emotions, a silent plea hidden beneath a mask of stoicism. I found myself drawn to the enigma that was Davide Corvo Bonanno, the man who had captured my heart against all odds.

A flood of memories washed over me as I studied his features in the photograph. The night we shared, our bodies entwined in passion and longing, seemed like a distant dream. I could still feel the heat of his touch on my skin, the whispered words of how much he wanted me. And yet, reality loomed large before me, reminding me of the barriers that stood between us.

A gentle exhale escaped my lips, a mixture of longing and tenderness as I traced a finger over Davide's image in the photograph. As if sensing my touch, the baby inside me kicked with surprising force. Knowing this little one would bring so much joy and adventure, I smiled. And yet, I didn't know their gender - wanting to be surprised when the time came. My life had been filled with routine and predictability, but this baby brought excitement and unknown possibilities.

I flip the page, and a tear escapes. It was the night of the gala after Davide broke the marriage arrangement. The Famiglia always have someone taking pictures. Carson was the photographer that evening and snapped the photo of Davide and I. At the end of the evening, he asked me when I was leaving. For a fleeting moment, I hoped he had changed his mind and was going to tell me he wanted to marry me. It was then Carson clicked the photo. He sent it to me and told me it was the only copy. I don't know if he saw what happened between Davide and me, but I was thankful for the photo.

We didn't have a photographer on the night of my going away party, so this was the last picture of Davide I would ever have. When our child was old enough, I would show them their daddy and the lie I would have to tell them for their own protection.

Chapter Sixteen

Davide

Seven long months had passed, each one spent hundreds of hours watching every second of the videos from the day Lucy vanished. The unknown redhead seemed to materialize out of thin air, her presence haunting and unexplainable. With each viewing, Justin's and my nerves were stretched thinner and thinner until they felt ready to snap under the weight of our desperate search for answers.

"Justin says he has nothing on the redhead," Luca growls.

"There has to be something. Did he find out where she went when she left the airport?"

"She took a taxi into the city and got out on 42nd Street. The camera follows her until she goes into a cafe. She walks towards the back, where the bathrooms are, and never comes back out. We think she slipped out the back. After that, she vanishes," Luca explains.

My hand slams against the chair arm with such force that it leaves a deep indentation. "She can't just disappear into oblivion," I growl through gritted teeth. There has to be a camera, a witness, anything that can give me a clue to her whereabouts. But all I see is an empty, silent void, mocking my desperate need for answers.

Luca's face twists into a scowl as he responds. "I know, but she did. And now I can't shake this terrible feeling that we may never see Lucy again." His voice cracks with emotion as he continues, "If she was taken for ransom, they would have contacted us by now. And if she ran away, the extensive network of cameras in the city would have captured her and pinged Justin's program." I see dread settle over Luca's features. "The only other explanation is that she has become a victim of unspeakable violence." This chilled me to my core, and my hands tremble with fear and anger.

The thought of Lucy's death was unbearable. I could feel her presence lingering in the air, filling me with a desperate hope she was still alive. My mind refused to accept the reality, clinging to any thread of possibility. I needed her to be alive, to beg for her forgiveness on my knees before it was too late. The weight of my guilt and regret crushed my chest as I frantically searched for any sign of her.

Nana's words echoed in my mind, her wisdom and intuition proving to be true. I was a stark contrast to my father and grandfather - their promiscuity and disregard for commitment were foreign concepts to me. The mere thought of being physically intimate with another woman made my stomach churn uneasily. Lucy was more than just my partner. She was my soulmate - no one else could ever come close to the love and connection we shared. She was the one and only. My heart and soul intertwined with hers forevermore. Corvo agreed. She was our mate.

The desire to make her mine consumed me, to marry her and defy the strict rules of The Famiglia. Giovanni's recent marriage to Angelina had sparked a change within him, causing him to approach The Commission with a proposal to modernize their archaic regulations. I couldn't comprehend his motives at the time, but now it all made sense. This woman had captured my heart, and I would do whatever it took to make her my wife, even if it meant going against the traditions of our powerful organization.

I would not give up. "Luca, she is alive. I just know it. We have to keep looking."

Luca's voice cracks. "It is so hard. If she was so unhappy, I would have moved heaven on earth to keep her close. Sometimes I hate The Famiglia and all our fucking rules. Before, I never thought much about it. But now I see what Giovanni was talking about. The women in our society are nothing but second-class citizens."

I knew I needed to come clean about my feelings for Lucy. "Luca, I have come clean. I love your sister so fucking much. The thought of spending eternity with her as my wife was a dream. But deep down, I knew it was just a matter of time before I followed in the footsteps of my father and grandfather. The memory of my mother's shattered heart every time he came home, reeking of cheap perfume and sex, still haunts me. And the sickening truth? He didn't just confine his infidelity to The Disorderly House. He brought his mistresses right into our own home, violating our sacred space like it was nothing. However, that didn't stop him from spreading his seed across half of New York City. And the real kicker? Our family doctor was always on call, providing him with medication for countless communicable diseases. He may have succumbed to cancer on paper, but in reality, it was syphilis that ate away at his brain until there was nothing left but Swiss cheese. That's the legacy my dear old dad left behind, and I can feel it creeping up on me every day."

Luca's mouth dropped open. "Wow, man, I had no clue."

The words spill out of his mouth like poison, dripping with disdain and bitterness. "No one else knew the truth, only Nan and me," I spit, my voice cracking with emotion. "She suffered through endless torment, and there was nothing she could do about it. There is no escape from The Famiglia."

"Davide, you are unlike your father or grandfather," Luca stresses.

"A wise woman beat that into my head already."

Luca's lip turns up in a smirk. "Nan?"

I nod. "She asked a question which I hadn't even thought of."

"What?"

"How many women have I been with since the marriage agreement? How many women have I been with since the broken agreement? And how many women have I been with since Lucy's disappearance?"

He raises an eyebrow. "How many?"

I shook my head at his question. "None." My voice is barely above a whisper. "After I broke the agreement, I went to The Disorderly House, but I couldn't bring myself to follow through. Every time I closed my eyes, I saw Lucy's face, her sweet smile and gentle touch. She was and is all I wanted." The memory of her haunted me, pulling at my heartstrings and reminding me of what I had lost. My overwhelming regrets drowned out any chance of finding pleasure or distraction at that infamous establishment. My desire for Lucy was all-consuming, and nothing could quell it.

Luca steps closer, his warm hand resting on my arm. His eyes are filled with concern and sincerity as he speaks. "She loves you, and when she overheard you saying you didn't want her, something shattered inside her." He pauses, shaking his head. Sadness painted his features. "I've never seen her so broken before." His words hang heavy in the air, emphasizing the weight of the situation. "I can't think of anyone better to be her husband than you. You are a kind and honorable man, even if you don't think so."

A tense silence fills the air as he speaks those words, but I know deep down that his tune will change once he hears what I have to say next. He'll probably fly into a fit of rage and unleash his anger on me, and I won't even try to fight back. I messed up, no doubt about it, but I can't bring myself to regret the time spent with Lucy. It seems like just yesterday when her velvety walls clamped tightly around my cock, perfectly molded to fit me like a glove. Even after all this time, the memory of her heat and passion still lingers on my skin, a constant reminder of what we shared.

I am about to open my mouth when Andrea and Danti waltz into the room. Well, shit, I'm not going to spill my guts in front of all of them.

"Told you he would be here," Danti says, punching Andrea in the arm.

"Damn, man, learn to control your strength," Andrea growls, rubbing his arm.

I know all too well the excruciating pain he can inflict. I shudder to even imagine the force behind his blows, the weight of his massive frame bearing down on his victim. I've witnessed firsthand the destruction he's capable of, his mammoth fists connecting with brutal precision and leaving our enemies in pieces. Danti Lucchese, our group's most imposing member, stands at a daunting 6'7" and weighs an intimidating 275 lbs of pure, rippling muscle. He is every bit deserving of his family's inner animal, the Bear. With dark brown locks that cascade down to his broad shoulders and piercing stone-grey eyes, Danti exudes a primal aura that draws women like moths to a flame. They crave the chance to see if his physical prowess extends beyond his fighting abilities - particularly regarding the size of his manhood. It is not like we stand around flicking out our dicks to see who has the largest, but over the years, we all have been naked at some point. Danti has complained countless times about his struggle to find a woman who can handle all of him. However, I felt he'll keep searching for his unicorn.

"Stop being a pussy," Danti says.

Andrea flips him a bird and walks over to the liquor cabinet, pouring a large tumbler of Luca's expensive bourbon into it. He takes a big drink before plopping onto one of the leather chairs. "So, any news?"

He doesn't have to explain what news he is asking about. For the last seven months, it has always been about Lucy. "No," Luca says.

"We are missing something," Danti says, pouring his drink.

I grit my teeth. "I know, but what? Every millisecond of the videos has been viewed at least ten times. Hell, it has been viewed fifty times. She just disappeared into thin air."

We are interrupted by Victoria. "Mr. Gambino, there is a young lady here who says she has to speak with you."

"Who is it?" Luca asks.

"Sophia Croft, Sir."

"I don't know a Sophia Croft. Do any of you know her?" he asks.

"The only Croft I know is Consigliere Croft," Andrea replies.

"I can't seem to remember seeing his wife or daughter?" Luca says. "Victoria, escort her in."

A few seconds later, she returns. "Sophia Croft."

Victoria gracefully steps back and, through the doorway, sways a young woman with an air of familiarity. I struggle to remember where I've seen her before, but my attention is drawn to her striking appearance. Standing about five foot six, her wavy shoulder-length hair cascades in golden brown waves. Her hourglass figure is accentuated by ample breasts, a narrow waist, and curvy hips that sway with every step she takes. She wears a pink flower dress that hugs every curve of her body, making her look even more alluring. And as my eyes trail down, I can't help but notice how the four-inch pink heels elongate her already long legs. She's undeniably beautiful, but in my mind, she pales compared to my Lucy.

"Fuck me," Danti groans beside me. I glance towards him and see he basically eye fucking her.

With a smile, she walks in and over to Luca, holding out her hand. Luca takes it and shakes it.

"Mr. Gambino, thank you for seeing me," she says, then turns towards us. "Mr. Bonanno, Colombo, and."

She stops and gasps the moment she sees Danti. He steps forward, takes her hand in his, and brings it to his lips. Never breaking the eye connection, he kisses the back softly. A bright pink blush blooms across her cheeks. "Mr. Lucchese."

"Danti, call me Danti."

She smiles and lowers her gaze. "Danti."

I look over at Luca and who pulls up his shoulders. He is as surprised at the interaction as I am. "Miss Croft, would you like a cup of tea?" Luca asks.

Sophia jumps and pulls her hand from Danti's grasp. "Please."

"I will be right back," Victoria says.

"Miss Croft, please sit and tell me why you needed to see me?" Luca asks.

"Please, call me Sophia, but I don't see Mr. Genovese. Normally, you are all together."

"He is home with Angelina. She is close to her due date," I say.

"Oh, that is right. I will have to call him and ask him if he would like me to come over and check on her as well," Sophia says.

She moves with a fluid grace, her steps purposeful and elegant as she glides to the chair. With a gentle sway of her hips, she lowers herself onto the plush seat, crossing her ankles and arranging her hands on her lap. The movement evokes memories of my mother, entertaining guests with effortless poise and charm. Every inch of her posture exudes grace and dignity like a swan serenely gliding across a still lake.

"Mr. Gambino."

"Please call me Luca, Miss Croft."

"Luca, please call me Sophia. I know you and others have been searching for Lucy. Over the years, I have seen her many times at the events at The Famiglia. I've never got to interact with her, though I always wanted to."

"Okay, but why are you here?" Luca asks.

"I think I saw her today," Sophia says.

With a burst of energy, I dash around the wooden desk and turn to face Sophia, my heart pounding. The urgency in her voice compels me to move faster as I ask, "Where exactly?" My gaze locks onto hers, searching for any hint or clue that could lead us to our destination.

"She was leaving a doctor's office in Brighton Beach," she answers. The room fills with audible gasps.

Danti stomps over and stares down at Sophia. "WHAT THE FUCK WERE YOU DOING IN BRIGHTON BEACH?"

Chapter Seventeen

Davide

Sophia glares up at Danti. "I am finishing up my residence. The clinic I am working at is in Brighton Beach."

"Are you a doctor?" Andrea asks.

"No, I am finishing up to become a midwife."

"Midwife?"

"My goal is to become a certified midwife, skilled in safely delivering babies on my own. Once I have completed my training, I aspire to work at the society hospital," she confidently responds. "Women within The Famiglia deserve and demand choices, especially in fields typically dominated by men. Pregnant women find it easier to trust and feel comfortable with female doctors and midwives."

Danti's voice turns into a low, guttural growl as he stares at her with narrowed eyes and a clenched jaw. The intensity of his gaze is suffocating, causing grown men to tremble and soil themselves in fear. "Does your father have any idea what you're risking by working in the heart of Russian territory?" he seethes, venom dripping from every word. The threat in his tone leaves no room for argument.

Sophia stands tall and takes a determined step closer to Danti. She plants her hands firmly on her hips, emphasizing her powerful will and defiance. Her chin tilts up, challenging him with her gaze. "He does," she retorts sharply, her voice tinged with frustration and determination. "Despite knowing the risks, I take every precaution. I am trained in self-defense and carry Pearly in my purse." There is a fire in her eyes, a fierce determination to protect what she holds dear.

"Who the fuck is Pearly?" Danti snaps.

Sophia stalks over to her purse and snatches it up, her hand diving inside to retrieve a sleek pink pearl handle 9mm Kimber. Her movements are swift and precise as she chambers a round, the click of the bullet echoing in the room. She levels the gun at Danti's chest with deadly accuracy, her eyes ablaze with unyielding determination. "This is Pearly, and I know exactly how to use it."

The air in the room becomes heavy as Sophia stands tall, her gun pointed unwaveringly at Danti. A palpable tension fills the space between them, each second stretching out like taffy. I am frozen in shock, unable to process the sight of a woman standing up to him with such unwavering defiance. Danti's face is a mask of stone, his jaw tightly clenched as he stares back at Sophia with dangerous intensity.

In a calm voice, Danti says. "Put the gun down."

Sophia's fingers wrap around the cold, metal grip of the gun, her knuckles turning white from the pressure. Her voice is like steel - unbreakable and unwavering. "Apologize for being an asshole." The weapon trembles slightly in her grasp, a physical manifestation of the fiery rage burning within her.

Danti's eyes flicker with anger before he lets out a scoff. "Apologize? To you? You are nothing but a foolish girl who doesn't know her place. Hasn't your father instructed you on who the boss in the society is?"

I can see Sophia's hand trembling slightly from the tension in the room, but she doesn't back down. "I may be young and a woman, but I am still part of The Famiglia. my father has informed me of the archaic thinking of the men inside the society."

"What have you done to prove yourself worthy of that title? Because by the sound of it, you don't understand the workings of The Famiglia and my standing within it."

Sophia takes a deep breath before answering. "I have completed my training as a midwife and am ready to serve The Family by bringing new life into this world."

Danti's expression softens slightly at her words, though his tone remains cold and crosses his arms over his chest. "And what makes you think that is enough to earn my respect?"

"I don't need your respect. But I do demand it as part of The Famiglia."

The room falls into a suffocating silence, holding its breath in anticipation of Danti's response. A tense stillness fills the air, heavy with unspoken words that hang like a guillotine blade over our heads. We all wait with bated breath, bracing for whatever comes next from the unpredictable Danti.

"Ding, ding, ding," Andrea says with a smirk. "Go to your corners. Sophia is here to give us information she has on Lucy."

Danti puckers his lips, his expression turning sour as he crosses his muscular arms over his broad chest. His piercing gaze is fixed on Sophia, who responds with a sly smirk and returns to her seat. The tension between them crackles in the air like a brewing storm waiting to unleash its fury. I can feel the heat of their animosity radiating towards each other, making the room feel stifling and uncomfortable.

"As I was saying before, I was so rudely interrupted. I was on my way to the clinic in Brighton Beach. A woman was walking down the steps as I neared. When she turned to go in the opposite direction, Helen, one of the nurses in the clinic, came running out. She called out, Lucy, and when the woman turned, she looked just like Lucy except she had deep red hair."

My heart raced. Had the redhead we saw leaving the bathroom and disappearing been Lucy in disguise? But how had she sent the text from her phone from Rome? And it was confirmed that her seat was occupied on the flight to Rome. How could that be possible when the redhead left the terminal after the plane departed?

"How sure are you it was, Lucy?"

"Other than the hair color and the fact she is very pregnant, I would say ninety-five percent sure."

I stand there. The revelation hit me like a ton of bricks. Pregnant. Lucy was pregnant. A surge of conflicting emotions washed over me - shock, disbelief, fear, and even a hint of guilt. Guilt for considering breaking off our engagement, for hesitating about marrying her. And now this. Was this my child, or had she met someone else, and it was theirs?

Andrea's smirk had vanished, replaced by a look of curiosity mixed with concern. He knew how tangled and dangerous the web we were caught in could be. "What do you want to do about this?"

Sophia leaned forward, her eyes flickering between me and Luca. She seemed almost on edge, as if waiting for an explosion that could shatter the fragile peace we were balancing right now. Her words were measured, laced with a hint of urgency. "We need to act swiftly and decisively. If Lucy is pregnant, it adds a layer of complexity to the situation. We cannot afford any missteps."

I could feel The Raven stirring within me, its whispers urging me to take control and eliminate any threats before they could harm her. But I pushed those dark thoughts aside, focusing on the task at hand. With a tornado of churning turmoil, I finally say. "We need to gather more information."

Andrea nods in agreement, his expression grave. "We need to find out where Lucy lives in Brighton Beach."

"And we need to contact Dominik," Danti says.

I whip around and glare at him. "Why the fuck do we want him to know Lucy is in his territory?"

Danti's eyes narrow dangerously as he meets my glare with a challenging one. "Because if Lucy is pregnant and on Russian turf. Dominik will see it as a sign of disrespect if we come onto his territory to get her." The tension in the room becomes palpable as everyone absorbs the gravity of the situation at hand.

I clench my jaw, weighing the risks and benefits of involving Dominik, the powerful leader of the Russian mafia. The fragile balance between our factions could easily tip into an all-out war with just one wrong move. But this was Lucy, my supposed fiancée, possibly carrying my child caught in the middle. Despite swallowing the bitter taste of pride, I nod curtly at Danti.

"Fine." I concede to Danti's assessment of the situation, but my tone leaves no room for argument. "Contact Dominik. Tell him we need to talk about a delicate matter."

"Sophia, I know this goes against HIPAA, but we need to know all of Lucy's medical history and what address she put down on her paperwork," Luca says.

She sighs and nods. "I will get the information, but the clinic is closed for the evening."

"Do you have a key?" I ask. "I can't wait until tomorrow morning to get the information."

"Davide, we can't go into Dom's territory now. We must wait until we have all the facts before we call him," Danti says.

"I don't give a flying fuck. My sister is there, and I am going after her."

Danti looks at Luca and then at me. "And what happens when you are seen on their turf?"

"This could start an all-out war. Tension is already high with the missing shipments, and it would only take one incident for it to explode. I want to get Lucy back safe and sound, but we must use our heads," Andrea says.

"I don't care. They are mine, and I am getting her back," I say, grinding my teeth.

Luca pounds his fist on the desk. "What do you mean, they are yours?"

Taking a deep breath to steady my simmering anger, I meet Luca's intense gaze head-on. "I meant Lucy and the baby. The night of her going away party, we were together." I clarify, my voice firm and brooking no room for misinterpretation. My fists clench at my sides, the tension in the room so thick it feels suffocating.

Luca pounces from behind the desk. His eyes narrowed to slits, and a fierce snarl escaped from between his bared teeth. The primal instincts of his inner lion have taken over, and he fixates on me with an intense focus. With every ounce of my being, I know that whatever punishment he has in store for me. I deserve it tenfold.

I brace myself for Luca's wrath, knowing I had betrayed his trust by being with Lucy that night. His lion eyes bore into mine, a mixture of hurt and rage swirling within them. But before he could unleash his fury, Danti steps in between us, his towering presence commanding attention.

"Enough," he says, his voice cutting through the tension like a knife. "This is not the time for infighting. We have a delicate situation on our hands, and we need to handle it with caution."

Luca's fists unclench slightly, his fierce gaze flickering between me and Danti. I can see the struggle in his eyes, torn between his loyalty to me as a friend and his anger at my betrayal. Taking a step back, he finally speaks, his voice laced with barely contained emotion.

"This is not over, Davide." The heavy weight of the situation may fracture friendship.

I force a weak nod, my heart heavy with guilt for the immense betrayal I have inflicted upon him. The hope of salvaging our friendship lingers like a flickering flame in the back of my mind, but I know deep down that it may never be repaired.

Andrea leans back in his chair, his cold eyes assessing the volatile situation unfolding before him. "We need to tread carefully here, Davide," he interjects, his tone cautionary, yet tinged with a hint of authority. "Rushing in without a plan will only lead to more chaos and put all of us at risk."

The Raven inside me stirs restlessly, its dark whispers taunting me to heedless action. But I push down the primal urge to lash out recklessly. In this deadly game, strategy and cunning were just as lethal as brute force.

With a steely resolve hardening my features, I meet Andrea's gaze head-on, determination burning in my eyes. "You're right." I swallow my pride and acknowledge the wisdom in his words. "We need a plan, and we need it fast."

Turning to Sophia, I lock eyes with her, silently urging her to hurry. We needed to obtain the information about Lucy's whereabouts. "Tomorrow is fine. Call Luca and give it to him as soon as you get it."

Sophia nods in understanding, her expression grave yet resolute. "I will do my best to gather the information you need." She stands and gives me a nod.

Luca rushes towards Sophia, enveloping her in a tight embrace. I glance up at Danti, his jaw clenching as he struggles to contain his seething rage. His eyes flicker with fiery intensity, daring anyone to challenge him at that moment. I allowed myself to smile for the first time since Sophia broke the news.

"Sophia, thank you so much for bringing me this information," Luca says, his voice breaking with overwhelming emotions.

"I just hope I am not mistaken."

"In my heart, I know it is her."

She picks up her purse and looks around the room. "I promise I will call as soon as I get in."

"I'll walk her out," Danti says, stepping over and offering his arm. "If that is okay with you, that is?"

She inhales deeply, her chest rising and falling with determination. She then nods confidently, her gaze locked with his as she slips her arm through his. I observe quietly from the sidelines as walk out of the room.

As Sophia and Danti disappear down the hallway, a heavy silence settles over the room. The tension is still thick in the air, each of us grappling with the weight of the situation at hand. I turn to face Luca, his expression a mixture of concern and raw emotion. With a deep breath, I take a step towards him, bracing myself for whatever repercussions may come.

Chapter Eighteen

Lucy

"I want to lick every inch of you." He kisses up my neck, taking my earlobe between his plush lips and suckles.

I moan out, grasping the sheets. "Yes, Davide, yes."

His hands and tongue glide over my body, tracing every curve and dip with feather-light touches, sending electric waves of pleasure down my spine. I can't resist the urge to arch my back, fully surrendering to his touch. The heat between us builds, fueled by the sensual dance of his hands on my skin. Every inch of me feels alive, wanting more of his skilled caresses.

"You're so beautiful, Lucy."

I'm lost in his gaze, in the intensity of his words. "I need you so badly."

The electric connection between us is undeniable as his lips find mine, igniting a fire within me. I can feel the warmth of his body against mine as we mold together, my legs instinctively wrapping around his waist to bring him closer. Every touch feels like a binding promise, a commitment I am not entirely sure I am ready for. With his arms tightly holding me and his breath mingling with mine, all doubts fade away at this moment, and all I want is him - body, mind, and soul.

He whispers in my ear. "I love you, Lucy. More than anything." The words send a wave of emotion crashing over me. My heart swells with love, fear, and uncertainty.

"I love you too, Davide." My voice is barely audible as I say my heartfelt words. He seems satisfied with my response, and he continues to explore my body with a ferocity that borders on desperation.

His lips trail down my stomach, leaving a trail of fire in their wake. When he reaches my slick, wet heat, his breath hitches and he murmurs,. "You smell delicious." I can feel the heat radiating from his body as he leans closer, his words causing me to shiver with anticipation. "I bet you taste even sweeter." The air is heavy with desire as I wait for his next touch, my body yearning for the sweet release only he can provide.

My legs part with a desperate hunger, beckoning for him to devour the intoxicating essence nestled between my thighs. I trail my fingers over my taut nipples, igniting a fiery ache that courses through my entire being. A wave of anticipation washes over me as I yearn for his mouth to join in on this carnal feast, sending me spiraling into ecstasy.

My body trembles and quivers as his lips devour my folds, sending delicious shivers coursing through me. His tongue delves deep within me, tracing every inch of my most intimate places, igniting a fire that spreads like electric currents throughout my entire being. I am lost in the overwhelming sensation, my mind consumed by the raw intensity of his touch.

"Davide, I'm going to come."

As our eyes lock, I am captivated by the intense warmth and depth of his chocolate-brown orbs. The passion between us ignites and I feel my body respond with a sheen of arousal glistening on his lips and chin. With a commanding tone, he urges me closer, beckoning me to him with a bite on my swollen, throbbing clit. The sensation sends shivers down my spine as pleasure courses through every inch of my being.

Those words cause my orgasm to explode. Shivers of pleasure pulse through every inch of my body. I can barely catch my breath as the waves of pleasure wash over me. Davide's face is buried between my thighs, his tongue and lips working their magic, bringing me to heights I never thought possible. The look in his eyes, the intensity of his touch. It all overwhelms me. I can't help but feel an overwhelming sense of vulnerability, of wantonness, as he commands me to come on his tongue.

"Are you ready for my cock?"

"Yes, oh Davide, yes."

Davide's eyes were dark with desire as he guided the head of his erect cock towards my entrance. My heart raced with anticipation and fear. This was the moment I had been waiting for when our bodies would become one.

His voice dripping with a dangerous edge, he growls. "Is this what you wanted, Lucy?" His eyes bore into me, sending electric pulses of desire and fear down my spine. I could feel his breath on my skin as he leaned in closer, his words laced with a seductive menace that sent shivers through my body.

I could only nod, my throat constricted with emotion. He slid into me inch by agonizing inch, his thick, unyielding member stretching me beyond capacity. My head fell back in a haze of pleasure-pain as he engulfed me, our bodies merging and molding into one entity that was both foreign and intensely intimate.

"Do you feel that, Lucy? Feel my cock inside you? It's yours now, forever."

I nodded again, my eyes still closed, too lost in the sensation to speak. Suddenly, I heard a crash. Sitting up, I looked around my dark room and realized I was all alone. It had been a dream. Davide wasn't here, even though my body still tingled from its intensity.

As I gasp for air, my hand rests on my swollen belly. The little one inside me stirs restlessly, their tiny movements reminding me I am not alone in this moment of panic. A sharp kick against my stomach startles me, but it also brings a sense of comfort and connection. They are here with me, a living being growing and thriving inside of me. This small life gives me hope and purpose, even amid chaos and uncertainty.

"Hey, little one."

The eerie silence is shattered by the unmistakable sound of footsteps. My heart lurches into my throat and pounds violently against my chest. A chill creeps up my spine as I realize that there is an intruder in my home, invading my sanctuary and threatening my safety. Panic sets in as I search for a weapon, ready to defend myself at all costs.

I jolt out of bed and frantically grab my phone, fumbling to turn on the flashlight. The thundering sound of footsteps echoes closer and closer, the anticipation from my dream replaced by pure terror. This is wrong. I shouldn't be shaking with fear in my own home. Every creak and rustle sets me on edge, my heart pounding against my ribcage like a prisoner desperate for escape.

My feet shuffle towards the source of the noise, a steady rhythm echoing in my chest. Each step feels heavy and deliberate as if I am walking through sludge. My heart thuds loudly against my ribcage, threatening to burst out of my chest. As I near the living room, I pause and call out into the darkness, my voice shaky with fear. "Is someone there?"

My request is met by silence. I flip on the light and look around to find it empty. After leaving the light on, I proceed to the kitchen and turn it on. Again, the room is empty. I go to the back door and gasp as I see it open with glass shards on the floor. I stand frozen in shock at the sight before me. The glass door leading to my backyard is shattered, with large shards scattered all over the floor. Fear grips my heart as I realize that someone has broken into my home. I automatically want to call Luca to come save me. No one within The Famiglia calls 911. We have our own security and do not want cops to stick their noses in our business. But I can't call Luca. I will have to deal with this myself. Taking a deep breath, I close the door and lock it, even though it is useless. The glass near the latch is broken out.

Without hesitation, I pivot on my heels and stride towards the closet, reaching for the broom and dustpan. The sound of the shattered glass crunches beneath my feet as I sweep it up, avoiding any sharp shards. My mind races as I consider how to cover the hole until it can be repaired. I sift through all my belongings, searching for something to serve this purpose. Suddenly, it hits me - the wood piece used to separate the crib pieces. I had stashed it away in the hall closet, thinking it might come in handy one day. With a determined nod, I retrieve it and bring it over to the broken window, thankful for its existence at this moment. I pull open my junk drawer and pull out several screws and my electric handheld screwdriver. The piece of wood is too big, but it will do. Once it was in place, I ensured the door was locked and left the kitchen, leaving the light on. I went to the front door and ensured it was locked. The knob was locked, but the deadlock was not. Had I forgotten to lock it before I went to bed? I can't remember.

I walked out of the living room, my heart still pounding from the unexpected intruder. My eyes scanned the room, looking for any sign of a struggle or anything that could explain what had happened. The atmosphere was eerily quiet as if nothing had happened.

A chill runs down my spine as I feel an eerie presence lingering in the shadows. My heart races as I make my way to the bedroom, on high alert and ready to defend myself at any moment. Every sense is heightened, every muscle tense, as I prepare for a possible attack from the unseen threat lurking in the darkness.

In the bedroom, I find everything as I had left it. The rumpled sheets and the discarded clothes told the story of the passionate night I had just experienced in my dream. The memory sent a shiver down my spine, and I couldn't help but feel a pang of longing for the man I had dreamed about.

Every item in the room was arranged, and nothing was out of place or missing. Suddenly, a sharp pain radiated through my lower abdomen as if a tiny foot had kicked me. "Ouch.". The little one inside me must have given me a hard kick in the bladder, making their presence known with a jolt of pain. Regardless of the discomfort, I couldn't stop smiling at the feeling of life growing within me.

I rub my hand over my belly and sigh. "Alright, mommy is going to use the bathroom and then we will get a little more rest."

As I enter the bathroom, my hand shakes as I reach for the light switch. The flickering fluorescent bulb illuminates a horror show before me. Written on the mirror in what appears to be blood are words that send chills down my spine. *You are mine.*

My heart races and my breath catches in my throat as I realize I might not be alone in my home. Every instinct in my body screams at me to run, but I am paralyzed with fear. Who or what is watching me?

Every creeping sensation, every hair-raising feeling of being watched and followed...it all comes crashing down as I realize it was this person all along. But why? What twisted motivation drove them to stalk and haunt me? The fear and confusion weigh on my chest, suffocating me with each thought.

My hands are shaking. I grab a towel and try to wipe away the words in the mirror. But they won't budge. It looks like it's written in dried blood. I try to calm my racing mind, telling myself it must be some kind of sick prank. But deep down, I know that this isn't a joke.

I finish using the bathroom, my heart racing with fear and desperation. I snatch up my phone from the nightstand, feeling the weight of my fate in my trembling hand. My finger hovers over Davide's name, a lifeline that could save me or destroy me. The burner phone had been my last resort, a desperate attempt to find some way out of this suffocating life. But now, with imminent danger looming, I couldn't risk calling anyone, not Davide, Luca, or any of my old so-called friends. They were all tied to the Famiglia, and one call could unravel all my careful plans to escape, especially now that I was carrying a forbidden child, a disgrace in the eyes of The Famiglia and the Gambino family. Going back was not an option. I was alone in dealing with the threat.

Chapter Nineteen

Davide

"Andrea, will you call Giovanni and get him up to speed?" Luca asks, never taking his eyes off me. He is beyond pissed, and he deserves to be so. I fucked up royalty. It wouldn't be my reputation that would be wrecked. It would be Lucy's.

The original founding fathers decided the rules and traditions of The Famiglia. They were men who sought to protect their families and communities during a time of unrest and political instability. Many believe that the first organized crime family came into being in the 19th century. However, they are off by five hundred years.

The genuine history of The Famiglia dates back to the late 15th century, during the Renaissance period in Italy.

The original founding fathers were merchants and traders who saw an opportunity to gain power and control by using their business connections and financial resources to establish a protection network for their families and allies. And over time, this network evolved into what we know today as The Famiglia.

It wasn't until the early 20th century that our organization became known as a criminal entity rather than just a group providing protection.

Another important tradition within the family is loyalty. We expect it from our members and those who are allied with us. Loyalty would be crucial for such an organization to function effectively.

This brings me to my actions. I messed up, but it was more than just that. I endangered the safety of not only myself but also of those around me. The rules and traditions of The Famiglia were to be followed by the letter. As a founding son, Luca and I are looked upon as an example. It wasn't the fact that I had sex with a woman. Hell, I could fuck a woman on the table in the middle of a society event, and no one would bat an eye at me. But I didn't fuck just any woman. I fucked a daughter and sister of a founding son. And more than that, I took her virginity.

To The Famiglia, Lucy was now nothing, but a damaged commodity. With her virtue stripped away, she could never hope to secure a marriage within the upper echelons of their society. She would forever be an outcast, shunned from attending prestigious functions or utilizing their resources. Her reputation was irreversibly tarnished, leaving her a pariah in the eyes of those who once revered her.

I didn't know how to fix this. I finally got my head out of my ass and realized I could be faithful to Lucy. However, I can't marry her.

"Davide," Luca says, his jaw clenched. "How long have you had your sights set on Lucy?"

"Six years."

Out of nowhere, Luca lunges towards me, his strong hands gripping my throat and slamming me against the wall with a vicious force. I gasp for air as his fingers tighten around my windpipe, cutting off my oxygen supply. The pressure builds, my vision blurring and darkness creeping in until I feel like I'm suffocating in his grasp.

"Six years! Lucy was sixteen!"

"No, Luca!" I gasped, struggling to catch my breath. "I swear I didn't touch her until the going away party." My voice cracked with desperation, pleading for him to believe me as my heart raced in fear for his reaction.

"You fucked with the wrong girl, Davide," he snarls, his eyes flashing with anger. "You may be one of the founding sons, but you aren't untouchable."

Despite the pain, I attempt to speak. "I know what I did was wrong. I messed up, and I won't let it happen again. I'll do everything I can to earn her forgiveness."

Luca doesn't seem inclined to let me go. "Forgiveness from her? Or from me? You've dishonored my sister, and you'll pay."

A tempest of rage consumes me in his grip, a blazing reminder of my colossal mistake. The weight of my errors presses upon me, threatening to crush my resolve. But I refuse to be extinguished by his wrath. I must find a way to mend the shattered pieces, even if it means shattering the very foundations of my existence.

"Luca, please... I know I've done wrong. I know I've dishonored you and your family, and I will never make excuses for my actions. I will make this right, I will earn Lucinda's forgiveness, and I will restore the honor of your family. I swear it."

Luca's grip on my throat loosens slightly, his eyes still burning with anger.

"We are bound by the rules. There is nothing you or I can do to make this right. My sister is unwed and pregnant," he says and tightens his grasp, applying more pressure to my neck. "Did you force yourself on her?"

"NO!"

The air is thick with Luca's seething rage, crushing my chest and choking off my oxygen. The truth weighs on me like an anvil, a final nail in my coffin. But I can't go down without trying to make things right. My lungs scream for air as I push out the words, knowing they could be my last.

"Luca, I swear, it wasn't like that. I never forced Lucinda, and I would never do such a thing. We both consented, and it was our decision."

His piercing gaze bore into me, searching for any hints of deception on my face. After what felt like an eternity, he let me go, and we locked eyes, the palpable tension between us suffocating and all-consuming. Silence hung in the air like a thick fog as we stood there, unsure who would break first under the weight of our unspoken thoughts.

"You better be right, Davide," he warned, his voice low and dangerous. "I will not hesitate to end you if you've lied to me."

I met his gaze, my heart pounding in my chest. I knew what I was risking, but had to take a stand. I had messed up, but I couldn't let this situation ruin everything I had built over the years.

"I swear it, Luca. We both wanted it, and nothing forced my hand. I will make this right and prove that I will love and care for Lucy and our child forever."

Underneath his roiling blue eyes, Luca continued to scrutinize me. A potent concoction of outrage and incredulity brewing within. His jaw flexed with a silent internal struggle before he gave an almost imperceptible nod. Behind that gesture lingered the aftertaste of resentment and wariness, hinting that his trust hadn't stopped playing hard-to-get just yet. But there was something else, too. The begrudging offer of an opportunity, as if saying, 'You've got one shot. Don't mess this up.' The electricity in the room buzzed softly in anticipation at this fragile truce we'd brokered, its underlying current whispering a hint of a chance.

He takes a step back and shakes his head. "Davide, there is no way you can fit this. Her life is ruined."

Desperation claws at my heart. This couldn't be the only time since the beginning of The Famiglia that something like this has happened.

"What the hell happened in here?" Andrea asks as he walks in. He looks between Luca and me, trying to figure out what went on while he was calling Giovanni.

"Just clearing the air," I say.

"Yeah, what he said," Luca grunts.

Andrea shakes his head and places his cell on Luca's desk. A moment later, Danti walks back in with a bloody nose and a shit-eating grin. I had never seen his dimples so pronounced.

"What happened to you?" I ask.

"Ah, just a little love tap," he said, grinning even bigger.

"Alright, Giovanni wants to talk to all of us," Andrea says.

"How is Angelina?" I ask.

"Big and sassy. She keeps telling the baby it is evicted and to come out," he answers with a chuckle. "Andrea has filled me in on what Sophia told you."

"Do you know her?" Luca asks.

"Yes," he replied with a hint of hesitation. "Sophia is bright, driven, and not afraid to speak her mind. Everything that goes against the traditional values and expectations of a daughter in The Famiglia. Her fiery spirit and unwavering determination remind me so much of Lucy."

"Do you think it is possible Sophia saw Lucy?" I ask.

"Well, Davide, you tell me. Did you have sex with Lucy?" Giovanni asks in a no-nonsense tone.

"Yes. The night of her going away party. I tried to fight my feelings but couldn't resist when she asked me to be her first."

Luca growled and balled his hands into fists. I knew he was hanging on by a thread, and at any moment, he was either going to beat me to death or draw his gun and shoot me.

"Giovanni, we need to call Dominic and tell him we are coming onto his territory," Luca says.

"I wouldn't advise to call him until we are absolutely certain that the woman Sophia saw was, in fact, Lucy," Giovanni cautioned. His deep voice held a hint of concern. "Andrea mentioned Sophia would try to obtain her address tomorrow when she goes to work. It may be difficult to wait, but for everyone's well-being, especially Lucy's, we must be completely sure before taking action." The air in the room seemed to grow tense with anticipation as they waited for further information. Giovanni's words hung in the silence like a heavy curtain, reminding them of the gravity of the situation.

Corvo's desperate rattling echoed through my being, his fervent pleas urging me to set him free. His relentless chants reverberated within, a relentless drumbeat of determination propelling us toward Brighton Beach. Each word resonated with unyielding resolve: *"Go now, find Lucy. She belongs to us. Go get her. She is ours."*

The words were forced through Luca's gritted teeth as he fought to control the anger simmering just beneath the surface. His fists clenched tightly at his sides, his body tense and ready for a fight. "Fine. We'll wait until tomorrow," he spat out, the tension in his voice and body language almost palpable.

"Davide, what are your intentions toward Lucy?" Giovanni asks. This is the first time he has not been present for something as important. Thank God for cellphones and speakers.

"I want to marry her and to take care of her and our child when he or she is born. But I don't see how I can do this. The rules are black and white concerning who founding sons can marry. Lucy, pregnant, even with my child, is no longer a virgin and cannot pass the test."

Of the five of us, Giovanni was the most knowledgeable of the intricate rules and traditions that governed The Famiglia. His mind was a steel trap, retaining every detail of the massive book that held them all - a weighty tome that could break a man's back with its twenty-pound heft. It had been entrusted to the Genovese family for centuries, who guarded it with their lives. And Giovanni himself had delved deep into its pages, studying its contents with a fervor bordering on obsession. So it was no surprise when he pulled out an obscure rite of blood for blood on his wedding night, using it to protect his new bride Angelina from the prying eyes of The Commission during the first time they had sex. Such was the power and importance of this book in our lives. As I watched Giovanni give up the right for the chance to spend their first time together in private, I couldn't help but wonder if there was something in those pages that could help me marry my own love, Lucy. For the first time since learning of her potential pregnancy, a glimmer of hope ignited in my heart for our future together. Perhaps buried within the depths of that heavy book lay the key to our happiness and survival as a family.

"I don't want to get your hopes up, but I faintly remember something concerning an issue like this in the book. Let me get Angelina settled for the night, and I will try to find it," Giovanni says, disconnecting the call.

The adrenaline surged through my veins at the thought of marrying Lucy and becoming a true father to our child. Every fiber of my being screamed with the certainty that it was my child. Lucy would never betray me by sleeping with another man. I could feel her heart pouring out to me that night, baring her soul and confessing her undying love. The intensity radiating from her eyes threatened to knock me off my feet, leaving me weak and breathless with devotion to this woman who held my world in her hands.

"I think we need to get some rest tonight," Andrea states as he looks at each of us. "Davide, Luca, do I have to put security on both of you? Or will you wait until tomorrow until we have the information we need? We don't need either of you to be seen inside the Russian territory."

As much as I wanted to go to Brighton Beach and search every damn house until I found her, I knew it would cause problems. "I'll stay home."

"I will, too," Luca says through gritted teeth.

"We will meet back here tomorrow morning and wait for Sophia to call," Andrea says.

I pick up my glass and down the rest of the bourbon. I look up at Luca, and I can tell how he feels. It was a mixture of relief that we might have found her and terror about what would happen once she was back home. "Luca, I promise in my life I will fix this."

"I hope so, Davide. I really hope so."

With a heavy heart, I walked out of the office toward my car where Hamm was waiting. I climb into the back and sink into the leather.

Chapter Twenty

Davide

As I stare out the car window, the city lights flash past in a neon blur against the night's deep ink blackness. The bustling streets are alive with energy and movement, each building and streetlight a tiny star among the dazzling skyline. Every nerve in my body is frantically urging me to tell Mici to take me to Brighton Beach, where I can begin my desperate search for Lucy. The urgency and fear fueling my mission drive me forward, my heart racing and hands trembling as we speed towards home.

Seven agonizing months have slipped by, devoid of her presence or the warmth of her touch, plunging me into a tormented abyss. Her essence haunts my every waking moment and lingers in the fabric of my dreams. I would not rest until she was safely back in my arms.

Giovanni was right that going into Russian territory alone and not knowing where she might be was stupid. However, I couldn't help but think of it.

I still couldn't believe she had been close to us all this time. She had the means to go anywhere in the world. Why had she selected Brighton Beach? She knew it was in control by the Russian Bratva. Years ago, she wandered into their territory by mistake while taking photos. She ran into the leader, Dominic Mogilevich, and one of his associates. They scared the hell out of her, and who knew what they would have done with her if she hadn't told them who she was? Dominic was a sadistic motherfucker, but he knew the shit storm which would have happened if one hair on Lucy's head was harmed. For months after the encounter, Luca told us that Lucy woke up with nightmares. Her screams resonated throughout the mansion. Every time I heard about it, I wanted to kill the fucker.

So why had she decided to hide there? She was very bright, dangerously so. Maybe she knew it would be the last place we would go looking for her.

My heart ached with regret, knowing I was why she ran away. My insecurities had consumed me, clouding my judgment and leading to my biggest mistake. When she told me she loved me, I should have held on tight and never let go of her, pouring all my love into her. As painful as it is, I understand why she didn't return home when she found out she was pregnant. She didn't want me to reject her again. That night of the party, I made it perfectly clear I would never tie myself to her.

I couldn't help but wonder how Dom would react when we told him about our plans to enter his territory. Would he outright deny us or try to manipulate us against it? Our determination to proceed only grew stronger at the thought. Even if he refused us, we were prepared to face whatever challenges came our way. After all, his denial would only mean more heavily trained armed men accompanying us into Brighton Beach. Nothing could stand in our way of bringing Lucy back home safely.

My blood boiled in Dom's presence, a seething hatred bubbling within me. Each encounter with him felt like two bulls locking horns, our animosity palpable and explosive. I refused to trust that conniving bastard, always keeping one eye on him as he slithered around, waiting for his next opportunity to strike.

The Famiglia may operate covertly, but their influence reaches every aspect of life. Yet, there are certain lines they refuse to cross or tolerate. Unlike their Russian counterparts, they vehemently denounce any involvement in the despicable trade of human trafficking. The women and men we have working at the Disorderly House did so of their own free will. Over the years, many of them had met their husbands or partners within the walls of the house. Two decades ago, it was decided to embrace the life choices of our members. We had some ancient rules governing us, but somehow didn't condemn homosexuality. If a worker inside of The Disorderly House found a partner, The Famiglia happily released them from their job and gave them the million dollars placed in a holding account at the time of their employment. Each woman or man coming to work for The Famiglia had an account set up for them. At the end of their defined term of service, the funds were released for them to use in any way they saw fit.

My phone beeped with a message.

> Marco: We need to meet ASAP

> Davide: Where do you want to meet?

> Marco: Leave the back gate unlocked.

> Davide: On my way home. Will be arriving in thirty.

> Marco: I will be there in an hour.

Marco was a member of The Famiglia and a mole within the Russian Bravta. He went deep uncover seven years ago. He wasn't the only mole the organization had. We had someone deep into every organized crime group in the world. It was our way of staying ahead of the game and ensuring we always had the upper hand. Their loyalty was unwavering, as they had sworn an oath to protect and serve The Famiglia at all costs.

As the car pulled up to the iron gates of my estate, I instructed Mici to stay back. The subtle click of my shoes against the gravel echoed through the grounds as I made my way towards the back gate, my mind consumed by thoughts of Lucy and the perilous journey that lay ahead.

I entered the code, unlocked the gate, and stepped back, waiting in the shadows for Marco to arrive. The minutes stretched on, each feeling like an eternity as I scanned the darkness for any movement. Finally, the sound of footsteps approaching broke the silence, and Marco emerged from the shadows, his features set in a mask of grim determination.

"Davide," he greeted me with a curt nod, his eyes scanning the area for any dangers.

"Do you want to come inside?" I ask.

"I can't chance it. It is too volatile right now," he answers.

"What is going on?"

"Someone is trying to take over the Bratva in New York."

"Dom is too powerful to allow that to happen."

"I haven't figured out who it is, but whoever it is, they are smart. Too damn smart. All the robberies from our gun shippers were not sanctioned by Dom. Well, at least not yet. Dom has had some issues with his shipments. Several containers full of guns have come up missing, and several of Dom's were killed. Evidence found at the scene points to you."

"I haven't sanctioned any attacks on Dom."

"I know. This bastard is pure evil. What he did to those men almost made me sick. Dom went crazy when he saw their bodies and saw the evidence that pointed to you. Thankfully, I was able to stop him from coming after you."

Rage boils inside me like hot lava, bubbling up and spilling over as I curse under my breath. My heart sinks as I realize the twisted fate that has unfolded - just when I had a glimmer of hope of getting Lucy back, this shit happens. But it couldn't get any worse, right? Wrong. The place where Lucy thought she would be safe is now a breeding ground for danger, with Dom's merciless enemies lurking in the shadows, waiting to strike.

Marco's words echoed in my mind, each one like a stab to my already tormented soul. The thought of someone trying to take over the Bratva in New York sent shivers down my spine, knowing the chaos and bloodshed that would follow. If Dom's enemies were making a move, it meant that Lucy was now caught in the crossfire of a deadly power struggle.

I clenched my fists, the muscles in my jaw tensing as I tried to process the magnitude of the situation. The walls were closing in on me, suffocating me with the weight of my mistakes. Lucy needed me now more than ever, and I had promised myself I would do whatever it took to bring her back safely.

"Do you have any leads on who might be behind this?" I asked Marco, my voice strained with a mix of urgency and frustration.

Marco shook his head, his expression grim. "Not yet, but I'm working on it. We need to tread carefully and watch our backs at all times. This is not just a turf war; it's a battle for supremacy that could shake the very foundations of organized crime in New York. The shadows are whispering secrets of betrayal and deceit, and we must decipher their twisted messages before it's too late."

I nodded, a steely resolve hardening within me. "I won't let them destroy everything we've built. Lucy's safety is my priority, but I won't rest until this threat is neutralized."

Marco's eyebrows knit together. "Lucy?"

"Yeah. Sophia Croft believes she saw Lucy outside a clinic in Brighton Beach."

"Lucy is in Brighton Beach?"

"We haven't confirmed it yet. Sophia is going to get her address from her file at the clinic. Marco, if it is Lucy, she is pregnant." Marco's mouth drops open, but I go on before he can say anything. "And the baby is mine."

Confusing paints over his face. This was how it was going to be with everyone within The Famiglia.

"Once Sophia confirms it is Lucy, Luca is going to call Dom. We didn't want to go into Brighton Beach without him knowing. However, now, with what you have informed me, this has gone a lot tricker."

Marco's eyes widened in realization, the gravity of the situation sinking in as he processed my words. The news of Lucy's possible whereabouts and her pregnancy threw a curveball into an already volatile game, one that threatened to tip the scales of power in unpredictable ways.

"We need to act fast," Marco says, his voice laced with urgency. "If Lucy is indeed in Brighton Beach, we cannot afford to waste any time. Dom must be informed immediately, and we must proceed cautiously to ensure her safety."

I nodded in agreement, the weight of responsibility heavy on my shoulders. The thought of Lucy carrying my child amid this chaos only fueled my determination to protect her at all costs. But with unknown enemies lurking in the shadows and Dom's wrath hanging over our heads, every move had to be calculated precisely.

Marco and I exchanged a knowing look, a silent understanding passing between us as we prepared to plunge headfirst into the treacherous web of lies and deceit that had ensnared Lucy. As I turned to leave, my mind raced with thoughts of the dangerous path ahead - a path littered with the remnants of shattered alliances and broken promises. The darkness of the night seemed to mirror the turmoil within my soul, each shadow whispering words of caution and foreboding.

Marco's footsteps echo behind me as I hastily lock the gate, my heart racing with anticipation. With every step towards the house, a sense of urgency washes over me. Tomorrow will be a dangerous day, and I must be prepared. As I pass the guard stationed at the garden doors, I bark out my warning: "Stay vigilant. We have received credible threats against the family." My voice is sharp and commanding, starkly contrasting the fear and determination churning within me. This will be a battle, and I refuse to let my loved ones fall victim to it.

"Oh, course, Mr. Bonnano."

The gentle creak echoed through the den as I pushed open the heavy oak doors. My eyes immediately fell upon Nan, sitting serenely in her favorite chair. The soft glow from the lamp on the side table illuminated her face as she sipped from a delicate tea cup and turned the pages of her book. The familiar scent of chamomile and honey wafted through the air, enveloping me in its warmth. Despite the chill outside, the den felt cozy and inviting, with its plush armchairs and shelves lined with books. It was indeed Nan's haven, and I couldn't help but feel at peace in her presence.

She looks up, and her face breaks out into a smile. "Davide."

"Mom," I say as I walk over and sit across from her.

She places her cup and book on the table. With a ferocity in her eyes, she reaches out and grabs my hand tightly. "What have you heard about Lucy?" she demands, her voice trembling with fear and desperation.

"Yes."

Panic erupts on her face as she urgently asks, "Where is she? Is she okay?" Her normally composed features are now marred with deep lines of worry and fear.

"We believe she is in Brighton Beach."

Her hand shoots to her mouth, stifling a sharp gasp that escapes with a strangled cry. "Is she being held captive by those barbaric savages?"

The words slipped off her tongue with a sharp sting, laced with years of pain and anger. She had every reason to call the Russians barbaric savages, for they were the ones who had taken her cousin when she was just sixteen and sold her into the darkest corners of the sex trade. Every memory of their frantic search and eventual discovery of her cousin, ravaged by drugs and disease, haunted her like a ghost in the night. Her mother had tried to save her, but the addiction had already consumed her. And then, when they finally found her again, it was too late. She was another young life lost to an overdose. The mere mention of those Russian savages left a bitter taste in her mouth, a reminder of the horrors they had inflicted upon her family.

"No, Mom, she is not being held captive. She went to Brighton Beach on her own."

"Why would she do that?"

"Because we wouldn't look there for her."

"When are you going after her?" she asks.

"We are waiting for confirmation that it is truly her. Then Luca is going to call Dom."

"Fuck Dom. The Famiglia has an army that could decimate every single one of those Russian bastards," she seethes through clenched teeth.

"Mom, we have to make sure Lucy is not harmed. There is something else I need to tell you." I rub my hand across hers. "Lucy is pregnant, and the baby is mine."

Tears form in her eyes. "When did this happen? Davide, The Famiglia will not allow you to be a father to that child."

"Giovanni is poring over the ancient rules, searching for any loophole or advantage that could secure our future. I will not be denied my love for Lucy and our child. We will defy all odds, overcome obstacles, and declare our unbreakable bond to the world. Nothing will stand in our way."

Chapter Twenty-One

Sophia

My hands quiver uncontrollably as I speed towards the clinic in Brighton Beach. Every muscle in my body is tense, ready for action as I approach the building. But this time, I'm not just heading to work - I'm on a mission to gather information about one of our patients. The gravity of the situation weighs heavily on me as I prepare to dive deeper into this dangerous game.

While I was growing up, hushed mentions of "The Commission" and its inner workings were always present in dinner conversations with my father. So when news of Lucy's disappearance reached our family, I wasn't surprised. My father was recently elected as the Consigliere, replacing the previous one who was removed after attacking Mr. Genovese's fiancée, Angelina. As the daughter of a high-ranking member of The Famiglia, I knew better than to ask too many questions. Lucy and I didn't move in the same circles, but I had seen her at a few of The Famiglia events.

While the months dragged on, I persistently bothered my father for any updates or leads on her whereabouts. But each time, his face fell, and he shook his head regretfully.

She had vanished without a trace, like a ghost haunting our memories. Every corner of our city had been searched, every contact questioned, but she seemed to have disappeared into thin air without explanation. And with each passing day, it became more doubtful that she would ever be found.

I might not be a founding daughter, but now that I was the daughter of a Consigliere, I was held to a higher standard than other daughters within The Famiglia. At the time when I started working towards becoming a nurse/midwife, I was just a girl whose family was a member of The Famiglia. As the leader and decision-maker of all aspects of our family, my father granted me permission to go to college. Once I was licensed, I would work at Mount Sinai Hospital. To the general public, it was just another hospital. However, Only The Famiglia owned and operated the hospital. In the mid-1800s, they built the facility to care for the members' medical needs. As the hospital grew, the doors were opened to the public, but members of the organization were given priority.

When I disclosed to my father that my final training would be held in the heart of Brighton Beach, I noticed the panic in his eyes. Brighton Beach, infamous for being controlled by the Russian Bratva, was not a place he wanted me to be. After much discussion and safety precautions, he reluctantly permitted me to proceed with my plans. However, there were strict rules I had to follow: my gun, which I knew how to shoot with accuracy, must be accessible. A high-tech tracker was placed in a necklace, which I always had to wear. I also had to check in upon arriving and leaving the area. The car I was driving could not be traced back to me or anyone within The Famiglia. Finally, my phone was also untraceable.

After thinking I saw Lucy, I quickly went to the Gambino mansion. Even though my father was on The Commission, Luca Gambino was her family. He was also head of the Gambino family and one of the founding sons, who was royalty. The Commission was the law branch of the organization. It was composed of four elected Consigliere and the five founding sons. When one of the members broke the law, they were brought before The Commission for them to pass judgment and execute whatever punishment they deemed appropriate.

I pulled my car into the parking space beside the clinic, adrenaline coursing through my veins. No matter how much it tore me apart, I had to do this. The memory of Luca's pained expression when I told him I thought I saw Lucy twisted like a knife in my gut, propelling me forward with a fierce determination. If I could reunite them, it would be worth any stress I might be feeling.

As I walk into the clinic with a sense of purpose, my heart races as I try to keep my composure. The familiar scent of antiseptic and desperation clung to the air, mingling with the hushed whispers of anxious patients awaiting their turn. As I made my way toward the records room, I couldn't shake off the feeling of unease that was gnawing at the edges of my mind.

"Sophia."

I turn to see Dr. Richardson walking out of her office. "Good morning, Dr. Richardson."

"Please call me Janice when we are not with patients."

"Okay, Janice."

"Please come into my office," she says.

I follow her into her office, and she motions for me to close the door.

"Have a seat, Sophia."

I drop into the chair in front of her desk, trying to steady my violently trembling hands as I place them awkwardly in my lap. My heart pounds so hard it feels like it might burst through my ribcage, and I can barely catch my breath as I wait for her to speak.

"Sophia, I just wanted to take a moment to express my appreciation for your exceptional work performance. Your vast knowledge and comforting bedside manner have not gone unnoticed. The mothers you have assisted with have been raving about your skills and dedication. Your presence has brought a sense of calm and confidence to the delivery room or their homes. This makes it a more positive and memorable experience for our patients."

A rush of warmth flooded my cheeks, a rosy blush spreading like a delicate watercolor painting across my face. I could have been better at accepting compliments, constantly feeling self-conscious about my appearance. At five foot six, I wasn't petite by any means; my ample breasts and curvaceous hips were a source of both pride and insecurity for me. As a young girl, I was often ridiculed for my weight, but over time, I learned to tune out the hurtful comments. Instead, I embraced my curves, and from the appreciative glances of men, I knew they appreciated them, too. My body was a work of art, with each curve and contour telling its story. As I stood there blushing under the warm sun, I couldn't help but feel grateful for every inch of myself that made me unique.

"Thank you. I really love what I am doing."

"When are you taking the AMCB?" she asks.

"I already have."

Her mouth falls open. "You have? When?"

"A few weeks ago," I reply. The exam could be taken any time after finishing classes, but most decided to take it after completing their practicals. This gave them time to prepare for the rigorous test, which determined whether we were officially ready to become certified nurse-midwives. Thanks to my photogenic memory, I was able to ace the exam.

"Excellent."

"I have no doubt you aced it. You are a natural, Sophia. Your dedication and passion for this field shines through in everything you do. I hope you will consider coming on board with us."

I couldn't help but smile at her words, feeling a swell of pride in my chest. It wasn't just about the exam but the lives I could touch and make better through my work. The thought of helping those in need and guiding mothers through the miracle of childbirth fueled me in a way nothing else could. However, I already had a position waiting for me. I would be working under Dr. Julie Bianchi at Mount Sinai Hospital.

"Janice, thank you for all the kind words and the offer. However, I have been offered and accepted at a hospital in upstate New York, and I accepted. It is closer to my family."

"Congratulations. I understand wanting to be close to family, but I am sad not to have you here. Alright then, I wanted to talk to you today. There's a special case, and I believe your skills and compassion are exactly what this patient needs."

My interest was piqued as I leaned in, eager to hear more about this mysterious case. Janice hesitated for a moment, as if debating how much information to disclose.

After discovering what she wanted, I would slip into the records room and try to find Lucy's patient file. I had no clue what name she was using, but I did know she was in the office yesterday, so I could look at the patient list from yesterday and narrow it down.

"This patient is one of our mothers who is all alone, and she has the markers for preeclampsia. She is twenty-eight weeks old. During her visit yesterday, I noticed swelling in her feet and legs. Her blood pressure was 140/85, and her urine sample had protein."

"Any headaches or blurry vision?"

"No, but I am worried about her. She stated she had no one to lean on during this time. I think it would be best to check her regularly at home. Would you be willing to make a house visit?"

"I would love to check on her."

"Great, let me get her file. I'll call her and tell her someone will come by to do the checks." She quickly gets up and walks out of the office.

Once she is out of the office, I grab my phone and shoot Luca a text.

Sophia: I am at the clinic, but the boss has me check on a patient.

Luca: How long will that take?

Sophia: I don't know. It is a house visit, so it could take a few hours. I promise I will get the information to you as soon as possible.

Luca: Please hurry. All of our plans are based on what you find out.

Janice walks back into the room. "Here is the file." I slipped the phone into my jacket pocket before she saw it. She walks around and opens the folder. "Her name is Lucy Mitchell, twenty-four, and she lives on 2nd St. This is her first pregnancy."

Her name is Lucy. Could this be Lucy Gambino? If so, I could get her out of Brighton Beach without the Russians knowing she was here. Also, Janice stated she was here yesterday, which is when I thought I saw Lucy.

I needed to get information I wouldn't see in the file. "I am trying to place her. What does she look like?"

"She is around five foot seven with brown eyes and red hair that is dyed."

"How do you know she dyes her hair?" I was confused how she knew Lucy's hair was not natural.

The corner of her top lip curved up. "Well, I am her obstetrician."

The puzzle pieces in my mind clicked and shifted, trying to make sense of the information. What connection could there possibly be between being an obstetrician and knowing someone's true hair color? My thoughts spun like a tornado, searching for an answer. Then, like a bolt of lightning, I realized. "Janice."

She giggles and gave me a wink. "She is a blonde. Now, let me call her and see if she would be okay with a home visit."

She called Lucy and began the conversation by asking how she was feeling. Janice listened and when Lucy stopped, she asked if it was okay for a midwife to come cheek on her this afternoon.

With a sigh of relief, she carefully placed the phone back onto its cradle. "She's agreed to a visit. Be sure to take a kit to collect blood and urine samples." Her tone turned serious as she added, "But monitor her blood pressure and other symptoms. If they worsen from yesterday or she shows signs of distress, don't hesitate to call 911 and get her to the hospital immediately." The responsibility was heavy in the room as they prepared for their follow-up visit with the patient.

The hospital chosen by the clinic was a dismal, crumbling building. The thought of taking Lucy Gambino there sent a shiver down my spine. I couldn't risk her life in that place.

"I will." I accept the file from Janice and left her office. I wondered if this was Lucy. When I didn't return to the clinic, I knew Janice would try to find me and Lucy. However, The Famiglia and their long reaches in every walk of life would put up barriers to prevent her. We would be like ghosts vanishing.

As I made my way to Lucy's house on 2nd St, my mind raced with thoughts of the possibilities that lay ahead. If this Lucy Mitchell turned out to be Lucy Gambino, I might save her from a fate entangled with the dangerous Russian mafia. My responsibility toward her safety and well-being sat heavily on my shoulders.

Arriving at her house, I knock on the door, feeling a mix of nerves and determination coursing through me. The door creaks open, revealing a young woman with striking red hair and warm brown eyes. It was her. This was Lucy Gambino. Suppressing a gasp of surprise, I composed myself and greeted her with a friendly smile.

"Hi, Lucy. I'm Sophia, the nurse-midwife from the clinic. Janice sent me to check on you after your appointment yesterday." I tried to keep my voice steady despite the whirlwind of thoughts in my mind.

Lucy smiled and welcomed me into her warm, comfortable home, nothing like her childhood home. My home was large and spacious, but her childhood home was massive.

The Gambino estate was a gigantic mansion surrounded by tall fences and iron gates. Security was stationed at the gates while other guards patrolled the grounds. The mansion was built in the early 1800s. Over the years, the family kept up with the times, ensuring the home was renovated to meet technological advances.

I follow Sophia into the living room, and we sit down. As I look around the room, I notice several pictures of Luca, her parents, and Davide. "How are you feeling today, Lucy?"

"I'm a little tire." I look at her face and see the dark circle under her eyes. Roaming over the rest of her body, I notice the swelling in her legs and feet.

"Did you not sleep well last night?"

She shakes her head and grimaces.

"Do you have a headache?"

"A little one."

Warning bells sound in my head. "Well, let's begin with taking your blood pressure. Lie back and put your feet up."

Lucy does as I instruct, and I place a pillow under her swollen legs. I open the medical bag and take out the blood pressure cuff and stethoscope.

"I love how you decorated your home. Have you lived here a long time?" I hope the small talk would easy her fears about me.

"Less than a year. I love how it turned out." She grimaces in pain, her eyes roll back in her head.

Listening to her response, I couldn't shake the feeling she was worse than yesterday. Lucy's words seemed genuine, but there was an underlying tension in the air that I couldn't quite place. The blood pressure reading on the monitor flashed before me, showing numbers dangerously high.

"Lie still, Lucy." My concern was growing by the minute. However, I didn't want her to know the extent of my worry. As I noted the readings in her chart, a movement caught my eye - a glint of metal tucked under the edge of the couch. Why did she have a gun under the couch? Had something happened to her?

I move back and look directly into her eyes. "Lucy, your blood pressure is extremely high. With the amount of swelling in your legs and your headache, I think it would be best if you got you to a hospital immediately."

"No, I don't want to go."

"Lucy, you have preeclampsia. It is serious, and its complications, such as liver and kidney damage, can threaten the life of you and your baby. Preeclampsia can also cause a decrease in the number of blood cells called platelets and damage to the placenta, the kidneys, or the liver. If your blood pressure increases even more, you can have a seizure."

Lucy's face falls, and tears form in her eyes. "I want nothing to happen to my baby, but I can't."

I don't know why she ran away from her family. However, she needs to put the needs of her baby before her reasons. Looking over, I see a picture of her with Luca, Davide, Andrea, Danti, and Giovanni. I pick it up.

"You look happy."

She looks at me and gives me a sad smile. "I was."

I could see the pain and conflict in Lucy's eyes as she gazed at the photo in my hand, memories swirling in her mind. There was a story behind that smile, a tale of a past that seemed both distant and yet so vivid in her heart.

As she wiped away a tear, I reached out and placed a comforting hand on hers. "You can still have that happiness, Lucy. It's not too late to make things right for yourself and your baby."

Her eyes met mine, full of uncertainty and fear. "But it's complicated, Sophia. So much has happened."

I nodded understandingly, knowing her life was entwined with complexities beyond my imagination. The weight of secrets and regrets seemed to hang heavy in the surrounding air, suffocating the possibility of redemption.

"Sometimes, we must confront our past to pave the way for the future. You have people who care about you. Luca and Davide haven't stopped searching."

She jerked back and gasped. "How do you know their names? Are you really a midwife?"

"I am a midwife but also a daughter of The Famiglia."

"How did you find me?"

"By accident. I am interning at the clinic and saw you walking out yesterday."

"You manipulated Dr. Richardson into deceiving me, didn't you?" she seethed through gritted teeth, her eyes blazing with accusation and anger.

I shook my head. "No, Lucy. I was going to look into the files to see if I could figure out where you lived. However, Dr. Richardson called me into her office and asked me to come check on you. I didn't know for sure it was you until you opened the door. Everything I told you about your health is true."

Chapter Twenty-Two

Lucy

My gaze lingers on the woman, my mind sifting through memories to recall if I had ever seen her before. I scoured through images of past events and gatherings at The Famiglia compound, searching for a glimmer of recognition. She was undeniably beautiful, with a kind face framed by cascading waves of hair and a warm, welcoming smile. Unlike many of the pencil-thin daughters of the society, Sophia's figure held curves in all the right places, giving her a sensual allure.

I knew Luca was still looking for me. Even though he was eight years older than me, we were extremely close. But there was no way Davide was. He made it clear he couldn't have a relationship with me. Had Sophia told him I was pregnant?

"How do you know they are still looking for me?"

"When I saw you, I went to Luca," she answers. "Davide, Andrea, and Danti were there."

"Did you mention I was pregnant?"

"Lucy, I will not lie to you. I told them. Of course, everyone was shocked, especially Luca. He wanted to come to Brighton Beach last night and start looking for you. Andrea and Danti tried to reason with him. Then wham, Davide proclaimed that you and the baby were his."

That couldn't be true. Davide wouldn't say that in front of everyone, especially Luca.

In disbelief, I tried to understand the possibility of Davide claiming me and the baby as his own. It felt like a cruel joke, a twist in fate that I never expected. Questions swirled in my head, doubts and fears clawing at my heart.

My gaze drifted back to Sophia, silently pleading for answers she might not have. Was he genuinely claiming me and the child growing inside me, or was there more to this unexpected declaration?

A flicker of hope ignited within me as Davide's unexpected words resonated with my deepest desires. Amid chaos and darkness, was there a small glimmer of hope for us to overcome the odds and create a path together? Did he think he could be faithful to me if we married?

Sophia's gaze softened as she observed the whirlwind of emotions warring within me. She reached out, her hand resting gently on mine as if offering silent comfort in uncertainty. "Lucy, I know this is a lot to take in, but I have seen glimpses of Davide's emotions. There was something different in his eyes when he spoke of you, something raw and unguarded. He didn't care if Luca was going to beat ever the living shit out of him. He stood his ground."

I couldn't believe what Sophia told me—that Davide had boldly claimed me and the baby as his own, standing his ground against Luca. This revelation shook the very foundation of my world, leaving me teetering on the edge of disbelief and hope. Could it be that Davide, the man I loved with all my heart, was finally ready to acknowledge our bond?

Sophia's words evoked a mix of emotions in me: happiness, relief, and fear of the uncertain future in our dangerous world. The Bonanno Crime Family was one of the founding fathers of The Famiglia.

However, amidst all the uncertainty and chaos swirling around me, one thing remained crystal clear - my love for Davide. My heart was his, despite all the complications and hidden risks. The thought of Davide standing up against Luca, risking everything for me and our unborn child, filled me with awe and gratitude. Though there was a bigger mountain standing in our way of being together. The rules of The Famiglia were clear when it came to me not being pure and Davide being a founding son.

"Davide wants to protect you, Lucy. I can see it and hear it in his voice," Sophia murmured softly, her voice carrying a sense of conviction that resonated within me. "But I am so worried about your health. I may be new as a midwife, but the signs of preeclampsia are obvious. Not only is your blood pressure extremely high, there is swelling in your feet and legs. Also, you have a headache, and it looks like you haven't been sleeping well."

Her eyes drifted to the cushion, and I remembered I had put my gun under it. After last night's break-in, I couldn't go back to sleep. Every little sound made me think that whoever left me that note was back. Sophia's concern was genuine. I glance around the room, taking all the pictures, pillows, throws, and little objects I had picked up. Over the last seven months, I had made this house deep in enemy territory my home. But I couldn't put my child in danger by either the intruder or my health issues. It was time to go face the music, as they say. I didn't know what The Famiglia would do to me for breaking the rules, but I needed my family, and I'm willing to face whatever punishment The Commission puts forth.

I reach down and pull out the gun. "Last night, someone broke into my house."

Sophia's eyebrows raise almost to her hairline. "Oh, my God. Did they harm you?"

"No, I didn't see who it was, but they left me a note."

"Lucy, we need to get you out of here."

"I know. I lied about my headache. It is bad, and I am having problems with my eyes."

"Fuck. Alright, I don't want to chance driving you to the hospital, and I'll be damn if I take you to the one near here. You need to be a Mount Sinai where Dr. Bianchi can see to your care."

This was it. "How do you think to get me there?"

"I can call the hospital and have them send an ambulance here. If, by chance, you have come under the radar of the Russians, at least it wouldn't look strange."

"Will you come with me?" I ask.

"Of course. I'll leave my car and ride with you," she says.

"But what if the Russian comes nosing around or Dr. Richardson?"

"The car is clean. There is no way it can lead back to me," she says, then holds up a cell phone. "This phone is a burner. The number is erased from memory as soon as I make a call. There is no way it can be traced back to me or The Famiglia."

"Alright, make the call. I'll put it on speaker so you can hear the conversation."

A wave of relief washed over me as she spoke. She clearly understood the importance of transparency in all aspects of her actions. Her words held a sense of determination and understanding, reassuring me that things would be handled with honesty and openness from here on out.

Sophia puts down her burner phone and takes out another phone, this one pink with sparkles. After she dials the number, she puts it on the coffee table.

"Hello," a woman answers.

"Dr. Bianchi, this is Sophia Croft."

Croft? As in Consigliere Croft? Why was she in Brighton Beach, working in a woman's clinic?

"Sophia, how are you? I can't wait for you to start," Dr. Bianchi says. "When do you think that will be?"

"How does today sound?" Sophia replies.

A few seconds pass by before Dr. Bianchi speaks again. "What is happening?"

"I have a patient. She is twenty-four, and she is twenty-eight pregnant. Her blood pressure is 160/90, her feet and legs are swollen. She is also having headaches."

"She needs to be brought here immediately," Dr. Bianchi says. I had been going to her as my doctor for years. She treated all her patients professionally and compassionately. She was the one who had given Angelina's purity exam, and even though she was attacked by Peter Martin, she remained calm. "Do you have any magnesium or hydralazine in your bag?"

"No. I only have a basic pack," Sophia answers.

"What is the patient's name?" Dr. Bianchi asks.

Sophia's eyes bore into mine with a steely gaze, her lips pressed into a thin line. "This is a matter of utmost confidentiality," she says in a hushed tone, her words dripping with caution and warning. "I cannot disclose the patient's identity until she is physically present." Her guarded demeanor sends shivers down my spine, making me wonder what dangers could be lurking behind her carefully measured words.

Dr. Bianchi's tone turned sharper. A sense of urgency tinged her voice. "I understand the need for discretion, Sophia, but without crucial information about the patient, I cannot fully prepare for her arrival and begin the necessary treatments. Time is of the essence in cases like these."

Sophia's jaw tightened as she glanced at me. A silent conversation passing between us. She took a deep breath before responding firmly, "I assure you, doctor, the patient in question requires immediate attention. We will be coming shortly; her condition demands urgent care."

A beat of silence hung in the air before Dr. Bianchi relented with a sigh. "Very well, Sophia. Give me the address, and I will send an ambulance. It will bring her to Mount Sinai as soon as possible. I'll make sure everything is ready on our end. It should arrive within thirty minutes, depending on the traffic. Keep her feet elevated."

As the call ended, Sophia turned to me with a mix of worry and determination in her eyes. "Lucy, you cannot come back here. We can't take a lot, but there is room for a bag or two. What would you like to take?"

I swallowed hard, the gravity of the situation sinking in as I realized I may never set foot in this house again. My eyes swept over the familiar surroundings, trying to decide what was essential. "I don't have to take any clothes. The most important things are the photos of my family and the small jewelry box on my dresser. There is a duffle bag in the closet in the bedroom."

Sophia rushes around the room, collecting all the photos and the photo book. When she walks out of the room to retrieve the jewelry box and duffle, I glance around the room again. My framed photographs hang on the walls. They were the most tangible things I had from my old life. The shell game I played with them worked, and when I hung them up in this house away from everyone and everything I knew, they gave me a sense of peace.

"I've got your jewelry box," Sophia said as she returned to the room carrying the duffle bag. "Is there anything else you want to bring?"

I gaze up at the captivating photograph of the underside of the Brooklyn Bridge. The strong, towering concrete pillars are adorned with vibrant graffiti, telling stories and representing a culture that thrives in this bustling city. As the sun dips below the horizon, its warm rays cast a golden glow over the bridge, adding to its already mesmerizing presence.

"Lucy, they are too big to take in the ambulance."

"I know," I say, my voice breaking.

She looks at me and then at the photograph. "Can we take them out of the frames and roll them up?"

A flutter of hope bubbles inside me. "Yes!"

As I swing my legs off the couch, ready to get up and help, Sophia blocks me with her hands on her hips. "Don't you dare move," she hisses, her stance rigid and threatening. The air around us crackles with tension, and her eyes burn into mine with an intensity that makes me freeze in place. I know better than to disobey her command.

With a swift movement, I rushed to put the legs back on the couch. In a flurry of movement, she hastily removed all the photographs from the walls, delicately removing them from their frames and carefully rolling them up one by one, each layer adding to the bundle in her arms.

"I need something to hold them together," she says.

My mind races to think what I might have that would do the trick. Then it hits me. I reach back and pull the ponytail holder from my hair. "This might work."

She takes it and rolls over the tube of images. Walking back over, she places it beside the duffle. "Is there anything else? I believe there is a little room left in the bag."

My future was uncertain, and its weight hung heavy on my mind, but I couldn't imagine needing anything else. The meager contents of my bag were worth more to me than all the riches in the world. Each item held a special significance and reminded me of my journey to reach this point.

The sound of approaching sirens outside signaled the arrival of the ambulance. Sophia met the EMTs at the door and took charge, giving them my vital stats.

I was quickly placed on the gurney and was wheeled out of the house. "Sophia."

"I'm right behind you."

A feeling of relief washed over me. In the short time I was with Sophia, I knew she was looking out for my best interests. Once the EMTs had me in the back of the ambulance and hooked up to monitors, Sophia leaned over and whispered in my ear, "I put your gun in my bag."

I had forgotten all about it but was happy she hadn't. As we sped through the streets toward Mount Sinai, I couldn't shake off the unease in my chest. What if they couldn't get my blood pressure down? What if they would have to deliver my baby? It was too early. I couldn't lose my baby...our baby.

The sirens wailed in the background as the ambulance raced through the chaotic city streets towards Mount Sinai. My heart pounded in my chest, a mixture of fear and determination gripping me as I lay on the gurney, clutching Sophia's hand tightly.

Her words about my gun echoed in my mind, a stark reminder of the dangers lurking around us. I knew that Sophia was fiercely loyal and protective, but even she couldn't shield me from every threat that loomed ahead. Once I was back within The Famiglia's keen eyes, they would know I broke their rules.

The ambulance screeched to a halt outside the emergency entrance, and a team of medical staff rushed out to meet us, with Dr. Bianchi following behind. Well, here it begins.

"Sophia, how is the patient?" she asks as she approaches the open doors. Her eyes land on me, and they grow huge. "Lucy."

Chapter Twenty-Three

Davide

"Damn it, Davide, you are wearing out the rug with your pacing," Danti says with a smirk.

"Fuck you, asshole. Why is it taking so long for Sophia to give us the information? It has been hours since she texted."

"She was having to check on a patient in the home. I know she will call when she gets the information," Luca says. "I am just as anxious as you are."

"Anxious? Anxious! The woman I love and our unborn child are in danger. They are deep in Russian territory. Fuck, he tried to keep her once. If he finds out she has been living there for seven months, he will claim her and do what God knows what with her."

I clench my fists, feeling the rage bubbling inside me like a dark storm threatening to break loose. The very thought of Lucy in danger ignites a fire within me that I struggle to contain. Every second that ticks by feels like an eternity, each moment stretching into infinite torment.

Danti places a hand on my shoulder, his gesture more comforting than his words. "We will get her back, Davide. We will not let them lay a finger on her. She is family."

Family. The word echoes in my mind, resonating with promises made and blood ties that bind us together. Lucy is my heart, the one who brings light to the darkness that lurks within me. I cannot bear the thought of losing her. I would do anything to make her my wife and care for her and our child.

Suddenly, the shrill sound of the phone cuts through the tension in the room. Luca pushes the speaker. "Hello."

"Luca, this is Sophia."

"Sophia, have you news about Lucy?" he asks.

"Have you seen her? Do you have the address?" I say.

"Is that you, David?" she asks.

"Yes."

"We are all here except for Giovanni, but we can get him on the phone if we need him," Luca says.

"Alright. As you know, I went to a patient's home this morning, which was Lucy's."

My heart nearly bursts as I struggle to process the news. "You've seen Lucy? How...how was she? Did she even recognize you?" My words spill out in a desperate rush, my voice shaking with anticipation and fear.

"I think it would be best if we talked face to face," she says.

"Did you not tell Lucy we are looking for her?" Luca asks. "We can't come to Brighton Beach without Dominic's permission."

"She is not in Brighton Beach. I need you to come to Mount Sinai."

"Why is she at Mount Sinai? Did something happen?" I ask.

Danti rushes closer to the phone. "Are you hurt, Sophia?"

"Don't get your panties in a twist, you grumpy bear. I can take care of myself," Sophia says.

"Don't you dare disrespect me like that, little girl," Danti snarls, his voice dripping with a mixture of anger and desire. We all knew about his dark obsession with being a Daddy Dominate and domination in general. He relishes in the power he holds over women who crave to be treated like little girls. Hell, all five of us founding sons enjoyed having women submit to us.

Lucy said nothing for several moments. I didn't know what she was thinking right now about his comment. She clears her throat. "I need Luca and Davide to come to the hospital."

My heart plummets like a lead weight, fear gripping my insides as I realize she can't say it over the phone. What if Lucy is injured or worse? A chilling thought shatters through me - what if something is wrong with the baby? Panic claws at my chest, and I struggle to catch my breath as I wait for the worst news imaginable. Corvo cries out from his cage in his low, gurgling voice. My pain is his pain.

"We will be there as fast as possible," Luca says, his voice cracking.

"I'll meet you on the 2nd floor desk."

The phone disconnects with a sharp click, sending Luca tumbling into his chair like a lifeless puppet. His face drains of all color, leaving behind a sickly pallor that matches the feeling in my gut. I know how he feels, but my own guilt and self-loathing add extra weight to the crushing emotions. It's all my fault, and I can feel it weighing me down like a heavy stone around my neck.

"Luca, Davide, your car is ready," Andrea says in a soothing voice. "We are coming with you."

My mind was a whirlwind of emotions and senses. Just as I had finally let myself open up entirely to her, the fear of losing her consumed me. The thought of her being taken away from me left me in a state of turmoil.

Somehow, Luca and I get into the back of the vehicle. Our breaths come in ragged gasps as we hurtle towards the hospital, the deafening roar of the engine drowning out any attempts at conversation. The air is thick with tension and fear as we all try to expect what awaits us at our destination.

Luca's words cut through the air like sharp blades, his voice dripping with venom as he spat out each syllable. "If she dies. I will never forgive you." His ordinarily calm demeanor was replaced by a cold, unfeeling mask of rage and grief.

I swallow the lump that has formed in my throat. "If she does, I don't want you to forgive me. I want you to kill me."

Luca turns toward me, his face full of hurt and shock. "You want me to do what?"

"I can't bear the thought of living without her. Luca, I admit I've made countless mistakes and done things that I deeply regret. But this time, it's different. This time, it's about Lucy and our baby - they are my reason for living." My voice cracks as tears threaten to spill down my cheeks. "I will do whatever it takes to make things right, no matter how long or how hard the journey may be."

Luca's gaze softens as he takes in my words, his icy exterior thawing slightly at the raw vulnerability laid bare before him. His grip on the steering wheel tightens, knuckles turning white with the intensity of his emotions. "I understand, Davide. I know how much she means to you."

The hospital looms into view, a stark monolith against the backdrop of the city. Upon reaching the entrance, a bustling scene unfolds with doctors in motion, patients on wheels, and machines mimicking my heartbeat.

The car stops in front of the entrance, and I don't wait for my guard to rush toward the doors. I didn't care if my enemies were waiting for me.

As tall glass doors slide open, I am surprised to see Giovanni and Angelina standing just inside. He reaches out and grasps my hand.

I glance down and see her enormous pregnant belly. Would I be able to see Lucy this large with my child?

"Gio," Luca says, stepping up beside me. "How did you get here so quickly?"

Giovanni's face lit up as he looked down at Angelina. "We were here for Angelina's weekly checkup. The doctor thinks it will only be a few more days."

"Good," I say and head towards the elevators. I push the button and am thankful that one of the doors opens immediately. I step inside, and the others follow. The ride is quick, and as soon as the doors open, I see Sophia standing waiting for us at the 2nd-floor desk. She looks shocked to see all of us.

"Sophia, tell me, what is going on with Lucy?" I ask.

"Not here. I have a room for us to talk in private." She turns and starts walking down the hall.

We follow Sophia down the sterile hospital corridor, the harsh fluorescent lights casting eerie shadows on the walls. My heart pounds in my chest with each step, anxiety and dread coiling in the pit of my stomach like a nest of vipers. I exchange a look with Luca, his expression mirroring my inner turmoil as we trail behind Sophia.

She leads us into a small consultation room, the air heavy with the scent of antiseptic and fear. I close the door behind us, shutting out the noise of the busy hospital wing. Sophia stands by the window, her arms crossed tightly over her chest, taking a deep breath before turning to face us.

"Lucy is here because..." Sophia's voice falters momentarily, her gaze flickering between Luca and me.

My heart froze in my chest, anticipating her reason for being here, leaving me breathless.

"She's here because she has preeclampsia," Sophia finally reveals, her voice barely above a whisper. "Dr. Bianchi is running tests, and Lucy is currently stable but not out of danger."

My chest tightens at the news, my worst fears coming to life before my eyes. The room feels like it's closing in on me, suffocating me with its sterile walls and the weight of impending doom hanging in the air.

Luca steps forward, his brows furrowed in concern. "Is she going to be okay? Can we see her?"

Sophia nods, her eyes filled with empathy. "She's stable for now, but they're keeping her under observation. You can see her individually, but please try not to overwhelm her."

"What about the baby? Is it okay?" I ask.

"It is fine now. However, we are worried if the preeclampsia gets worse, it will cause us to take the baby. It is very early, and we want it to stay where it is for the next two months," Sophia explains.

My heart clenches at the mention of our unborn child, a surge of protectiveness washing over me like a tidal wave. The thought of losing both Lucy and the baby is unbearable, driving me to the edge of desperation. I take a deep breath, trying to steady my racing heart as I step forward.

"Can I see her first?" I ask, my voice barely above a whisper. The weight of guilt and fear hangs heavy in the air, threatening to suffocate me with every passing second.

Sophia nods solemnly, her expression softening with understanding. "Of course, Davide. Follow me." She leads me down the corridor, each step echoing like a drumbeat in the hushed atmosphere of the hospital wing. The scent of disinfectant mingles with the tang of anxiety, creating a sharp taste in my mouth that mirrors the bitterness in my soul.

We stop outside a closed door, beyond which lies Lucy - the woman I love with every fiber of my being, the woman carrying our child, the embodiment of my hopes and fears intertwined. I stand rooted to the spot, my hand hovering over the door handle as if afraid of what I might find on the other side. Sophia gives my shoulder a reassuring squeeze before stepping back, leaving me alone to face whatever awaits me.

With a steadying breath, I push open the door and step inside. The room is bathed in the pale light filtering through the curtains, casting a soft glow over Lucy's prone form in the hospital bed. She looks so tiny and fragile amidst the sterile white sheets. Her face was peaceful in repose, despite the IV lines snaking from her arms.

My heart constricts at the sight, a surge of raw emotion welling up within me like a storm threatening to break free.

I quickly cross the room, dropping to my knees beside her bed as if pulled by an invisible force. Gently, I take her hand in mine, marveling at the warmth and softness of her skin against my own calloused fingers. The rise and fall of her chest beneath the thin hospital gown is a reassurance, a reminder that she's still here, still fighting.

I brush a strand of red hair away from her face. "Lucy, you have to be strong, amore mio. For us, for our baby."

Her eyelids flutter open at the sound of my voice, revealing the verdant depths of her gaze clouded with pain and weariness. A faint smile tugs at the corners of her lips, a flicker of determination shining through the exhaustion that threatens to overwhelm her.

Her voice, barely more than a whisper, calls out to me. "Davide, I'm scared."

The words pierce through me like a knife to the heart, igniting a fierce protectiveness that blazes within me like a wildfire. I lean in closer, my forehead resting against hers as I drink in her scent, which is uniquely her.

I whisper words of comfort and love, my voice an inaudible murmur that fills the silence of the room. "I'm here, Lucy. I won't leave your side. We'll get through this together, I promise." My hand tightens around hers, a silent vow etched in the touch that binds us together in this moment of uncertainty and fear.

Lucy's gaze meets mine, a storm of emotions swirling within the emerald depths of her eyes - fear, love, hope, all warring for dominance in the fragile sanctuary of her soul. She squeezes my hand weakly, her fingers trembling against mine as she draws a ragged breath.

"I don't want to lose our baby, Davide. I can't bear the thought of... of..."

Her words falter, choked off by a sob that escapes her lips in a raw rush of anguish. I feel my heart shatter at the sound, the pain of her fear and vulnerability like a physical blow to my chest. I gather her into my arms, cradling her close as tears prick at the corners of my eyes. "Shh, Lucy, you're not alone. I won't let anything happen to you or our baby." I kiss her forehead gently. The scent of her hair, like sunshine and wildflowers, ground me in this moment of uncertainty and dread.

We stay like that for what feels like an eternity, wrapped in each other's arms as the world outside fades away into insignificance. The beeping of machines, the distant murmur of voices - all of it pales in comparison to the bond that binds us together in this crucible of fear and hope.

Eventually, Lucy's sobs quiet into sniffles, her grip on me loosening as exhaustion takes its toll. I pull back slightly to look into her eyes, my heart breaking at seeing her vulnerability before me. Her tear-streaked face, once so full of determination and strength, was now etched with the weariness of battle fought on multiple fronts. I brush away her tears gently, my touch a silent promise of protection and solace amidst the storm raging around us.

"I love you, Lucy," I say, my voice barely above a whisper, yet filled with an intensity that echoes through the confines of the hospital room. "You and our baby mean everything to me. I want everything with you. I want you to be my wife. I want to live every day basking in your love. I could never be unfaithful to you, and I'm so sorry it took me so long to figure that out."

Lucy's gaze meets mine, a glimmer of gratitude shining through the pain and fear that clouds her eyes. She leans into my touch, seeking comfort in the warmth of my embrace, as if drawing strength from our connection.

"Davide," she murmurs, her voice a fragile thread weaving through the room's silence. "I'm scared, but I want everything with you, too."

I kiss her forehead, a tender gesture that speaks volumes of my love and devotion for her in the depths of my being. The weight of my confession lingers in the air, mingling with the scent of antiseptic and the soft lilac perfume that clings to Lucy's skin. It feels like a dam has burst within me, releasing a torrent of emotions I've kept contained for far too long.

As I gaze into her tear-filled eyes, I see a glimmer of something akin to hope shining through the storm clouds of uncertainty. I have to prove to her that I'm all in.

"I promise you, Lucy," I whisper, my voice hoarse with emotion. "I will never let you go. I will protect you and our baby with every breath."

She nods slowly, a small smile playing on her lips as she reaches out to cup my cheek in her delicate hand, her touch a balm to the turmoil raging within me. "I believe you, Davide," she replies, her voice stronger now, infused with a quiet resolve that steals my breath away. "Let's face whatever comes our way together as one."

At that moment, the weight of guilt and fear that had threatened to consume me lifted, replaced by a newfound determination to be the man Lucy deserves—a man who will stand by her side through thick and thin, come what may. The love shining in her eyes is a beacon of hope amidst the darkness that once clouded my soul.

    As we sit entwined in each other's arms, a sense of peace settles over us like a soft blanket, cocooning us in our shared resolve to face the challenges ahead. The beeping of machines and distant sounds of footsteps fade into the background, leaving only the steady rhythm of our hearts beating as one.

Chapter Twenty-Four

Lucy

The familiar, comforting scent of home fills my nose as I take a deep breath. Home is not a place, but a person - Davide. For months, I had prayed to hear the words of his commitment to me, and now they finally echo in my mind. My heart swells with joy while my brain tries to replay every moment leading up to this one. I can still feel the cool tiles beneath my feet as I left the pool house, where Davide had just professed his love for me but said he could never marry me.

For seven endless months, I have been adrift in a churning sea of despair and hopelessness. Each crashing wave threatens to swallow me whole, dragging me deeper into the suffocating darkness surrounding me. But I refuse to give up, clinging desperately to any shred of hope as I struggle to stay afloat amidst the tumultuous waters.

"Are you sure, Davide?"

He pulls back and places his large hands on my face. His dark brown eyes with flecks of gold stare deep into my eyes.

"With my whole heart and soul, I meant everything I said. I am so sorry for doubting my feelings. I never wanted to hurt you. I've loved you for so many years, even before it was acceptable. Don't tell your brother that. He is still pissed at me."

A broad and genuine smile spread across my face. It was not a mere façade, but a genuine expression of joy. As I basked in the warmth of that simple emotion, the heavy burden of despair lifted off my shoulders, its weight lessening with each passing moment. The corners of my mouth turned upwards, revealing dimples and crinkles at the edges of my eyes. All my worries melted away at that moment, and I felt as light as a feather floating in a gentle breeze.

"How is he?" I knew my disappearance would be harrowing for Luca.

He pulls his hands from my face and sits back. "He hasn't stopped looking for you. Neither did I. We poured over every nanosecond of the video from the airport. I spent weeks in Rome trying to track down any lead. It wasn't until recently that we figured out you had used a disguise." He gives me a smirk as he fingers my red hair. "Red hair. Please tell me this will grow out. I miss your blonde hair."

"It will, and I'm missing it as well. Is he here?"

"They are all here, including Angelina."

"Angelina? Has she had her baby?"

"No, but she is due any day now. Giovanni is going crazy."

"I want to talk to Luca before I see everyone else. But will you stay?"

"I'm never leaving your side," he declares.

He leans down and brushes his lips over mine. As we part from the kiss, a sense of peace washes over me, knowing that Davide is here to stay by my side. I take his hand in mine, feeling the warmth of his touch, grounding me in reality. With a deep breath to steady my nerves, ready to face Luca and explain my sudden disappearance.

"I'm ready to face him."

He squeezes my hand and gets up. As he walks over to the door, I try to calm my nerves. I don't need to get overly excited. Dr. Bianchi explained in detail the complications of preeclampsia. My baby is only twenty-eight weeks old, and it is way too early for it to be born. Until my blood pressure is brought down to an acceptable number, I will be stuck here.

"Lucy," Luca mutters and cautiously walks toward the bed.

"Hey, Lu," I croak as tears escape my eyes.

With a gentle sigh, he lowers himself onto the edge of the bed. We both rush forward, wrapping our arms around each other in a tight embrace. My big brother's powerful arms enfold me, creating a sense of security and comfort like no other. My worries and fears melt away in his presence as we hold on to each other. At this moment, there is no place safer than in his arms.

"I'm sorry," I whispered against his chest.

"Don't do it again. My heart can't take it."

"I promise."

He gently releases me from our hug and gazes into my eyes. A small smile plays on his lips as he speaks. "All is forgiven." His words are like a gentle breeze, carrying away any lingering tension between us. I feel a weight lifted off my shoulders and a sense of peace wash over me now that our disagreement has been resolved. The warmth in his gaze melts away any doubts or worries I had before.

I glance at Davide, his strong hand reaching out to take mine. I feel a wave of warmth and relief wash over me. "Even after everything that happened with Davide?"

"Lucy," Luca hisses. "This is between Davide and me and, unfortunately, The Commission. He was well aware of the rules, yet he broke them." Anger flashes in his eyes as he grinds his teeth together.

My heart explodes into a frenzied rhythm, panic coursing through my veins like wildfire. I know what this means. The Commission will stop at nothing to control me. Will they tear me away from my family? Banish me from Davide's side? Dear God, will they rip my precious baby from my arms and leave me empty and broken?

"DAMN IT. I TOLD YOU NOT TO UPSET HER!" Sophia yells as she rushes into the room, pushing Luca out of the way. "Luca, Davide, get out!"

"No, Davide, don't leave me," I cry.

"I'm not going anywhere," Davide says, holding my hand.

"If he is staying, so am I," Luca growls.

"Oh, no, you're not. Get out," Sophia commands.

I purposely avoid making eye contact with him, feeling the weight of his presence lingering in the room. Suddenly, I hear a deep, exasperated sigh and hear his heavy footsteps as he storms out, leaving a palpable tension behind.

The monitor by the bed beeps loudly. I glance up and see the numbers and cringe. My blood pressure was in the danger zone once again.

"Lucy, I am going to give you a dose of hydralazine, and Davide, can you help her onto her left side?" Sophia instructs.

Davide wraps his hand under my back and gently rolls me to my side. Sophia places a pillow behind me. The monitor alarm keeps sounding and with each beep, I become even more scared my pressure won't go down.

"Shh, my love. Take a deep breath and relax. I'm here, and you are going to be alright," Davide says as he places his hand on my belly. "Our precious little baby is safe."

I do as he says, take deep breaths, and allow the tension to leave my body. As if it knew I needed it, our little one gave me a powerful kick.

Davide pulls back his hand and stares down. "Was that what I think it was?"

"Yeah. It wanted to let us know it was okay," I say.

He gently rests his palm on my swollen belly and leans in close. "Hello, little one," he coos. "I am your daddy, and I already love you more than words can express. But for now, you need to stay put a little longer. Mommy and I will do everything possible to protect and keep you safe. So please, settle down so Mommy can rest after her long day."

As Davide spoke those tender words to our unborn child, a rush of overwhelming emotions flooded through me. Tears flowed freely down my cheeks, a mixture of relief, love, and sheer gratitude. The baby inside me, our precious little one, was surrounded by so much love and protection. I felt Davide's unwavering devotion to me and our baby, his words soothingly to my anxious soul.

The monitor's beeping faded into the background as Davide continued to speak softly to our child. His deep voice was filled with tenderness and a fierce determination to keep us safe. With each word he uttered, I felt a renewed sense of strength and courage blossoming within me.

"Davide," I whispered, my voice barely above a breath. "Thank you... for being here, for loving us so deeply."

He turned his gaze from my belly to meet my eyes, his own filled with an intensity that took my breath away. "Lucy," he murmured, his voice a low, soothing rumble. "I will always be here for you, for our baby. You are my everything, the light in the darkness that guides me home. I promise to protect and cherish you with every fiber of my being for as long as I draw breath." His words wrapped around me like a warm embrace, filling me with a sense of security and love unlike any I had ever known.

In that moment, amidst the monitor's beeping and the hushed whispers between us, I felt an unbreakable bond forming between us. Davide, our unborn child, and I were now intricately woven together by threads of love, hope, and a fierce determination to overcome whatever challenges lay ahead.

As Davide leaned in to kiss my forehead gently, I closed my eyes and let myself get lost in the overwhelming wave of emotions crashing over me. The love that flowed between us was a force of nature, unyielding and pure. In that intimate space, surrounded by the beeping of machines and the soft murmur of his words, I found solace in his unwavering presence. Despite the storm that raged outside these hospital walls, Davide was my anchor, grounding me in a reality where our love and our family were the only things that truly mattered.

As I opened my eyes to meet his gaze, a sense of determination flickered in his dark brown eyes. "We will face whatever comes our way together, Lucy," he said, his voice a steady reassurance that washed away any lingering doubts in my mind. "No matter what challenges lie ahead, I will stand by your side, ready to protect you and our child with everything I have."

His words resonated deep within me, stirring a newfound strength and resilience that I didn't know I possessed. With Davide by my side, I felt invincible, as if together we could conquer any obstacle that dared to cross our path. The monitor's beeping seemed distant now, a mere background noise to the symphony of emotions that enveloped us in this intimate moment. I reached out and intertwined my fingers with Davide's, feeling the warmth of his touch seep into my soul like a comforting embrace.

In that hospital room, amidst the sterile smell of disinfectants and the soft glow of the bedside lamp, time seemed to stand still. The two of us were bound by love and the unspoken promise of a future together. Our unborn child fluttered within me, a gentle reminder of the life we had created out of our shared love.

As I gazed into Davide's eyes, a sense of peace settled over me. His presence was a constant reassurance, a pillar of strength that held me steady in the face of uncertainty. In his eyes, I saw my reflection mirrored back with such tenderness and devotion that it took my breath away.

Silence enveloped us, the only sound in the room between our intertwined breaths and the soft hum of the machines. Davide's eyes held mine, myriad emotions flickering within their depths. As if sensing the moment's weight, he leaned in closer, his warm breath caressing my skin as he whispered, "I love you, Lucy. With all that I am and all that I have. You, our baby... you are my world."

Tears welled in my eyes at his heartfelt words, a profound sense of gratitude washing over me. In that intimate moment, I knew with unwavering certainty that Davide's love would be my guiding light no matter what trials lay ahead. His steadfast devotion was a shield against the uncertainties swirling around us, a promise of hope and strength in the face of adversity.

Davide's gentle hand caresses my cheek, his voice a warm and soothing balm to my troubled mind. "My love," he murmurs, "close your eyes and let yourself drift into peaceful slumber." The soft timbre of his voice wraps around me like a comforting blanket, easing away any remaining tension as I allow myself to sink into blissful sleep.

Chapter Twenty-Five

Davide

My gaze remains locked on her peaceful, slumbering form. Every inhale and exhale seems to revive my spirit, like a cool, refreshing drink amid a scorching desert. She is the oasis that quenches my soul's thirst, bringing much-needed respite from the dryness of life. Her delicate features are like a painting come to life, each detail more captivating than the last. I can't help but feel a sense of awe and gratitude for this calming presence in my life.

The soft rise and fall of her chest and the peaceful expression on her face all fill a void I never knew existed. Lucy, my Lucy, is so innocent and in slumber. I can't help but think of the darkness surrounding me, contrasting sharply with me I her light. How could someone like her ever belong to someone like me? Yet I doubt her love for me.

As I brush a lock of hair from her face, a sense of dread washes over me. The Raven inside stirs, restless and hungry for chaos. It whispers dark thoughts in my mind, telling me I am not meant for love and happiness. I am the harbinger of death, the hand that deals destruction without mercy.

But looking at Lucy, so fragile yet so physically and emotionally strong, I wonder if there is a chance for redemption within me. Maybe her light can overpower my darkness, allowing our love to shine like a brilliant star in the night sky.

A hand touches my shoulder, and as I look to see who it is, I see Angelina's smiling face. She holds her finger to her lips and motions for me to follow her. I glance down again at Lucy's sleeping face and force myself to leave. We step out of the room.

"Giovanni and the others want to have a meeting. They need you to attend," Angelina whispers, looking back toward Lucy's. "I will sit with Lucy until you return."

I don't want to leave Lucy, but I need to see what is so important they would pull me from her. "Okay, but if she awakes or something happens, come get me immediately."

"I will, I promise."

"Where are they?" I ask.

"Down the hall, the last door to the left," she answers.

"Thank you."

I can feel my heart racing as I glance one last time at the hospital door. My mind is flooded with thoughts of what could go wrong in the meeting ahead. Angelina's presence next to Lucy gives me some sense of comfort, but the two guards flanking the door remind me of the potential danger that lies ahead. With a deep breath, I reluctantly make my way towards the meeting room, unsure if I am truly ready for whatever may come.

As I approach, I see the two guards standing vigilantly at the door. They nod in recognition and step aside to allow me entry. My brothers sit around a small table. Our shared bond is not forged through blood but by our unbreakable loyalty to each other. We exchange nods before taking our seats, the air thick with anticipation and unspoken understanding.

"Davide, how are you holding up?" Giovanni asks.

"By a thread. Thanks for allowing Angelina to sit with Lucy," I say, giving him a weak smile.

"Allow, did he just say allow?" Giovanni chuckles. "Angelina would have me by the short hairs if I told her she couldn't sit with Lucy."

A warm chuckle escaped my lips at Giovanni's playful comment. I couldn't believe that this was the same man who used to be so guarded and distant. But now, with Angelina by his side, I could see a spark in his eyes that hadn't been there before. It made me wonder if I also looked different now that I had finally let go of my fears and confessed my unwavering love for Lucy. The weight of secrets and doubts had lifted from my shoulders, allowing me to fully embrace the joy and lightness that came with being with the one I loved.

The door opens, and Dr. Bianchi walks in. "Gentlemen, thank you for allowing me to speak to you directly concerning Lucy."

My eyes wander across the table to Luca, who sits with a tired, weary expression etched on his face. Time has taken its toll on him as if he has aged ten long years in just a few brief moments. Deep lines crease his forehead, and shadows linger under his eyes, giving him a worn and weathered appearance. My heart aches at seeing him, my dear friend who has endured so much.

"Luca and Davide, listen carefully. Your dear Lucy is in a very precarious health situation at the moment. The results of the tests I've run confirm her diagnosis of preeclampsia, a potentially life-threatening condition for both mother and baby. We are giving her what medication we can to lower her blood pressure and lower her chances of seizure."

"When can I take her home?" I ask.

Luca springs to his feet, his hands balled into tight fists that tremble with fury. "I WILL NOT LET YOU TAKE HER TO YOUR HOME. SHE WILL LEAVE WITH ME, HER BROTHER, AND TO OUR HOME!" His voice booms with determination, the muscles in his jaw clenching as he stares at me.

"Over my dead body," I growl.

"That can be arranged," he snaps.

"Try it, asshole." I stand and am about to go around the table when a loud crash sounds. I look over to find Dr. Bianchi holding a metal coffee decanter and glass from a picture lying on the floor.

Her voice drips with malice as she speaks, her teeth clenched tightly together in controlled rage. With a sharp glare first at Luca, then at me, she slowly raises an eyebrow, her threat hanging in the air like a blade poised for its next strike. "The next time," she hisses. "It'll be someone's head. I won't bother to fix the damage."

I have never encountered a woman with the same boldness and confidence as Lucy, who spoke to me this way. Her words were like a sharp blade, cutting through the tension and challenging us to do what was right for Lucy's health. And as I watched her stand firm against us, I couldn't help but admire her bravery and determination.

"As I was saying, Lucy's condition is life-threatening not only for herself but for the baby as well. We need to make her environment as stress-free as possible."

"And I can do that," I say. "Both her and I want to be together. I am going to marry her as soon as possible."

Luca's laughter echoed cruelly through the room. "You think anyone will want Lucy now that you've defiled her?" he sneered, his eyes glinting with malice. "She's nothing but a tainted whore, and no one will ever love or marry her." His words struck like stinging daggers, leaving a bitter taste in the air and a sense of despair in the hearts of those who heard them.

"I didn't take her virginity. We gave ourselves to each other."

Luca's voice rises to a fever pitch as he throws his hands up in exasperation. "Whatever, Davide Bonanno. You may be the Don of the infamous Bonanno crime family and revered as a founding son of The Almighty Famiglia, but it doesn't change the fact that you refuse to marry anyone who isn't pure. And now that my baby sister is pregnant, you can forget about marrying her." His eyes flash with anger and disappointment at his former mentor and leader.

"But he can," Giovanni says, then looks at Dr. Bianchi. "Doc, we need a few minutes of privacy, please."

"Alright, but remember what I said. Lucy cannot be under any stress, period." She looked at Luca and then at me before leaving the room.

I turned quickly toward Giovanni. "How?"

"Yesterday, I started looking through the ancient rules. I figured this wasn't the first time something like this had happened before. Nothing has changed in the male libido in the last five hundred years. Hell, probably from the beginning of time. They were as sex-crazed back then as we are now. So they wrote in a rule to override the virginity clause if they *jump the gun* and had sex with their attended."

My heart raced with this news. "So I can marry Lucy?"

"Yes, and no."

"What do you mean, yes and no?" I ask.

"You can marry her, but first blood has to be shed and witnessed by The Commission," Giovanni explained.

First blood? They couldn't witness that because it happened seven months ago.

"But Lucy's virginal blood was already spilled," Luca says, glaring at me with his hand fisted.

"The rule is not talking about virginal blood. Blood needs to be spilled by the prescribed punishment."

"What type of punishment?" I ask. I would do anything for us to be together.

"Lashing by a cat o' nine," Giovanni replied.

"Damn," Danti drew out.

"The man gets five, while the woman gets twenty-five," Giovanni mutters.

There was no way in hell I would allow Lucy to be subject to that. Fuck, just when I thought we found a way for Lucy and me to be together, it was ripped away. "No. I won't allow Lucy to be subject to that. I'll leave The Famiglia before I let that happen."

"You can't leave," Andrea says.

"I'll give the family to a cousin or someone."

"Davide, calm down. There is a clause called surrogato sanguigno, blood surrogate. You spill your blood in place of hers," Giovanni explains. "That is similar to what I did to have Angelina and my first night together. The male member can invoke surrogato sanguigno. You then will take the additional twenty-five lashings."

Without hesitation, I say. "I'll do it. Hell, give me a hundred if it means I get to spend my life married to Lucy."

I looked at each of my brothers, hoping to convey the sincerity of my remark. Giovanni looked like he already knew what my answer would be. Andrea and Danti gave me a look of pride. I finally glanced at Luca, and I saw forgiveness. Luca and I were always the closest. However, since he found out that Lucy and I had sex before her disappearance, he looked at me as the enemy. I've missed my friend.

"I take a hundred lashings if it meant I could marry Lucy."

I look at each of my brothers. Giovanni smiles and nods. Of all the others, he understood my position. I was just thankful he found the clause. Andrea and Danti both look concerned. Thirty lashings with a cat o'nine were going to be painful and most likely leave permanent scars. However, it wouldn't be anything like the pain and scars on my heart if I couldn't be with Lucy.

My eyes moved to the last brother. Luca and I had been close friends until he learned about Lucy and me.

Luca's eyes burned with a mixture of anger and disbelief. "You're willing to endure that level of punishment for her?" he asked, his voice tinged with a hint of astonishment.

I nodded solemnly, my gaze unwavering. "I've never been more sure of anything in my life. Lucy means everything to me, and I'll do whatever it takes to be with her."

A heavy silence settled over the room as the weight of my decision hung in the air. Luca's jaw clenched as he processed my words, his expression a blend of frustration and concern.

Finally, after what felt like an eternity, Luca spoke up. "I am still hurt by this, Davide. But I can't think of a better man to marry my sister."

His unexpected support touched me deeply, and a sense of relief flooded me. Knowing Luca would be there for us meant more than words could express.

As the tension in the room eased with Luca's unexpected show of support, I felt a surge of gratitude towards him. Despite the rocky road that led us here, his acceptance meant the world to me. I knew that winning back his trust would take time, but having his blessing to marry Lucy was a step in the right direction.

With newfound determination, I turned to Giovanni. "Let's make this happen. I'll endure the lashings if it means Lucy and I can finally be together."

Giovanni nodded in agreement, his eyes reflecting understanding and respect. "We'll need to prepare for the ceremony according to the ancient rules. We have to call a meeting with the entire Commission and advise them you have invoked surrogato sanguigno. After the meeting, a date and time will be set for the punishment. The Commission must witness the blood surrogate ritual before you can marry Lucy."

I took a deep breath, steeling myself for what lay ahead. The prospect of enduring such punishment was daunting, but the thought of a future with Lucy made it bearable. Love had a way of pushing boundaries and defying obstacles, and I will face whatever lay ahead for the chance to be with her.

"If there is nothing else, I want to return to Lucy," I say.

"You go ahead. I'll call the meeting and let you know when it is," Giovanni says.

"Have it as soon as possible. I want to marry Lucy as quickly as I can."

"Alright, brother," Giovanni says, slapping me on the back. "I'll go get my wife."

"Is there anything you need from home?" Danti asks.

"Maybe a change of clothes. Oh shit, I forgot to call Mom."

"We will tell her. Do you want her to come here?" Andrea asks.

"Do you really think you can prevent her from coming?" I reply with a chuckle. Ever since Lucy's disappearance, my mother had been a constant encourager that we would one day find each other again.

Andrea's lip twitched with a grin. "No, I don't see Nan staying away, especially when she finds out Lucy is back and is in the hospital."

Danti and Andrea exited the room, leaving Luca and me alone. He moves slowly, deliberately around the table, stopping to stand in front of me. Physically, we are equal - same height and build - but his muscles bulge under taut skin, evidence of his determined efforts in the gym since the attack that left him marked with a jagged scar on his face. From that moment on, he vowed to always be prepared for any potential danger. Every morning and evening were dedicated to intense workouts, honing his body into a weapon of strength and protection.

"Davide, I vow to keep my emotions in check around you. It's no secret that I am still deeply wounded, but I understand the importance of moving on. Having both Lucy and you in my life is something I hold dear and will continue to strive for."

"I want you in our life. You are going to be our child's uncle. Having no brothers or sisters means you will be the only uncle."

A smile breaks across his face. "And I plan on being a kickass uncle. I'll spoil them rotten, jack them up on sugar, and return them to you and Lucy."

I had to chuckle over the remark because I could see him doing just that. "Alright, let's go see how she is doing."

Chapter Twenty-Six

Lucy

"*I'm never leaving your side. I'm never leaving your side. I'm never leaving your side.*"

Davide's words echoed through my mind, repeating repeatedly in my dream. As I slowly opened my eyes, the hazy edges of sleep dissipating, I expected to see his face before me. But instead, my gaze fell upon the familiar features of my best friend, Angelina. Her platinum blonde hair cascaded over her shoulder as she leaned in close, concern etched on her delicate features. The memory of Davide's voice filled me with a longing ache, and I wondered if it had all just been a dream or if it had really happened. Reality and dreams blurred together, leaving me feeling uncertain and unsettled.

"Lucy," she whispers, taking hold of my hand.

"Angelina, it is so good to see you. Wow, are you big?"

She gently rested her hand on the round, protruding curve of her belly, feeling the weight and movement of the life growing inside. "This little one seems quite cozy in here," she chuckled, rubbing her palm in a circular motion.

A joyous, carefree laughter bubbled up from within me. At the bittersweet going away party, Angelina had pulled me aside to reveal her exciting news—she was pregnant. As the months passed, I couldn't help but imagine what it would have been like to experience this journey alongside my dear friend. To share our cravings and anxieties, to exchange our hopes and dreams for our growing bellies and future children. It would have been a comforting bond during such a tumultuous yet miraculous time in our lives.

I look around the room and panic when I don't see Davide. Had it been a dream? My heart races, and my lungs limit the amount of air.

"Shh, Lucy, you are okay?" Angelina says as she strokes my hand.

Fighting to get enough air, I struggle to say. "Davide."

"He is just down the hall. The guys are having a quick meeting. He will be right back, I promise. Now, take deep breaths. In, out, in, out."

I do as Angelina says, breathing in and out, trying to calm my racing heart. The sound of Angelina's soothing voice and the rhythmic pattern of my breaths brought a sense of peace to my restless mind. As the panic slowly ebbed away, I felt a warm hand on my shoulder and turned to see Davide standing there, a concerned expression clouding his handsome features.

"Lucy, what happened? Are you alright?" he asked, his dark brown eyes searching mine for any sign of distress.

I took a deep breath and managed a slight nod. "I... I thought it was all a dream. You were here one moment and then gone the next," I whispered, feeling the weight of uncertainty lift off my chest.

Davide's gaze softened as he reached for my hand, his touch grounding me in reality. "I'm here, Lucy. I promise I'm not going anywhere," he reassured me tenderly.

A wave of relief washed over me at his words, knowing I could always find solace and comfort in Davide's presence. Despite the uncertainties and dangers that lurked in the shadows of our world, his unwavering support and love were constants I could rely on. As I gazed into his eyes, a sense of calm settled within me, dispelling the lingering doubts that had plagued my mind moments before.

Angelina stood up from her chair, her belly swaying as she approached the door. "I'll leave you two alone," she said with a knowing smile before she turned and walked out of the room.

Alone with Davide, I felt a surge of emotions welling up inside me. Our bond was undeniably forged through trials and tribulations that strengthened our connection. As he sat beside me, his presence enveloped me like a protective shield, shielding me from the chaos of our tumultuous world.

"Davide," I began, my voice barely above a whisper as I struggled to calm down. "Why were you meeting with the others?"

His lips crash against mine, igniting a spark that spreads like wildfire through my body. The electricity between us crackles and hums, sending shivers down my spine. This moment, the one I've dreamed of for so long, is nothing like I imagined. Davide's low growl sends a surge of desire through me as he pulls back, his molten chocolate eyes burning into my very soul. I am powerless under his intense gaze, surrendering myself to his every touch.

He pulls back his heavy breath, as is mine. "You are a very dangerous creature, my love."

"I could say the same thing."

He sits back and smirks. "How are you feeling?"

"Better," I say, then look at the monitor. My blood pressure was 129 over 80, much lower than before my little nap. I sighed with relief, hoping whatever Dr. Bianchi was doing would help me have a full-term baby. I turn back to Davide. "My pressure is down."

He looks up at the numbers, and I see relief in his features. "I hope it stays that way. Before I answer your question, I have one of my own."

"Okay."

He slides off the bed and drops to one knee. He couldn't really be doing what I think he is doing.

Taking my hand in his. "I know I have fucked up in the past, and I don't deserve your love. But I promise you I will spend every moment forever loving you. Will you marry me, Lucy?"

Tears welled in my eyes as I gazed down at Davide, kneeling before me with a vulnerability I had never seen in him before. The weight of his words hung heavy in the air, their sincerity piercing through any doubts or fears that had clouded my heart. At this moment, surrounded by the beeping monitors and sterile hospital room, all that mattered was the man offering me his love and devotion so openly.

My hand trembled in his as I mustered the courage to speak, my voice barely above a whisper. "Davide... yes, yes, I will marry you."

His eyes lit up with joy, a smile breaking across his face as he stood up and pulled me into his arms. The warmth of his embrace enveloped me, cocooning me in the sense of belonging and security that I had longed for. In that fleeting moment, all the uncertainties and dangers of our world melted away, leaving only the promise of a future filled with love and commitment. Davide's lips found mine again, sealing our unspoken vows with a kiss that spoke volumes of his devotion. As we lingered in each other's embrace, the weight of his love anchored me to the present, grounding me in a reality where we faced whatever challenges lay ahead together.

"But how can we marry?" I ask. The Famiglia rules are very clear.

The sudden sound of footsteps approaching interrupted our moment, and Davide reluctantly pulled away, his gaze never leaving mine. The door swung open, revealing Dr. Bianchi standing in the doorway.

"I'm glad to see you're feeling better, Lucy. There is still concern over your blood pressure and the amount of protein in your urine. But I am encouraged by the results of the medicine so far. I want to do an ultrasound to check on the baby's progression."

The clinic had been so busy I had only had one ultrasound during my pregnancy. The thought of another excited me. Also, this would be the first time Davide would see his child.

A nurse wheels in the machine, and Dr. Bianchi prepares it. I couldn't contain my excitement at the thought of seeing our baby on the screen for the first time together. Davide stood by my side, his hand intertwined with mine, a mix of nervousness and anticipation flickering in his dark brown eyes. The room seemed to hold its breath as Dr. Bianchi placed the cold gel on my belly and started moving the wand around to capture an image of our little one.

And then there it was. The little figure was taking shape on the screen, and a fluttering heartbeat filled the room with wonder and awe. Tears welled up in my eyes as I gazed at the screen, overwhelmed by the realization that this precious life growing inside me was a part of both Davide and me.

Davide's grip on my hand tightened as he watched intently, his gaze softening at the sight of our unborn child. A mixture of emotions played across his features - pride, joy, and a hint of vulnerability that touched my heart. Seeing him in this moment, witnessing the raw emotion reflected in his eyes, I felt a surge of love and gratitude wash over me. Despite the uncertainties and dangers, this moment connected us and gave us a break from the troubles of our world.

Dr. Bianchi's voice broke through my reverie, her tone gentle yet tinged with concern. "Everything looks wonderful so far, but we'll need to monitor your blood pressure and protein levels closely. Would you like to know the sex?"

I looked at Davide and tried to understand what he wanted. Did I want to know? Yes, but if he didn't, I would wait. "Do you want to know?" I asked.

He smiled and nodded his head. The excitement of finding out the baby's sex danced in his eyes. I looked up at Dr. Bianchi. "We would like to know."

She moved the wand, and a few seconds later, she stopped. "It is a little boy."

"A boy?" Davide asks, excitement in his voice.

"Yes. Congratulations. I can see us discharging you tomorrow if you continue keeping your blood pressure down. However, I would like to see constant monitoring. Where will you be staying once you are discharged?" Dr. Bianchi asks.

"She will be with me," Davide answers.

My head snaps back, my eyes locking onto his. My mind races with a million thoughts and emotions, like a storm raging inside me. How could I stay with him when we couldn't be married? Would I just be his secret lover, hidden away from the world? But then why did he even propose to me in the first place? It's all so muddled and tangled, like a knot too complex to unravel.

"I can see if Sophia wants to move in and see Lucy's medical needs. She is a licensed midwife and already is well aware of her medical issues," said Dr. Bianchi.

Davide looks at me, concern written all over his face. "Would that be okay with you?"

I liked Sophia, and knowing she was looking out for me and my baby's best interests gave me a sense of peace. "Yes, please."

"Great," Dr. Bianchi says with a reassuring smile. "I will go speak with her now." Her voice is gentle, like a soothing balm for the worried mind. "Remember to keep your stress levels low, nourish your body with healthy food, stay hydrated, and most importantly, find moments of happiness in your day." With a nod, she turns and walks towards the door, leaving behind a sense of warmth and comfort in his wake. I take a deep breath and try to follow her advice, feeling grateful for such a caring doctor by my side during this difficult time.

Once the door shuts, I reach out and grab Davide's hand. "How can we marry?"

He leans down, his warm breath tickling my skin as he gently presses his lips to mine. When he pulls back, his eyes twinkle with joy and determination. "The meeting with the others was Giovanni informing me and the rest that he had discovered a long-lost clause in the ancient rules that permit us to unite in marriage."

As I take in this monumental development, a sense of hope and excitement floods my heart. Every fiber of my being thrums with anticipation for our future together, bound by this newfound loophole in tradition. I couldn't wait to be Mrs. Davide Bonanno and raise our child as a family.

Chapter Twenty-Seven

Davide

My car pulls through the large iron gates, adored with my family crest—the mighty raven with golden wings and a jeweled crown. Lucy is nestled beside me, her head resting on my chest.

After telling Lucy we could marry, her stress level dropped considerably. My mother arrived with the ring, and I didn't waste one moment slipping onto her finger. It looked perfect on her. I had jewels my ancestors collected through the centuries. However, the engagement my father gave my mother seemed tainted. After his death, Mom removed the ring after the funeral and placed it in the safe with all the other jewelry he gave her over the years. Each piece was not a giving of love but an outward expression of his dominance over her. There were also pieces of jewelry in the safe, and after everything calmed down, I would go through with my mother and Lucy to see what we wanted to keep. The pieces tainted by my grandfather and father would be gotten rid of.

I haven't told Lucy what I had to do to be able to marry her. After it was over, there would be no way I could hide the damage the whip would make. My back was covered in a massive tattoo of my family crest. It would be damaged with the lashing, but after I healed, I would have it repaired. Any scaring then would be covered by a tattoo.

"Davide, when are we getting married?" Lucy asks.

"If your health holds, I would love to marry you on Saturday." Before leaving the hospital, I took Dr. Bianchi to the side and asked her if she thought Lucy would be up to a traditional Famiglia wedding. She felt Lucy would be fine, but wanted Sophia to always be near. I asked if it was safe for Lucy to get the tattoo. The primary concern with a pregnant woman getting a tattoo is with unsanitary conditions.

As one of the founding sons, I was trained by a professional tattoo artist to ensure that every piece of equipment that would touch Lucy's skin was thoroughly sterilized. I would double and triple-check, taking every precaution to protect her health. The tattoo would be placed at the top of her left breast, a smaller version of our family crest. The intricate design of a black raven with its wings curled around as if protecting her heart, crowned with shimmering gold to symbolize its reign over her. And after our son was born, I had plans to expand the artwork.

The other part of the ceremony involved her kneeling at my feet and kissing my family's signet ring. In Italian, she will proclaim to the other four founding sons and the rest of The Commission, Padrone del mio cuore, corpo e anima, Master of my heart, body, and soul.

Lucy moves so she can look at me. Unshed tears are in her eyes. "Saturday?"

Placing my hands on either side of her face. "I would marry you this very moment. However, we must do the traditional way."

"So, we are having a Famiglia traditional wedding?" she asks.

"Yes. A small ceremony in the chapel on the compound, followed by the marking ceremony, then your declaration to me," I say with a wink. Lucy doesn't have a submissive bone in her body. Having to kneel before me was going to be difficult for her. "Then I bring you home and make love to you in our bed."

Her pupils widen with desire, and her tongue darts out to moisten her lips hungrily. I feel her body tremble, not from the cold air around us, but from the electric arousal coursing through her veins. I know that if I were to slip my hands down her tight yoga pants, I would find her slick and ready for me. The thought alone makes my heart pound and my erection throb with aching anticipation. Although we have only been intimate once before, the intense memories of that passionate encounter still ignite a fire within me, yearning to be reignited in another heated moment together.

She shuts her eyes, and my name escapes from her full lips like a desperate plea. Each syllable is laced with longing, dripping with aching desire. She whispers it like a prayer, hoping I'll somehow hear it and rescue her.

As Lucy's eyes flutter open, her gaze meets mine and holds it captive. I can see the unspoken words and thoughts racing through her mind, the love and longing she feels for me written all over her face. Her eyes fill with questions and concerns, and I know she's hesitant to voice them. But I won't let her doubts stand in the way of our love.

"Lucy," I begin softly, my voice filled with reassurance. "I promise you I will do everything in my power to protect you, to make you happy, and to be the best husband and father I can be. I won't let my past or my family's history dictate our future. You are my one true love, and I will always put you and our family above everything else. Our love is strong, and it will only grow stronger with each passing day."

I reach over and gently cup her cheek in my hand, the warmth of her skin rejuvenating my soul. "We will stand together, facing every challenge that comes our way. We will raise our children with love and respect and teach them to value family and faith above all else. With me by your side, you will never have to face the world alone."

Lucy's eyes well up with tears, and her lips tremble as she presses them against mine. It's a passionate embrace, filled with the intensity of our love and the promise of our future. I feel her heart race in tune with mine, and I know we will always be together.

As we pull apart, I can see the doubt and fear in her eyes, as well as the strength and resilience that have brought us this far. And I know that together, we can overcome any obstacle that lies ahead.

We drive up to my, no our home. The tension in the car is palpable, but I can't help but feel a mix of excitement and anxiety about the events to come. Over the years, Lucy had only been at my home a handful of times. When my father was still alive, Lucy was too young to attend the parties he threw. After his death, Mom didn't want to have them anymore. Years of seeing her husband flirt and sometimes fuck other women at the parties left her hurt.

As we pull up to my family's sprawling compound, a feeling of comfort and tension washes over me. My mother and Sophia stand on the front steps, their figures silhouetted against the warm glow of the doorway. Lucy and I were excited to have Sophia stay with us until our baby was born. Luca and I had boldly called her father and asked permission to have her be our live-in midwife. We promised to explain this in more depth later, but we knew it was necessary to bring this situation before The Commission. They didn't know I would appear before them this afternoon to declare my intentions to marry Lucy Gambino. At that time, I would invoke the rite of surrogato sanguigno. The consigliere members of The Commission are not aware of the rule. Giovanni will explain the rule as well as show them it in the original text of The Famiglia. A vote to allow the marriage will happen next.

The strategic choice of having an odd number of members on The Commission ensured that ties would never arise. The elite group comprised the five sons from the founding families and four carefully elected consiglieres. I was well aware of my brothers' loyalty, and their votes favoring the arranged marriage were merely a technicality. But even with the outcome predetermined, the formality was necessary to solidify our power and strengthen our connections within the underworld.

I offer a hand to Lucy and help her out of the car, feeling the weight of her body against mine as my arm wraps around her waist. I search her face for any hint of pain or discomfort. "Are you alright?" I ask, concerned for her well-being. The warm summer sun beats down on us, casting a golden glow on our skin as we stand outside the car. Lucy's eyes meet mine, filled with gratitude and trust in my support. Her soft breaths rise and fall in rhythm with mine, a comforting reminder of our unspoken connection.

"Good," she answers with a smile.

"Alright then. Let's get you in the house so my mother can fuss all over you."

Lucy giggles, and the sound fills my heart with joy.

"Lucy, dear, welcome home. I've got your bedroom all setup and the closet full of clothes," my mom says. "But I thought you might like to go sit in the sunroom. Sunlight is good for you. We will have lunch in about an hour."

"That sounds lovely."

"Once you get settled, I'll do your vitals," Sophia says. "I want to see where we are at so we can adjust."

We enter the grand foyer of the mansion, and Lucy's eyes widen in awe at the opulence of our home. I know that she's already a part of this life, but I can see that the reality of it all is still setting in. The thought of her becoming my wife and then my wife and mother to my child fills me with an overwhelming sense of pride and responsibility. I can already picture us as a family, our love and connection growing stronger with every passing day.

As we make our way to the sunroom, I can't help but feel a sense of excitement and anticipation about the future. We have so much to look forward to, and while there may be challenges along the way, I know we will face them together, side by side. I can already feel the bond between us growing stronger, the love and trust we have for each other deepening with each passing moment.

In the sunroom, Lucy sits on a plush loveseat, her eyes taking in the view of the sprawling gardens. I can see the wheels turning in her mind, the thoughts and questions swirling around in her head. But I know that with time and trust, we will be able to overcome any obstacles that come our way.

Sophia checks Lucy's vitals and smiles when she sees the number. "Your blood pressure is still a little high, but much better than yesterday."

"Thank you, Sophia. Are you all settled in your room?" I ask.

"Yes, Davide. The room is lovely. Thank you."

"Nan, Sophia, would you mind giving Davide and me a moment alone?"

"Certainly. We will go check on lunch," Mom replies. She stands and locks her arms with Sophia. They walk out of the room, chatting away.

I scooped Lucy up and settled her on my lap when the door clicked behind them. Her shoulders slumped, and she nibbled on her lower lip while avoiding eye contact. "What's wrong, sweetheart?" I asked softly, stroking her hair.

"Lucy, tell me what is bothering you. I can't fix it if I don't know."

Her voice was a timid whisper as she spoke, her uncertainty palpable in the way she hesitated before asking, "Are we not going to share a bedroom?" The softness of her words was matched by the gentle tone of her question, as if she were afraid of offending or disappointing. Her eyes darted nervously around the room, searching for any sign of displeasure.

It took me aback for a moment. Then I remembered what my mom said: "We haven't had a typical relationship, and that is all because of my stupidity. I love you so much and would do anything to make you feel comfortable in your new home. I thought you might want your own bedroom until we are married."

"Davide, we have spent too much time apart. We have gone about this relationship in the eyes of The Famiglia ass-backward, so why start doing things the way rules dictate? I'm tired of sleeping alone. I want to share our life together."

"I want that too, so much," I declared, pulling her close and burying my nose against her sweet skin. Drinking in her essence, Corvo sighed with contentment. Never in my life had my inner Raven been so at peace. She was mine and his. We would protect her with everything we were. I pulled and looked deep into her soulful eyes.

Lucy nodded, tears glistening in her eyes as she wiped them away. "Thank you, Davide," she whispered, her voice trembling.

I stroked her hair, my thumb brushing against her cheek as I looked into her eyes. "You're the love of my life, and I want to be with you always, in every way."

With a smile, she leaned into me, her arms wrapping around my neck. I held her close, the warmth of her body comforting me in a way that nothing else could. The world outside faded away for a moment, and it was just us together in the sun-drenched room.

"Alright then," I said, a smile tugging at the corner of my lips. "Let's go and see what Mom has cooked up for lunch."

We stood up, Lucy still in my arms, and walked towards the door. As we exited the room, I couldn't help but feel a surge of pride and love for her. We were taking a step forward in our relationship, one that wouldn't be dictated by the rules of The Famiglia but by our love for each other. I knew that there would be challenges ahead, but as long as we had each other, we would face them together, side by side.

After a wonderful lunch, Sophia checked Lucy's blood pressure and was happy with the numbers.

"I am loving these numbers," Sophia says. "Keep up with everything. We are not out of the woods yet."

"I will," Lucy says.

A wave of relief washed over me as I finally received the news that Lucy was recovering. My lungs expanded fully for the first time since hearing about her life-threatening condition, and I could feel my heart settle. Our son's life had been in danger, too, and now he would have the chance to live and grow alongside his mother and me. A son - our son, a beautiful little boy who would bring joy and love into our lives. As I imagined my son's future, I knew it would be different from mine. He would learn from the example of his strong, resilient mother and me how to love fiercely and unconditionally. At that moment, my heart swelled with pride and love for my family, and I could not wait for our future together.

Offering her my arm. "Let me show you our home."

Her face lights up, and a bright smile breaks out. "Our?"

"Oh baby, yes, ours," I say with a wink before turning to my mom. "Have the staff move all of her stuff to our room."

"As you wish, Davide," my mother replies, her eyes twinkling with excitement for us.

We take a leisurely tour of the mansion, Lucy's eyes wide with wonder and awe at every turn. She asks questions about the artwork and antiques, her curiosity piqued by our family's rich history. I answer her questions, sharing stories of our ancestors and the legacy we have built. We laugh and reminisce about the past, our hearts growing fuller with each passing moment. Even though we had many of our ancestor pictures through the mansion, there was one that was absent. That was of my father. After his death, I took down everyone and burned them. My mother deserved a happy life without being reminded of her past every time she saw his face.

Our room is beautifully decorated with soft colors, luxurious fabrics, and comfy furniture. The king-sized bed, dressed in crisp white linens, takes center stage, inviting us to claim it as our own. My mom must have done this before we arrived. She knew where Lucy belonged.

Lucy takes it all in and turns to me, her eyes filled with gratitude and love. "This is more than I ever could have imagined," she mumbles, her voice trembling with emotion.

"And it's all because of you, my love," I reply, gently cupping her cheek in my hand. "You're the one who makes this house a home."

As we stand there, wrapped in each other's embrace, I can't help but feel a sense of pride and contentment wash over me. I've lived in the shadows for years, always watching out for my family while keeping my true self hidden. But now, with Lucy by my side, I feel like I'm finally emerging from the darkness.

With a smile, I lead her to the bed and help her settle in. "I need to go to the compound to inform The Commission of our wedding."

Her forehead creased. "They won't deny us, will they?"

"No, love. Giovanni found a rule which allows us to marry. They can't deny the rule made by the founding fathers. Now take a nap, and when I return, we will take a walk through the gardens, then have a quiet dinner for two on the terrace."

"And after?" she asks, biting her lower lip.

"After I plan on christening this bed."

Chapter Twenty-Eight

Davide

Mici drives toward The Famiglia Compound. I couldn't say I was nervous about going before The Commission. Not my fellow founding sons, but the four consigliere. I knew I had the backing of Andrea, Danti, Giovanni, and even Luca. I was uncertain about the others' response to my intention of marrying Lucy, who they considered unclean.

A copy of the original *Stirpi Della Bestia, Bloodlines of Beast*, was entrusted to the Genovese family and housed in The Commission's chamber. Throughout the years, the Commission has used it for rule clarification. Today, I would refer to an unknown rule.

I was nervous because I didn't know Giovanni would be there. Earlier this morning, I received a text letting the others know Angelina was having contractions.

Giovanni's absence may result in a tie vote. There has always been consensus in every situation over the years. We relied on the book and its rules to guide us. Hopefully, today will be the same.

We approached the heavy iron gate, its surface adorned with intricate designs of the five founding family animals.

With its wings spread wide and talons gripping the gate's bars, the great dragon was flanked on either side by a proud raven and a fierce lion. Its tail coiled tightly around a mighty bear and a cunning wolf, symbolizing the family's strength and unity. The engravings on the gate glistened in the bright sunlight, each telling its own story of ancient battles won and glorious triumphs achieved. People felt a mix of pride and respect as they entered through the slowly opening gate, stepping into a world filled with history and tradition.

The Famiglia compounds embody the essence of security, formidable fortresses crafted to safeguard those inside. Encircled by an imposing eight-foot stone wall, their unwavering strength and invincibility are immediately evident. Every inch of the wall is blanketed with cutting-edge motion detection sensors and cameras, instilling a sense of constant vigilance and alertness. As privileged members of The Famiglia, we possess access to the most advanced security systems known to man, setting us apart from any other place in the world. Only two other compounds can rival our unparalleled level of protection and sophistication, a testament to our unwavering commitment to safety and protection.

Beyond the towering walls, stretching as far as the eye could see, lay a sprawling complex of buildings. The central structure, known as the main building, was a grand architectural marvel that served as the heart of The Commission. Its imposing stone walls were adorned with intricate carvings and statues, exuding an air of majesty and power. Within its walls, the chambers of The Commission held court and made decisions that shaped the lives of its members.

The main building had a state-of-the-art industrial kitchen and pantry, ready to cater to up to five hundred guests. On the other side stood essential facilities such as security, an armory equipped with the latest weapons, a fully equipped gym for physical training, and a well-stocked clinic for any medical emergencies.

But the imposing judicial building caught the eye. It was a formidable structure with its tall columns and grand entrance. Inside its halls, justice was swift and merciless for those who dared to break the rules set by The Commission. Here, members were brought to face judgment and receive punishments for their transgressions.

As one stepped inside the compound, one could feel the heavy weight of authority and power hanging in the air. A constant reminder of the Commission's control over its members. It was a place where rules were strictly enforced and every move monitored. This was the heart of the Commission, a symbol of strength and dominance in their world.

I parked my car outside the compound, feeling a rush of adrenaline as I stepped out and walked towards the intimidating entrance. The heavy wooden doors loomed large before me, a silent barrier between me and The Commission. My footsteps echoed in the corridor as I made my way inside.

As I entered the chamber, I saw the four consiglieres seated around a large oak table, their expressions unreadable. Andrea nodded at me in acknowledgment. Danti's gaze was distant and calculating, while Luca's usual stoic gleamed on his features. Giovanni's absence did not go unnoticed, leaving a gnawing sense of unease in the pit of my stomach.

I took my place at the table, feeling the weight of centuries-old traditions pressing down on me. The Stirpi Della Bestia lay open before me, its ancient text a reminder of the bloodlines that ran deep within our veins. Lost in our thoughts, each of us awaited the start of the meeting, the silence in the chamber palpable. Tension filled the air, coiling like a predator, ready to strike any weakness.

Finally, Danti cleared his throat, breaking the suffocating silence. "Davide, you have called this meeting with The Commission. Speak your mind," he said, his voice steady and commanding.

I squared my shoulders, steeling myself for what was to come. "Gentlemen, I come before you today to address a matter. I wish to discuss my intention to marry Lucy Gambino."

A collective murmur rippled through the chamber at my revelation. "We understand that Lucy Gambino is pregnant, and if this is true, she is no longer able to wed a founding son," Consigliere Jackson Patterson said.

The words ripped from Luca's throat like a savage roar, his eyes blazing with fury. "She's the daughter of a founding father and the sister of the head of the Gambino family. So watch what you say about her."

"Yet she whored herself out," Consigliere Williams sneered, his words laced with disdain.

My vision is consumed by a thick, blood-red haze. The mere mention of Lucy's name in such a degrading manner ignites a primal rage within me. I can hear Corvo, my inner demon, chanting in his cage for the death of our enemy. With determined fury, I launch myself towards Consigliere Williams, his sneering face taunting me. Before he can even utter a sound, my hands are around his neck, squeezing with all my strength. Through gritted teeth, I growl out my words. "She is not some cheap whore. She is destined to be my wife and the mother of my son." A fierce determination fuels my grip as I refuse to let him speak ill of her again.

The room seems to tilt on its axis as Williams struggles against my grip, pushing and clawing at me in defiance. The air crackles with tension as the other Consiglieres leap to their feet, their expressions ranging from shock to anger.

"Stop this madness!" shouts Andrea, his voice cutting through the chaos like a knife.

Danti moves swiftly, grabbing my shoulder and pulling me away from Williams with surprising strength. "This is not the way, Davide."

I take a step back, breathing heavily as my chest heaves with pent-up emotions. The taste of blood fills my mouth from where I've bitten my lip in the heat of the moment.

Williams coughs and splutters, glaring at me with malice burning in his gaze. "You have lost your mind."

In that instant, a surge of regret floods through me. This is not what I envisioned. Lucy's honor should not be defended through violence, but through reason and respect.

The room falls into an uneasy silence as we try to regain our composure. Andrea breaks the quiet tension by addressing the Consiglieres.

"I understand that this is how we normally work. Someone who is with a child cannot marry a founding son.

However, the founding families made allowances for this situation," Andrea says in a measured tone.

"What do you mean?" Consigliere Croft asks.

Gaining some control, I know I need to make my case to the others. "Giovanni has found a provision in the ancient text that allows the couple to atone for transgression."

"Atone? How do they do that?" Consigliere Croft asks.

"First blood has to be shed and witnessed by The Commission," I answer.

"She is expecting, so she is no longer a virgin," Croft says. His tone was one of confusion, not one of malicious.

"The rule is not talking about virginal blood. The blood comes from the prescribed punishment."

"What type of punishment?" Williams asks.

"Lashing by a cat o' nine," Andrea replies. "The man gets five, while the woman receives twenty-five."

The men were purely shocked. They did not expect this. "However, I am invoking surrogato sanguigno, blood surrogate clause. I spill my blood in place of hers. I will take the additional twenty-five lashings in her stead."

As the room fell silent, I could feel the stares of my fellow consiglieres boring into me, weighing the gravity of my offer. It was not a decision I took lightly, but I would do whatever it took to save Lucy's honor and ensure our union.

"You would accept twenty-five lashes for her? Even though you will not be bound by the ban against your marriage?" Consigliere Jackson Patterson asked, his voice filled with disbelief.

I nodded, my resolve unwavering. "I will do whatever it takes to protect my future wife and unborn child. The blood surrogate clause is a part of our traditions, and I will honor it."

Although the consiglieres were visibly shocked and taken aback by my offer, they remained silent for what felt like an eternity. The room's heaviness grew more palpable, the tension thickening with each passing second.

Finally, Danti broke the silence, his voice grave but calm. "Davide, your commitment to Lucy and your unborn child is admirable, but we must consider the implications of such a decision. This will not be a simple task. It will require much physical and emotional endurance. Are you certain you wish to proceed with this plan?"

I took a deep breath, forcing myself to stay composed as I answered, "Yes, I am." My eyes never left their faces, making sure they understood the depth of my devotion. "I have made my decision, and I stand by it. In order to uphold the honor of my future wife and child, I will take the lashes and agree to the blood surrogate clause."

"Then I call for a vote. I vote yes," Luca says, never taking his eyes off me.

"Yes," Andrea says.

"Yes," Danti booms, giving me a wink.

I predicted yes for these votes, but now the others come and I have no idea how they will vote.

"Yes," Williams reluctantly states, his resentment toward Lucy still glaring in his eyes.

"Yes," Croft says.

"Yes," Lee Butler says.

The room fell silent as we awaited the final vote, which would either uphold or shatter our tradition.

Finally, Jackson Patterson speaks up, his voice echoing throughout the chamber. "Yes."

"With a unanimous vote, Davide, you can marry Lucy Gambino," Consigliere Croft states. "Does the book state when the first blood must be drawn?"

"It has to be done before the wedding. If possible, I would like to do it tomorrow evening."

Croft looks around the room, and each member nods. "Alright, tomorrow evening at eight, we will meet at the Tombs of the Blooded."

The meeting ended unanimously in favor of my blood surrogate clause proposal. Although this decision weighed heavily on my heart, I knew it was the only way to protect Lucy's honor and secure our future together.

The four consigliere leave the room, leaving the four of us. "Who do you want to give you the lashings?" Andrea asks.

I had thought of this, and there was only one person I wanted. It was his right because I had broken his trust in me. I turned toward Luca. "I want you."

Luca shakes his head. "Davide, you cannot ask me to do this. You know the pain the lashings will bring, and I cannot be the one to inflict such pain on you."

I take a deep breath, gathering the strength and courage to make my case. "Luca, this is not a request. This is my decision. I have chosen you because I trust you more than anyone else. I know you will ensure I feel every lash and every ounce of pain. This is the least I can do for betraying your trust."

He looked at me, his face a mix of emotions: first confusion, then anger, and last, deep concern. Eventually, he nodded. "Alright, I will do it. But know that I will not hold back."

"That is all I ask."

Chapter Twenty-Nine

Lucy

It was like I had entered a dream. Davide's heady, woody fragrance surrounded me, creating a comforting cocoon that wrapped around my body. I felt a new tranquility and contentment. Like an invisible blanket, the scent seemed to seep into every pore, engulfing me in its embrace. It was as if the very essence of Davide had materialized and was now permeating my being.

I open my eyes, momentarily unaware of my surroundings. But as my eyes focus from my deep sleep, I see him sitting in a chair. It wasn't a dream. He is here.

Davide's penetrating gaze met mine, and time seemed to hold its breath momentarily. His dark brown eyes, usually so intense, softened as they locked with mine. He stood and walked over to the side of the bed. I felt a shiver run down my spine as he reached out a hand and gently brushed a lock of hair away from my face. The touch sent electric currents through me, awakening every nerve ending in my body.

"Davide," I say. It comes out and I am barely able to contain the rush of emotions swirling inside me. It was as if the universe had conspired to bring us together at this moment, erasing all doubts and fears plaguing my heart.

His fingers traced a pattern on my cheek, his touch both tender and possessive. "Lucy," he says, his voice a low rumble that resonated deep within me. In that instant, I saw a vulnerability in his eyes that contradicted the fierce exterior he often presented to the world.

As I gazed into those depths of his eyes, I felt a sense of longing and desire, an unspoken connection that bound us together in ways I couldn't fully comprehend. Davide's inner turmoil seemed to mirror my own, the struggle between duty and desire etched on his face.

"I've missed you." His voice barely audible but laden with raw emotion. At that moment, the weight of his words hung heavy in the air, each syllable declaring something unspoken yet understood between us.

I reached out to touch his hand, the warmth of his skin searing through mine. "I've missed you too," I say, the truth of my words ringing true in the air around us. "Did The Commission give us permission to marry?"

"Yes, they did," he says. For a moment, something flashed in his eyes. Did something else happen?

"David, is something wrong?"

"No, my love. We will be married on Saturday evening in a traditional Famiglia service."

"Traditional?" Did he mean everything a daughter of The Famiglia was taught since she was old enough to understand?

His full, sensuous lips quirked up in a half smile, revealing a flash of straight white teeth. His dark brown eyes sparkled with mischief, reflecting the dim light in the room like glinting gems. With each movement of his expressive brows and the subtle playfulness in his gaze, he exuded an irresistible charm that left her heart fluttering.

"Yes. The ceremony will be in the chapel on the compound. Father Loren will bless our union. After the ceremony, I will mark you with my family's crest over your heart. Then, as a sign of our devotion, you will kneel before me and kiss my ring. Give me your pledge. Padrone del mio cuore, corpo e anima, Master of my heart, body, and soul."

My mind had removed this part from memory, but now it all came rushing back. How archaic and unnecessary this ritual seemed to me now. Why should I have to kneel before Davide, the only man who owned my heart, body, and soul, while others watched? It felt like a performance, a display of ownership for all to see. My cheeks flushed with embarrassment at the thought of being in such a vulnerable position. It was an antiquated tradition that held no meaning in this modern age.

"Davide, I understand signifying tradition, but I am not sure about this particular aspect. Kneeling before you in front of others and making such a symbolic gesture feels like a performance rather than express our love."

His expression shifted, his brows furrowing as he processed my words. For a moment, there was a flicker of something unreadable in his eyes before he composed himself, masking whatever emotion had surfaced.

"Lucy, I know this may seem outdated to you. But in our world, such rituals are more than just tradition. The traditions symbolize our unity, strength, and commitment to each other. The public display of allegiance is not meant to diminish your independence or autonomy, but to solidify our bond in the eyes of our Famiglia. It is a testament to our shared values and unwavering dedication to each other."

I listened to his explanation, trying to reconcile my modern beliefs with the ancient customs of the Famiglia. While I understood the importance of tradition and unity within the organization, I couldn't shake off the unease that crept into my heart. The idea of submitting to Davide in such a public manner felt like a betrayal of my own principles, a surrender of my agency and identity.

"Davide, I respect our traditions and the significance they hold for our family, but I can't help but feel conflicted about this particular ritual. As you know, I am not like most Famiglia daughters. Luca encouraged me to follow my dreams. I love my independence."

Davide's gaze held mine, his intense stare unwavering as he processed my words. He briefly showed emotion in his eyes before regaining his composed and authoritative look, which always earned him respect. I could sense his internal struggle between honoring tradition and respecting my desire for independence.

"Lucy, I understand your concerns. Your independence and strength are some of the qualities that drew me to you in the first place. But please understand that these rituals do not diminish your spirit or autonomy. They are a part of who we are, a reflection of our shared history and values as a family."

I nodded, acknowledging his words while still wrestling with my own convictions. The weight of expectation bore down on me, the weight of generations past dictating my actions and decisions. In Davide's eyes, I saw the conflict mirrored, the struggle between duty and desire playing out in silent communication between us. As much as I longed to honor our traditions and stand by Davide, a part of me rebelled against the idea of sacrificing my autonomy for the sake of unity. It was a battle within myself, a clash between loyalty to my heart and allegiance to our Famiglia.

In that moment of tense silence, Davide reached out and took my hands in his, his touch grounding me in the present. His eyes bore into mine with an intensity that spoke volumes, a silent plea for understanding and acceptance.

"Lucy," he breathed, his voice tinged with a vulnerability I had rarely seen. "I know this is a lot to ask of you. I understand that the weight of our history and traditions can be suffocating at times. But please trust me when I say that our bond transcends these rituals. What we share goes beyond words or gestures; it's a connection that defies tradition and expectation."

I think about his words. It wasn't like I didn't like the idea of being on my knees. Actually, I loved the thought of it.

"Davide," I started. My voice was a whisper as I struggled to articulate the thoughts swirling in my mind. "It's not that I disagree with our traditions, it's just..." He watched me as I paused, his eyes reflecting a glimmer of uncertainty.

"I give my heart, body, and soul to you." With this confession, a blush spread across my cheeks at the bold admission. A spark ignites in Davide's eyes as he registers my words, his hands tightening around mine. My heart pounds against my ribcage, a symphony of anticipation and desire that echoes with every beat.

"I want to submit to you, Davide, but only to us." The vow hung heavy between us, intertwining with the electric current flowing through our clasped hands. "My words and submission should be put on stage for The Commission to see and hear."

"Lucy." Davide rasps out, the sound of my name carrying a hint of raw need lacing his deep baritone. His gaze darkens, intently focused on me.

A wicked smirk played upon my lips, and I tilted my head coyly as I slid off the bed and onto the floor before him. Positioning myself to kneel between his long legs, I traced my fingers teasingly up along his muscled thighs to rest close to his growing arousal beneath his tailored pants.

Davide sucks in a sharp breath at the contact and watches me with hooded eyes. My grin widens as I unzip him slowly. As his impressive length springs free from its confine, my fingers dance on the shaft, sending shivers rippling through his muscular frame.

"Mio Dio, Lucy." Davide groans at the teasing sensation, edging closer to a tipping point. Leaning forward, my hot breath fans over him, making him twitch under my attention.

I run the flat of my moist tongue over his swollen tip, causing Davide's grip to tighten involuntarily into my hair. I murmur against his pulsing length. "Oh, you taste so good."

Davide's voice was rough with desire as he groaned my name.

I take him in, inch by inch, relishing the gasp that tumbles from his lips. As I move rhythmically, taking him deeper with each stroke, an onslaught of pleasure surges through both of us. Pleasure spun with anticipation and need.

I looked up at him, meeting those intense eyes that expressed more than words ever could. At this moment, we were submitting to something far more significant than tradition or expectation. We were surrendering to our primal instinct. Our carnal desires for each other.

I could tell Davide was more than just excited. He was overwhelmed. His breathing became ragged as I continued to pleasure him, my hands working in tandem with my mouth. I could feel the tension building within him, the anticipation of release growing stronger with each passing second.

"Lucy, I can't take much more of this." His grip tightens around my hair even more. I smile around him, not letting him see the satisfaction in my eyes. I loved the power that came with bringing him to his knees.

"Then don't." His breathing became even more ragged, his hips bucking up in response to the pleasure coursing through him.

Finally, he could hold on no longer. With a primal roar, Davide came, his release spurting into my waiting mouth. I swallow every drop, savoring the taste of his passion. His orgasm left him panting and weak in my grasp, and I couldn't help but feel a rush of power and satisfaction at the control I had just exerted over him.

As I pull away, I look up at him with a smirk, knowing that I had just proven a point to him and me. It wasn't about submitting to tradition or expectation, but rather about finding a balance between our desires and our expectations.

"Lucy..." Davide says, still catching his breath. His gaze is soft and filled with reverence, and I know he understands the depth of what we have just shared. In that moment, I feel an unbreakable bond between us, transcending the boundaries of our roles and responsibilities.

We are seated on a charming terrace, surrounded by vibrant flowers of every color imaginable. The scent of blooming jasmine fills the air, adding to the idyllic atmosphere. Our plates are filled with an array of delectable dishes, each more delicious than the last. As someone not skilled in the culinary arts, I am blown away by how flavorful and satisfying each bite is. After seven long months of less-than-stellar meals, this experience is a much-welcomed treat for my taste buds. Moans of pleasure escape my lips with every bite.

"Damn, woman, you are killing me."

I look down and see the outline of his massive cock straining against his black pants. Putting down my fork, I stand and walk to him. His eyes never leave mine as I pick up the edge of my dress and straddle his lap. The thin layer of wet satin panties allows me to feel his cock. My pussy clenches with the memory of how it felt when he was inside me. I can feel his hardness pulsating through his pants, and I can't help but run my fingers over the bulge. His eyes are filled with desire, and I can tell he wants me just as much as I want him.

"Lucy, I can't take much more of this." He groans and adjusts himself.

I give him a seductive smile. "Well, lucky for you, we're not done yet."

I slide off his lap and take his hand, leading him to a nearby secluded corner of the terrace. The dim light and the water fountain sound create a sexy ambiance that gets me even more turned on. I press my back against the wall and look up at him, my eyes filled with lust.

"Fuck me, Davide."

He doesn't need any more encouragement. His hand is on my throat, his other hand gripping my hip as he pushes me against the wall. I moan as I feel his pant-covered dick rub against my already-wet panties. He's still clothed, but that doesn't seem to matter right now. All I can think about is feeling him inside me.

"You want it, Lucy? You want me to fuck you right here where anyone could walk out and see us?" His breath is hot against my ear, sending shivers down my spine.

"Yes, Davide. I want you to fuck me hard and fast like you've never done before. I need you to claim me, to make me yours in a way that leaves no doubt who owns me, body and soul."

My hands grasp the back of his neck, pulling his lips down to mine. The kiss is intense, our tongues dueling as our passions build. With a loud groan, he breaks the kiss and pulls away, smirking at my flushed cheeks.

"As you wish, mia bella."

He lifts me into his arms and carries me towards behind hedges, where we can find some privacy. The cool night air hits my skin, and I shiver in anticipation. He lays me down on the soft grass, the stars twinkling above us.

With a gentle kiss to my lips, he pushes my dress up over my waist, revealing my lace panties. He looks down at me, his eyes burning with desire, and I can feel my heart pounding.

He hooks his fingers in the waistband of my panties and teasingly pulls them down my legs. I lift my hips to help, unable to contain the anticipation coursing through me. He tossed them aside, then unzipped his pants and shoved them down his legs. His thick dick bounced against his stomach. It was as glorious as I remembered. He falls to his knees and positions himself at my entrance.

"Davide," I whisper, my voice shaky with need. "Please."

He looks at me, his eyes dark and hungry, and then he thrusts into me in one smooth motion. I gasp, my body arching up to meet him as he fills me. He's not gentle. He can't be. I have dreamed of nothing but him and this for seven long months.

I wrap my legs around his waist, pulling him even closer as he moves inside me. Every stroke is a catalog of our desire, a testament to our power over each other. His hands grip my hips, his fingers digging into my skin as he thrusts into me with increasing intensity. My pussy clings to him, the walls of my core squeezing his cock with each movement, urging him on.

"Lucy, you feel so good," Davide groans, his head falling back as he loses himself in our passion. "You are mine, Lucy. Only mine."

I moan, my voice barely audible over the sounds of our lovemaking. "Yes, I'm yours, Davide. Yours forever."

His hips continue to move, each thrust like a promise etched into my being. I can feel the heat building, the desire intensifying with every passing moment. I need this to release the tension coiled within me for so long.

I reach down, grabbing his rock-hard ass, pulling him even deeper into me, wanting nothing more than to feel every inch of him. His erection slides in and out of me, hitting all the right spots, sending shockwaves of pleasure coursing through my body. The sensations are overwhelming, and I can feel myself starting to tremble.

"Davide, I'm so close."

His eyes lock onto mine, his face contorted with passion, and he picks up the pace, thrusting into me with more intensity than before. "Come for me, Lucy. Let go with me."

With those words, I lose myself at the moment. My body shuddered, my muscles tense, and I knew without a doubt he was the master of heart, body, and soul.

Chapter Thirty

Davide

"This is our most exclusive crib. It is solid brass with a 24-karat gold overlay," the saleslady says as two others wheel the ornate crib in front of us. We deserved the very best, and money was no object.

I woke up this morning happier than I ever thought I would be. Lucy was snuggled up against me, and my hand lay on her belly. Our son was moving, and every now and again, I could feel him pushing either his hand or foot against my hand. He was so strong already, and I couldn't wait to see him.

Tonight, I will take the final and most excruciating step to ensure Lucy and I can marry under the strict rules of The Famiglia. Every lash from the whip will slice through my skin like a hot knife, leaving me writhing in agony. But for love and honor, I am willing to endure any torture. I felt bad about keeping it from Lucy, but she didn't need the stress of worrying about me. Tomorrow, I will tell her because there is no way I can keep it from her. I will need help put on fresh dressing on the wounds.

After Sophia did her morning checkup on Lucy, I informed them we were going shopping. Lucy needed clothing since she had only brought a few things from the house where she was staying. It would be too dangerous for us to go back to it. Thankfully, she could bring the items that meant the most to her. Her prized photographs were currently being reframed. Once that was done, I wanted her to place them wherever she wanted to in our home. My home is now hers, and I want her to change whatever she wants.

I spent the morning making multiple phone calls, determined to create a unique and luxurious shopping experience for us. After much effort, I arranged for a renowned specialty baby boutique and a boutique for maternity clothes to open their doors exclusively for our private use.

Lucy relaxed on a comfortable sofa at both stores, her feet propped up, while the staff brought each item to her. Everything in the store was top-of-the-line. The owner was a member of The Famiglia, and all the wives of the society purchased all the necessities for the organization's next generation.

"Do you like this one?" I ask.

A small, shy smile played at the corners of her lips. "I can't help but think it's a bit pretentious," she mused, her voice soft and hesitant. Her eyes flickered with uncertainty as she spoke, unsure if she should express her thoughts.

"Nothing is too good for our child."

"Nan, do you think it will look good in the nursery?" Lucy asks.

"Yes. However, it needs some work. It hasn't been used in over thirty years," Mom answers.

Wrapping my arm around Lucy's shoulders, I pull her closer. "I'll hire a crew to renovate the room however you want."

She turned and looked deep into my eyes, which glistened with unshed tears. "I want your opinion as well. This room will be where we bring home not only this child but our others."

When I thought I couldn't be happier, Lucy said something like this: She has given me the two greatest gifts I could ever ask for. One was our son, and the other was her unbelievable love for me. I was just coming to grips with having her back, and I didn't think about having more children. Oh, but how I wanted to fill our home with the laughter of our children.

"I will be there for every decision."

She places her hands on my face and pulls it down toward hers. "I love you, Davide," she breathes, her voice a sultry whisper that sends shivers coursing down my spine. Her lips are a tantalizing inch away from mine, and I no longer resist the magnetic pull.

"I love you too, Lucy." My words hang heavily in the air before getting swallowed by the heat of our kisses. Soft, lingering, exploratory—our tongues mingle and dance in an erotic ballet that leaves us both breathless.

I was so lost in the kiss that I forgot where we were until my mom cleared her throat.

"Ahem," Mom's pointed throat-clearing successfully breaks our passionate embrace. Lucy blushes, a rosy hue painting her cheeks as she looks away shyly. I couldn't help but chuckle at the situation—caught in a moment of intimacy by my mother.

"We'll... uh, are you getting the crib?" she asks with a twinkle in her eyes.

With a confident smile, I face the sales lady and make my final decision. "Yes," I declare firmly, meeting her gaze. "We will take the complete collection." The woman's eyes light up with delight, her lips parting into a pleased grin.

"Excellent choice, Mr. Bonanno," she praises, brimming with enthusiasm. "And congratulations on the impending birth of your son."

She steps away, and I take Lucy's hand in mine, gently kissing her knuckles as I bring it to my lips. "You make it very hard for me to focus on anything else when you're around," I confess with a smile.

Lucy giggles softly, her eyes sparkling with affection. "I can't say I mind too much. Being here with you feels like a dream."

Leaning in, I press another tender kiss to her lips before pulling back slightly to gaze deeply into her eyes. "You are my dream, Lucy," I whisper, my voice laden with sincerity and love. At that moment, surrounded by luxury and anticipation for our future together, I knew nothing else could compare to the happiness she brought me. Our journey was just beginning, and I promised to cherish every moment we shared as husband and wife, parents, and partners in all things. Hand in hand, we left the boutique, our hearts full of joy and hope for the life we were creating together. As we stepped out into the bustling city streets, I knew that no matter what challenges lay ahead, as long as we faced them together, we would always find our way back to each other. With Lucy by my side, I felt invincible, ready to take on whatever the future held. And with our precious son on the way, our family was bound by a love that would withstand any trial or tribulation.

We climb into our vehicle, and Mici heads to our next destination. I knew Lucy was thrilled.

"Where are we going?" she asks.

"It's a surprise."

Her eyebrows furrowed, and her lips formed a deep pout as she crossed her arms over her chest. I couldn't help but smile at how adorable she looked when she was angry. "I told you, I hate surprises," she grumbled.

Mom and Sophia were trying their best not to laugh. She looked so adorable.

"Love, I promise you will love the surprise." Reaching over, I picked up one of the water bottles and handed it to her.

A heavy sigh escaped her lips as she lifted her gaze to meet mine. The anger that had been burning in her eyes was now replaced by a gentle warmth, and I couldn't help but feel grateful for the woman who held my heart in her hands. Her touch was soft and delicate, yet with a strength that could move mountains.

"Thank you, and I'm sorry. These hormones send my emotions in every different direction," she mutters.

I wrapped my arm around her shoulders and pulled her closer. Placing a kiss on top of her, I whispered. "I love you and all your hormones."

As she leans against me, her chest rising and falling steadily, my inner raven, Corvo, coos with pure joy. He loves her just as much as I do.

"Lucy, hold still for a moment. I want to take your blood pressure before we continue on to our next surprise,"

Sophia says with a gentle smile, reaching into her backpack and pulling out a medical cuff. She moves to Lucy, the sun highlighting the freckles scattered across her cheeks. With practiced ease, she wraps the cuff around Lucy's arm and begins to inflate it, her movements quick and efficient. The soft sound of the air released from the cuff fills the air as she finishes the test.

"How is it?"

"It's higher than this morning, but with all the running around we've been doing, that's to be expected."

Lucy fidgeted, nervously twisting her hands together. "Do you think we should go home?"

Sophia placed a reassuring hand on her arm. "No, it's still above average, but much better than two days ago. I think another stop won't be too taxing."

Her voice was heavy with exhaustion, a soft sigh escaping her lips as she leaned against my shoulder. Her head felt warm and heavy against my skin, her breath's gentle rise and fall lulling me into a peaceful daze. We both closed our eyes, finding comfort in each other's presence.

Several minutes later, we pulled through the estate gates. As we drove through the estate gates, the grandeur of the property never failed to impress me. The sprawling lawns, manicured gardens, and elegant façade of the mansion stood as a testament to the family's success and power. Lucy stirred beside me, her eyes fluttering open as she took in the familiar sight.

"Where are we?" she asked, her voice tinged with curiosity. A few seconds later, she recognized where we were.

As we pulled up in front of the house, I saw three other cars belonging to Andrea, Danti, and Luca. They were here to welcome the newest member to The Famiglia and the next leader of the Genovese Family.

Lucy looks at me with eyes full of excitement. "Is Angelina home already?"

"Yes. Giovanni brought her home this morning. I thought you might want to visit her and the baby."

She throws her arms around my neck and peppers kiss all over my face, whispering thank you between each one.

My hands gently hold her face, my fingers tracing the delicate curves of her features. I peer deeply into her eyes, entranced by their depth and beauty. A warmth spreads throughout my body, like the sun's rays on a bright summer's day, reaching all the way to my soul. It is a love so pure and intense that it fills every corner of my being, making me feel alive and complete. "I love you."

"As I love you," she murmurs against my lips.

Someone raps on the window, breaking the mood. "Alright, Romeo, you already knocked her up," Danti says.

Not taking my eyes away from Lucy, I flip him off. The asshole is going to pay for that comment.

The door opens, and Sophia bounds out of the car. She comes up before Danti and jabs her finger into his chest.

"You big jackass. Don't say things like that," she growls. "She doesn't need to get upset."

I turn to face Lucy, curiosity piqued by the mischievous smirk on her lips. Despite Danti's comment, she remains unfazed and seems entirely enthralled by their interaction. Her eyes sparkle with fascination as she watches our banter unfold before her.

"When did that happen?" she quietly asks.

"Just a few days ago. He walked into the room, and boom. The fireworks exploded between the two of them."

I step out of the car and assist Lucy out. We stop and watch.

Danti's lips curled into a sly, confident smile. "Now, now, Fifi," he drawled, his voice dripping with amusement. "Don't get your delicate panties all twisted up." His eyes glinted mischievously as he taunted her, his sharp wit always one step ahead.

"Fifi? Are you calling me a dog?" Sophia growled, balling up her hand into a fist, and without a moment of hesitation, she punched him in the nose.

Danti grabs his nose as blood sprays. "Damn, Fifi, bloodthirsty much?"

She arched an eyebrow and lightly shrugged her shoulders in exasperation. "I could have aimed for a more sensitive area, but I suppose you desire to bear children in the future," she bites out with a hint of sarcasm. Her words were laced with a mixture of annoyance and amusement as she playfully threatened Danti.

He steps closer, leans down, and whispers something in Sophia's ear. A ray of expression plays out on her face before she turns on her heels and stomps off.

Danti watches with fascination. "I'm going to marry her."

I slap him on the shoulder. "Good luck with that."

Lucy wraps her arm around mine. We walk towards the front door, and as we near it, Giovanni opens it. He looks as if he hasn't slept in days.

"Welcome, everyone," he says, opening the door wide. When Lucy gets close, he looks at her with a smile. "It is so nice to have you home."

"It is nice to be back," she replies.

"Move out of the way, Gio," Danti says. "We are not here to see your ugly face."

Giovanni shakes his head and guides us to the living room. As soon as I walk in, I spot Angelina sitting on a loveseat, holding the baby wrapped in a crimson red blanket with the emblem of The Famiglia stitched. It was customary for all babies born into founding families to be wrapped in a blanket like this when the other families came to visit for the first time.

With a graceful stride, Lucy crosses the room and sits beside Angelina. I can't seem to take my eyes off of her. She radiates an ethereal beauty as she leans over and gazes at the baby in awe. A lump forms in my throat, and I imagine that it will be our turn to experience this same joy and wonder in just a few short months.

Giovanni walks up behind Angelina and places his hand on her shoulder. "Thank you for coming today. Angelina and I are beyond excited to introduce our son, Massimo Drago Genovese."

"Oh, Angelina, I love the name," Lucy coos, running her finger along Massimo's cheek.

I watch them for several minutes. They were animately talking about the baby and other things no man wanted to hear about.

I feel a hand on my shoulder. When I turned, I saw it was Luca. He motions for me to follow him out of the room. We leave the living room and walk down the hall to Giovanni's office. The others were already there with a glass of bourbon in hand. Andrea hands a glass to me while Danti hands one to Luca.

We turn toward Giovanni and raise our glasses. "May your son inherit our legacy, a tapestry of shadows and moonlight. May he learn the art of silence—the Omertà that binds us. For every secret whispered, he shall know its weight, its power. To Massimo."

As we sit, we slam down the bourbon, the amber liquid burning our throats. The room feels suffocating, the weight of the impending event heavy and oppressive. A sense of looming doom hangs in the air, enveloping us in a thick blanket of tension.

"Davide, are you sure you want to go through this?" Luca asks.

"I want to marry Lucy, and this is how I can make it happen."

Luca sighs. "Alright then."

Chapter Thirty-One

Davide

As the car pulled through the gates of The Famiglia, the compound was void of light. Tonight, no one was allowed access except the Commission, our personal guard, and the doctor. After receiving the lashings, I will receive medical care to prevent infection. Even the Disorderly House was closed to members tonight, and the workers were told not to come in.

Mici revs the car to a screeching halt in front of The Commission building. The headlights cut through the darkness like spears, illuminating eight ominous figures standing in front. Four are shrouded in black cloaks, blending into the shadows, while the other four stand out in vibrant crimson. They were the members who made up The Commission. I am a member as well, but not tonight.

I hated leaving Lucy, but I wanted this behind us. To keep her mind occupied during my absence, I arranged for a designer to come to our home with a rack of wedding gowns in her size.

I stepped out of the car, pulling on my crimson cloak, as the chilly night air instantly sent a shiver down my spine. The weight of what would come hung heavily on my shoulders, but I knew there was no turning back now. The familiar faces of The Commission regarded me with stoic expressions, their eyes unreadable in the darkness.

Without a word, I followed them into the building, the heavy wooden doors closing behind me with a resounding thud. The air inside was thick with tension, each step echoing ominously in the silence. With each turn, I still myself for what is about to come. The winding passageways of The Commission building were a labyrinth of traps and false leads, designed to ensnare any intruders with their confusing layout. Each hallway seemed to lead to a dead end or circle back upon itself, creating an endless maze that could easily trap and disorient even the most skilled infiltrator.

As I entered the dimly lit Tomb of the Blooded, where the lashings would take place, I couldn't help but feel a surge of defiance rising within me. The Raven stirred restlessly in my soul, eager for release, but I suppressed its dark urges with practiced control. I needed to do this for Lucy. This was the only way we could have a life together as husband and wife within The Famiglia.

Giovanni, Danti, Andrea, Luca, and the four consigliere take their positions in a semicircle in front of the pillory pole. Over the years, I have witnessed several men shackled to the pole, and punishment for their crimes against The Famiglia has been dispensed. I have seen a man receive a lashing, and images of his back afterward are still vivid memories.

"David Corvo Bonanno, why are you here this evening?" Consigliere Jackson Patterson asks.

Straightening my back, I looked straight into his eyes. "Primo sangue." My voice was hard and void of any emotions. "I also invoke Surrogato Sanguigno."

"Very well, let us begin."

I remove my jacket and shirt and lay them on a nearby chair. I step over to the punishment pole and place my hands next to the shackles. Danti steps over and secures my hands in cold metal. He pats my shoulder and gives me a supportive smile.

Luca steps forward, his face grim and pained by what he is about to do. I glance down at his hand, and in it is the cat o' nine. The handle is wooden and shaped so it can be held comfortably by the person inflicting the punishment. The nine leather straps are knotted at the ends to cause even more damage.

He leans down. "Davide, please don't do this. There has to be another way."

I give him a reassuring smile. "You know there isn't. This is not about me, this is for Lucy and her future within The Famiglia."

He clenches his jaw, and I can see in his eyes that he knows I am right. As much as I would like to say fuck The Famiglia, I can't. The organization was part of a bigger picture. He reaches into his pocket and pulls out a leather bit.

"This will help," he says.

"Thank you." I open my mouth, and he places the leather between my teeth. He walks behind, and I hear him letting out a deep sigh.

The first lash sliced through the air, followed swiftly by a searing pain across my back. The whip tears into my flesh, each strike like fire igniting my nerves. I bit down hard on the bit to stifle any sound that threatened to escape. I could hear the gasps of the others in the room. Even the hardened members of The Commission seemed taken aback by the brutal display.

As Luca continued his task, delivering blow after blow, I focused on a single thought. Lucy. She was the reason for enduring this agony, for facing this brutal punishment without flinching. The future we could have together, free from our past mistakes, fuelled my resolve.

With each strike, the Raven within me cawed and clawed at its cage, desperate for release. But I held firm, refusing to let it sway me from my path. This was a trial I had to endure, a sacrifice I had to make for the woman I loved.

Finally, after what felt like hours, Luca dropped the whip to the ground, his breathing ragged. I slumped against the pole, my back a burning torture of cuts and welts. Danti released my hands, and I stumbled to the nearest chair, collapsing onto it. My body felt like it was on fire, but I knew it would soon heal in time.

The Commission members remained in the room, watching me with sympathy and awe.

Consigliere Patterson steps forward. "Primo sangue has been shed. The marriage between you and Miss Gambino will be recognized by The Famiglia. Anyone speaking against your union will be punished."

"Thank you."

"Davide, are you alright?" Giovanni asks, his voice laced with genuine worry.

I looked up at him, my expression as hard as a stone. "I will be."

Andrea and Danti rush to my side, their faces etched with worry. "We need to get you to the doctor," Andrea says. They hoist me up, my body screaming in protest as the pain intensifies tenfold. Every step feels like a sledgehammer hitting every bone in my body, sending violent vibrations through my entire being. I grit my teeth and try to push through, but each movement only amplifies the agony coursing through me.

We somehow make it out of the tomb, and they drag me toward the hospital we have within the building. The doctor is ready to tend to my wounds when we walk inside. He doesn't say a word nor question how or why my back is how it is.

Once I am stretched out on my stomach, the doctor begins. I haven't seen the damage, but it seems to take forever for the doctor to clean and stitch up the worst spots.

"You must apply the antibacterial creme to the wounds twice a day. Try to leave the bandages off as much as possible. If you are wearing a shirt, you need to cover up the wounds until they heal."

I nod in acknowledgment, the pain still reverberating through every fiber of my being. As the doctor finishes tending to my wounds, I slowly sit up, feeling the pull and sting of each movement. Andrea and Danti offered their support, helping me get dressed once again. Despite the agony, a sense of relief washed over me. The lashings were over, and Lucy and I could finally have a chance at a future together.

After leaving the hospital room, Luca approaches me with a solemn expression. "Davide, I know this wasn't easy for you. But your sacrifice will not be forgotten."

I meet his gaze, gratitude flickering in my eyes. "Thank you, Luca. I did what needed to be done."

As we return to the main hall of The Commission building, the weight of what transpired settles upon me. The path ahead would still be fraught with challenges and dangers, but I will face them all for Lucy.

Suddenly, Mici ran toward us. "Davide, Marco is on the phone. It sounds bad."

I take the phone, placing it on speaker for the others to hear. "What is wrong, Marco?" He doesn't say anything but in the background, it sounds like World War Three has broken out. Multiple gunfire and explosions echoed through the call. "Marco?"

"Davide, all hell has broken loose in Brighton Beach."

"What is happening?"

"Dominick is dead. His right-hand man has staged a coup. He has the majority of Dominick's men on his side."

"Who is he?" I've always seen the man by Dominick's side. He was the same height as Dom but bulkier, with a scar across his right cheek and evil eyes.

"Ivan Volkov. His father was ex-KGB and was murdered in a coup of rival families. Ivan was injured during the fighting."

"Do you have any reason why he is doing this?"

"No. It was him all along. He orchestrated the missing shipments on both sides, pitting us against each other like puppets. The man close to Dominick called me after the murder and said Ivan was nuts. Going on about how the Little Sparrow got away."

Why did that sound so familiar? "Little sparrow?"

I feel a hand grasp my arm. When I look, I see it is Luca, who looks as if he has seen a ghost. "Did he say little sparrow?"

"Yes."

"Davide, that is what Dominick called Lucy when she found herself lost on Brighton Beach all those years ago," Luca says.

I shake my head as a chill runs through my body. Was Ivan talking about Lucy? "Luca, call Lucy."

Luca pulls out his phone and dials. It rings and rings, but she doesn't answer.

I disconnected the call and dialed the guard who was watching over Lucy. The call rang and rang. I took off running, forging through the unbelievable pain on my back. Nothing was going to stop me from getting to Lucy.

"Davide, wait up," Luca says, rushing beside me. "You're hurt."

"Don't fucking care. I have to get to her."

Busting through the doors of The Commission, I saw my car parked out front. I jump in the back, with Luca, Danti, Andrea, and Giovanni piling behind me. Mici jumps in the front seat, and we take off and go down the driveway. The momentum of the car pushes me back against the seat, and I groan out in pain. "FUCK."

"Davide, you need to take it easy, or you're going to bust open the stitches," Danti urges.

"She is more important than my fucking back."

We speed through the streets, weaving through traffic with blaring sirens echoing in the background. The news broadcasts fill the car with talk of chaos in Brighton Beach, but I can't focus on that. I have one priority: Lucy.

The car screeches through the open gate, and I see the bodies of my men lying on the ground. When we reach the front of the house, my heart stops. The guards are lying dead, and the front door is standing wide open. I jump from the car, gun drawn, and rush into the house with the others behind me.

"Lucy!" I listen, and nothing. My heart hammers in my chest. "Lucy!"

A desperate cry of "Davide!" echoes through the empty house, clawing at my heart and sending shivers down my spine. I sprint toward the source, my feet pounding against the wooden floor, until I come upon the sight of my mother sprawled on the ground. White wedding dress stained with blood. She reaches out to me with trembling fingers, her eyes beseeching for help. My breath catches in my throat as I take in the horrific scene before me.

I drop down and groan with pain. "Mom, what happened?"

"He took them."

"Took who?"

"Lucy and Sophia."

"Who took them?"

"I don't know. He had a scar on his face and called Lucy, little sparrow."

Chapter Thirty-Two

Lucy

"Oh, Lucy, the dress is perfect," Nan says with a warm smile

She is right. The dress is everything I have ever wanted in a wedding. The long, flowy sleeves and sharp "v" of the neckline would give Davide access to put his tattoo on me above my left breast during the marking ceremony. With a high waist, it showed off my baby bump, but with a touch of elegance.

I turn and give the designer a large smile. "This is the one."

"Wonderful, dear. It looks lovely on you and fits you like it was made for you."

"Thank you."

After I slip back into my comfortable clothes, Sophia performs her usual evening check, smiling satisfiedly as she reads the numbers. Despite the busy day with extra activities, my blood pressure remained acceptable. For the first time in a week, I allow myself to believe that our precious baby will enter this world strong and healthy. A rush of warmth and joy fills me, wrapping me in a cozy blanket on a cold winter night.

The realization that I am about to marry Davide, with the blessing of The Famiglia, still feels surreal. It's like every dream I ever dared to have is coming true. My heart swells with overwhelming joy and disbelief. I never could have imagined this moment in my wildest fantasies. And yet, here I am, three days away from becoming his wife. The love between us is palpable and undeniable. From how he looks at me, I know he loves me just as fiercely as I love him. At this moment, there is no room for doubt or fear. Only pure, unadulterated happiness and the promise of a future filled with love and devotion.

Sophia puts her instruments in her medical backpack and pulls out her phone. As she scrolls through her social media feed, she gasps.

"What is it, Sophia?"

"The house in which you were living in Brighton Beach has been burnt to the ground."

I lean over, and she shows me her screen. The news feed shows the charred remains of the little house I poured myself into and made my home. It was my safe haven when I thought all was lost with Davide.

"Who would have done this?" I say, shocked by the news.

"That would be me, Little Sparrow," a deep voice calls out.

My heart races as I spin around to face a man with piercing, ice-cold eyes standing in the doorway. My blood runs cold as I take in the sight of the gun glinting in his hand. The words he speaks, "Little Sparrow," send shivers down my spine. I gasp for air, struggling to process the memories flooding back. The last time I heard those words was when Dominick and his henchman caught up to me in that dark alleyway in Brighton Beach all those years ago. As I study the man's face, it hits me with a jolt of fear - this is one of Dominic's men.

A sinister smile breaks out across his face. "Oh, so you remember me, Little Sparrow."

"How did you get in here?" I ask.

"Bonanno's men were weak and unprepared. I am not."

"What do you want?"

He steps closer and reaches out. As soon as he does, Nan jumps in front of me.

"You will not touch her," she growls.

Without hesitation, he backhands her, causing her to fly against the rack of wedding gown. She lands hard against the stone fireplace.

"Nan," I cry out. I go to reach for her when I am jerked back against my assailant.

"I've waited for you for a long time, and no one will stand in my way. Not the Bonanno's guard, not the old woman, and especially not Dominic Mogilevich. The asshole thought he could tell me no. Well, he is no longer in charge."

"What do you mean?"

"I killed the motherfucker because no one is going to stand in my way to get you. You are mine," he says, then looks down at my belly. "And don't worry about that. I'll raise him or her as my own."

My heart is pounding in my chest, and I can barely swallow past the lump in my throat. I search for any weapon, any way to protect myself and my unborn child. The man releases me, and I step back, my eyes darting around the room for an escape route.

Sophia grabs a clear glass vase from the windowsill and swings it at his head. He dodges it gracefully and lunges at her, wrapping his arm around her neck in a chokehold. I watch helplessly as she struggles to break free, her eyes pleading with me to do something. He shoves her to the ground.

As he approaches me again, a sadistic grin is on his face, and I remember his name, Ivan. Needing to escape, I spot the leather-bound ledger on the table and snatch it up, hoping to use it against him. He freezes momentarily, his eyes widening as he realizes what I've got. I pounce on this hesitation, throwing the ledger at him with all my strength. It hits him squarely in the face, and he stumbles back, clutching his nose. I seize the opportunity to run towards the door, but he's faster.

He grabs me from behind and wraps his arm tight around my waist, pulling me back against him. I struggle and kick, trying to break free. He whispers into my ear, "I've waited for so long, little bird. I'm not letting you escape again."

I'm trembling with fear, not just for my own life, but for my unborn child. The man tightens his grip on me, making it hard for me to breathe. He's so strong, and I'm so weak, withering under the weight of my pregnancy. My mind races, trying to devise a plan to save us both. The room spins, and my head pounds, and then a sharp pain cuts across my stomach. I hunch over, grasping my belly. Oh no, something is wrong with the baby. I can't lose our little boy.

"Let me check on her," Sophia pleads.

"No," Ivan barks.

"Please. I am her nurse. She has a condition, and if it goes unchecked, she could die."

I glance up at Ivan and plead with tear-filled eyes.

"Alright, but you can do it in the vehicle. We need to leave now," he says, gripping my arm and pulling me.

My eyes dart to Sophia, who gives me a slight nod before reaching for her trusty physician backpack. I know all too well that it holds not only the instruments to monitor my preeclampsia, but also a hidden compartment where she keeps Pearly. Her cherished pearl-handled handgun. We share this bond of being sharpshooters, always prepared for any danger that may arise.

"What is that?" Ivan asks.

"My medical bag," Sophia replies.

Ivan looks over at one of his guys. "Search it."

The guy grabs the bag and begins looking through it. He pulls out a scalpel and throws it to the floor. "It is clean."

"Hurry, before we're caught," he hisses, yanking me through the blood-soaked house. Davide's men lay scattered on the floor in gruesome heaps. The stench of iron and death permeates the air. An ominous black SUV screeches to a halt outside. "Get in now!" His voice is low and dangerous as he shoves me towards the vehicle, his grip like a vice on my arm.

Sophia climbs in, and I follow. Ivan gets in beside me, and the vehicle takes off when the door closes. Panic fills me as we speed down the long driveway and onto the street.

"Lucy, take deep breaths for me," Sophia says as she pulls out the blood pressure cuff and secures it to my arm. "In for two seconds and out for four seconds."

I try to follow her instructions, but the fear and adrenaline make it difficult. My heart races, and my breath catches in my throat. The SUV takes a turn too fast, and I lurch against Ivan. He squeezed my arm again, clarifying that he would not let me escape.

"I won't let you take away my child," I whisper through clenched teeth.

"Your child?" Ivan chuckled, placing his hand on my stomach. "No, Little Sparrow. This is mine now."

"No," I say, shaking my head. "I won't let you do this. Davide will come for us."

A sinister grin breaks out across his lips. "Davide Bonanno and the late Dominic Mogilevich are or were nothing but weaklings, their brains no brighter than a flickering candle. For years, I've been swiping their precious merchandise right from under their noses, selling it to the highest bidder, and manipulating them into blaming each other for the losses. Despite my blatant disrespect and sabotage, these fools did nothing but cower in fear and let me continue to run rampant. It was both pathetic and infuriating to see such feeble *mafia bosses* unable to defend their own territory."

"Why me?"

"You were mine since the day you stumbled into that dark alleyway. The moment I saw you, I knew I had to have you. But Dominic intervened and sent you back to your brother, denying me what was rightfully mine. That's when I started plotting my takeover of the Bravta, all for the sole purpose of claiming you as my own. I became obsessed with you, watching your every move for years. I even made trips to Italy just to ensure your loyalty to me. And then fate brought you to Brighton Beach, a clear sign you were meant to be with me. You even changed your hair to match my favorite color, red, which only enhances your natural beauty in my eyes."

I glance at Sophia and see she is feeling the same way I am. Ivan is definitely crazy.

"Then what happened to Dominic?" I ask, trying to distract myself from the horrifying thought of what might be happening to my baby right now.

Ivan laughs manically. "He got in my way. I couldn't have you without getting rid of him first. It was an accident, really. I didn't mean for things to go so far. But once I had the chance to take him out, I knew I couldn't let anyone else get in the way. You're meant to be mine."

The SUV accelerated as he spoke, never breaking its monstrous pace. His gaze never left me, and I could feel his eyes burning into my skin and drilling into my soul.

"Please," I whispered, my voice barely above a whisper. "Please, don't hurt my baby."

Ivan's eyes softened for a moment, but only for a moment. "Oh, I won't hurt your baby. I will protect it. I will be its father, just as I am yours."

I recoiled in disgust, my stomach churning. "You're sick. You're worse than a monster."

He smiled a cold, predatory smile that made my skin crawl. "And you are my prey. You always have been."

My heart pounded against my chest, and I felt like I was suffocating with fear. I glanced at Sophia, and she mouthed the words "stay calm."

I took a deep breath, trying to steady my nerves. I had to put on a brave face for Sophia's sake and mine. We were in this together, and there was no escape for either of us. I need to remain calm so I can be of help when the time comes to escape. Closing my eyes, I think of Davide. I replay every second of our reunion. I can't help but think of the last few moments we spent together, how his dark brown eyes locked onto mine, filled with a love that still lingers in my heart. I remember how he would hold my hand, his strong fingers intertwined with mine, as if trying to etch his love onto my skin, something that would never fade away. I can still feel the warmth of his touch, the comfort it brought. My eyes well up with tears, but I shake my head to clear my emotions. I need to focus. There's a life inside of me that depends on me.

Sophia gently pats my hand, trying to reassure me. Her eyes are just as determined as mine, fixed on the road, alert for any sign of danger. "Lucy, take a deep breath," she says, her voice filled with resolve.

I take a deep breath, trying to follow her advice. What could be happening to my baby? I take another deep breath, and suddenly, something occurs to me. Davide, the face of the Bonanno Crime Family, is bound to come for us. He will protect his legacy and his people. His soul may be tainted by the darkness of the Famiglia, but in his heart, he's my soon-to-be loving husband, a caring son, loyal friend, and fierce protector of our unborn son.

I glance at Sophia, and in her eyes, I see the same determination that burns within me. We nod to one another and brace ourselves for whatever lies ahead. This is our reality now - a fight for survival.

The SUV takes a sharp turn, and I lurch against Ivan again. He holds me fast, his grip like an iron vice. I can feel his breath against my neck, hot and stale. I try to shake him off, but his hold is too strong.

"Please," I beg, "leave my baby alone."

Ivan laughs, a cruel sound that echoes in my ears. "Your baby is already mine."

My heart sinks, and I feel like I'm drowning in despair. How can this be happening? How can I have a child with such a monster?

Just then, the SUV screeches to a halt. Ivan opens the door, and I stumble out, my legs shaking. The air outside is chilly, but I can't feel anything but the cold, hard grip of fear.

Sophia gets out, too, by my side. We stand together, our faces pale, our eyes wide with terror, as Ivan leads us toward the dark, looming structure before us. I reach out and take Sophia's hand. Together, we will get away.

Chapter Thirty-Three

Davide

Why did Ivan take Lucy? Had they run into each other while she was in Brighton Beach? But why was he calling her Little Sparrow? I was missing something, but I don't know what.

These questions have been playing in a loop in my brain for the last twenty-four hours. The Famiglia doctor checked out Mom. Other than a slight concussion and a head wound, she was going to be okay physically. Mentally, though, she was beating herself up for not protecting Lucy.

As soon as I found my home destroyed and Lucy gone, I wanted to go to Brighton Beach, guns blazing. However, my brothers talked me out of it. As much as I hated to admit it, they were right. We needed as much intel as possible to get Lucy and Sophia out of Ivan's hands. Marco, my contact within the Bratva, had gone radio silent since he called with his news. Without his intel, we were blind.

As I gaze out the window, the evening sky ignites in a blaze of red and orange. The deep hues paint the horizon with an almost otherworldly glow. It's as if Mother Nature herself is throwing one last obstacle in our path, taunting us with her unpredictable power. My heart clenches with worry as I try to navigate through this added challenge on top of everything else.

A monstrous hurricane barrels towards us with fierce determination. Its winds rage at a dangerous Cat3 level, but the forecasters warn that it will only gain strength and become a Category 4 beast before landfall. The eye of this tempest will strike with unrelenting force, aiming straight for the shoreline and Brighton Beach, leaving nothing in its path undamaged or standing.

Ivan was somewhere in Brighton Beach, holding Lucy and Sophia captive. Not only were they in danger from Ivan and whatever his plan was, but they were also on the path of this killer hurricane. Of course, the name of the hurricane was Nyx, the Greek goddess feared by Zeus.

I couldn't shake off the feeling of dread that clawed at my insides. The impending storm was a cruel twist of fate, adding another layer of chaos to an already dire situation. Nyx, the goddess of night and the formidable force of nature, seemed to mirror the darkness that threatened to swallow Lucy and Sophia whole.

But I refused to let despair take hold. I clenched my jaw, steeling myself for the battle ahead. As the storm loomed closer, its shadow stretching over the city like a shroud of doom, I made a silent vow. No matter what obstacles stood in my way—be it Ivan or the wrath of Nyx herself—I would find Lucy and Sophia. I would bring them back safely, no matter the cost.

As we waited with bated breath for updates, a team of skilled workers diligently restored the once beautiful house and grounds to their former glory. The memory of my men who were ruthlessly taken from us in the attack weighed heavily on our hearts, but their families were being looked after and provided for by The Famiglia. With so many of our own lost, The Famiglia had dispatched a contingent of highly trained guards to protect the property and ensure our safety as we prepared for the inevitable strike against Ivan. Their presence brought comfort and reassurance amidst the chaos and uncertainty.

"Davide, we have someone at the gate wanting to speak to you?" Danti announces, coming into the room. He and the other founding sons had taken residence in my home. I didn't know if it was to have a centralized location for information, or if they were making sure I didn't go to Brighton Beach alone. Either way, I appreciated them being here. Sophia's father was also staying. After we found out that Lucy had been kidnapped as well as Sophia, Giovanni called Consigliere Theo Croft. The five families were very aware of the dangers of being part of the mafia. The men who became part of The Commission also knew the dangers. That is why all of us have security details. The amount of men on guard the night of the attack should have been enough. When I get her back, I will never make that mistake again.

"Who?"

"Vladimir Mogilevich. He is Dominic's brother."

"What does he want?"

"He says he will only speak to you personally."

"Is he alone?"

"He has only one man with him."

"Search them and take any weapons."

"Are you sure?" Luca asks.

"Not really, but we need to hear what he wants?" I reply.

I nodded to Danti to let Vladimir Mogilevich and his companion in. As they entered the room, I could feel the tension crackling in the air. Vladimir's steely gaze met mine, his expression unreadable. He looks around the room and takes in the others. Beside him stood a burly man whose eyes darted around the room warily.

"Davide Bonanno," Vladimir's voice was smooth but laced with an underlying uncertainty, then turned toward the others. "I see you have aligned with the other families. It is a pleasure to meet you all, Mr. Genovese, Mr. Colombo, Mr. Lucchese, and Mr. Gambino."

"They are assisting me in getting my wife back," I say. Lucy isn't legally my wife, but in the eyes of these men, she is.

"And I might be of help with that. I have come to you bearing a proposition."

I gestured for them to sit, my gaze never leaving Vladimir's face. "Let's hear it then."

He leaned forward, his hands clasped together on the table. "Ivan has murdered my brother to take over the family. His actions of taking your wife have endangered the delicate balance between our organizations. I propose a temporary alliance between our families to take him down."

I raised an eyebrow in surprise. The Mogilevich and Bonanno families had always been rivals, locked in a perpetual power struggle. The idea of working together seemed almost absurd, but given the gravity of the situation, I knew desperate times called for desperate measures. Ivan had not only threatened Lucy and Sophia, but had also disrupted the fragile peace between our families. As much as I despised aligning with the Mogileviches, I couldn't ignore the opportunity to strike back at Ivan and rescue my loved ones.

"Under what conditions would this alliance operate?" I asked, my tone guarded.

Vladimir leaned back in his chair, a calculating glint in his eyes. "We will share intel and resources to bring Ivan down. Once he is out of the picture, we go our separate ways, no blood debts owed."

I mulled over his proposal carefully. Trust was a scarce commodity in our world, and forming an alliance with an old enemy was risky. But with Lucy and Sophia's lives hanging in the balance, I knew I had to put aside personal vendettas for now.

"I will agree if you know that our main objective is to rescue Lucy and Sophia," I finally replied.

"But I am the one who will kill the motherfucker who took my brother's life. The ones who have elected to follow this asshole are fair game," Vladimir states in a voice with no room for negotiating.

I look at Luca, Danti, Giovanni, Andrea, and Theo. Agreeing to this without going before The Commission was going to be an issue. However, no one outside of the Society knows anything about The Famiglia. Each of my brothers gives me a slight nod of support, as does Theo. Whatever happens with The Commission after this, we will face this united. The only thing I was having issues with was that I wouldn't be the one to make Ivan suffer for laying his hands on Lucy. The need for blood was almost unbearable, yet I could let it pass. Ivan would die, and there was no doubt Vladimir would make him suffer.

"We have a deal," I say, holding out my hand. Vladimir takes it and shakes it. The deal is made, and I must now just trust that he will stand by it.

"Then let us begin," Vladimir says and motions to the man beside him. He opens a briefcase and pulls out a set of maps and drawings. I motioned for him to place them on the large table in the middle of the room. Once they are laid out, Vladimir begins, "This is where Ivan is. From the Intelligence I have received, he believes his plan has gone off without a hitch."

"Doesn't he think you will take revenge for killing your brother?" Danti asks.

"I haven't been here in many years. I run the family business in Russia. He might have forgotten I even existed. Dom and I only spoke privately. Last month, Dom told me about some suspicious activities that were happening. Even though there was evidence Bonannos was responsible for some shipments coming up missing, he didn't believe it was you. Dom had become unsure of the loyalty of some of his men," Vladimir says.

I looked at the map and saw that the house where Ivan had Lucy was actually over the line into Manhattan. The large house was sitting right on the fucking beach in the direct line of the hurricane. "Fuck. Giovanni, how long will it be until Nyx makes landfall?"

He begins typing on his tablet and studies the information. The Famiglia has access to multiple weather satellites and radars.

"Fuck. It has picked up speed and is coming in fast, Davide. The storm's outer edge could land within the next few hours. We need to act quickly. There is a mandatory evacuation," Giovanni says.

I glance at Vladimir, who remains calm and collected, studying the maps intently. "What do we do? Time is running out for Lucy and Sophia," I say, my voice trembling with fear.

Vladimir meets my gaze, his eyes hard and determined. "Ivan won't leave. He thinks he is invincible. We strike now, catching Ivan off-guard before the brunt of the storm hits. We'll split into two teams: one to neutralize Ivan's men and take Ivan hostage, and the other to rescue Lucy and Sophia. Once we have them safe, we can focus on taking down the rest of Ivan's operation and figuring out who is still loyal to the Mogilevichs. The information I have is that Ivan's loyal followers are under fifty men, maybe less. The ones still loyal to the family have been biding their time until I arrived."

"How would they know you would come?" I ask.

Raising an eyebrow. "Because it is what family does."

"Vladimir, I must inform you that Lucy is with a child and facing severe complications. Sophia, a skilled midwife, has diligently monitored her blood pressure and provided care to keep both mother and baby safe. We must be fully prepared for the worst in case her condition has deteriorated since she was taken. Her trusted doctor and an ambulance will be on constant alert, ready to whisk her away to the nearest hospital as soon as she is found."

"Do what you must," Vladimir says, his features softening. "Now, round up your men. Mine are waiting at a warehouse on the western edge of Brighton Beach."

"Do you need weapons?" Andrea asks.

A small grin forms on his lips. "Het. We are covered."

"We will meet you at the warehouse in four hours," I say.

"Good. I will leave these for you to familiarize yourself with the house and warehouse location." Vladimir turns and leaves with the man who never spoke a word.

After he is escorted out, I turn to the others. "We need everyone we can get. Giovanni, is it okay if the other family members come to your home so we can secure one location inside of all of them?"

"Of course."

"Alright, everyone, get your family members to Giovanni's. Put on extra security, and all those left, have them meet us here in an hour and a half. I know it is not much time, but we must make this happen. Theo, I know we have gone through The Commission, but we need The Famiglia guard."

"Let me make a call," Theo says. He pulls out his phone and dials. Moments later, he sits it down on the table. "Gentlemen, we have a situation. As you know, Lucy and Sophia were kidnapped. The founding sons are mounting an attack to rescue them. There is no time to come before The Commission in a formal meeting."

"What is the request?" Consigliere Butler asks.

"We need the Grande Armie," Theo answers.

Fuck, how had I forgotten about them? The Grande Armie was the most skilled and deadliest group in the world. The Grande Armie was an elite squad of assassins hand-picked by The Commission. They were the last resort in any situation and were only called upon in the most desperate circumstances.

"The Grande Armie?" Butler repeated in disbelief. "You want to call them in for this? We're talking about kidnapping here, not a full-scale war."

"I know, but we're running out of time," Theo said. "And this is no ordinary kidnapping. Ivan Mogilevich has crossed a line by taking not just anyone. He took a founding daughter, someone who is the future wife of a founding son and also the mother of the next generation of The Famiglia."

"He also took your daughter," Butler said.

"Yes, he did. My daughter has studied hard to help wives of The Famiglia to give birth to the next generation."

"Is there anything else we need to know before we hold an election?" Butler asked.

I look at everyone, silently asking if I should tell them about Vladimir and his proposal. Even if the others didn't like it, we had the majority votes. "We have received vital intel of where Lucy and Sophia are being held. We need the extra manpower to rescue them."

"That is great news. We will prepare the tomb for Ivan," Consigliere Patterson said.

"We won't be the ones who will be dealing with Ivan," Luca states.

"Why not?" Butler asks.

There was no sugar coating, which would make this go down any easier. "Because Vladimir Mogilevich wants revenge for the death of his brother."

A deadly silence fell. It was so quiet Theo looked down to see if the call had been disconnected.

"How do you know Vladimir Mogilevich wants revenge?" Butler asks.

"Because Vladimir was just my home," I reply and pause before continuing. "For his assistance, I agreed to allow him to take justice for his brother's death."

"What authorizes you to make a deal with our enemy?" Butler snaps.

How dare he speak to me like that. Corvo, who has been on edge since Lucy's kidnapping, slams against his cage door, breaking free. His darkness cloaks over me. I unleash a roar that would send fear down the strongest of men. "I am Davide Corvo Bonanno, leader of the Bonanno crime family and a founding son of The Famiglia. You, Lee Butler, are only an elected Consigliere of The Famiglia with limited rights. But none of those rights allows you to question my authority."

Silence fills the room. The men stand frozen, unable to process the transformation before them. Once calm and collected, Corvo's voice now echoes with the primal power of the Raven. It was a sound they had never heard before, leaving them shaken and afraid.

"What are you planning?" Butler finally manages to ask.

"We need to act fast with the Grande Armie and Vladimir's assistance," I say, my voice reverberating with the same intensity as Corvo. "Ivan's men have not yet realized the full extent of the storm. If we catch them off-guard, we can save Lucy and Sophia and neutralize Ivan's loyal followers. It is not only my authority as a founding son, but our duty as The Famiglia to ensure the safety of our own."

"How are you going to explain Grande Armie?" Butler asks.

"The Grande Armie are wise enough to disguise themselves as the personal guard of any founding son. When Vladimir was here earlier, he didn't even question why the other crime families were here. So, if this is your last stupid question, I say we vote."

Chapter Thirty-Four

Davide

Our convoy of black, fortified SUVs hurtles through the desolate streets of New York. Mandatory evacuations have emptied the coastline, leaving only a few brave souls to face nature's wrath. Gale-force winds batter our vehicles, and torrential rain obscures our vision as we barrel down the abandoned city streets. I watch horror as the drivers navigate debris and fallen power lines. Their lightning-fast reflexes dodging whatever obstacles the storm has thrown in our path.

Without delay, we gathered our supplies to rescue Lucy and Sophia right after the vote. Dr. Bianchi and Dr. Amato were immediately summoned, ready to handle any potential medical crisis. With our loved ones safely guarded at Giovanni's stronghold, a small army stood watch to protect them at all costs. We raced towards The Famiglia compound, which boasted an armory that would make any military drool with envy. It is stocked with enough weaponry to take on an entire nation.

The Grande Armie joined us at the armory, and we filled them in on the situation. I clench my jaw. My gut coils with tension as I anticipate the confrontation with the Russian mafia. The scent of gun oil fills the air, mixing with the acrid tang of fear that hangs heavy over us all. The men around me exchange grim glances, their hands resting on the handles of their weapons. We are a formidable force, united by a common goal and bound by loyalty to each other and The Famiglia.

As we gear up for the imminent battle, I glimpse Lucy's face in my mind's eye. Her delicate features are etched with worry, her eyes haunted by the uncertainty of our situation. I steel myself against the flood of emotions threatening to overwhelm me and focus on the task. We will not rest until she and Sophia safely return to our arms.

The convoy screeches to a halt outside the warehouse, and I step out into the howling wind and rain, my senses on high alert. I glance around and notice no lights on any of the buildings near us or any street lights. The storm must have knocked out the power.

Suddenly, the door opens. "Do Americans like standing out in the middle of a storm?" Vladimir says with a smirk.

For some reason, I like this Russian. "Het."

"Ah, do you have Russian blood running through those veins?"

"No, fucking way. I am a hot-blooded Italian."

Vladimir lets a booming laugh. "Come, let's get ready."

As Vladimir leads me inside the warehouse. Instead of darkness, the warehouse is bathed in light. "We have generators."

We make our way deeper into the heart of the compound. Men armed to the teeth stand guard, their eyes cold and watchful. My inner demon, The Raven, stirs within me, its hunger for vengeance palpable.

Vladimir turns to me, his gaze sharp. "We must proceed with caution. Ivan will not give up Lucy and Sophia without a fight."

"We are ready."

"Then let's go finish this." He turns and yells out to his men in Russian, and they quickly get to their feet and begin getting into the many SUVs. Large bay doors open, and the force of the storm pours in.

I turn back to Luca. "I won't stop until she is safely back with us."

"Neither will I. My little sister loves you so much, and I can see that the feelings are mutual. You are a good man, and I consider you my brother."

"Me too. Now load up."

As we load up into the SUVs, the tension in the air is as thick as the storm raging outside. The engines roar to life, drowning out the howling wind, and we set off toward our destination with grim determination etched on our faces. My mind races with thoughts of Lucy and Sophia, their safety paramount above all else.

The convoy moves like a well-oiled machine, each vehicle keeping pace with the others as we barrel through the rain-soaked streets. As we near Ivan's house, a sense of foreboding settles over me like a shroud. I grip the handle of my weapon, my knuckles turning white with tension, ready for the confrontation that awaits us.

As we approach the mansion, the storm intensifies, the wind howling like a pack of wolves, shaking the very foundations of the house. The sky is a blanket of darkness, lit only by occasional lightning. The air is thick with tension, a palpable sense of anticipation as we prepare for the inevitable battle ahead. It's a war, not just between two families, but between two worlds, two ideologies.

We park our vehicles in a line, forming a barrier against the storm and the enemy. The sky roars in protest as the rain lashes down, pelting against the windows of the cars. As I inhale deeply, gun oil and rain mingle in my nostrils. I'm not afraid. This time, it's not for me. I'm fighting for Lucy, Sophia, and the family I was a part of. I'm fighting for the Bonanno name, the Bonanno legacy.

After a last look at our vehicles, I stepped out into the storm. The wind whipped at my clothes, and icy chilly rain blew on my face. I turned to my brothers, ready to face whatever awaits us on the other side of this storm.

We trudge through at least a foot of water as we approach the mansion. This will only get worse by the minute. The storm surge was predicted to be over eight feet, and that was before the hurricane even hit. I press on towards the looming mansion, my heart racing as I see no one at the post. Ivan's incompetent guards are nowhere to be found, leaving him vulnerable to our attack. A twisted grin spreads across my face as I realize this can only benefit us.

The Grande Armie begins their assault alongside Vladimir's men, each movement calculated and precise, almost like a dance. It was a dance, a lethal one. They were instructed on the objective of the offense. Lucy and Sophia were our priority, and Ivan was Vladimir's.

We launch our attack in a coordinated strike that catches Ivan's forces off guard. I can see the fear in their eyes as we take control of the mansion, their entire operation falling apart like a house of cards.

The Grande Armie was a sight to behold, a force of precision and destruction. Every movement was meticulously choreographed to inflict maximum carnage on their enemies. No mercy, no hesitation, just relentless pursuit of the kill.

We round the corner to find Ivan, the rogue leader, tied to a chair. It shouldn't have surprised me, but it does. Sophia and Lucy have guns pointed at him. I recognize the pearl-handle gun as the one Sophia owns. However, the one Lucy is holding is not hers. It was a gold Glock-T. She is sexy as hell.

"Who is that woman holding my brother's gun?" Vladimir whispers.

"She is my wife."

"Damn. I was hoping she was single. I've never seen a woman hold a gun like she does. Does she know how to shoot?"

I smirk at the question. "Yes, she is deadly."

Vladimir's hand slams into my back, sending a shock of pain through my body. The ache I was barely containing now ignites into a blazing inferno, consuming me from the inside out. I know some of the stitches have pulled open with all the movement. I take a deep breath, and Lucy looks over her shoulder as I do. She looks pale and tired. What can of hell had this motherfucker put her through?

"Kill the fucker, kill the fucker, kill the fucker," Corvo chanted.

"Davide," she says with her eyes full of unshed tears. She takes one more glance at Ivan and raises the gun.

"Lucy, stop."

"He deserves to die."

"Yeah, babe. But let us handle it."

She looks back at me and then back at Ivan. I watch her clench her jaw as she considers it. She takes several deep breaths before lowering her arm. "Fuck it. Sophia, let's get out of here."

Vladimir's men grab Ivan and start dragging him out of the room.

"Little sparrow, I know you love me," he yells.

Lucy shakes her head. I move to her and pull her into my arms.

"Get me out of here."

"Gladly, my love."

Luca comes over and places a kiss on top of her head. "Hey, Lulu."

Lucy looks up and gives him a weak smile. "It is about time."

She sways on her feet, and suddenly, her eyes roll back. I catch her before she collapses on the floor.

"SOPHIA!" I scream.

She tucks her gun in her waistband before picking up her backpack. "Put her on the couch. I need to check her blood pressure."

I gently put her on the couch and step back, allowing Sophia to check on Lucy. She places the blood pressure cuff on and growls after a few minutes. "FUCK! WE NEED TO GET HER TO A HOSPITAL ASAP."

"Dr. Richardson is waiting down the street," I say.

"Then let's get the fuck going. Her blood pressure is dangerously high."

Ignoring the pain, I picked Lucy back up and took off through the mansion. As we neared the door, I saw the storm had increased in power. The water was now up to the second step, which meant it was at least two feet. Driving through this was going to be very slow going or even impossible. I will if I have to carry Lucy the five blocks to the ambulance.

We finally reached the vehicles and piled in, soaking wet but determined. I laid Lucy on the seat, and Sophia sat down beside her. She hooked up again to the blood pressure monitor and listened to her heart.

"Davide, we have to hurry."

"I know, Sophia. Mici, get us to the ambulance as quickly as possible."

"Okay, boss," he said, putting the vehicle in gear and pulling away. As we drove away from the mansion, I saw that the water level had risen even further, and the wind was picking up speed. We were clearly leaving a war zone behind us, and I couldn't shake the feeling that this was just the beginning.

"Is she going to be alright?" I ask.

Suddenly, Lucy shook violently. "What is happening?"

"She is having a seizure," Sophia answers.

"What can I do?"

"Just help me keep her on the seat."

Sophia reaches into her backpack and pulls out a vile amount of medicine and a syringe. "What is that?"

"Carbamazepine. It is to help with the seizure. We need to stop it before it does any damage to her brain."

Oh my God. I can't lose her now. Then a thought hits me. "What about the baby?"

Sophia looks at me with concern. "I don't know. We need to get to the hospital as soon as possible. We don't have time to worry about that right now. I'll do everything in our power to ensure she's okay."

The fierce wind howls like a beast, rocking the vehicle as if it were a mere toy in its grasp. My heart races as I watch Mici expertly navigate through the treacherous water and debris mercilessly strewn across the road. Despite his skill, I know one wrong move could send us tumbling into a watery grave. As the storm's full force looms, I can only imagine the catastrophic devastation that awaits us.

Sophia sighed, and I saw that Lucy had quit seizing. "Help me roll her to her side in case she vomits."

I gently roll her and rub my hand down her cheek. My beautiful girl has been through so much, and there is no one to blame but me. "Why is not waking up?"

"I don't know. I hope it is her body taking time to heal itself. Once we get her in the hospital, we will have more answers. For now, we monitor her."

I take her hand in mine, wanting her to know I am with her. Looking out the windshield, I breathe a sigh of relief when I see the flashing lights of the ambulance ahead. We pulled up beside it, and the ambulance's back door opened as soon as we did. Dr. Bianchi and Dr. Amato climbed out wearing raincoats and rubber boots. I opened the door as they approached.

Dr. Richardson looks in and sees Lucy lying on the seat. "What happened?"

Sophia comes forward. "She is in eclampsia. Her blood pressure is held at 160/110 even after the dose of nifedipine. She seized ten minutes ago, and I gave her carbamazepine."

"Alright, we need to get her in the ambulance and to the hospital," Dr. Bianchi says. "Can you carry her?"

I nod and turn to lift her. Once I have her in my arms, Dr. Amato removes his raincoat and drapes it over her body. I step down from the SUV, water coming up to my knees. Slowly, I shuffle over to the back of the ambulance. Dr. Amato climbs in, takes Lucy from my arms, and then places her on the gurney. Dr. Bianchi climbs in, and they hook her up to the machines and put an oxygen cannula on her.

The space is cramped with the two doctors and the gurney. There isn't a space I could squeeze into. At the second, I knew I would have to let them take her, and I would follow.

I stood outside the ambulance, the rain pounding against my body like a thousand needles. Dr. Bianchi's eyes revealed anguish as she glanced back at me, her face illuminated by the flashing lights of the emergency vehicles. I knew it was time for me to let them take Lucy. I couldn't risk jeopardizing her safety or the life of our unborn child.

With a heavy heart, I waved to Dr. Bianchi through the closing doors of the ambulance, watching it pull away from me. I felt a profound loss and helplessness as it vanished into the stormy night. I was alone, with no one to turn to. I only hoped that the skilled doctors inside the ambulance could save Lucy and our baby.

I turned and walked back towards the vehicles, feeling the rain sting on my skin and the icy wind biting at my bones. As I looked around, the streets were flooded. The wind was howling, and the storm showed no sign of letting up. I knew it would be a long and dangerous journey.

I climbed back into the vehicle, and Mici took off. As we drove through the storm, I couldn't help but worry about Lucy and our baby. I prayed they would be okay and that we would all endure this ordeal unscathed.

After what felt like hours of driving, we finally arrived at the hospital. Mici pulled up to the emergency entrance, and I jumped out of the vehicle, my heart pounding with fear and concern. I sprinted towards the entrance, ignoring the rain that pelted my face. As I entered the hospital, I couldn't help but feel a sense of relief that we had finally made it. The hospital was chaotic, with people rushing around in a state of urgency. Nurses and doctors were busy attending to patients, and beeping machines filled the air.

I spotted Dr. Bianchi in the crowd and ran towards her, desperate for an update on Lucy's condition.

"How is she?"

"She's stable for now," Dr. Bianchi says calmly and professionally. "We're doing everything possible to stabilize her and monitor the baby's heart rate. It will be a tough road ahead, but we're hopeful."

As I stood there, watching the doctors and nurses attend to Lucy,

I couldn't help but feel a sense of helplessness. I wanted to be with her, to hold her hand and comfort her, but I knew I had to stay strong for both of us. With a deep breath, attempting to calm my nerves, I nodded to Dr. Bianchi.

"Thank you. I'll be here if you need anything."

With that, I stepped back and watched as the medical team continued to work on Lucy. For what felt like an eternity, I paced the halls of the hospital, my mind racing with worry. Luca, Danti, and Andrea finally made it to the hospital. Giovanni went home to check on the family. They told me that all of Ivan's men were dead, and Vladimir had taken Ivan to make him pay for murdering his brother. After completing the mission, the Grande Armie packed up and drove off.

Finally, hours later, I saw Dr. Bianchi walking towards me. My heart was in my throat as I braced myself for any news.

"She's stable. Her blood pressure is under control, and the seizures have stopped. We'll keep her sedated for now to give her body time to rest. We've also stabilized the baby's heart rate. Over the next few days, we will closely monitor them and try to guarantee a successful outcome."

I let out a sigh of relief, gratitude, and fear. "Thank you, Doctor. You don't know how grateful I am."

"It's what we're here for. Why don't you go home and rest?"

"No. I have been away from her too much. My place is beside her."

Chapter Thirty-Five

Lucy

The low rumble of his voice pierces through the shadows, pulling me out of the terrorizing nightmare that had consumed me. I force my eyes open, my heart lurching with relief as they focus on Davide's familiar face. In an instant, a wave of safety washes over me. My protector is here, and I know he will undoubtedly keep us safe, no matter where we may be. As I lay there, Davide's hand rests gently on my swollen belly, rubbing soothing circles as he speaks to our unborn child, promising them a world full of love and protection.

"You are going to love your mommy. She is the most beautiful woman in the whole wide world. Her smile can light up a room, and she has a wicked sense of humor. Don't tell her this, but she is a better shooter than I am. When you get old enough, she will be the one to teach you. Your mommy is also so fucking brave. Shit, I guess I should watch my mouth around you. Your mommy will tan my ass if you start saying bad words."

A giggle escaped, and as soon as it did, Davide whipped his head toward me. "Hey," I croak, my mouth dry.

"Oh my, God, Lucy," he cries, placing his hands on either side of my face before placing a sweet kiss on my dry lips.

As Davide's lips meet mine, I feel a rush of tenderness and love wash over me. His touch is like a balm to my soul, calming the storm within me. I gaze up at him, his dark brown eyes filled with concern and care, and I know at that moment that he would move mountains to protect us.

With a gentle smile, I cup his face in my hands, feeling the roughness of his stubble against my palms. "You always know how to make me feel better," I whisper. "How is everyone? Is Nan okay?" The last time I saw her, she was lying in a pile of wedding gowns in a pool of blood.

"Nan is fine. We lost the men at our home during the initial attack. However, during your rescue mission, none of our men were killed. A few had minor bullet gazes, but nothing serious."

I let out a sigh of relief. "How is Sophia?"

"Mad as a wet hen," Davide chuckles. "Danti is driving her crazy."

I look up into his eyes. "Thank you for coming for us."

Davide's expression softens, his eyes reflecting his love for me. "I will always be here for you, Lucy. No matter what challenges come our way, we'll face them together," he vows, his voice unwavering.

I nod, feeling the weight of his words seep into my being. "I know you will, Davide," I reply, my voice stronger now. We are a team, you and I. "And soon, our little one will be part of this team, too." I place his hand over my belly, feeling the warmth of his touch seep into our child's world.

Davide's gaze shifts to where his hand rests, a myriad of emotions swirling in his eyes. "I promise to protect both of you with everything I have," he murmurs, his voice filled with determination.

As I watch him, a sense of gratitude fills me. To have a man like Davide by my side, ready to face any challenge that comes our way, is a gift beyond measure. Despite the dangers that lurk in the shadows of our world, I know that as long as we stand together, nothing can break us.

At this moment, I realized that today was our wedding day. It was the day I had dreamed about for so long, and Ivan took it away from us.

As I realized what today was settled in, a mix of emotions flooded through me: anger at Ivan for disrupting our wedding day, sorrow for the loss of what could have been, and fierce determination. Davide's hand on my belly felt like an anchor, grounding me in the present moment.

"We may have missed our planned day, but that does not change anything," Davide's voice broke through the turmoil in my mind. "We will still have our wedding, Lucy. Nothing and no one can take that away from us. Our love is stronger than any obstacle thrown our way."

His words wrapped around me like a shield, filling me with renewed hope. With him by my side, I felt invincible. The thought of becoming his wife, legally bound to him in every sense, made my heart swell with anticipation.

I looked into his eyes, seeing the determination and love shining within them. "I am ready, Davide," I whispered, feeling a sense of calm wash over me. "Let's do it. Let's finally become husband and wife, no matter what obstacles come our way."

Davide's eyes sparkled with love and relief, his grip on my hand tightening ever so slightly. "Lucy, you are my rock, my guiding light in our chaotic world. I promise to cherish you, protect you, and stand by your side through all the trials and joys that life brings."

His words echoed through my heart, filling me with unwavering trust in our future together. With a determined smile on my face, I nodded at Davide. "Let's make this official, then. Let's seal our love before those who matter most to us, our family. I know the traditions and customs of The Famiglia require us to wed. However, couldn't we do another version? Would the priest come to the hospital and perform the ceremony? We can wait until the baby comes for you to mark me, but I am ready to pledge my heart, body, and soul to you."

Davide sits motionless, and I wonder if I said something wrong. Have I overstepped my place?

Suddenly, his arms are around me, pulling me into his chest. "I want the same thing."

I wrap my arms around him, and when I rub my hand up his back, he lets out a hiss. At that moment, I freeze, guilt washing over me as I realize I must have hurt him with my touch. "Davide, I'm so sorry," I whisper, pulling back to look into his eyes with concern. His face is contorted in pain, but he offers me a reassuring smile.

"It's alright, Lucy. It's nothing," he reassures me, though I can see the facade of strength he puts up for my sake.

I reach out tentatively, tracing the path of his muscles carefully. "Let me take a look," I offer, worry clouding my thoughts. As I lift the hem of his shirt slightly, my breath catches at the sight of his back covered in angry red welts. What caused this? I studied it closer, and suddenly, I knew.

"Davide..." I murmur, my voice cracking. "What happened?"

"What had to be done. For our marriage to be accepted by The Famiglia, first blood had to be spilled."

"I'm seven and half months pregnant. I am definitely not a virgin. So, I can't pass the virginity test."

"Yes, however, Giovanni found a clause with the rules which allows the intended to spill the first blood."

He allowed himself to be whipped so we could be married. A sob escapes as I think about how bad the pain must have been.

I couldn't believe what Davide had done for us, for our love. The sacrifice he had made, enduring such pain and humiliation to ensure that The Famiglia accepted our union. Tears streamed down my cheeks as I looked at the welts on his back, each mark a testament to his unwavering commitment to me.

"Davide," I whispered, my voice trembling with emotion. "I had no idea... I would never have asked this of you."

He turned to me, his eyes filled with a mixture of pain and tenderness. "Lucy, you are my world. I would do anything for you, for us. This is a small price to pay for the happiness and safety of our family."

His words pierced my heart, filling me with deep love and gratitude. I touched his cheek, wiping away the tears that fell silently from my eyes. "Thank you," I murmured softly.

Davide took my hand, his touch warm and reassuring. "There is no need for thanks, Lucy. It was a choice I made willingly for our future together. Let us focus on the present and the happiness that awaits us."

As we stood there, our gazes locked in a shared understanding of the trials we had overcome and the strength of our bond, I felt a sense of peace settle within me. Davide's sacrifice was a clear testament to his love for me, a love that knew no bounds or limits.

I smiled at him through my tears with renewed determination and a heart full of love. "Let's make our union official. Our love will prevail over any obstacle that comes our way," I declared, feeling a sense of unity with him that filled me with hope for the future.

Davide nodded, his eyes shining with unwavering devotion. "Together, we are unstoppable, Lucy. Nothing will stand in our way."

Nothing is impossible with unlimited money and being members of the found families of a secret organization. Davide and I will be married here in my room in two hours. Dr. Bianchi wanted me to remain in bed for the next twenty-four hours to make sure my blood pressure stayed down and I had no more seizures. I'm not going to lie, but I am a little disappointed. However, in the end, I will marry the man who is the love of my life.

"Come on, lover boy. Let's go make arrangements and get cleaned up," Luca said, placing his hand on Davide's shoulder.

His grip on my hand tightens as he shakes his head in disbelief. I can feel his fear and desperation emanating through our intertwined fingers, mirroring my own anxiety. It's as if the moment he releases me, I will fade into nothingness once more, lost in the abyss.

"Go on with Luca. Sophia will stay with me. I promise I will be okay until you return."

Davide closes his eyes and takes several deep breaths. He is fighting his feelings and Corvo, his inner Raven. Finally, he opened his eyes and gave me a small smile. He squeezes my hand once more and gets up. He walks to the door, and as soon as he opens it, Nan is standing there. When he sees her, his shoulders relax. He leans down and whispers something in her ear. She gives him a smile and pats his cheek.

Davide leaves, and Nan turns toward me. Her head is banged, and she has two black eyes. Yet, she is wearing one of the biggest smiles I ever saw. She is carrying a large white box. She places the box at the foot of the bed and pulls me into a tight hug. "I've been sick with worry," she cries.

"Me too." I pull back and look at her. Now that she was closer, I could see the damage Ivan caused. Her lip had been busted open and was still swollen. "Are you okay?"

She smiles and pats my hand. "Just a bump on the head and a few bruises. It is going to take more than a crazed Russian to take me out. Now, I hear you are finally going to become my daughter. Unfortunately, the gown you loved so much was damaged and beyond repair. So I brought this for you to wear."

She delicately hands me the box, her eyes sparkling with anticipation. I eagerly open it, my fingers trembling with excitement. As I peel back the layers of soft tissue paper, my breath catches in my throat. My eyes widen in awe as I take in the sight before me. It was a stunning satin nightgown. The fabric shimmered under the light, adorned with intricate lace floral patterns that seemed to dance across the bodice. Next to it is a delicate bed jacket, its edges lined with matching lace. It's like something out of a fairytale, fit for a queen.

"Oh, Nan, I love it," I cry, throwing my arms around her.

"Good, my dear Sophia, help me get her out of that dreadful hospital gown."

As Nan and Sophia help me change into the exquisite satin nightgown and bed jacket, I can't help but feel a sense of anticipation building within me. The soft fabric glides over my skin like a caress, enveloping me in the sense of comfort and elegance I had never experienced before. With each delicate lace detail and shimmering thread, I feel like a princess preparing for the most important moment of her life.

Once I am dressed in the beautiful ensemble, Nan steps back to admire her handiwork with a satisfied smile. "You look absolutely stunning, dear. Davide won't know what hit him when he sees you in this."

I can't contain the smile that spreads across my face at her words. My heart flutters with excitement at the thought of finally marrying the love of my life, surrounded by those who care for us. As Nan and Sophia help me arrange my hair and add a touch of makeup, I feel a sense of calm settling over me, ready to face whatever challenges come our way.

The door opens once again, and this time, Davide walks back in. His eyes widen in awe as he takes in the sight of me in the exquisite gown, a look of pure adoration crossing his features. He crosses the room in quick strides, his hands reaching out to cup my face gently.

"Lucy, you are the most beautiful woman I have ever seen," he whispers, his voice full of emotion. "I am the luckiest man alive to have you as my wife."

Tears prick at the corners of my eyes as Davide's words wash over me, filling me with warmth and love that transcend any pain or hardship we have faced. I reach up to place my hand over his, holding it against my cheek as I gaze into his dark brown eyes, seeing nothing but unwavering love and devotion reflected back at me.

"Alright, let's get this party started," Danti booms, walking into the room with Andrea, Giovanni, and Luca behind him. Davide moves so he can stand beside me.

Adorned in tailored suits and stern expressions, the Commission members followed closely behind Father Grayson. Their presence reminded us of the strict rules and rituals that governed our unconventional founding son's wedding, necessary for it to be recognized by The Famiglia.

"Davide, Lucida, are we ready to start?"

"Yes, Father," Davide answers.

"Alright then," Father Grayson says.

The ceremony was the same one that all founding sons, through the ages, took part in. As archaic as it might sound,

I pleaded my obedience, loyalty, and undying love to Davide.

"I pronounce you man and wife," Father Grayson declares as he gives us the sign of the cross.

Davide leans and kisses my lips, sending chill bumps down my whole body. Dr. Bianchi already told us that sex was out of the question until six weeks after birth. Well, I guess we will save money on electric bills with all the cold showers.

Davide pulls back, and I see I wasn't the only one affected by the kiss. He leans down and whispers. "Are you ready?"

I nod. He assists me out of bed, and once I am steady on my feet, he walks over to a tall, high-back chair. It was brought in from the Famiglia compound. The chair was ornate, hand-carved African Blackwood. It was the same one all founding sons sat in during this part of the ceremony.

Davide sits down and stares at me with such intensity I can feel it in my bones. I slowly walk to him, and I lower myself to my knees when I am in front of him. Bowing over as best as I can with a protruding belly, I wait for him to present his family's ring to me.

He places the black onyx ring with the Bonanno crest before me. I raise my head and look him in the eyes as I kiss the ring. This man is more than just my husband; he is my everything. The words I am about to say used to make me ill. However, with Davide, I am safe with giving my all to him.

"Padrone del mio cuore, corpo e anima," Master of my heart, body, and soul.

Chapter Thirty-Six

Davide

Six-Weeks Later

We made it. Today, Dr. Bianchi was going to induce Lucy, and by day's end, we will have our son in our arms.

For the last six weeks, Lucy has been a trooper, staying in her bed. As much as she hated it, she wanted our son to be born healthy and strong. She is destined to be an exceptional mother.

Sophia remained living in our home to monitor Lucy twenty-four/seven. Her ever-loyal companion had been a constant presence in our home during these long weeks. Her watchful eyes and reassuring presence had brought a sense of calm amidst the anticipation brewing within me. I knew Sophia would take good care of Lucy.

Once again, we found ourselves in the hospital, this time in a reserved birthing suite for The Famiglia. The three-room suite includes comfortable birthing beds with soft colors and recessed lighting. The patient's room, second bedroom, and adjacent sitting room have Wi-Fi and a flat-screen television. These suites even offer the mothers' salon services, such as haircuts, styles, manicures, and pedicures.

"Lucy, Davide, are you ready to see your little bundle of joy?"

"YES!" we both yell.

She laughs and looks over at Sophia. "Would you like to do the honors?"

"Yes, please."

Sophia comes over and inserts misoprostol into Lucy's IV. When Sophia did her daily check yesterday, Lucy was already 4cm dilated. After a scan, it was confirmed that she wasn't in active labor. I was concerned, but Sophia reassured me it wasn't unusual.

As we waited for the misoprostol to take effect, I couldn't help but feel a mix of excitement and nervousness coursing through me. The first time we held our son was a thrilling yet terrifying experience. I glanced at Lucy, her eyes shining with anticipation and a hint of anxiety. She reached out for my hand, squeezing it tightly as another wave of contractions washed over her.

Minutes felt like hours as we waited for the moment to arrive. Sophia stood by, her presence a comforting anchor in the whirlwind of emotions that threatened to overwhelm me. At last, after what felt like forever, Dr. Bianchi said it was time to begin pushing.

Lucy's grip on my hand tightened even more than she bravely began the arduous task. With every push, determination was etched on her face. I felt a surge of pride and love for this incredible woman who was bringing our child into the world.

After what felt like an eternity of waiting, our little bundle of joy arrived, crying out his first breath. Dr. Bianchi and Sophia worked seamlessly to clean him up and place him on Lucy's chest, her eyes brimming with tears of joy and relief.

I couldn't tear my gaze away from the tiny, perfect being we had created together. His cry was a beautiful melody to my ears, a promise of new beginnings and endless possibilities. I reached out a trembling hand to touch his soft cheek, overwhelmed with emotions I never knew existed within me.

Lucy looked up at me, her eyes shining with unshed tears, and whispered. "He's so perfect, Davide. Our little miracle."

I leaned down to press a tender kiss on her forehead before turning back to our son. "What shall we name him?"

Lucy smiled through her tears and replied. "Gabriel Corvo Bonanno."

At that moment, as I gazed down at little Gabriel, a surge of emotions overwhelmed me. The weight of responsibility settled on my shoulders like a heavy cloak, but it was a burden I welcomed with open arms. For the first time in my life, I felt a sense of purpose beyond the shadows of The Famiglia, beyond the darkness that lingered within me.

As Lucy held Gabriel close to her heart, I vowed to protect and cherish them with all I had. The Raven within me stirred restlessly, but in the presence of my newborn son and the love shining in Lucy's eyes, its whispers faded to a mere murmur.

I reached out to stroke Gabriel's cheek, marveling at the softness of his skin and the innocence in his eyes. A sense of fierce determination welled inside me. A resolve to shield him from the darkness that had haunted my past.

"Gabriel Corvo Bonanno." It was a name that carried the weight of our family history and the promise of a new beginning. As I looked at my son, a sense of fierce protectiveness washed over me, mingling with a deep-rooted love that I never knew I could feel.

At that moment, as Gabriel gripped my finger with his tiny hand, I silently vowed to shield him from the shadows that had clouded my life. The Raven within me stirred its hunger for darkness, momentarily quelled by the presence of this innocent life in my arms.

Lucy's eyes met mine, shimmering with unspoken emotions and a deep understanding that transcended words. She knew the demons that haunted me, the battles I fought within myself every day. And yet, in her gaze, I found solace and acceptance.

We were beginning a new chapter, with unknowns but also lots of love and support. As Gabriel let out a soft coo, breaking the tender silence that enveloped us, I felt a surge of determination coursing through my veins. I would break the cycle of darkness that had plagued my family for generations. I would be the father that Gabriel deserved, one who would protect him at all costs and guide him with love and compassion.

As Lucy looked at me with pride and adoration, I knew we were united in our mission to create a different future for our son. The weight of The Famiglia and its dark legacy still loomed over me. However, at that moment, holding my newborn son in my arms, I felt a glimmer of hope flicker to life within me.

With a newfound sense of purpose burning in my soul, I silently vowed to be the father Gabriel needed. I would shield him from the shadows that threatened to engulf us, fiercely guarding his innocence and nurturing his spirit.

I would teach him how to embrace his inner Raven and, with its help, be stronger for whatever life throws his way.

Everyone leaves the room, allowing Lucy and me to enjoy these precious moments with Gabriel. I don't deserve them. They are light while I am in darkness. However, nevermore will allow darkness to rule me. I choose the light.

The End

All About

Amber Joi Scott
Wicked Writing Wench

Amber Joi Scott or the Wicked Writing Wench, born and raised in the South with a snarky attitude and kiss my ass mentality. Also, being born in the month of August, she embraces her Leo sign, letting her inner lion roar through her writing.

She lives in the beautiful Shenandoah Valley with her big, burly husband and their many animals. Raising her children to be polite, hardworking young adults is and will always be her biggest accomplishment. When deciding on her pen name, she dedicated all her writing to her children by using parts of their names as her pen name.

She doesn't plan to stop writing anytime soon and hopes that people fall in love with her characters as much as she has.

Also By

Amber Joi Scott
Wicked Writing Wench

The Famiglia Secret Society Series

The Dragon: Book One

https://mybook.to/feu72cp

The Raven: Book Two

The Bear: Book Three ~ Coming 2025

The Wolf: Book Four ~ Coming 2025

The Lion: Book Five ~ Coming 2025

Hot Erotic Mafia Romance

Bound Series

Bound to the Family

https://mybook.to/1mrKN

Bound Together

https://mybook.to/lK0rWB

Bound and Dangerous

https://mybook.to/MXGAKXE

Bound and United

https://mybook.to/c7HILJK

Mafia Romance

Heart of the Mafia

https://mybook.to/DmRyF

Deadly Secrets

https://mybook.to/GKUFa

Broken Lullaby

https://mybook.to/355vkxR

Hot Erotic Romance

Trust and Obey

https://mybook.to/YKZr

Sweet Romance

In a Heartbeat

https://mybook.to/jLU3

Wishing Upon a Snowflake

https://mybook.to/p9CXQO9

Where to Follow

Wicked Writing Wench

www.facebook.com/amberjoiscott
www.twitter.com/amberjoiscott
www.instagram.com/amberjoiscott
www.amberjoiscott.com
www.amazon.com/Amber-Joi-Scott/e/B01NAC09UZ

Milton Keynes UK
Ingram Content Group UK Ltd.
UKHW021935151124
451262UK00015B/1787